Pride Publishing books by S. J. Coles

Single Books
Blood Winter
Straight to the Heart
Dark Summer
The Devil You Know

Collections
My Bloody Valentine: Blood Red Roses
Sun, Sea and Small-Town Secrets
Enemy Territory: My Iron Knight

I0646149

THE DEVIL YOU KNOW

S.J. COLES

The Devil You Know
ISBN # 978-1-80250-949-6
©Copyright S.J. Coles 2022
Cover Art by Kelly Martin ©Copyright May 2022
Interior text design by Claire Siemaszkiewicz
Pride Publishing

THE
DEVIL YOU
KNOW

Dedication

For Shez, a fount of valuable legal advice.

Chapter One

Hilary took a deep breath. His shirt, new on that morning, was sticking to the small of his back. He looked up at the Hart-Gosfords' Mayfair townhouse and told himself, yet again, that it was just another case.

You can do this.

He straightened his back, let out the breath and pushed the intercom.

"Yes?"

"Hilary Whyte from Gunnerson and Gains to see Mr. Hart-Gosford."

The gate buzzed and swung open. Hilary transferred his briefcase from one hand to the other so he could wipe his palms on his trousers as he climbed the steps to the front door. Before he could knock, it was opened by a short, stiff-necked man with a smart suit and a grim expression. The scar of an old piercing marred one eyebrow and another, more jagged, bisected the fleshiest part of his neck. The marks, combined with the crew-cut, made him more look like private security than house staff, though it didn't surprise Hilary that the Hart-Gosfords felt the need for both.

"This way."

Hilary resisted staring at the minimalist paintings and crystal sculptures as he followed the butler into a well-appointed parlor. It was best not to appear daunted by such things, even though just one of these pieces was probably worth more than he made in a year, even now.

Tall windows flooded the room with weak spring sunshine. Two women with the same shade of platinum hair looked up as he entered. The younger, who sat on the edge of a mauve love seat, wore a carefully schooled expression, the sort executed best by those who spent a lifetime practicing it. But Hilary detected strain in her slate-gray eyes. The older woman managed to look down her nose at Hilary, even though she barely grazed five feet in her thin-heeled patents. Her eyes, a shade paler than her daughter's, were sharper than cut glass.

"Mr. Hilary Whyte, ma'am…for Master Dominic."

"Thank you, Merriweather," the younger woman said, her accent crisp. "Some coffee, I think. Coffee, Mr. Whyte?"

"Yes, thank you," Hilary said, finally spotting the other figure in the room. Dominic Hart-Gosford stood with his back to them as he poured whiskey into a tumbler on a chrome sideboard. Even at this distance, Hilary could see that his hair had darkened since school, now a brown just this side of black. He'd also added yet more muscle to his six-foot-three frame. Hilary fought to keep his face neutral.

"*You're* the solicitor Walter recommended?" the older woman said, examining Hilary like he was something she'd just stepped in.

"That's right."

"This is simply not acceptable—"

"Mother—"

"No, Amelia," the older woman cut her off. "This simply will not do. You...Mr. Whyte. How old are you?"

"I'm twenty-nine, Mrs. Hart."

She lifted an eyebrow. "I was not aware Walter Gunnerson had a sense of humor—or that he would have such poor taste as to use my son-in-law's murder trial as a chance to exercise it."

"I can assure you, Mrs. Hart, I am a fully qualified solicitor with years of experience in criminal defense."

"How can you possibly have *years* of experience?"

"By dedicating almost every waking hour to my profession since I was eighteen years old," Hilary replied without inflection. "Mr. Gunnerson supplied you with my trial record, I believe?" Mrs. Hart narrowed her eyes. "If that is not enough to reassure you, you are more than welcome to apply to the senior partners for a change of counsel. But, in the meantime, there is rather a lot to be done. So, if you don't mind..." Hilary indicated the open door.

"I suggest you don't get too comfortable," Mrs. Hart said, then swept from the room.

"I'm sorry for my mother," Amelia said, standing and clasping her manicured hands together. "This is a trying time."

"I understand," Hilary said with a careful smile. "But it will take at least a few hours for your mother to try to have me removed from this case. In the meantime, my time is best served speaking with your husband."

"Yes, of course." She glanced back at Dominic. He stood, gazing out of the window, his drink untouched in his hand. Hilary took in the broad shoulders, the trim waist, the controlled stillness in his stance and hurriedly suppressed the memories that threatened to surface before they could show on his face.

Amelia stepped forward, lowering her voice. "My husband is innocent, Mr. Whyte. Whatever you think you know, you must believe that."

Hilary smiled but did not speak. Amelia left as Merriweather appeared with a silver tray of coffee and china cups and set it down.

"You sure you don't need me, sir?" he said, his eyes on Hilary.

"I'm fine, Merriweather. Thank you."

Merriweather withdrew, closing the door behind him, and Hilary fought the impression that the room had shrunk.

Dominic finally turned around. Hilary had told himself many times in the last few weeks that he'd forgotten what this man looked like—that he'd successfully wiped the image from his mind, along with the sound of his voice. But as he took in the eyes, blacker than midnight, the hard, almost cruel set to a jaw that would otherwise be considered handsome, it was like Hilary was again sprawled on the PE changing room floor, that same face hanging over his, bloodied lips twisted and mocking, his fist raised for another blow.

"So, it really is you." Dominic didn't speak loudly, but it was like a stone had dropped into the silence of the room. "I could have laid a considerable amount of money on never seeing you again."

"Well, I guess we would have both lost that wager. Shall we?" Hilary said, indicating the sofas and coffee.

"I'm good," Dominic said, lifting his glass. "You help yourself."

Hilary sat, ignoring the coffee, even though his veins were clamoring for caffeine. Fear that the coffee pot would shake in his grip was too real. Instead, he opened his briefcase and began laying the paperwork out on the narrow glass table. "It probably would have been better to meet at the office for this—"

"Too many flapping ears," Dominic said. "My mother-in-law has some trust issues, to say the least."

"We can manage here if you're more comfortable. But just so you know," he said, pulling a device out of his case and laying it on the coffee table, "I'll be recording every session."

"Still have trust issues of your own, I see."

"So," Hilary said, switching the recorder on, not meeting Dominic's eye, "I'm up to speed on all the known facts of this case. This meeting is for me to get to know your side of the story in more detail and to help you prepare for what happens next."

Dominic gazed at him thoughtfully. "I've been trying to remember... What was it we called you? In school?"

"That isn't—"

"Lilywhite. That was it, wasn't it?"

Hilary took a moment to steady his voice. "Let's get one thing straight right from the start, Mr. Hart-Gosford," he said levelly. "Our personal connection is one of the reasons why Walter Gunnerson wanted me to represent you. But all he knows is that we both attended St. Edmund's."

Dominic lifted his fine, black eyebrows. "If the good Mr. Gunnerson knew the truth, he might wonder why you agreed to take this case at all…as I do."

Hilary looked him in the eye. "I'm capable of not allowing the past to affect my judgment. But if you insist on bringing it up, it will become a problem. Understand?"

He sipped his drink. "I understand."

"Good. And now that's on record," Hilary continued, nodding at the recording device, "perhaps we could discuss your case?"

"There's nothing I would like more." Dominic's smile widened and he unbuttoned his suit jacket and lowered himself onto the sofa, draping one arm along the back and crossing his long legs. "Where do we start?"

Hilary took in the mocking slant to his mouth. "I think we need to start by establishing just how serious this is."

"I am aware of the seriousness of the situation."

"I'm not sure you are. You have been charged with double murder. First degree. If you're convicted, you will go to prison for life."

"I know you won't allow that to happen."

"But you have means, motive and no alibi."

"I didn't do it."

Hilary examined Dominic for a long moment—his strong limbs held so still, his cool expression…

"From the top, then," Hilary continued, sliding the witness statements over the table. "On the morning of Thursday, the twenty-third of November last year, a postal worker attempting to deliver a package to

Number 4 Kensington Gardens found the front door open. He rang the bell, but there was no answer. He pushed the door ajar, thinking to leave the package on the mat. It was then he saw the murdered body of Dean Wood on the stairs and called the police. When the police arrived, they discovered Dean's twin sister, Lizzie, the resident of the property, in the living room, also dead. Lizzie had been shot seven times. Dean twice. The neighbors never heard a thing, so the police believe a silencer was used."

Dominic was watching him over the rim of his glass as he sipped his drink.

Hilary looked away. "Lizzie's neighbors say Dean quite often came over to cook dinner for them both. But there was no set routine for this, so it's believed Lizzie was the intended target." Dominic's gaze dropped to the papers on the table, but he didn't speak. "Feel free to contribute at any point," Hilary said after a pause.

"Thank you. I will."

Hilary repressed his impatience and placed the crime scene photographs on top of the witness statements. A young, brunette woman lay on her back, her head twisted at an awkward angle. Her eyes were wide and staring. Blood soaked her sun-yellow top almost black and stippled the skin of her face and neck. A young man with a similar build and coloring was sprawled on a staircase, the treads and banister smeared with blood where he'd tried to drag himself up.

Dominic looked at them, his own eyes unreadable. "Do I really need to see these?"

"Lizzie Wood worked for you?" Hilary said, tapping the picture of the dead girl.

"I believe so. Or, rather, not me…Amelia. Some sort of low-level admin in one of the charities. I'd never met her."

"Never?"

"No."

Hilary laid out another photo. It was of Dominic at a formal occasion, resplendent in an elegant dinner suit and black tie, a glass of champagne in hand and a fixed smile for the camera. He was amongst half a dozen other people in front of a banner emblazoned with the slogan *Homes with Hart*. Amelia, looking stunning in an azure ball gown and flashing white smile, was on his right. Lizzie Wood, looking shy, despite her professional updo and designer playsuit, stood at his left elbow.

"I explained this to the police," Dominic said. "I go to dozens of these things. I try not to speak to people unless I have to. I rarely remember them."

That'll be the drink. Hilary pushed the thought aside. "Lizzie was fired from Homes with Hart about a month before she died."

"I believe so."

"Do you know why?"

"I didn't then. I do now. She'd been making fraudulent expense claims."

Hilary laid a bank statement on top of the other papers. "Lizzie Wood was in a considerable amount of debt—credit cards, payday loans. There's even some evidence that she'd resorted to some less-than-legal solutions more recently."

Dominic swirled his whiskey and didn't speak. Hilary pointed at a highlighted transaction on the bank statement. "This cash deposit was paid into her account the week before she died. Ten thousand pounds."

"The police told me all this. I still don't know anything about it."

"You're sticking to your story that Lizzie Wood wasn't blackmailing you?"

Dominic put the glass down on the table with a definitive click. "I have answered all these questions several times already, Mr. Whyte."

"I have read your answers to the police, but now I'd like you to answer me. And, for the sake of the case, please realize that the truth is more important than looking innocent."

Dominic leveled a hard look at him. "I did *not* know this woman. She did *not* blackmail me. How and why that money ended up in her account, I can't explain. An examination of my own accounts has revealed no large withdrawals. There is nothing to connect me to any of this."

"Except your DNA at the scene."

Dominic sighed and crossed his legs the other way. "One hair…just one. No skin cells, no fingerprints — no other more interesting forms of DNA."

Hilary tried to decide if there was a spark in his eye.

"The hair is pretty damning, Mr. Hart-Gosford," he continued. "It was found under Dean Wood's body. How did it get there?"

"I don't know."

Hilary turned to the next page of his notes.

"Lizzie and Dean died around eleven p.m. on the night of the twenty-second of November. You were supposed to be at a banquet with your family and their guests at Brentwold Hall that night. There were several high-profile guests, including some prominent politicians and foreign dignitaries, so they had security cameras installed in the banqueting hall."

"I take it the police finally got a warrant for the footage?"

"They did."

Dominic stood in one fluid motion and returned to the sideboard. "Sure you don't want something stronger?"

"I'm fine," Hilary said, taking the opportunity while Dominic's back was turned to pour himself some of the now-cooling coffee. A couple of mouthfuls and he found as Dominic returned that he was able to meet his eye without flinching. "Why weren't you at the banquet, Mr. Hart-Gosford?"

"For fuck's sake, Hilary," he said as he resumed his seat. "Call me Dominic."

"Mr. Hart-Gosford. Please answer the question."

He sighed. "You still have that stick up your arse, I see. But, either way, my statement to the police is the truth."

"'*Changed your mind at the last minute*' is not going to cut it with me."

"It will have to."

Hilary laid down his pen. "Not a single traffic camera picked up your Bentley leaving London that day. You never even left town."

"I never said I did."

"So from the time you were last seen leaving your mother-in-law's art gallery at just after four p.m., to when your security cameras picked you up returning here at a little after eight the following morning, where were you?"

"Walking."

"Just walking?"

"That's right."

"But you didn't make a single payment on any of your credit cards and had your phone off the whole time?"

Dominic glanced at his left hand. "You're married, yes?"

Something sharp went through Hilary's chest. He glanced at his platinum ring then busied himself with papers. "Engaged."

Dominic raised his eyebrows. "She makes you wear an engagement ring?"

"How is this relevant?"

"Best decision I ever made, marrying Amelia," Dominic said after a pause. "We are partners...in everything. Eloise may be an overbearing harridan at times, but I am more a part of their family than I was ever a part of my own." He drained his glass and looked away. "But belonging to a family like this...? There's a price. The world watches everything — where you shop, where you eat, who you see." He met Hilary's eyes again, something dark glittering in the black depths. "Sometimes I need time to myself."

"It is very, very unfortunate that you chose that particular night to go dark."

"I didn't kill anyone."

"So tell me where you were."

"You're just going to have to trust me."

"Were you drinking? On drugs?"

"Excuse me?"

"When someone won't admit the truth to their solicitor, it's for one of two reasons. They're guilty or they're ashamed. Sometimes both."

"I told you that I just wanted to be alone."

"I'm not here to judge," Hilary said levelly. "There is literally nothing you could say that would shock me—"

"I highly doubt that."

"But anything the prosecution might find out, I need to know first. Only then can I prepare for it coming up in court."

"So you think the only possible explanations are that I was either murdering these two people or shooting up in a smack den? Good to know my lawyer has so much faith in me."

"You're not giving me much to work with."

A corner of Dominic's mouth twitched. "I've read your trial record. I believe you're more than capable of winning this without anything so trivial as an alibi."

Hilary clenched his jaw. "So we've covered motive and opportunity. Let's move on to means. Forensics have determined the murder weapon was a semiautomatic nine-millimeter handgun. Do you own a gun, Mr. Hart-Gosford?"

"You know I don't."

"You don't possess a firearms license," Hilary returned coolly. "That's not the same thing."

Dominic looked away. "No. I do not own a gun."

"But your wife does," Hilary said, pulling out a copy of her license and laying it on top of the photographs of the victims. "Three, in fact. Semiautomatic nine-millimeters."

"That's correct," he said with a hard look. "Which must have been known by the killer."

"Why does she own these weapons?"

"She is a sportswoman..." Dominic indicated the awards and trophies in the glass cabinet by the window. "And, before you ask, she keeps her weapons locked securely at her gun club."

"Your wife was filmed at the banquet all night, so we know she couldn't have done this. But now I must ask if you have ever fired these guns yourself?"

"Once or twice…at the range, with Amelia. But I don't like guns."

Hilary raised an eyebrow. "Do you have access to them? The truth, please. The police and prosecution will be making inquiries at the club as we speak."

Dominic smiled. "Not…officially."

"And…unofficially?"

Dominic gazed into his drink. "If you know the right people to tip, there are always ways around paperwork."

"So you've accessed her guns without her present?"

"No. But she sometimes takes friends to her club. Only members and their list of pre-approved guests are allowed to fire the weapons. But she has intimated that there are ways around it."

"Why aren't these friends on her list?"

"You'd have to ask her that."

Hilary scribbled more notes. "You haven't mentioned the security cameras at the gun club," he said. "Is that because you know there are ways around those, too?"

"I assumed that if there was footage of someone accessing my wife's guns on the night of the murder, we wouldn't be sitting here right now."

"It's true. The security cameras at the club were malfunctioning the night of the murder."

"Either way, Amelia's guns are accounted for."

"Yes. Mrs. Hart-Gosford gave her guns up to ballistics soon after your arrest. Were you made aware of the findings?"

"The police said they had been fired recently. But Amelia went to the club for a few rounds before leaving for Brentwold, so that doesn't mean anything."

"And the fact that they had been cleaned?"

"Amelia takes good care of her weapons."

Hilary drained the coffee and set the cup back on the tray. "I think it's time we talk about your plea."

"What's to talk about?"

Hilary met his eye squarely. "It is my duty to inform you that, from a legal point of view, your best option, at this stage, with this evidence—"

"I'm not pleading guilty."

"If you just let me explain—"

"I will not say I'm guilty just to make your job easier."

Hilary was unable to stop the color from heating his face and cursed his pale skin for the millionth time. "It's not about making my job easier. It's about getting the best possible outcome for my client—in this case, you."

"The best possible outcome is me walking away from this sordid mess with my name cleared."

"I can only do that if the proof exists."

"So do your job. Find it."

"Mr. Hart-Gosford," Hilary said, dredging together his last scraps of patience, "if you plead guilty before this goes to trial, I'm confident we can get the charge down to manslaughter with diminished responsibility—"

"What do you mean by 'diminished responsibility', exactly?"

Hilary started to gather the papers, his gaze lowered. "There had been one payment already.

Blackmailers rarely stop at one. You were under pressure. You were scared. Possibly…intoxicated." Dominic clenched his fists. Hilary went on like he hadn't noticed. "If we can make a case for this being a spontaneous act," Hilary went on, "committed whilst your capacity was compromised, and you admit to it, there's a good chance you'll be looking at ten years, tops. Less with good behavior."

"If you wanted to get your own back, Hilary, why not just join a Twitter? Write a blog? Sell your story to *The Sun*? It would be a lot less troublesome than trying to get me to plead guilty to a crime I didn't commit."

Hilary straightened and met Dominic's eye. "As I said, it is my job to present the best legal options available to you. If this goes to trial and we lose, you will go to prison for the rest of your life."

"So don't lose."

Hilary turned off the recorder. "You need to be realistic."

"I am all too well acquainted with realism," Dominic said, an edge to his voice.

"The plea hearing is in two days' time. You need to think about it."

"I've done all the thinking I need to."

Hilary surveyed him narrowly. "Going to trial means everything coming out. Everything. Your arrests, the news reports, the rumors, the photographs you thought your family had buried. The prosecution will find it. All of it."

"I'm not afraid of the truth. None of it means I killed anyone."

"Maybe not. But it will still affect people's judgment of you. The jury's judgment. They aren't supposed to read up on you, but they will. You need to be aware of that—and that is what we need to mitigate."

"Mitigate?"

"If you want people to believe you're innocent, start acting innocent."

Dominic smiled. "Anything you say, Mr. Whyte."

* * * *

That same smile sent shivers over Hilary's skin from every file photo and social media post he scoured that evening. His glass stood empty on the bedside table, but he resisted reaching for the half-full bottle of Grey Goose next to it, realizing that the alcohol was dulling his senses but not his frustration.

Dominic's arrest records were only the start. In Hilary's exasperated state, it seemed that the entire Internet was made up of stuff about Dominic Hart-Gosford being a first-class twat. His boats, his cars, his helicopter... His impulse purchases, gambling debts and the tumultuous relationship with his politician father... His entitlement, his drug abuse and his borderline alcoholism...

Not only that, but all the hits on all the articles had jumped significantly since the date of his arrest.

The sound of the front door opening jerked him from his reverie. He heard Jasper staggering around the living area, bumping into the corner sofa like he always did when he tried to move around in the dark after he'd been drinking. Hilary had suggested moving the sofa a hundred times, but Jasper insisted it was in the perfect position to have sex whilst watching TV, so it remained where it was.

Jasper opened the bedroom door a crack then pushed it wide when he saw the light was on.

"Babe," he said, his handsome face twisted in concern. "You're still up?"

"Yeah," Hilary said, removing his glasses and rubbing his eyes. "This new case. Good night?"

Jasper shrugged one shoulder, staggering a little as he pulled his shoes and socks off. "I swear these things get worse every time. It's like the more money you make for them, the more validation the bloodsuckers need from you."

"My heart bleeds," Hilary said with a smile as Jasper shrugged out of his shirt.

"You know what I mean," his fiancé moaned as he crawled between the sheets. He smelled like woody cologne and Jack Daniel's. He began nuzzling at Hilary's neck, running a hand up his thigh under the covers. "Have I told you you're gorgeous today?"

"Jasper," Hilary started, "it's late."

"We're awake, aren't we?"

"You're drunk."

"So?" Jasper mouthed his jaw then caught sight of the laptop screen. He went still. "What the—?"

Hilary shut the laptop.

"*He's* your double murder case?"

"Yeah. Him."

"Dom Gosford? The prick who bullied you at school?"

"It doesn't matter."

"Like fuck it doesn't," Jasper said, sitting up and spilling the pillows on the floor, his flushed face suddenly serious. "You can't represent this guy, Hil."

"I've got to."

"Surely there some sort of conflict of interest or something."

"Not when the link is so tenuous. Besides, I'm a professional—"

"I know you are," Jasper said, taking his hand. "But they shouldn't be making you work with that man, not after what he did."

"No one knows about all that."

"Well, perhaps they should."

Hilary gave him a look.

"Is he guilty?"

"He says not."

"Fuck…"

"I can do this," Hilary said, setting the laptop aside. "Gunnerson's mentioned the junior partnership twice since assigning the case."

"Still—"

"Jazz. I can handle it."

"You've got nothing to prove, you know," he said. "Not to him. Not to anyone."

"I know that."

Jasper visibly hesitated.

"What is it?"

His fiancé sighed. "It's just it's really not the best timing, with the wedding and everything."

Hilary reached for patience. "Not everything's about the wedding."

"If you end up representing a convicted double murderer, it will be."

"I'm not the one who wanted our wedding to be a publicity campaign," Hilary said, yanking the covers up. "Just remember that."

"Do we have to have this argument again?"

Hilary bit back his instinctive retort, knowing where the argument would go. Jasper's face softened.

"We've got the ski trip to look forward to, haven't we? Less than six weeks for that. The wedding may be for the public, but everything else is for us."

Hilary sighed, picking at the cover.

"You said all you ever wanted was to look around you and know you'd gotten somewhere with your life. I will give you that, Hil. I swear. We just need to get through the wedding first."

"I know…"

"Forget it all for now," Jasper went on, running his foot up Hilary's leg. "If you say the case won't interfere, I believe you. Just promise me you'll win?"

"I'll do my job," Hilary said, bringing his fiancé's head down and brushing a kiss over his lips. "If Dom Gosford can resist being a complete arsehole, that is."

"Yeah, well, don't count on that."

Jasper kissed him hungrily, pushing him down into the pillows and climbing on top. Hilary sank into the feel of his weight, allowing the pleasant sensations to chase the day away. Jasper moaned and thrust his erection against Hilary's leg and Hilary pushed a hand between them to tend to it. Jasper gasped and fumbled for the bedside lamp, knocking Hilary's glass onto the floor then plunging them into darkness.

They fumbled to shed their remaining clothing and Hilary parted his legs and pulled Jasper close, arching up as Jasper pushed his length against his arse.

"Oh God," Jasper breathed in the dark. "I'm too close for that, Hil. Suck me off?"

Hilary allowed himself to be rolled on top and made his way down Jasper's body, kissing and licking the sculpted chest and the firm abdomen that was known to swooning movie fans around the world. Jasper cried aloud when Hilary took him into his mouth. He threaded his hands tight in Hilary's hair and thrust, once, twice then was coming in his throat.

He dropped his hands away and was snoring even before Hilary had sat up. He looked at Jasper's face, his stylishly disheveled hair and perfect cheekbones just visible in the low light, then closed his eyes and took his own cock in hand to finish himself off.

He froze when dark eyes, sparking with a hint of danger, rose in his mind. He hurried for the bathroom, splashing cold water on his face until his pulse slowed.

He stared at his reflection. He'd not seen that look in his eyes for years, but it was as familiar as the slant of Dom Gosford's mocking smile. He blinked until his breathing calmed then switched off the light and returned to bed.

It was still a long time before he fell asleep.

Chapter Two

"And this is your final decision?"

"It is." Dominic's voice was even deeper over the telephone.

"Fine. 'Not guilty' it is." Hilary caught his researcher's eye. Beck grimaced in sympathy. "I'll see you at the courthouse. Wear a conservative suit and a dark tie. Blue, if you have it."

"I don't."

"Then buy one. Can your wife come?"

A pause. "I was not aware PR was so integral to a murder trial."

"It's more important in some cases than others," Hilary said, earning a smirk from Beck. "There will be a press conference outside the court after the hearing. It would be good if you could be seen to be supported, especially by women."

"Amelia's coming, as is Eloise."

"Good. See you there. Get the tie." He cut off the speaker phone and shook his head.

"Jesus, sir. I think we've hooked a live one here."

"Think the old man's testing me?" Hilary said as he handed Beck some files.

"He's always testing us," Beck said sagely. "But that's how we know he needs us."

"Good to know. Can you start drafting our timeline? And get Simon to check the report dates. I'll be back after the hearing."

Beck nodded. "It's done. Good luck, boss."

"Thanks. I'll need it."

When he arrived at the courthouse, Hilary went straight to the marble-tiled bathroom and surveyed himself critically in the mirror. He made sure that not a strand of his strawberry-blond hair had escaped its short tail and tugged his cuffs down to better conceal the swallows that were tattooed on the insides of his wrists. He was in his dove-gray suit with a tie in a soft green that Jasper said brought out his eyes. He pushed his glasses up his nose and took out his silver studs, putting them in his pocket. Judge Fotheringham was a progressive sort, but even she barred male counsel appearing in court with any more jewelry than a wedding band. He fiddled with his engagement ring a moment, then straightened his back. He left the bathroom, not analyzing why his appearance mattered more to him than usual, and made for the courtroom.

Dominic was approaching along the corridor— Amelia on his arm, Eloise at his shoulder. Hilary was gratified to see that he was wearing a dark suit, perfectly tailored to his broad shoulders and trim waist. He strode with the fierce confidence of someone who knew where he was going but with the stiffness of someone trying to leave something behind.

Hilary noted with satisfaction that he'd worn a navy tie. The dark tones accented his coloring and, combined with his grim expression, made him look at least somber, if not humble.

His focus landed on Hilary and stayed there as the party approached, despite the small gaggle of press that scurried alongside, firing questions as they held out mics and recording devices.

"What are you pleading today, Mr. Hart-Gosford? Why did you kill Lizzie Wood? Why do you hate women, Mr. Hart-Gosford? Were you abused as a child, sir?"

Hilary sent up a silent prayer then stepped forward, inserting himself between his client and the reporters.

"Ladies and gentlemen, we are not answering questions at this time. My client will give a brief statement outside as soon as his plea has been entered. Thank you." He held his arm out in a practiced maneuver that kept the reporters back whilst allowing the Hart-Gosfords to pass into the nearest anteroom.

"Thank you, Mr. Whyte," said Amelia as soon as they were alone.

"I'm afraid we should prepare for a lot of this sort of thing before this is over."

"We understand that," Amelia said, glancing at her stiff-backed husband, who was staring out of the window with his face set in hard lines. "We are prepared. The important thing is proving Dominic's innocence."

"I feel you should know, Mr. Whyte," Eloise Hart said, peering at Hilary from under her starch-stiff sweep of platinum hair, "I have a meeting with Walter Gunnerson this afternoon."

"Yes, ma'am. He told me."

"I thought it only courteous to inform you that I will be asking to have you removed from this case."

"Mother, you didn't!"

"Dominic needs the best representation there is," Eloise said firmly. "I will not accept anything less."

"I'm sure Mr. Gunnerson will agree with you," Hilary said with his warmest smile. "Now," he went on, checking his watch, "we should be taking our places."

He held the door open, and Amelia and Eloise filed out, but he pushed it to again before Dominic could leave.

"Stand when I stand," he murmured. "Sit when I sit. No smiling."

"Why would I smile?"

Hilary held the deep, black gaze for a moment longer than he had to, just to prove that he could, then opened the door again.

The courtroom was already full, the chatter buzzing like an excited swarm of bees in the air, building in volume as they entered. All eyes were on Dominic as he moved to the front of the wood-paneled chamber. Laurette Augustine caught Hilary's eye from where she sat at the prosecutor's table as he followed his client down the aisle. She raised her eyebrows minutely and Hilary gave a half-shrug. Augustine shook her head and turned to whisper to her co-counsel as Dominic and Hilary took their seats.

"All stand for the Honorable Mrs. Justice Fotheringham."

There was the shuffle of fabric and the scrape of chairs as everyone stood. The murmuring hushed as the judge entered and took the bench. She was a small woman, with wiry, graying curls, but her eyes behind her thick-lensed glasses were sharp as knives. She opened her files, peering at the papers as the announcer instructed everyone but the defense and prosecution to sit.

"Plea hearing for Case 367-L CW, The Crown vs. Dominic Marcus Hart-Gosford," the judge intoned and raised her head, her inscrutable gaze moving from Dominic to Hilary and back again. "Is representation for Mr. Hart-Gosford present?"

"Yes, my lady," Hilary said. "Mr. Hilary Whyte of Gunnerson and Gains representing Dominic Hart-Gosford."

"And the plea, Mr. Whyte?"

It seemed like the room held its breath.

"Mr. Hart-Gosford is not guilty, my lady."

"Very well," Judge Fotheringham said after a hesitation so brief no one but the counsel seemed to notice. "Parties to file all evidence and witness lists by the end of the month. The trial will commence in six weeks." She banged the gavel and excited chatter broke out on all sides while she called for the next case.

Six weeks. Hilary cursed silently then ushered the family toward the door. Augustine caught his sleeve before he could follow them out.

"Hilary…a word."

Hilary gave the Hart-Gosfords a reassuring nod then followed Augustine to an empty office. She shut the door behind them and stood in front of it with her arms crossed.

"He's really doing this then?"

"He's innocent."

Augustine cocked an eyebrow. "You should know a lost cause when you see one, Hilary Whyte."

"If it were a lost cause, you wouldn't be here."

Augustine frowned. "Defending this is madness. Lizzie Wood worked for the guy's wife. We can prove

31

any number of things that would be worth blackmailing him over, not to mention the stuff we know about but can't prove. And he has no alibi."

"You have no murder weapon."

"We have his DNA at the scene."

"One hair. It could have come from anywhere."

"We both know the jury won't see it that way."

"The hair is either a coincidence or a lab error," Hilary said, glancing at his watch.

"You believe that?"

"I can make the jury believe it. That's all that matters."

"Hilary," Augustine said darkly, "the powerful rich guy killed a barely managing girl after she tried to beat him at his own game, for God knows what sordid reason. He killed her brother, too, just for *being* there. They'll throw away the key."

"I know the prosecution service doesn't want this to go to trial any more than we do," Hilary said after a pause. "But the difference between you and the Hart-Gosfords is the family think any amount of bad press is worth him not going to prison. So we fight."

"This case will make your career, Hilary," she said softly, "but only if you win. And that's a big if."

"So I take it you have an offer?"

Augustine pursed her lips. "We have an offer."

Hilary listened to her speak, schooled his face to neutrality and rejoined the family in the corridor.

"Mr. Hart-Gosford," he said, "could we have a word in private?"

"What did she want?" Eloise said.

"It would be best if I discussed this with Dominic alone."

"Nonsense" — Eloise clutched her handbag strap tighter — "we are in this together. Tell us what the prosecutor said."

"It was an offer, wasn't it?" Amelia said, her eyes wary.

"Mr. Hart-Gosford —"

"What was the offer?" Dominic asked.

Hilary glanced at the keen-eyed women, sighed and lowered his voice. "They're offering manslaughter with diminished responsibility. Seven years. You'll be out in four. *If* you change your plea."

"Out of the question," Eloise began.

"Dominic is innocent," Amelia insisted, her eyes bright with anger. "He will *not* plead guilty."

Dominic stared at the wall without speaking.

"Mr. Hart-Gosford," Hilary said, "I really must insist on a word in private."

Amelia and Eloise launched into protests, but Dominic nodded. "Very well."

Dominic sat in a chair in the anteroom, crossing his long legs and folding his hands in his lap.

"Go on then," he said. "Give me the spiel."

"This is a good offer," Hilary said. "Better than I thought we'd get. And accepting it is the only way to guarantee you don't go to prison for the rest of your life."

"You've never lost a case. Why start with mine?"

"I've never let a case with this little chance of winning get to trial in the first place."

Dominic narrowed his eyes. "You think I did it, don't you?"

Hilary hesitated. "I strongly advise you to take this offer."

Dominic eyed him for a long time. "I thought you said you wouldn't let your personal feelings affect your judgment?"

"That's not what I'm doing," Hilary said coolly. "I'm doing my job."

Dominic brushed at his trouser leg. "You've changed since school. Is it so hard for you to believe that I have, too?"

"I will turn the deal down if you tell me to," Hilary replied after a long moment. "But not because your family wants me to."

"My family and I are united on this."

"I want you to think about it," he said. "Seriously think about it."

"I take it you know all the reasons why the prosecution service doesn't want this to go to trial?" Dominic continued, examining his fingernails.

"Because they think you're guilty but can't prove it."

"More than that," Dominic replied, weaving his fingers together around his knee. "The Ministry of Justice wants to present itself as blind to rank and prejudice. But the hard truth is, when the names of the rich and influential are dragged through the mud, it upsets the balance…the precious unity. And no one comes out of it well."

"If someone commits a crime, they should be punished, no matter how much money they have."

Dominic's eyes went right through him. "I haven't committed any crime."

"We can't prove that."

Dominic tapped his finger off his knee. "Your fiancée. Does she believe in you?"

"He's a he. But yes. Yes, he does."

Hilary tried to decide if something changed in Dominic's eyes. The silence stretched on for a moment longer than was comfortable, but Hilary couldn't even begin to think why it was there, let alone how to break it.

"My wife believes in me," Dominic said eventually. "Believes in my innocence. That kind of belief has power." He shifted forward in his seat, looking up at Hilary through his thick, straight eyebrows. "I need *you* to believe in me, Hilary Whyte."

"The offer is on the table for twenty-four hours," Hilary said, heading for the door. "I suggest you think about it—for your own sake, Dominic. Not your family's."

The start of a smile that did not reach his eyes turned up the corner of Dominic's mouth. "At least you're calling me Dominic."

Hilary opened the door. "I will call you in the morning for your decision."

"Oh, and Hilary." Hilary looked back. A smile of a different kind transformed Dominic's face. "You really do look very fine in a suit."

Fire lit under Hilary's belly. He clenched his jaw, fighting confusion. He yanked the door wide. "The press is waiting."

Dominic continued smiling as he strode through the door to join his family.

"Hold hands with Amelia as I speak," Hilary instructed as they approached the entrance. "And remember not to smile."

Amelia already had her arm through Dominic's as they passed into the weak sunshine and the flashing of a dozen cameras.

"Mr. Hart-Gosford has this morning entered a plea of not guilty," Hilary stated in his clearest, most level voice. "The trial will commence in six weeks' time, when we look forward to getting the chance to prove his innocence. My client will now make a short statement, after which we ask for privacy for him and his family at this difficult period."

Hilary stepped to the side as a dozen people shouted questions at the same time. Dominic stepped forward, his unfathomable gaze sweeping the crowd.

"I want to thank my family for their support," he said, his voice loud and firm enough to cut off the barrage of questions. "I also want to thank my legal team for their tireless efforts." His focus landed on Hilary and again that tickle of something uncomfortable started up under his belly. "Their belief is sustaining me during this time of doubt and fear. But I know, in the end, the truth will win the day. Thank you."

The Hart-Gosfords pushed their way through the crowds of reporters to where Merriweather was waiting, holding the door to their limousine open. Hilary caught up to Dominic just before he climbed in.

"Promise me you'll think about it," he said earnestly.

"I'll think about it, Hilary," he said, smiling. Merriweather gave Hilary an inscrutable look then Dominic climbed into the car.

Hilary watched the limousine pull out into the traffic with the uncomfortable feeling spreading out from his belly into his chest. He'd had clients flirt with him before—men, women, married, single. In his experience guilt, desperation or arrogance manifested in strange and often inappropriate ways. But...Dom

Gosford? *Married*, straight Dom Gosford? Dom Gosford who had once been the best person in the world at convincing Hilary he was less that worthless?

He must have read it wrong. That was the only explanation.

But even that didn't explain the tickle of electricity Dominic's look had sparked in Hilary's chest.

He felt sick. He hurried to his car, breathing deep until the unwelcome sensations passed.

Hilary spent the rest of the day fielding phone calls from the Crown Prosecution Service, court scheduling clerks and Beck, who was out following up on the witness statements. He only ate because his PA Janice brought him a panini at mid-afternoon and stood over him until he took a bite. His personal phone buzzed with notifications and messages, many from Jasper. The third time he'd tried to ring, Hilary had canceled the call, fired off a text—*Busy. Talk later*—and turned the phone off, something he'd never done before in the whole of their relationship.

He didn't let himself analyze why.

He was so engrossed with background checks and evidence lists that Janice had to clear her throat to make him aware of her presence as the clock ticked toward six p.m.

"Mr. Gunnerson wants you, sir."

Hilary downed his cooling coffee, sent the three draft emails still sitting open on his computer screen and followed her.

Walter Gunnerson was a squat, round man with a receding hairline and small eyes that were comically enlarged by a pair of bottle-bottom glasses with bright red frames that made him appear almost childlike. The other senior partners had attempted to get him to switch to contact lenses a number of times, stating that it would make him look more professional, but he insisted that he found it useful to be consistently underestimated.

Though prosecutors rarely made that mistake twice.

From the knowing look directed his way as Hilary walked into his vast, drafty office, Hilary deduced that Gunnerson not only knew everything about his case but probably had already figured out how it would end. He knew better than to ask, even though his employer had the unnerving capacity to be right most of the time.

"*The law is a tool,*" he'd said to Hilary when he'd joined the firm. "*You only learn how to handle it by using it yourself.*"

"Mr. Gunnerson," Hilary greeted him. "Good afternoon, sir."

"Good afternoon, Hilary," he said, indicating one of the worn leather chairs in front of his desk. "Though it really is evening, now."

"You're right, sir. Busy day."

"I hear Hart-Gosford went with 'not guilty' after all."

"That's right, sir. Though the prosecution has come back with an offer I've urged him to consider."

"Yes, I heard that, too," he said, carefully tapping a sheaf of papers together with his small, stubby hands. Mr. Gunnerson rarely did anything by email. "It's highly unlikely that he'll take it, just so you're aware."

"I gathered as much. But at least we have it on record that we made him think about it."

"Indeed." The old man leaned his leather-patched elbows on the table, peering at Hilary over the top of his glasses. "I take it you would like to know how my meeting with Mrs. Eloise Hart went?"

"I think I can guess, sir."

A smile stretched the thin lips. "Eloise and I go back a long time — longer than either of us cares to remember, truth be told. I know better than to not at least make a show of addressing her concerns."

"Of course, sir. And if you believe her son-in-law would be better represented by someone else —"

"Oh, heavens, no," Gunnerson said. "The only chance that boy has of winning over a jury is with you."

"Thank you, sir."

The set look on his boss's face told Hilary that he wasn't fooled. "It's a rite of passage, Hilary, attempting to prove the innocence of someone one wouldn't get caught dead in a ditch with."

Hilary suppressed a grimace. "My personal feelings don't come into the matter."

Gunnerson chuckled. "Well, the best of luck with that. And, just so you know, I've scheduled a case review with the whole bally lot of them, just to smooth the ruffled feathers. It's probably best you aren't present."

Hilary nodded with relief. "Yes, sir."

"Have you been allocated a barrister yet?"

"Not yet. But I've been trying to set up a meeting with Tarrant."

Gunnerson raised his bushy eyebrows. "That would be a coup."

"I haven't even got as far as her under-secretary yet. But she's worked with Judge Fotheringham for years. And she represented the Braithwaites in their criminal negligence case last year."

"And won, if I remember."

"Yes. But, as I say, her office hasn't returned my calls."

"Let me see what I can do," Gunnerson said, scribbling something on a sheet of his monogrammed notepaper. "I've worked with Anna a couple of times. She may let me put a word in her ear."

Hilary resisted smiling with some effort. "Thank you, sir."

Gunnerson leaned back in his chair. "The Harts have been clients here for generations, Hilary. They are a very good family to have on our side—a very bad one not to."

"I don't intend on getting on the wrong side of anyone," Hilary said with conviction. "But I won't lie to them, either. There's not enough truth available in this case to sugarcoat what's left."

"The prosecution won't do them any such courtesy. We can't afford to, either, as much as Eloise might disagree."

"I have to be honest, sir. Making a jury believe this man is innocent is going to be...a challenge."

"Do *you* believe it?"

Hilary hesitated. "It's what he's told me."

Gunnerson surveyed him narrowly. "It would be helpful if you could bring yourself to believe him—not vital, but helpful."

* * * *

Hilary sighed as he sat back at his own desk, removed his glasses and rubbed his eyes. A headache was starting up at the base of his skull—never a good sign so early in a case.

And now his desk phone was ringing.

He picked up the receiver. "Hilary Whyte."

"Hil, for fuck's sake. When exactly were you going to get back to me?"

Hilary schooled his voice. "I told you, I'm busy, Jazz."

"When were you going to tell me the trial clashed with the ski trip?"

Hilary winced. "As soon as I got the chance."

"Mum spent a fortune on this. The whole wedding party is going," Jasper said. "Not to mention the press. How's it going to look if one of the grooms bails?"

"It will look like one of the grooms has to work."

"This was important to me, Hil. To all of us."

"It's just another photo opportunity," Hilary snapped as his work mobile started to ring. "The press will get enough of that at the bloody wedding. Look… I've got to go—"

"Don't hang up. Not after saying that."

"What do you want me to say, Jasper? I don't even like skiing."

"This is not fair," Jasper said, and Hilary's chest clenched to hear the genuine hurt in his tone.

"You're right, and I'm sorry," Hilary managed as the other phone stopped ringing and four more emails popped in to join the queue of fifteen unopened ones that had landed in his inbox since his meeting with Gunnerson. "I just… You know stuff comes up. Murderers don't consider their timing and neither do the courts. It happens with your film shoots, too."

"My shoots don't usually involve me sacking you off to spend time with abusive men from my past."

Hilary blinked. "Where did that come from?"

"You've done nothing but research this guy for weeks."

"I have to know what the jury will know."

"And that's really all it is?"

"What else would it be?" Hilary said, angry heat flooding his chest.

Jasper made an impatient noise. "You've always avoided talking about school and about him. And now he's back in your life and it's like he's the center of everything. Maybe he was all along."

"You're overreacting."

"I just don't want you to get sucked into anything that's gonna bring back bad memories."

"Dom Gosford was a wanker at school. That's no secret." Hilary took a breath. "And, yeah, I was in a bad place because of that—because of him—for a long time. But I've worked through it all now. He's just another client."

Jasper didn't say anything.

"I'm sorry about the holiday," Hilary said, managing to sound sincere. "I'll make it up to you. Let's go for dinner the night before you fly out. That place off the Strand you like?"

"Vincenzo's? You hate that place."

"This is for you. Get Marcia to tweet about it if you'd like. I'll pose for some photos."

"You'd be okay with that?"

Hilary sighed as three more emails pinged in. "Yeah. Sure. Now I really have to go."

"You're still coming to my folks this weekend, right? The tasting?"

Hilary looked at the pile of files on his desk with a sinking heart.

"Hil—"

"Yes, I'm coming. I might just have to work on the drive, that's all."

"I'll remember this the next time a shoot overruns, just so you know."

"Oh, I know you will," Hilary said, smiling.

It was Jasper's turn to sigh. "Love you, babe."

"Love you, too."

Hilary closed his eyes a moment, even though the desk phone was already ringing again. He waited until the dizzy spell had passed before picking it up.

"Hilary Whyte. Hey, Beck. Yes, I'm still working. How'd it go at the gun club?"

* * * *

Jasper was in bed by the time Hilary got home. There was a half-empty bottle of whiskey in the kitchen, the glass in the sink. Hilary slipped into bed without turning on the light and his fiancé's snores did not even change in rhythm. He was still asleep when Hilary got up six hours later to return to the office. Hilary didn't wake him to say goodbye, telling himself that Jasper would only be grumpy if he did.

Janice buzzed the intercom at a little after eleven to tell him Dominic Hart-Gosford was wanting a word with him. Hilary blinked at the phone blindly.

"Sir?" Janice said when he didn't reply.

"Send him in."

Hilary stood, straightened his tie and buttoned his jacket as Dominic entered. He caught a glimpse of Merriweather standing like a sentry on the threshold before the door closed between them.

"Mr. Hart-Gosford," Hilary said flatly. "How was your meeting?"

Dominic put his hands in his pockets. "I was disappointed not to see you there."

Hilary spent a fruitless moment trying to read his face. "Mr. Gunnerson thought it was better if I was not, so ideas could be expressed freely."

"Oh, they were certainly expressed freely." His smile widened. "Not that it mattered. It would seem you've made quite an impression on the partners of this firm. You're still on the case."

Hilary quashed a stab of disappointment. "And how is Mrs. Hart with the decision?"

Dominic's smile showed his canines. "Incandescent."

"I'm sorry to hear that."

"No, you're not."

Hilary indicated the chairs in front of his desk and sat. "Did you think about the offer?"

Dominic sat, gazing around at the shelves of legal textbooks and journals, the black-and-white photography taking up the remaining space, the record player in the corner with its neat stack of vinyl alongside. "I thought about it."

"And?"

Dominic folded his hands in his lap. "I can understand why you would have trouble believing in my innocence, Hilary," he started, speaking carefully and, for the first time, with contrition. "But I said I'd changed. That is the truth."

Hilary pursed his lips.

"What do you want to say?"

Hilary took a breath. "Your public record does not suggest that much has changed since you left St. Edmund's."

Dominic tilted his head. "What exactly is in the public record these days?"

"Gambling. Drunkenness. Drugs. Speeding. In debt to some nasty people, until the Hart family managed to settle that quietly. The only thing that seems to be missing is philandering." Hilary paused. "If we're laying cards on the table, I'd like to ask why that is?"

"Why what is?"

"There are rumors of affairs—but not many and none substantiated." Hilary leaned on the desk. "Are you happy with Amelia?"

"Of course I am."

"Huh."

"Is that so surprising?"

"So why the rest of the bad behavior?"

"It's all click-bait nonsense."

"All of it?"

Dominic raised an eyebrow. "Most of it."

"Unfortunately, it makes very little difference anyway," Hilary went on. "It's in the public domain. People have read it. Judged it. Judged *you*. And they will be the ones deciding whether you killed the Woods."

Dominic tapped one of his long forefingers off the arm of his chair. "Do you honestly think I could kill someone?"

You almost killed me. Hilary clamped his mouth over the words. "All I think is that if you take the prosecution's deal, you will lose four years of your life. If we go to trial, you could lose everything."

"Or walk away with a clear name."

"In legal terms, yes. Not necessarily in the eyes of the public."

"I don't care about the eyes of the public."

"Your family does. Do you think they'll continue to protect you after all this?"

Another pause. "What would you do?"

"I would take the deal," Hilary said without hesitation.

Dominic surveyed him for another long moment. "I'm not a murderer, Hilary."

"Honestly, at this point, it doesn't really matter if you aren't," Hilary said frankly "It's what you're willing to risk to prove it."

"I'll risk everything," he replied, voice dark and smooth as black coffee.

Hilary watched him in silence, taking in the firm set to his jaw, the black, unblinking eyes. He looked away with a sigh, ignoring the flicker that went over his skin. "Fine. I'll ring Augustine and tell her we're turning the deal down."

"And what happens then?"

"Then we go to trial in six weeks," Hilary said. "I will spend the time building the case—prepping witnesses, going over the evidence. You need to make yourself available if I or my researcher needs you. And, until the trial, you behave. Understand?"

He lifted one of his thick, black eyebrows. "'*Behave*'?"

"I'm serious, Dom," Hilary said, ignoring the squirming his knowing look had started in his abdomen. "Get caught even *thinking* about playing a card game or getting into a fight, and you might as well plead guilty now and save us all a lot of time."

"You just called me Dom."

Hilary cursed under his breath. "Do you understand what I'm telling you?"

Dominic nodded. "I understand."

"Good. Janice will be in touch to schedule our next review. In the meantime, I have rather a lot to do, so if you don't mind…"

"Can I ask you one more thing? Whilst we're being honest?"

Hilary fought wariness. "What?"

"Are you really gay?"

Hilary blinked. "Excuse me?"

"And engaged to Jasper Prince?" Dominic's eyes had hardened. "I was certain that couldn't be real. But there are plenty of photographs."

Hilary made sure his voice was level with an effort. "I'm sorry if me knowing everything about your personal life makes you uncomfortable, but it's how I can best do my job. Doing the same to me to put me on the back foot is not only unprofessional but pointless."

"I'm not trying to put you on the back foot. I was just curious."

"Why?"

"There were rumors at school," Dominic said, a little too easily. "But then there were always going to be rumors about any kid who dyed his hair and wore eyeliner. But you never came out."

Hilary flushed. "That's none of your business."

"I know that," Dominic said, standing. "I'm just wondering why you never said anything. You used to speak your mind about everything else."

"Is it any surprise?" Hilary snapped before he could stop himself.

Dominic's mouth turned down. "Perhaps not." He glanced at Hilary's ring. "He's a lucky man."

Hilary was groping for a response when a crash and raised voices had him on his feet. Dominic beat him to the door. The room beyond was in an uproar.

Merriweather was on the ground, twitching violently, bloody spittle dangling from his mouth, clawing at his neck as he struggled to breathe. Simon, the junior researcher, stood against the wall, frozen, his face white as a sheet while Beck knelt by Merriweather, her own face bloodless, loosening his tie with shaking hands.

"Move," Dominic ordered, pushing Beck back and kneeling in her place, fumbling at Merriweather's trouser leg.

"Call an ambulance," Hilary shouted while hurrying forward to help Dominic.

"I'm sorry," Simon quavered, eyes fixed on Merriweather. "I'm *so* sorry."

"Simon," Hilary shouted. "*Ambulance.*"

"I'm on it, boss," Beck said, pulling out her phone.

"Get back," Dominic said, pulling an EpiPen from the pouch strapped to Merriweather's ankle.

Hilary made room and Dominic stabbed the needle into Merriweather's thigh. Slowly, the butler's convulsions stilled. His breathing started to level. Dominic pressed a hand to his scarred face, a gesture so tender that Hilary was startled.

"Ambulance is on its way," Beck said, looking warily between Hilary and Simon, who still stood against the wall looking like he was about to cry.

"What happened?" Hilary demanded.

"I'm sorry, I forgot. I…" Simon glanced at the paper bag on his desk, the half-eaten peanut butter sandwich on top of it. Hilary stared at it, going cold.

"Simon—"

"I'm *sorry*—"

"Mr. Merriweather's allergy alert is on the front of every file," Hilary said, smacking his hand on the nearest folder, the yellow warning sticker in the corner. "How could you *forget*?"

"I'm sorry, sir," Simon choked, eyes wide.

"Don't tell me. You can tell Mr. Merriweather…in writing."

"Yes, sir. I will, sir."

"Get rid of that thing…outside. *Now*."

Simon grabbed the sandwich and hurried out of the door like he was being chased by a wild animal.

"Ambulance is here, boss," Beck said, answering her ringing phone and heading for the entrance.

Dominic stayed by Merriweather, checking his pulse with one hand whilst he continued to offer a reassuring pressure on his forehead with the other. The man was finally stirring. Hilary let out a shaking breath. Dominic's eyes met his. He opened his mouth to speak but the paramedics were swarming into the room and urging them both back.

"I'm fine, sir," Merriweather slurred, looking around blearily as they hefted him onto the stretcher. "Honestly, good as new. I don't need to go."

"Let them check you over," Dominic said, his face earnest. "I need you back fighting fit ASAP, understand?"

"Yes, sir," Merriweather said, trying to keep his eyes open as the paramedics stretchered him out of the office. Hilary followed them outside to the waiting ambulance. Dominic stood on the pavement, watching as Merriweather was loaded into the back.

"I sincerely apologize," Hilary said, voice tight. "We were well aware of Mr. Merriweather's allergy. Simon Bishop will be disciplined —"

"Don't be too hard on the boy," Dominic said as the ambulance doors were shut. "Merriweather could have said something or left the room. He probably chose not to."

"What? Why?"

Dominic watched the ambulance drive away in silence. When he finally replied, his voice was quiet, contemplative. "He's a proud man. Being rendered so vulnerable by something he has no control over... It's hard for him to accept."

Hilary searched Dominic's face, trying to see if anything lay behind his words. But he looked away and the spell broke.

"I trust you'll convey my answer to the prosecution?"

Hilary blinked, the topic change jarring. "If you're sure."

"I'm sure," Dominic said, his eyes earnest. He turned and, with a swirl of his long coat, disappeared into the crowds teeming up and down the pavement.

Chapter Three

Hilary sensed Jasper's look as he hung up a call and began typing another email while they bowled down the M25.

"I'll turn my work phone off when we get there."

"It's been all over Twitter, you know," Jasper said mildly. "And Facebook, Instagram, you name it. Gosford's already convicted—hung, drawn and quartered, even."

"Innocent until proven guilty," Hilary said, skimming the latest email from the court scheduling service. "Whatever the Internet thinks."

"Even him?"

Hilary took a breath. "Even him."

"Does it at least mean the trial will be over quickly?"

Hilary gave him an irritated look. "So it's done before the wedding, you mean?"

"Well, yeah," Jasper said with a shrug. "You don't want all this hanging over you on top of all that, right?"

Hilary let out a sigh. "You're right. And yes. It'll be over by then—one way or another."

They lapsed into silence as Jasper overtook a lorry. When they were back in their lane, he reached out to squeeze Hilary's knee. "You sure you're okay?"

"You don't need to keep asking me that."

"I know I don't *need* to," Jasper said patiently. "But I'm reminding you I'm here for you."

"You weren't this worried about me when I was defending Marshall Braun."

"Because I know you can handle lying, murdering pieces of shit. But you've never defended one you know before."

"I said already I can handle Dom Gosford."

Jasper opened his mouth to reply but Hilary's phone rang again, saving him from any further discussion.

When they were approaching the gates of the Princes' art deco manor house, Hilary frowned to see a small crowd of people milling in front. They turned as one as soon as they heard the car and surged forward to meet them as they pulled in.

"Jesus, Jasper," Hilary said, staring out at the grinning faces and the phone cameras. "Did Marcia post we were coming?"

"You would know if you read my feeds," he said, beaming at the fans as he edged the car toward the gates.

Hilary made an impatient noise. "But the *catering*, seriously? They care about the catering?"

"They care about us," Jasper said as he stopped the car.

"Jazz, no—"

But Jasper had already lowered his window. The crowd pushed forward, thrusting phones and cameras into the car. Hilary blinked in the flashing lights and swore under his breath.

"Hey, guys," Jasper said, signing a photo with the Sharpie he always kept in his pocket, handing it back and taking the next. "Thanks for coming. What's that? Yeah, we're really excited. Hilary? Oh, he's excited, too."

Hilary sent him a warning look, but Jasper was already pressing the control for the passenger window.

"Hilary! Hilary, so nice to see you together," a round-faced woman said, leaning through his window. "You guys are so cute." Hilary forced a smile as the cameras flashed and phones set to record were pushed through his window as more faces crowded around. "Are you looking forward to the big day? Any butterflies? How are you feeling?"

"Hungry," he said with another forced smile.

There was a ripple of laughter and Jasper waved as he crept the car forward. Cameras continued flashing through the rear window until the gate slid closed behind them.

"Nice one," Jasper said, kissing Hilary on the cheek as they got their bags from the boot. "Try to smile a bit more next time, though, yeah?"

Hilary bit off his instinctive reply when the front door opened. Jasper's mother and three of his cousins barreled forward and enveloped Jasper into a tight hug. His father stepped out and waited until the women retreated, still chattering, then shook his son's hand with a gruff greeting.

"They're at the gates again, then?" he said, peering down the drive.

"Yes, Dad. But they're harmless...promise. They just wanted selfies."

Stewart Prince raised a bushy eyebrow. "As long as they keep buying the merch, son."

"Hilary, dear," Jasper's mother said, squeezing Hilary's arm. "So good to see you. So sorry to hear you won't make Switzerland."

Ten seconds, Hilary thought. *She managed ten seconds before bringing that up.*

"I know. I'm so sorry, Fernella," he said, attempting to sound sincere.

"Oh well, I know what it's like to have such an important job," she said, her smile wide and blank. "We'll say no more about it."

I doubt that.

"I can't believe you're not coming, Hil," Josephine, the eldest cousin said, pouting. "I was counting on getting some pics for my blog. LGBTQ influencing is big right now."

"Leave him be, Jo," Jasper said. "I said you could livestream the ceremony, didn't I?"

She brightened and they all started talking at once as they ushered Jasper inside.

"Come in and have a drink, my boy," Jasper's dad said as Hilary shouldered his bag. "Your family is inside."

Hilary felt almost physically weak with relief when his brother and sister separated themselves from the throng of Prince cousins and in-laws in the huge, open-plan sitting area to draw him into a hug.

"Hil, thank God," Maxwell breathed in his ear. "What are your rates again? I'm this close to murdering some of these people."

"Max, shush," Minnie said, glancing around nervously, but the Prince family were all falling on Jasper, pressing champagne into his hand, seemingly oblivious to them.

"Oh, as if they'd miss just one," Maxwell whispered, his freckled face twisting. "There's at least a million, and they're not even all here yet."

"It's great to see you," Hilary said, squeezing his brother's shoulder. "Where are Mum and Dad?"

"In the kitchen," Maxwell said, his smile twitching. "Mum said she wanted to help. I think they just wanted some peace and quiet."

"Come on," Minnie said, taking Hilary by the elbow. "They can't wait to see you."

Being drawn into Rose Whyte's embrace and having her plant her usual bruising kiss on his cheek made something loosen inside Hilary.

"Good to see you, son," his dad said, patting his shoulder. "Sorry you caught us in here," he said, giving the chef a knowing smile. "This is where they keep the good plonk, after all."

"Arthur," his mother snapped. "We're very grateful to be invited, dear, as always."

"I know you are, Mum," Hilary said. "Thanks for coming. It means a lot. I know it's not exactly" — he glanced around the huge, chrome kitchen, thronging with caterers — "well, it's different."

"Free booze and food," Arthur said, snatching a pastry from a plate as a waiter carried it out. "What's not to like? Even if the family are stark raving bonkers."

"*Arthur*," his mum scolded again as Maxwell hid a snigger behind his champagne glass.

"I think we should get back, shouldn't we?" Minnie ventured, her expression tense. "They'll notice we're all gone."

"Not with Jasper around, they won't," Hilary said, glancing at the serving staff scurrying out of the door. "But it does look like they're serving."

Hilary took his place next to his fiancé at the twenty-seater dining table as the first samples were served. Jasper's father announced each course with the solemnity of a master of ceremonies, and the chef was called upon to describe each dish and what wine it would best go with.

"I think the salmon would be best for the pre-appetizer, Hil?" Jasper mused as he chewed.

"I don't mind," Hilary replied, topping up his wineglass and resisting checking his buzzing phone with an effort. "You choose."

"The honey saffron chicken does have the summeriness I want, though," Jasper went on, spearing the artful stack of chicken and pancake from the next plate along. "June wedding. Tradition. Summer. Sunshine. That's the vibe I want."

"Salmon is more elegant, dear," Fernella said, her three sisters and their seven daughters nodding and chattering in agreement.

* * * *

"And how's the big case going?" Stewart asked when they were finally back in the living area, the detritus from the meal cleared away and everyone loud and flushed with wine.

"It's going," Hilary hedged. "Early days, you know."

Stewart shook his large, leonine head as he held his glass out for a top-up from the waiter. "They should throw away the key, if you ask me."

"Dad," Jasper warned, "he's Hilary's client."

"Don't make me wrong," Stewart said, swallowing wine. "Bet Hilly knows that better than anyone. I remember Marshall Braun. Fucking psycho."

"Yes, he was," Hilary said without intonation. "And he went to prison...but with an appropriate sentence."

"Sure, you know best. Just tell me you're not gonna let this Gosford character get off scot-free?"

"Dad," Jasper cut in, giving Hilary's knee a reassuring squeeze. "Hilary can't talk about the case. You know that."

"Yes, yes. I did a turn with the Military Police as you well know. But come on, son," Stewart continued, clapping Jasper on the shoulder. "Marcia said they upped your offer for the new Bond movie? Are you going to take it? You'd be daft not to..."

Hilary squeezed Jasper's hand in thanks, even though his fiancé was already absorbed in an anecdote about Daniel Craig, so he slipped out of the open French windows. The night was cold and damp, but it felt good against his heated skin. Minnie and Maxwell sat smoking on the edge of the ornate pool, engaged in a murmured conversation. Hilary, as always, felt hesitant to intrude, so intent were they when they were together, but then Minnie looked up and waved him over.

"Where are the folks?"

"Gone to bed. Didn't they say goodnight?" Minnie said.

Hilary looked around the shadowy statuary. "No."

"Stewart had you in a corner," Maxwell muttered, smoke wreathing from his lips "I think they just wanted to slip away. They'll be at breakfast."

"Yeah," Hilary said. He nodded at the cigarettes. "Can I bum one?"

"Hilary," Minnie scolded, "you gave up years ago."

"Nights with the Princes don't count."

Maxwell snorted and Minnie held out her pack.

"Mum blamed us for you starting, you know," Maxwell said.

"I wanted to be in the club." Hilary took a cigarette with a half-smile, accepted a light from his brother and inhaled, closing his eyes as the nicotine stole through him. "It's not your fault the club feels this good. So, how's everything with you?" he asked, perching next to them.

"Good," said Minnie brightly. "My orders are picking up all the time. I'm interviewing for an assistant next week. The festival bookings are just starting. I think summer's going to be busy. I'll still have time to make your wedding cake, though. Don't worry."

"Did Jasper get back to you about the flavors yet?"

"Not yet," Minnie said, glancing at the shimmering blue of the pool.

Hilary swore under his breath. "I'll remind him. I like the chili chocolate but think he wants the honeycomb brandy. But I'll make sure he lets you know."

"Thanks, Hil," she said with a soft smile. "By Friday would be good…in case I need to cure the chili."

Hilary nodded and glanced to the blank-faced Maxwell. It was only then that he noticed the dark shadows under his brother's eyes. "Max? Did they drop your hours yet?"

"Not yet."

"You can't keep doing twelve-hour shifts, Max. You'll burn out."

"Tell that to the three other nurses off long-term sick."

"Still, legally—"

"How many hours did you work last week, Hilary?" Maxwell cut him off.

"That's different."

"Like buggery is it different," Maxwell said, topping up their glasses from a bottle of champagne he must have swiped from the kitchen. "You just get paid more so you're not allowed to complain."

"Tell us how it's *really* going, Hil…" Minnie said quietly.

"With the case or the wedding?"

"Both."

Hilary watched his exhaled smoke curl through the cold air. "It is what it is."

"Which one?" Minnie asked.

"Both," Hilary replied with a shrug.

"You think you can win?" Maxwell asked in a low voice.

"Honestly?" Hilary said, examining the glowing end of his cigarette. "I don't know."

"You've won everything else," Minnie pointed out.

"Every other case that went to trial was with a client who did what they were told."

Maxwell snorted again and stubbed his cigarette out on the pool tiles. "Can't believe you have to stand up in front of the world and tell everyone that Dom Gosford is a good bloke."

"I don't have to say that, luckily. Wouldn't fool anyone for a second." The twins exchanged a knowing glance and Hilary fought annoyance. "But I can say he claims he's innocent and make the best case possible. The rest is down to the jury."

"I remember when he set fire to your dorm," Maxwell said in a low voice. "Do you remember that?"

"I remember," Hilary said grimly. "Three of us ended up in hospital with smoke inhalation."

"And that fight in the changing room? You needed stitches, Hil."

Hilary winced. "That was both of us."

"But he started it." Maxwell shook his head. "And why? Because you were different—not some posh twat with a silver spoon up your arse. What a five-star dickhead."

"People change," Minnie said quietly.

"The Dom Gosfords of this world stay the same or they get worse," Maxwell responded, "but they don't get better."

"Max," she chided gently, "you never knew him."

"I know what he did to Hil," Max said, anger heating his voice. "That's enough for me."

"Let it go, Max," Hilary said gently.

"Why?"

"Because I have."

"Have you?"

"Would I be representing him if I hadn't?"

"If you feel like you have something to prove," his brother ventured, "then maybe."

"Hilary's a professional," Minnie insisted.

"I don't doubt *his* ability," Max replied sharply. "Just Dom Gosford's to act like a human being."

"Time will tell," Hilary said, finishing his own cigarette and stubbing it out next to Max's. "You guys get the money we sent for wedding clothes?" They looked at each other and didn't answer. "What is it?"

"We'd rather choose our own clothes," Minnie said softly.

Hilary blushed. "I know you would. But Jasper wants that designer. I'm sorry."

"Is anything in this wedding for you?" Maxwell said coolly.

Hilary met his brother's flaming green eyes with a quiet, level look. "It's just the game we have to play...for Jasper's career."

Maxwell shook his head. "I don't get it, Hil. I never will."

"You don't have to," Hilary said. "Please, just buy the suit and be there on the day. That's all I need."

"Of course we will," his sister said gently, squeezing his hand. "Mum and Dad are so looking forward to it. Honestly, when Mum heard that Ed Sheeran was playing, she nearly passed out."

Maxwell's face softened. "She did, it's true. Honestly, Hil, the wedding sounds like a dream." He looked in at the Prince family again, at Jasper laughing with his cousins at something on his phone. "Just not *your* dream."

"Marrying Jasper is my dream," Hilary said. "We've worked hard to get here...both of us. We're both ready for a life together. I'll put up with the circus for that. And in return, well" — Hilary shrugged — "he has to put up with me."

"Don't be silly," Minnie scolded. "He's the lucky one."

"So everyone keeps saying," Hilary said as his phone buzzed in his pocket. "But marrying a solicitor's no picnic. Ask Mum."

"Max, Min!" Jasper was stood at the door, beckoning. "Jo's got the best ideas for your speeches."

"Fucking Josephine," Maxwell muttered.

"Hey, that's my future cousin-in-law you're talking about," Hilary said, taking out his phone.

"That's not even a thing," Max said as he drained the champagne. "But for you, little brother...anything."

Hilary answered his phone with a smile. The twins filtered inside, and Jasper beckoned to Hilary.

"Five minutes," he mouthed, and Jasper frowned but went back in. "Beck. What did you find?"

"It's not good news, boss. Sorry."

"Nothing?"

"The Hart accountants are playing hard ball," Beck said helplessly. "The police haven't been able to find any obvious withdrawals around the time of the payment, but they have so many companies and subsidiaries, they could make ten grand disappear without much effort. Unless the accountants start cooperating with some affidavits, we won't be able to make a believable case for that money not coming from our client."

"Which means the prosecution can't prove it did either, at least," Hilary said, scuffing the tiles with his toe. "Anything on the brother?"

"Dean? Nothing," Beck said defeatedly. "He was just a normal guy. Under-chef in some East End Mediterranean place. Some minor debt, though nothing like his sister's. Single, no criminal record. Not even a parking ticket."

"So the poor sod really was just in the wrong place at the wrong time?"

"Looks like it," Beck said. "But, really, neither of these kids looks like any kind of threat to anyone. Lizzie worked for charities. She wanted to do good things…she just wasn't very good at keeping within a charity worker's salary."

"No reason to die…" Hilary murmured.

"We've seen murder done for less, I guess."

Hilary let out a sigh. "That brings us to the one angle we haven't considered…"

"What's that?"

"If Dominic Hart-Gosford didn't do it, who did?"

Beck made a disbelieving noise. "We can't rely on finding another suspect, sir. There's a reason they charged him."

"I know. But Lizzie was in with some fairly shady characters. It's at least worth a look. Even if we can't prove someone else did it, if we can at least establish that there was more than one motive, we're adding to reasonable doubt."

Beck sighed. "I'll see what I can find."

"Great. And what about this Sara Holden they've added to the witness list?"

"Lizzie's best friend, by the look of it. Loads of pics of them on social media. *Hashtag besties*," Beck added derisively.

"Just a character witness then?"

"Probably. But I'll keep digging. There is one thing, though…"

"What's that?"

"The hashtags, pictures, tagging with Sara… Everything stopped about a month before Lizzie died."

Hilary blinked. "Not besties anymore, then?"

"Maybe not."

"I don't suppose they were helpful enough to air their grievances online?"

"Not that I've found," Beck said regretfully. "But we should get access to Lizzie's phone records soon. If they fell out, there will be texts."

"Good. This is good. Sara must know something, or she wouldn't be on their list. If we can establish that she's not objective, it can only be to our advantage."

"We'll have to see what the texts say."

"Let me know when we get them. I'll talk to Gosford again in the meantime. You never know. Maybe he'll decide to tell me the truth this time."

"I do have one bit of good news. Anna Tarrant got back to us. She's agreed to meet to talk about the case. This Friday."

"You'd better not be joking."

"Boss, would I? About this, I mean."

Hilary smiled. "Great. That's really great. Something in our favor at last."

"Sorry it's not more. But I'll keep going."

"Thanks, Beck." Jasper had reappeared in the doorway with an impatient expression. "I gotta go. But I'll see you Monday."

"Take it easy, sir."

* * * *

Jasper was woozy and fumbling when they finally went to bed. He went down on Hilary with flushed feverishness. Hilary was so on edge and yearning for release that Jasper had him clutching the sheets and gasping in minutes.

"Beg, baby," Jasper slurred out of the darkness, teasing his entrance with a lube-slicked finger.

"Jazz, *please*."

Jasper chuckled as he took him deep into his throat and pushed two of his fingers in, sending sparks dancing along Hilary's ragged nerves. He came, trying desperately to keep quiet, aware of his parents in the next room.

Jasper crawled back up the bed and kissed him wetly, guiding Hilary's hands down to his straining erection. It took Jasper a long time to come, drunk and stupefied as he was. But finally, he moaned into Hilary's neck, shuddering as his hot seed spilled over his hands.

He was snoring in seconds.

Hilary wiped himself clean with a tissue, turned over and closed his eyes. He was so exhausted and his blood buzzing with wine that he expected to pass straight out. Instead, he lay there, staring into the darkness, his conversation with Maxwell repeating in his head.

"*You needed stitches, Hil.*"

He remembered the look on Dominic's face as he'd sat in his office.

"*I can understand why you would have trouble believing in my innocence, Hilary. But I said I'd changed. That is the truth.*"

Hilary sighed and turned over, making himself listen to the familiar, grating sound of his fiancé snoring until it distracted him enough to finally drop into oblivion.

* * * *

Hilary's parents were presiding over the coffee pots when Hilary came downstairs the next morning. Many of the Princes were already sitting around the table, swallowing painkillers with their Buck's fizz and pushing away the artisan breakfast feast with pale faces.

"We have staff for that, you know," Stewart Prince grumbled as he watched Rose hand coffees around.

"I like doing my bit," she said with a warm smile. "And you've done so much for us."

"Our pleasure, dear," Fernella said, sipping the coffee warily, like she thought it might be poisoned.

Hilary schooled his face with an effort as he took his seat next to Jasper's empty one.

"In fact, now that Hilary's here, we'd like to say a little something," his dad said. Hilary laid down his coffee cup as several pairs of eyes turned his parents' way.

"What's going on, Dad?" Maxwell asked.

"We were going to save our speeches for the wedding," Arthur went on, putting his arm around Rose and beaming under his bushy ginger mustache. "But I'm afraid I'd be too nervous in front of all those cameras. Besides, I'd rather say it here, amongst friends."

"Say what, Dad?" Hilary asked.

"We are immeasurably proud of all our children, that goes without saying," Arthur Whyte said, turning his smile on the twins, who both blushed under their freckles. "Max landing a position on an ICU at the Royal London, and now Min starting her own business and everything. Honestly, we couldn't be prouder. But I hope you two don't mind if we just focus on Hil a moment?"

"It's his day," Maxwell said, sending a genuine — if wary — smile Hilary's way. "Go for it, Dad."

Arthur took a deep breath. His eyes were shining, and Hilary's chest tightened.

"It's been a real dream come true, to see Hilary do so well," he began. "Winning a place at St. Edmund's. Then a law scholarship at Cambridge, not to mention getting the position with Gunnerson and Gains. I'm sure he won't mind me saying he's overcome some significant challenges to get where he is" — Hilary kept his face neutral but couldn't stop a blush from climbing up his neck — "and I honestly thought he'd reached a point where we couldn't ask for anything more for him. Then he met Jasper."

"Honestly, Jasper Prince," Rose said, pressing her hands to her cheeks. "I thought it must be someone with the same name. But no, *the* Jasper Prince..." She beamed, scanning the faces around the table with her eyes twinkling. "I've been a fan ever since *Stiches in Time*. And you've come so far since then!"

"He's still in bed, Mum," Hilary said.

"Oh," she said, blushing herself.

"No, no," Jasper croaked from the doorway, "I'm here." He managed a brilliant smile for Hilary's mother, and in that moment, Hilary felt like he could fall in love with him all over again. "Can't miss out on listening to someone talk about me, can I?" He pressed a kiss to Hilary's temple as he sat, and Hilary smiled in thanks.

"Well, as I was saying," his dad went on, "the only thing we still wanted for our Hilary was a partner worthy of him. And I think, in Jasper, that's exactly what he's found. Hilary deserves someone who makes him happy, makes him feel good. And that's what Jasper does. I want to thank him, and all of you, for welcoming Hilary and the rest of us, into your family."

"Glad to have you, old chap," Stewart said, raising his coffee cup in salute. He looked more than usually pale, the hangover heavy in his eyes. "And Hilary, too. I always said if Jazz insists on marrying a bloke, he'd better be a winner. Good-looking lawyer ticks the boxes, at least."

"Stewart," Fernella scolded, and Hilary looked away. But Arthur just laughed nervously and, finally, his parents sat and helped themselves to food.

"Fuck, I'm so sorry," Jasper said later as he steered the car onto the motorway. "Dad's a dick when he's hungover."

"It's okay," Hilary said as he typed an email.

"You don't sound okay."

Hilary patted Jasper's knee distractedly. "I'm fine. I'm just working. Long week ahead."

Jasper sighed but didn't speak again.

* * * *

Hilary arrived at his office well before eight the following morning, but Beck was already there, up to her elbows in tablets, laptops and paperwork.

"Tell me you took some of the weekend off," Hilary said, placing a takeaway coffee and a bagel on her desk.

"Did you?" she said, pulling the food toward her without looking up from her laptop.

"In a sense."

"Well, I hope you got some rest, because it's the last chance either of us will get for a while," she said, holding out a dozen heavy files. "Everything I've found makes the case less certain, not more."

"Well, we wouldn't want it too easy, would we?" Hilary said grimly. "Are these Lizzie Wood's phone records?"

"What I've gone through so far," she said, taking a wolfish bite of her bagel. "Nothing about blackmailing anyone. If she really was doing it, she used a burner that no one's found."

"Figures," Hilary sighed as he scanned the lines of texts. "Oh…"

"Yeah," Beck said around her mouthful. "She and Sara Holden did fall out. It was short and not sweet. Nothing world-beating. Over a bloke, it seems." She sighed. "It's so disappointing when people are predictable, isn't it?"

"Any indication of who he might be?"

"Lizzie specifically instructs Sara not to name him because 'she works for him'."

"Shit…"

"Yeah."

"But we're sure it's a man?"

"They both refer to a 'him'. Though Sara mostly calls him 'that slimy bastard'. Sara was warning Lizzie off."

"Do we think Lizzie was sleeping with this mystery man?"

Beck shrugged a shoulder. "I can't really tell. But I must admit I don't understand half the kids' lingo these days. Hoping Simon will be able to help when he gets in."

Hilary glanced at the empty assistant researcher's desk. "Where is Simon?"

"Don't ask me. You're the one who said that planting tracking software on a colleague's phone was illegal." She met his look and raised her hands. "I was just trying to give the kid incentive to turn up to work on time. Anyway, I'll dump it all on his desk when he gets in and see if he can translate. In the meantime, see what you make of it all. I've highlighted the interesting parts."

Hilary flicked through. "That's a lot of nasty words. Biologically inaccurate, too."

"Yeah, Sara didn't hold back. But Lizzie gave as good as she got. But 'bestie' clearly thought 'mystery man' was bad news."

Hilary pursed his lips. "Do we think Sara's going to identify Dominic in court as Lizzie's lover?"

Beck shrugged helplessly.

Hilary sighed. "At least we have evidence she's not objective." Beck gave him a pained look. "It's a start. And I've got a meeting with his highness at lunch. Maybe he'll tell me the truth if I confront him with this."

Beck's disbelief was evident on her face, but she refrained from comment.

* * * *

Hilary was pleased when he parked outside The Salisbury restaurant and found his palms were dry and his heart rate was only slightly elevated.

Just another client, he repeated to himself as he approached the restaurant. He took a breath, squared his shoulders and pushed open the swinging doors.

The broad, grim-faced form of Merriweather stood at the deserted maître d' stand, blocking the entrance to the dining room. He was slightly paler than usual but otherwise looked recovered.

"Mr. Merriweather. Feeling better, I trust?"

"Peachy, sir. Thanks for asking."

"I want to apologize again. My assistant has —"

"Forget about it, sir," Merriweather snapped. "I have."

Hilary attempted to glance past him into the restaurant. "I think Mr. Hart-Gosford is expecting me."

"Oh, he is, sir. I just wanted a word first, if I may."

Hilary blinked. "Of course. How can I help?"

He narrowed his eyes. "You do believe Master Dominic's innocent, right, sir?"

Hilary hesitated. "I really can't discuss your employer's case with you."

"I need to hear you say that you believe him."

"I am paid to believe what the client tells me."

"That don't assure me over much." He leaned forward, lowering his voice. "I know you knew him as a kid. Knew it weren't great between you."

"That has no bearing —"

"Like fuck it don't. Begging your pardon, sir." Hilary pressed his lips together and held the man's hard gaze. "I do know a bit about what he was like back then. And it don't sound pretty."

"And how do you know?"

"He told me some things. Some things I found out on my own."

"I see," Hilary said carefully. "Does your employer know you researched his past?"

"It's my job to know the family," Merriweather continued, tilting his chin. "Know all there is to know — the best and the worst. Get me?"

"I'm not sure I do."

"I'm paid to protect them," he went on. "Just like you. I know his dad snorted away all their money before Master Dominic could sit his A-levels. Know he was expelled from that fancy school of yours, too."

"I am aware of all this, Mr. Merriweather. But I'm a professional. I don't have his best interests at heart any less than you do."

"I *know* Master Dominic. Know him well. And I know he can be a prick. Bad temper, sometimes." Hilary kept his face blank with an effort. Merriweather's eyes glinted. "But it takes one reformed arsehole to know another. I'm grateful for the chance I was given by this family. Proud of what I made of it, too. The Harts gave that chance to Master Dominic, too. We both took it. Made it work."

"That's good to know," Hilary said.

"This is me telling you that he didn't do nothing," Merriweather said, "and that you better believe it."

Hilary surveyed him narrowly. "So where was he that night?"

"How would I know? I was at the banquet. I'm on tape…"

"But you've just said how well you know him. How you're paid to know everything, the best and worst, so you can protect him."

Merriweather interlaced his fingers. "That's right. But I weren't there that night, were I?"

Hilary continued to watch his face, trying to unravel what was going on behind his eyes. "You're on some of his arrest records. Witnesses said you intervened on several occasions — broke fights up before things went too far. Why weren't you with him that night, when he needed you most?"

"Like I said," Merriweather said, his words harder than stone, "I were needed at the hall. If I could give him an alibi, I would of done it."

Hilary raised his eyebrows. "You sound angry. Is it unusual for him to keep secrets from you like this?"

"I ain't his babysitter," Merriweather insisted. "But I *know* him — know the sorta bloke he is. He wouldn't do this."

"Well, I'm glad to hear he has such staunch support," Hilary said, starting to edge around him. "He needs all he can get."

"He's sorry for what he did to you, you know," Merriweather added in a low voice.

Hilary stopped. "Excuse me?"

"He wouldn't never admit it — leastways, not to me — but I can tell. He might tell you himself before this is over. But if it's gonna help you believe him, I think you should know."

Hilary stared at him, searching for a response. "Your employer is paying me for my time here," he finally said. "I think it's best I talk to him now."

"You do that, sir," Merriweather said, stepping aside. "I've said my piece. Just hope you take me at my word, for your own sake as well as his."

Hilary felt Merriweather's eyes on him as he moved into the busy restaurant. Dominic sat a table in the far corner, his long fingers interlaced on the tabletop, watching him approach.

"Hilary." He stood, raising an eyebrow, "glad you could make it."

"Mr. Merriweather stopped me at the door," Hilary said, looking back to where the man still stood to attention, his cold gaze now fixed out of the window. "Thankfully he seems quite recovered."

"It's not the first time and it won't be the last." He watched Hilary lay his iPad and phones on the table. "I trust he didn't make you uncomfortable?"

"No," Hilary lied, shutting his case and taking his seat. "He just wanted to make sure I was taking this seriously. I trust you need no assurance on that front?"

Dominic sat and spread a napkin on his lap. "No, Hilary. I know you are taking this very, very seriously." His eyes glinted. "Thanks for agreeing to meet here," Dominic went on as the waiter presented him with the wine list. "If I didn't have at least some of my meetings at a restaurant, I would never get the chance to eat." He ordered and the waiter held out the menu to Hilary.

"Just a water, please."

"You should eat," Dominic said as he poured water from a carafe into Hilary's glass. "Defending murderers all day must take a lot of energy."

"I thought you weren't a murderer?"

Dominic smiled. "A turn of phrase."

Hilary sipped his water and tapped his iPad. "I'm happy to meet wherever you want. But I want it on record that I've advised you that it's unwise to discuss your case in public."

"I own this restaurant," Dominic said as the waiter arrived with a bottle of pinot noir. Dominic tasted it, nodded and waved the waiter away. "I know for a fact that only people with problems bigger than mine eat here. They will be far too absorbed in their own troubles to pay us any attention."

Hilary glanced around the minor celebrities and Westminster bigwigs, turned back to the table without comment and handed the iPad over.

"I've emailed you all the progress reports and witness lists. Did you get a chance to read it all?"

"Yes."

"Anything to say about any of the prosecution's witnesses?"

"I don't think so."

Hilary repressed impatience, reached over and swiped the iPad to reveal a picture of a young Asian man with smart hair and a wide smile. "Adeel Bukhari. He worked with Lizzie at Homes with Hart. Know him?"

"I've probably met him, but I don't remember him any more than I remember Miss Woods."

"I'm willing to bet he remembers you," Hilary said, swiping the iPad again. The image of an overweight, middle-aged white man with a balding pate and chins spilling over his tight, gray collar appeared on the screen. "What about Frank Hermann?"

"Gun club security chief," Dominic said. "I've met him with Amelia once or twice."

"Is he going to testify that you took Amelia's guns that night?"

"He can't," Dominic stated. "I wasn't there."

"Well then, at the very least he'll be telling the jury about the lack of security. That you *could* have taken them and got them back without anyone knowing."

"Probably."

"This will give the prosecution grounds for stating that the crime was premeditated. That's not good news."

"The man takes bribes like sweets," Dominic said, putting the iPad down. "Look in his bank records. That must be enough to get his testimony discounted."

Hilary raised his eyebrows and started typing a text to Beck. "We'll look at that. They also have a couple of

Lizzie's neighbors on the list. Probably just to talk about her routine and Dean's visits. Then, finally…" Hilary reached over and swiped the screen again. A woman with honey-colored skin, thick black hair curling out from her head and with lips pressed together in a hard line glared out at Dominic like she knew he was there. "Sara Holden."

Dominic gazed at the image impassively then lifted his eyes to Hilary without comment.

"You don't know her?"

"No."

"Lizzie Wood's best friend. Any idea why she might be on the list?"

"Isn't it your job to know all this?"

Hilary took a breath for patience. "At first we thought character witness…to establish an impression of Lizzie and gain sympathy from the jury. Though her phone records now suggest that wouldn't be the wisest move on the prosecution's part."

"Why's that?"

"You really don't know?"

"I really don't know, Mr. Whyte," he said, leaning forward on his elbows. "Why? What are you wanting me to admit to this time?"

Hilary glanced around and lowered his voice. "I'm going to ask you one more time, Dominic. Did you know Lizzie Wood?"

"I will answer one more time. No."

Hilary searched his face. "You weren't sleeping with her?"

Dominic's eyes hardened. "Excuse me?"

"Sara and Lizzie fell out over a man Lizzie looks to have been involved with—someone Sara thought was bad news."

"And?"

Hilary paused as the waiter brought Dominic's steak and salad. Dominic began slicing the meat without meeting Hilary's eye.

"Dominic—"

"I don't know why that woman is on the list."

"I can't defend you against something if I don't know what it is."

"And I'm telling you there's nothing to know," Dominic said, spearing a bloody chunk of the meat.

Hilary sighed. "What about the brother? Dean?"

"What about him?" Dominic said, swirling his wine in his glass.

"Is he your link to Lizzie? To Sara?"

Dominic drank deeply and set the glass down. "You're asking me if I know the *brother* of someone I didn't know in the first place?"

"Sara must know *something*," Hilary insisted.

"Maybe she's pretending to know something."

"Why would she do that?"

"I don't know. Maybe she's misunderstood something. Or maybe she thinks she can make some money selling a story to the papers after the trial."

Hilary took the iPad back with a frown.

"Is that so unlikely?"

"No," Hilary admitted. "Sadly, not." He tried to meet Dominic's eye, but he wouldn't look up from his food. "None of this would matter if we could prove where you were that night."

Dominic wiped his mouth on the napkin and topped up his wine.

"There's really nothing you want to talk about?"

Dominic finally met his glance. "Many things, Hilary Whyte. But nothing to do with the case."

"Then what?" Hilary asked, the look in his eyes sending wariness sneaking up his spine.

"Do you love him?"

Hilary blinked. "What? Who?"

"Do you love him? Jasper Prince?"

It was a long time before Hilary could answer. "My personal life is not relevant."

"I'm trusting you with my whole life, personal and otherwise," Dominic said smoothly. "I think I deserve to know what sort of person I'm trusting."

"You had your time to object to having a queer lawyer," Hilary said, voice hard. "It would take a court motion to change that now. And I really don't think you'd survive the media blowback."

Dominic's eyebrows rose in what seemed like genuine surprise. "I don't object to having a gay lawyer, Hilary—just a publicity-hungry one."

Hilary took a moment to control his reaction. "Have I, in any way, indicated any interest at all in getting publicity?"

"How about instructing me how to live my life so it doesn't negatively impact on you?"

"So it doesn't impact on the *case*," Hilary snapped. "Whether you act on my advice is your responsibility, not mine. I get paid if you win or lose. Remember that."

"Oh, I will."

Hilary slipped his iPad back in his bag with icy calm. "If there's really nothing more you can give me about your alibi or Sara Holden, I'd say we're done here."

"It would mean a great deal to me if you would answer my question, Hilary…about your fiancé."

"Well, I'm not going to."

"It's not just idle curiosity, you know."

"Then what is it?"

Dominic withdrew his phone from his pocket. "I agree with Walter Gunnerson. I think you are the best person to plead my case, despite what you think of me.

But this…" He held out his phone. "This isn't a person I'm willing to trust with my future. I don't know who this is."

It was Jasper's most recent interview with *Hello!* magazine, featuring a photo of them smiling under an arch of roses. It was from their engagement photoshoot. Hilary felt color rise in his face when he remembered the amount of makeup they'd plastered on him, how they'd dressed him to make sure his tattoos didn't show, styling his hair so it fell in his eyes in a very attractive but very impractical way. He remembered the hours the photos had taken and how Jasper had been too drunk afterward to make love, even though the magazine had hired the most expensive suite in the hotel for them.

Hilary raised his eyes. Dominic's jaw was tight, but his eyes were deep and searching.

Hilary debated a long, silent moment. Then he shook his head.

"This," he said, nodding at the photograph, "is Jasper Prince and his fiancé, according to the Internet. This," he continued, searching through the photos on his own phone until he found a candid selfie Jasper had taken on their secret trip to the Maldives the year before. Jasper was tanned, his skin the rich amber it turned in the sun when he wasn't touched up with fake color. The lines in the corners of his eyes crinkled with his wide, bright smile and he had at least an inch of salt-and-pepper showing at the roots of his blond hair. Hilary was pink with sunburn, his face creased with laughter, his collar unbuttoned to reveal some of the lettering inked into his chest. His hair was down and frizzy with seawater and heat. It was the night Jasper had proposed. He laid the phone on the table. "This is the real us."

Dominic examined the photo in silence.

"We have to put on a show because of who he is," Hilary went on when Dominic still didn't speak. "His agent, Marcia, arranged that photoshoot, the interviews. She's the one who put out the story about him going down on one knee at the Savoy. It's all for his career—and, yes, for the public perception of gay marriage, too." He looked away. "But mostly for his career. But we *are* getting married...and we are in love."

Dominic lifted his gaze. "Really?"

"Really," Hilary said firmly.

"He just doesn't seem...your type."

"You don't know him...or me."

Dominic raised his eyebrows. "I know you want strength. Passion. Someone who knows you inside out and loves every last bit of you. The light and the dark."

Hilary's face heated further. "You know nothing of the kind."

"It's what we all want, isn't it?"

Hilary put his phone away, glancing around to make sure no one was paying attention. "We are not discussing this any further."

"It's so easy, Hilary," Dominic said softly, "to look up one day and wonder how you got there. To feel it's too late to get out. I get it. I do."

"*This* is what you want to talk about?" Hilary said in a fierce whisper. "You're getting tried for double murder, Dominic."

"I like to know my associates—whatever the circumstances." He drained his glass, not meeting Hilary's eye. "How do you meet a movie star, anyway?"

"If you're someone like me, you mean?"

"If you're someone like anyone," Dominic said mildly, pouring more wine into his glass.

Hilary chewed on that for a while then looked out of the window. It had started raining. "It was a little over three years ago. The firm I was working at represented Jasper's management company at the time. We met at one of the tedious parties we were both made to attend back then. I think I was the only one there who didn't want to talk to him about his films." He smiled. "I don't like superhero movies."

A corner of Dominic's mouth twitched. "So what do you talk to Jasper Prince about if it's not superhero movies?"

"Music," Hilary said. "He came into the room while I was going through the host's record collection. We had an argument about the Beatles versus the Rolling Stones."

"Who won?"

"Depends which of us you ask."

Dominic gazed at him thoughtfully and held out the bottle. "Are you sure you won't have some?"

Hilary checked his watch. It wasn't even two in the afternoon, but butterflies had hatched in his belly. He held out his glass. He gulped the rich, fruity wine and willed it to calm his nerves, wishing he could smoke.

"I do have my own question, Dominic."

"What's that?"

"Who do *you* think did it?"

"Pardon me?"

"If it wasn't you, someone wants to make it look like it was," Hilary said carefully. "Why?"

"How am I supposed to know?"

"Framing someone for double murder is a pretty serious undertaking. People usually know when someone hates them enough to do something like that."

Dominic dabbed his mouth with the napkin again. Hilary found himself noticing how full his lips were, how expressive, even when they were set in their usual hard lines. He raised his eyes hurriedly as Dominic said, "I don't know if you've noticed, but I'm not the most popular person."

"Anyone in particular you've pissed off recently? Anyone connected with your wife's charities or the Woods?"

"If there was, don't you think I would have mentioned them?"

"I don't know. Would you?"

"Honestly?" Dominic said, gazing out into the wet street. "I don't know how anyone could do anything so barbaric...to anyone. I'm hard pressed to think of a reason why anyone would do it at all, let alone just to make me look bad...worse," he corrected, eyes sliding back to Hilary.

Hilary drank again, even though he could feel his walls thinning. "You weren't exactly opposed to violence at school."

Dominic was silent a long time. "You've defended murderers, yes?"

"Yes."

"Then *you* know why people kill. I don't."

"Money. Love. Revenge."

"What?"

"The big three," Hilary said, staring into his glass. "The reasons people kill each other."

"Is that right?"

Hilary nodded. "Money being the usual one."

"How unromantic."

"It's not like on TV. Not many murders get to trial. It's usually all too obvious who did it."

"But not this time."

"No." He drew a deep breath and met the deep, black gaze. "So do you trust me to do my job again?"

"Is Ed Sheeran really singing at the wedding?"

Hilary winced. "I wanted The Offspring, but there you go."

Dominic smiled again. There was still a glint in the black eyes, but the sincere tilt to his lips transformed his face and, for an unnerving moment, Hilary wondered again just who this man had become.

Hilary drained his glass and stood. "I'll start work on our own witness list tomorrow. Make sure you're available for queries. And the meeting with Ms. Tarrant QC is at my office on Friday. Make sure you're on time."

"Who?"

Hilary frowned. "I sent an email."

"You'll have to refresh my memory."

Hilary sat again, frown deepening. "Ms. Tarrant... the barrister."

"I don't want a barrister."

It was a moment before Hilary could get his thoughts in line to answer. "It's not a case of *wanting* a barrister—"

"I want you to represent me."

Hilary rubbed his eyes. The headache was back. "I am your solicitor. I prepare the case. The barrister presents it in court."

"Not always."

"No, not always but most of the time. Presenting cases is their job. They do it best."

"I want you."

Hilary stared at him. "The only reason you would choose a solicitor over a barrister is if they have an equivalent amount of court experience. Most solicitors don't. *I* don't."

"Hilary," Dominic said, leaning forward, "I need someone to stand up in court who knows all the worst things about me but still believes I'm innocent. That is how I win."

"Tarrant's one of the best barristers in London, in the country—"

"I don't want her. I want you."

Hilary stared at his empty glass, the wine dregs staining the crystal like blood.

"If I insist, you have to, don't you?"

"Unless I file a motion for change of counsel."

Dominic's gaze flickered. "You wouldn't do that. Think of all the negative publicity, just before your wedding."

Hilary repressed a frustrated noise and stood again. "You're meeting the barrister, Dominic. There's no negotiation there. Friday. Two o'clock."

"I won't change my mind."

"You'll have to." Hilary picked up his briefcase. "And remember. Best behavior."

"Of course," Dominic said, emptying his own glass. He locked eyes with Hilary and ran his tongue over his lips, cleaning off the dark red stain. Hilary's blood rushed as his mind shied away from the memory of that same mouth sneering over him as he lay sprawled on the concrete floor of the changing rooms, the taste of blood in his mouth.

He left before he could let any reaction show on his face.

Chapter Four

"Is this really our witness list?"

Hilary glanced up at Beck's strained expression then back at the files on his desk. "We don't exactly have people queuing up to extol our client's virtues."

"But Eloise Hart and Bruce Merriweather?" she said, scanning the list with a deep frown. "Talk about faces that sink ships."

"I don't think our witnesses' personal appearances come into it."

"They bloody do," Beck countered. "They shouldn't, but they do—and you know it. Those two won't generate any sympathy from any human jury member."

"We need people who know him...are loyal to him."

"That gorilla of a butler was a stunt double after he was discharged from the army. Did you know that?"

"I did."

"Got addicted to painkillers after breaking his neck on set—in and out of rehab, criminal record for assault, battery..."

"I read your report."

"I know you did. And yeah, I know it's the best we've got. It's just prepping twats for trial is twice as hard as normal people, and you're still not allowed to hit 'em."

"If only you weren't so good at it," Hilary said with a smile. "At least we've got the forensics analyst — and the DI."

"I dunno, boss. We already know forensics is a virtual bust. And Inspector McGarry's danced this dance before. She knows what she's doing."

"She has a history with our client," Hilary said, signing off a subpoena order and pulling out another. "She's had him in her sights ever since she couldn't make that battery charge stick."

"Can't say I blame her," Beck murmured.

"Beck..."

"He beat up a gay guy, boss."

"Allegedly," Hilary hedged. "No witnesses. No charge."

"Because the family paid everyone off." Beck shook her head. "McGarry won't come in for prep, you know."

"We don't want her to," Hilary said, handing the orders over. "I don't want her to know what we're going to ask."

"Oh, she'll know."

Hilary tapped some more papers together and filed them away without answering.

"Fine," she said with a weary gesture. "So the DI with beef might work for us. But Eloise Hart always looks like she's smelling something rotten, boss. I really wouldn't use her."

"She was the last person to see Dominic that day. She's the only one who can testify to his mood when he left the art gallery."

"And she says it was good?"

"Yes. It was just a normal day—for that family, at least."

Beck pulled out her phone, searched for something then held it out. "You clearly missed the Twitter chatter at the time." The screen showed an image of Dominic storming out of the doors of the art gallery, his tie askew, flushed, his face like thunder. "It didn't exactly make headlines, but it went around the trolls and gossips, rumors of an argument about the banquet. Clarence Lavelle was on the guest list, some old crony of his dad's."

Hilary paused. "Isn't he under investigation for something?"

"Probably," Beck said with a sardonic look. "What politician isn't? But darling Eloise had also invited that West African ambassador they tried to nail for extortion last year. The click-baiters tried to make the whole thing political."

"Both Eloise and Dominic have denied any argument that day," Hilary said. "And the picture doesn't prove anything. Eloise can back him up, whatever the differences between them."

"I still think it's a bad idea," Beck said, turning to the last page of the list. She paused. "And you're certain you want the client on here, too?"

"If we don't put him on the list, it will look like we're scared to."

"Hearing that man talk in his own defense is the fastest way to make everyone believe he's guilty as hell."

"I'm hoping it won't come to that."

"I want it on the record right now that no amount of prepping will make that man sympathetic to the jury."

"Your objection is noted," Hilary said patiently. "Where are we with the accountant?"

"Janice still hasn't managed to arrange a meeting," Beck said, flinging the witness list back on Hilary's desk. "And it takes some doing to refuse Janice."

"Maybe I should just drop in on him before the meeting with Tarrant."

"You'll have to be quick about it," she said, looking at her watch.

"Why?"

"Their office told Janice he's on a flight to Dubai later today. I'll be surprised if he hasn't left already."

"Today?"

Beck nodded.

Hilary swore and grabbed his coat.

"Cutting it fine, boss. Tarrant will be here in an hour."

"If she gets here before I get back, can you make sure she gets a tea? Not coffee, tea. Earl Grey. And, for Christ's sake, keep the client and her separate until I get back?"

Beck nodded and Hilary raced from the office.

He left the thirteenth-floor offices in the Shard with less than twenty minutes to get back to his office, no more information than when he'd arrived and in an even worse mood.

999. Tarrant's here.

Beck's text came through just as the traffic slowed in a snarl around Piccadilly. Hilary swore in a way he hadn't done since uni and used voice command to reply.

Stall her.

She's not the problem. Client's here, too. They're in your office. We couldn't stop him.

Hilary slammed on his indicator and turned into the back roads to try to make up some time. The heavens chose that moment to open up and deluge the streets, slowing the already snail-paced traffic to almost a standstill.

* * * *

Anna Tarrant strode into the law office lobby, making for the front door, just as Hilary hurried in, shedding his dripping coat and trying to pull his wet hair into some semblance of order.

"Ms. Tarrant," he said. "I'm so sorry I'm late."

"More late than you know," she said. "If you want my advice, young man, you will get your client to change his plea before this trial starts. I've worked with enough murderers to know one when I see one. And he doesn't care who knows it, either."

She swept out, her long coat swishing as the door closed behind her.

Hilary made for his office. Beck gave him a helpless shrug as he passed her desk. He opened the door with anger searing his skin. Dominic sat in one of the leather chairs, one leg crossed over the other, not a hair out of place, a soft smile on his lips.

"What did you do?"

Dominic lifted an eyebrow. "I let the good QC know that her services were not required."

"That is *not* your call."

"My family is paying for this. My decision stands."

"You really have no idea what you've done, do you?"

"You're very wet, Hilary. Where have you been?"

"At your bloody accountants trying to get some answers."

Dominic tapped his fingers off his knee. "Did you get any?"

"No. And the man is leaving the country for six months. His deputy is making the court appearance. Do you have any idea how *that* looks on top of everything else?"

"Like the accountants don't think they have anything to account for."

Hilary glared. "I understand you are used to getting what you want, Dominic. What I don't understand is how you've not learned that that's not always a good thing."

Dominic stood. Hilary resisted the urge to step back with a gargantuan effort as he approached. "I believe in you, Hilary," he said in a low voice, thick, like treacle. "All I need is for you to believe in me in return."

"Do you know what it's like in prison?" Hilary said after a pause.

"I was rather hoping I wouldn't have to find out."

"Those men will tear down the fabric of your mind. They will destroy every last idea of safety and security you've ever had. Do you know what that's like?"

Dominic's eyes narrowed. "Do you?"

Hilary couldn't find his voice for a long moment. "If you're going to sabotage the case, you should at least have an understanding of the consequences."

"I'm not trying to sabotage anything. I just believe the jury will invest more in you than a white-wigged stranger who clearly hates my guts."

"And I don't?"

Dominic paused. "You hate me?"

Then. Now. Forever. Hilary managed not to answer out loud, but he was sure a blood vessel nearly burst under the strain.

Dominic's face tightened as he took in Hilary's expression. "You'll see, Hilary. Before this is over, you'll see."

"Why do you care what I think?" Hilary snapped.

"Because I have to. Otherwise, there's no point...to any of it."

Something about the look in his eyes went right through Hilary. He looked away and stepped behind desk. "Get out."

Dominic frowned. "Excuse me?"

"Out. *Now.* I need to deal with this."

"I understand you're angry. But if you cannot maintain your professional courtesy—"

"*Get the fuck out.*"

Hilary did not look up as Dominic banged the door shut behind him.

* * * *

"He...he *what*?"

"I know," Hilary said, pulling off his tie. "I swear this tosser will be the end of me."

"That's not funny, Hil," Jasper said with a frown.

Hilary pulled the band out of his hair and ran his fingers through it with a sigh. "It's just an expression."

"He has pushed you to the edge before and now he's clearly delusional. Sacking his own barrister?"

"He wants me representing him in court," Hilary said wearily, accepted a tumbler of iced vodka from his fiancé. "And he's not used to being told no."

Jasper poured himself a whiskey. "You can do it, Hil. I know you can. You just shouldn't have to."

"Doesn't look like I've got much choice. No other barrister's going to work with us after this."

"I'm sorry."

"No, *I'm* sorry. I didn't want to bring this home." He managed a weak smile as he unbuttoned his collar and took a deep breath. "Tell me about your day."

"Oh, it was boring," Jasper replied, downing the whiskey and pouring another. "Production meetings. Script review. Then a two-hour session with Mum and the wedding planner over lunch."

"What is there left to plan?" Hilary said, managing to keep the exasperation in his tone to a minimum.

"If that woman can charge for it, lots," Jasper said with a tired smile. "Then three hours with Marcia after that. The promo schedule for the *Raiders of the Lost Ark* remake is mad already and we haven't even started shooting yet. Oh, I booked Vincenzo's, by the way. The night before I fly. You're still coming, right?"

"Of course."

"No last-minute meetings?" Jasper narrowed his eyes. "Or protesting if I share a selfie?"

"I promise," Hilary said, laying his hand on Jasper's chest. Jasper's smile widened to a grin, and he leaned forward to nuzzle Hilary's jaw. Hilary sighed at the warm touch then, out of nowhere, he remembered

Dominic's deep voice and the intensity in his look. Hilary froze.

"Hil?" Jasper said, drawing back. "What's wrong?"

Hilary shook his head. "Nothing. Nothing, I'm just tired." He stepped away. "I think I'm just gonna listen to some records and go to bed."

"Okay," Jasper said. "If that's what you want."

Hilary filled his glass and went to the music room. He scanned the shelves of records—Jasper's small collection by the window, his more considerable one taking up all the remaining wall space. He ran his fingers along the faded spines, chose one, set it on the turntable and collapsed into the wide, comfortable armchair. He leaned his head back on the headrest as Chester Bennington's tortured tenor filled his ears. He sipped the vodka and closed his eyes, willing the music to clear his head. But if anything, his nerves felt more tightly strung than before. He hesitated then went to the door and opened it a crack. He heard the TV blaring in the sitting room and quietly closed and locked it, then retrieved a cigarette from the hidden drawer under the hi-fi. He opened the windows wide, letting in the cold air, lit up and sat back down.

He took a deep drag and finally started to relax as he finished it and dozed off.

He woke with a crick in his neck and the record spinning silently on the needle. The digital clock on the turntable read just after one a.m. He blinked blearily as his work phone buzzed and flashed on the table next to him. He noted the six missed calls and was instantly wide awake.

"Hilary Whyte," he answered.

"Ah, Mr. Whyte. Glad we finally got you."

"Who is this?"

"Custody Sergeant at Charing Cross nick. We've got one of your clients in the cells. He'd like a word."

Hilary's heart sank. "Which client?"

* * * *

Dominic sat straight-backed on the concrete bench. His shirt was rumpled, his dark hair disheveled, but he sat motionless, his gaze heavy but impassive as Hilary stepped into the cell.

"Hilary—" he started, but Hilary raised a hand.

"Not here," he said and gestured out of the door.

Dominic preceded him out. His client sent the custody sergeant a supercilious smile as they passed through the reception. Her only reaction was to lift an eyebrow, but the members of the public slouched in the waiting area all pulled out their phones to film them as they passed.

Hilary swore under his breath, took Dominic by the elbow and hurried him out through the door.

"Don't even think about it," Hilary snapped as a traffic warden bent to examine his numberplate.

He started the engine and pulled out, causing the traffic warden to jump back to avoid being caught in the spray from the curbside puddle. Hilary accelerated, his gaze fixed out of the windscreen, his jaw aching from clenching.

"Aren't you going to say anything?" Dominic's voice was low, teasing, thick with drink. Hilary didn't answer. Dominic sighed and sat up straighter in his seat. "I was looking forward to another of those verbal undressings you're so accomplished at. You know you're one of the very few people who speak to me like that?"

"And where the hell is your nanny?"

"Gave him the night off."

"Fucking impeccable timing."

"Why, Mr. Whyte… What unprofessional language."

"Six weeks, Dominic," Hilary snapped. "You only had to behave for six weeks."

"I've never been good at following rules."

"I'm trying to keep you out of prison. Did you really think a DUI was going to help this situation?"

"You don't care if I go to prison. You wouldn't care if I choked on my own vomit."

Hilary looked at him, the streetlight washing his glowering face orange, then turned his eyes front again. "It's my job to care."

"What a lovely lukewarm sentiment."

"What do you *want* from me, Dom?" Hilary snapped, braking at a red light.

"I want you to believe me."

"I do."

"No, you don't. You think I'm a monster. A killer."

Hilary ground his teeth, glaring at the traffic light, willing it to change. "If you really want a new lawyer, it can be arranged."

"That's not what I want."

Hilary shot him a look. "You're enjoying this, aren't you?"

"Enjoying what?"

The light changed. Hilary pressed the accelerator, his grip tightening on the wheel. "Just like school. Getting into people's heads…under their skin. Even if you're the one to suffer for it."

"Self-destruction and I have always been close acquaintances," Dominic said smoothly. "But you already know that."

Hilary shot him a look of pure loathing. "We're not in school anymore."

"I'm aware of that."

"So start acting like it."

Dominic leaned over, his whiskey-scented breath brushing Hilary's face. "Why is it so hard for you to understand what's going on here?"

A shiver went through Hilary, but he refused to turn his head. "I understand you're a spoiled, entitled bully who lashes out when the world gets too real," Hilary said. "Which is fine until the shit doesn't just land on you."

"Don't play the victim. It doesn't suit you."

"I was thinking of Lizzie and Dean," Hilary snarled.

"That's *nothing* to do with me."

The fierceness of his tone made Hilary look over. His black eyes blazed, his cheeks were flushed, lips turned down. Intense. Real. Hilary looked away hurriedly. "So *act* like it. Act like you're aware of what's going on. Act like you give a shit, for fuck's sake."

"You're one to talk."

Hilary yanked the wheel over and climbed the curb outside the gates of the Hart-Gosford townhouse. "Out."

"Now? When we're finally being honest with each other?"

Hilary got out of the car and pulled out his phone, ignoring the rain that soaked his clothes and plastered his hair to his head.

"What are you doing?" Dominic said as he climbed out of the passenger side.

"I'm getting your butler or whatever the hell he is to come and manhandle you to bed, night off or not."

"For the amount I'm paying you, I would hope you'd be the one to do that."

Hilary stared at him, the phone forgotten. "Fucking stop all of this, okay? Just stop. It's not going to work."

"I don't know what you mean."

"Yes, you do. You've always known how to get in my head. And yeah, in school, it worked. You fucked with me. You won." The darkness in Dominic's eyes shifted in the low streetlight. Heat surged up from Hilary's belly. The rain ran down his face, doing nothing to cool his burning cheeks. "But guess what? I was a queer, alternative kid at an all-boys boarding school. It was never gonna take much to mess me up. But I'm not that kid anymore. And you keep telling me you're not, either. So drop the campaign against my sanity."

"I never won," Dominic said in a low voice. "Not with you."

"I would have died before I let you know it."

Dominic swallowed. Hilary watched the muscles in his throat move, the look in his eyes raw and burning. He wanted to turn away, wanted to get in the car and drive, but he couldn't move.

"You never knew…never knew *why*…" There was a new rasp in Dominic's voice.

"Knew *what*?"

Dominic stepped forward, trapping Hilary against the car—and kissed him.

Hilary felt water close over his head. He smelled the sweet-salt musk of Dom Gosford's skin, the faint, herbal smell of whatever shampoo he used. He could taste rainwater and whiskey as he tilted Hilary's head back and swept his tongue between his parted lips. He felt the tenderness of the touch under his chin, of the fingers running up his arm. For several stunned moments he couldn't understand or stop any of it. He shivered, closed his eyes, opened his mouth and gripped onto an iron-hard shoulder to stop himself from falling.

Dominic made a low noise deep in his chest and Hilary slammed back to reality. He shoved Dominic away so hard that he stumbled. He fumbled with the car door, cursed as his fingers slipped in the rain, but then, finally, he was in. He turned the key and stamped on the accelerator. The car raced into the road. Thankfully the street was deserted, otherwise, he reflected later, he was sure he would have killed someone…or himself.

He watched Dominic shrinking in his rear-view mirror until he vanished in the veil of rain.

Hilary didn't stop speeding until he'd left Mayfair far behind.

He rode the lift to his and Jasper's floor with his body shaking. He had to concentrate very hard to unlock the door without making any noise. He hovered on the bedroom threshold, listening to the gentle grating of Jasper's snores. He gripped the doorframe tight but couldn't make himself go in. Instead, he went to the music room and shut the door. He sat in the armchair, telling himself he was only shivering because of his damp clothing, and stared out of the windows at the dawn spilling up over the sky like a stain.

The sound of Jasper moving around the flat woke him several hours later. The clock read just after nine. He cursed, wondering just how he was going to explain being late, today of all days. He dared a look at his work phone—a missed call from Janice, two from Beck...four from Dominic Hart-Gosford. There was even a voicemail.

Hilary's blood ran cold, but when he listened, it was just silence and a bleep as the call was cut.

Hilary deleted it and all records of Dominic's missed calls then hurried to the kitchen. Jasper looked up and frowned.

"Hil, I thought you'd gone to work?"

"Not yet," he said, grabbing a mug.

Jasper poured milk on his quinoa flakes and dried fruit. "Hey, are you okay?" he said, face changing. "You didn't come to bed."

Hilary felt the heat climbing up his neck and turned his back, fumbling with the coffee machine. "I'm fine. Just had to bail someone out."

Jasper lowered his spoon. "It was that dickhead again, wasn't it?"

Hilary didn't reply as the coffee streamed into the mug.

"What did he do now?"

"Best I don't talk about it."

"I don't fucking believe it. Who does he think he is? Getting you called out in the middle of the night?"

"It's nothing," Hilary said, grabbing the coffee.

"Nothing?" Jasper frowned. "If it was *nothing,* why didn't you come to bed?"

"I didn't think I'd sleep, so I just went to the music room. I didn't want to disturb you."

"Seems like that's happening a lot these days," Jasper said after a pause.

"Look... I'm late," Hilary said, making for the bathroom.

"This is becoming a problem, Hil," Jasper said, trying to follow. "You can't keep avoiding it."

"We'll talk later," Hilary said firmly and shut the bathroom door in Jasper's face.

He turned the water up to its hottest setting, willing it to sear away the memory of the night before. But it didn't matter how hard he scrubbed his skin or how many times he brushed his teeth, he could still feel Dominic...taste him.

He used his car's Bluetooth to phone Beck when he was sure he could control his voice.

"Boss, thank Christ. Where are you?"

"I'm on my way. Sorry, it was a...late night."

"Yes, I saw on Twitter."

Ice went down Hilary's neck. "What's on Twitter?"

"You hustling our client out of Charing Cross police station. Pictures *and* videos. And you should know that both Eloise Hart and Amelia Hart-Gosford have been on the phone three times each."

"I'll be there in twenty minutes."

* * * *

"The footage is everywhere," Amelia said, her face flushed, her fine-boned hands clasped in her lap tight enough that the tendons stood out under the fair skin. "All over social media. The news sites..."

"I am aware—"

"It's your job to *protect* Dominic from this sort of thing."

"I said this from the start," Eloise put in, her eyes sharper than needles. "This man is *not* up to the task."

"All due respect," Hilary cut in, raising his voice the barest notch. "I warned Dominic about managing his behavior. I can't be held responsible for his choices or for the fact that everyone now carries a camera phone and a desire to go viral."

"Mr. Whyte, I've had reason to comment already on your lack of respect—"

"Eloise." Dominic was sitting in the same leather chair, his elbows on the chair arms, his fingers steepled in front of his face. He showed no signs of his heavy night, apart from the weight in his gaze, which was fixed on the wall. "Mr. Whyte is right. It's not his fault. I had a hard day." He glanced at Hilary then away again. "I wasn't thinking."

"Well, clearly," Eloise said, venom in her tone. "You rarely do. But Mr. Whyte should have anticipated this and been prepared for it."

"I got the charge dropped," Hilary stated. "We can't stop the video from doing the rounds, but my advice is to not respond to it. No statements. Nothing. The fire will die if we don't give it any more fuel."

"That's your strategy, is it?" Eloise said.

"It's all we can do."

"He's right." Amelia put her hand on Dominic's shoulder. "It won't happen again, Mr. Whyte." Dominic lowered his hands but didn't speak. "I apologize for our manner. The news was a shock to wake up to, that's all."

Something bitter washed up the back of Hilary's throat. He felt Dominic's eyes on him but didn't meet them. "I understand this is a hard time. We just have to do the best we can—all of us."

"Well, I suppose we will have to be satisfied with that, then," Eloise said, retrieving her handbag from the arm of the chair. "Amelia? The fundraiser."

Hilary got to his feet as the women made for the door. Amelia looked back at Dominic, who had also stood but didn't follow.

"You go on ahead. I'd like a private word with Mr. Whyte."

Color suffused Hilary's face as Amelia's glance went between them. "Very well, dear. See you at dinner."

The door closed. They stood in silence, staring at each other.

"Shouldn't we talk about it?"

"There's nothing to talk about," Hilary stated.

Dominic raised his eyebrows. "Your recollection must be different from mine."

"You were drunk."

"Not that drunk."

"Unless there is a specific legal query I can help with," Hilary said firmly, "I would ask that you leave."

"You don't look well. Did you sleep?"

"Mr. Hart-Gosford—"

"Let's not go backward," Dominic cut him off. "I was Dom last night."

"I was angry last night."

"Just angry?"

"Please leave."

"I think we should talk."

"Let me make this crystal clear," Hilary said coldly. "The only way I would want to discuss last night further would be in the context of a sexual assault claim. Now, do you want to talk?"

"You kissed me back, Hilary."

Hilary pushed a button on his desk phone. "Janice, Mr. Hart-Gosford has apparently forgotten his way to the exit. Do you mind showing him?"

Dominic locked eyes with him until Janice opened the door. When he was gone, Hilary sank into his seat and put his head in his hands. Jasper tried to call. He didn't answer.

Chapter Five

"Hil?"

Hilary blinked. He was stood at the kitchen counter, a spoonful of porridge frozen halfway to his mouth. Jasper stood in the doorway, a line between his eyebrows.

"Hmm-m?"

"You okay?"

"Course," Hilary said, scraping the rest of his breakfast into the bin and filling the coffee machine.

"You're still not sleeping?" Jasper came up behind him, rubbed the small of his back.

"It's just the case," Hilary said as the coffee machine began to burble, filling the air with a rich, deep fragrance that he usually found comforting. "It's the evidence filing deadline tomorrow and, well…we don't really have any." Jasper didn't speak but continued to hover. "What is it, Jazz?"

"Can we talk?"

"What about?"

Jasper lifted a hand as if to touch Hilary's face then dropped it again. There was an unfamiliar wariness in the crystal-blue eyes that made nervousness churn in Hilary's belly. "You know what about. You've been acting weird for a while. Distant. I just want you to look me in the eye and tell me nothing's wrong."

"I'm prepping for trial. It's always intense."

"It feels different this time."

"How?" Hilary said exasperatedly as he filled his travel mug.

"I don't know... It just does."

Hilary screwed on the lid without raising his eyes. "Are you sure it's not you who's acting weird?"

Jasper frowned. "Me?"

Hilary shrugged. "Marcia seems to be getting more attention than usual, that's all."

Jasper's face was set. "She's my agent. I've got a lot on right now. You know that."

"Well, so have I."

He left without looking back.

* * * *

Hilary stared at his work phone. Dominic's contact info glowed on the screen. His thumb hovered over the call button, as it had done countless other times since he'd thrown him out of his office the week before. And, like all the other times, Hilary impatiently closed his contacts list down without calling.

"Boss?"

Hilary started, blinking at Beck who had stuck her head around the door. "Soz, boss. I did knock."

"Sorry. Million miles away," he said, laying the phone face down on his desk. "What is it?"

She frowned as she came forward. "Are you okay? You look wrung out."

"Trial in two weeks," Hilary said, glancing at the snowdrift of papers on his desk. "And we still have fuck all."

"This will cheer you up," she said, holding out the iPad. "Remember their witness Adeel Bukhari?"

"Lizzie's supervisor?" Hilary said, skimming the text messages on the screen and raising his eyebrows.

"Not just a supervisor, it seems."

"No," Hilary said, scrolling down. "Clearly not. Though...oh."

"Yeah. If someone spoke to me like that, supervisor or not, they'd know what I thought about it, that's for sure."

"Could Bukhari be the person she was arguing with Sara Holden about?"

Beck raised a shoulder. "Dunno. There's no proof, without a name. And I'm sure he'll deny it. But at least it's another arse in her life that isn't our client. And we can certainly prove he knew her—and that he's a twat."

Hilary gave her a look. "I may avoid using that exact phrase in court."

"Why?" she said, smiling slightly. "It's so accurate."

"Anything more on Sara Holden?"

Beck shook her head. "Think she's gonna say Lizzie got herself in over her head with something...or someone. It's not going to look good, that's for sure. But pretty confident she's not going to have anything definitive. There's certainly no trail between Sara and Hart-Gosford that I can find, even after Simon finished translating the Gen-Z lingo for me."

"That's something, at least," Hilary said and handed the iPad back just as Janice buzzed the intercom.

"Mr. Whyte, your sister's here."

"Thanks. Send her in." He stood and Beck opened the door. Minnie stepped into the room, smiling shyly at Beck, who leaned in and whispered something in her ear as she left.

"Min," Hilary said, trying for a bright smile, "what a nice surprise. What did Beck say?"

"She wants me to make sure you're okay, which luckily is the reason I came anyway," she said, putting her bag on the chair.

"Why is everyone wondering if I'm okay?"

"I tried calling a couple of times, Hil. Max did, too. You haven't rung back."

"I'm sorry," Hilary said, resuming his seat. "I'm snowed under. But *you're* both all right?"

"We're fine," Minnie said, perching on the edge of her seat and pulling a paper bag out of her handbag. The rich smell of butter and pastry made Hilary's stomach clench. "Here. I brought you some cannoli."

"You really didn't have to."

"I know what you're like when you're busy," she said, putting the bag on his desk. "That's all it is, right?"

Hilary felt sick but made himself open the bag and take out one of the rich, cream-filled pastries. "I promise."

"Not long until the wedding now," Minnie said with another small smile. "You excited?"

"Honestly? I'll be happy when it's over. Not least because the trial will be over, too. Then we've got a month sailing around the Atlantic with no phone signal. I *really* can't wait for that."

"It sounds lovely," Minnie agreed, her smile widening. "You deserve that, Hil. You deserve to be happy."

Hilary swallowed his mouthful of cannoli and smiled. He was spared replying by his desk phone ringing. He gave his sister an apologetic look.

"Sorry. We start prepping witnesses tomorrow and it's nonstop."

Minnie smiled and stood. "I'll leave you to it. Remember... Max and I are just on the end of the phone if you need us."

He thanked her and she smiled warmly and left. Hilary put the rest of the cannoli in his drawer, knowing he'd be unable to finish them, and answered the phone.

The witness prep went about as well as Hilary had expected. Eloise Hart listened with cold courtesy as Beck went through her testimony, gently prompting her to remain earnest but measured in her responses.

"You care about Mr. Hart-Gosford," Beck said in an impressively measured tone. "It's good if that comes across...but not too much."

"That will not be a problem," Eloise responded. "Can I ask..." she said, looking at Hilary and not Beck, "why Amelia is not testifying at her husband's trial? I know spouses can't be called by the prosecution, but surely it is unusual that she is not speaking up on Dominic's behalf."

"Testimony from a spouse is nearly always discounted by a jury," Hilary explained.

Eloise's eyes glinted. "My daughter knows Dominic better than anyone. She is the best person there is to help that jury understand the sort of man he is."

"She's helping in other ways, ma'am," Beck continued, "by attending every hearing, by being seen with him in public. Displaying her support in those ways is far more effective—"

"Excuse me, dear," Eloise cut in, giving Beck a sharp look. "I was addressing my son-in-law's solicitor."

Beck's face paled. Hilary stood. "Beck, would you give us a moment?"

"Gladly," his researcher said and strode out of the door, shutting it behind her with perhaps a touch more force than necessary.

"I don't appreciate being patronized by your secretary, Mr. Whyte."

Hilary took a second to rein in his own temper. "Miss Donavon is not my secretary. She's my senior researcher and your son-in-law's co-counsel. And no one knows more about prepping witnesses for trial."

"I do not need to be *prepped*."

"Eloise," Hilary said, sitting in the chair opposite her and meeting her gimlet-sharp gaze with a level one of his own, "you need to accept that you do not necessarily know what's best for Dominic. You need to accept that his legal team does."

"I would accept it if I believed it, Mr. Whyte."

"I have a motion for change of counsel filled out and ready in my desk," he said, fighting the memory of the smell of Dominic's skin, the feel of his powerful body, the strength held in check but vibrating through the touch of his fingers. "It would have to go before a judge, but I'm pretty confident Judge Fotheringham would grant it. If that is still what you want, it can be arranged."

Eloise narrowed her eyes. "Isn't it a bit late for such things?"

"It's very late. It would make it look like the solicitor no longer believes he can defend the case, which would make the prosecution very happy."

Eloise's eyes flashed. "Are you threatening us, Mr. Whyte?"

"No," he said. "I'm making you aware of your legal options — and the fact that there are very few. So either you start cooperating or I will be forced to take drastic measures."

Eloise let out a slow breath through her nose and stood. "I would like to reschedule the rest of this meeting." She lifted her handbag onto her elbow. "I need to talk to my daughter."

"Very well," he said, standing and opening the door. "Make another appointment with Janice on the way out. Oh, and one more thing," he said, and Eloise paused with a narrow look. "If you ever treat a member of my team like that again, I will bring a civil suit against you that will leave you in no doubt as to my ability to practice the law. Understand?"

The blood drained from Eloise's face and her nostrils quivered.

"That," he said, lowering his voice, "*is* a threat."

Eloise swept out with her head held high. Beck and Simon watched her go with raised eyebrows. When she was gone, Beck grinned.

"Jesus, boss. She was not a happy bunny. What did you say?"

"Don't get too excited," he said wearily, moving over to the refreshment counter and pouring a drink. "You're the one who has got to finish prepping her."

He turned back with his mug of coffee and froze. Dominic stood in the doorway. His hands were in the pockets of his long, black coat. Raindrops sparkled on his shoulders like jewels. He was smiling.

"I've just seen Eloise," he murmured. "You must tell me your secret."

"Mr. Hart-Gosford," Hilary started, aware of Beck and Simon pretending to be suddenly absorbed in their laptops. "I don't think we have a meeting?"

"We don't," he said. "I was just hoping for a quick word."

Hilary gripped his mug tightly, then preceded Dominic into the office and shut the door.

"How can I help?" he said stiffly.

Dominic lowered himself into a chair. "I've not come to make you uncomfortable," he said levelly, "so you can drop the formality."

"What do you want?" Hilary said and took his seat behind the desk.

"The trial starts next week. I just wanted to…" All trace of a smile was gone from Dominic's face. There were shadows under his eyes.

"The defense is filed," Hilary said. "We're readying the witnesses. We're as prepared as we can be. Now, if that's all?"

"Hilary, I…"

"What?"

For the first time Hilary could remember, he saw Dom Gosford look nervous. "Do you really have a change of counsel motion prepared?"

Hilary blinked. "Eloise told you?"

"Yes."

Hilary folded his hands on the desk. "Yes. I do."

Dominic blinked once, slowly. "I never… I didn't want…"

"Don't get arrested again, and I will have no reason to file it."

"I won't."

"Good. Is that everything?"

Dominic gripped the arms of the chair. "This is it, then?"

"This is it," Hilary said, aware of a sudden tightness in his throat. "See you in court."

* * * *

When Hilary opened the door of the flat that evening, his neck and head were aching and weariness heavy as lead had settled into his bones. The physical strain had never bothered him before, but now, the more tired he became, the harder it was to resist the memory of that kiss, of feeling Dominic's hard body against his. Anger swirled with fear in his chest, creating a black fog he recognized all too well.

He shed his coat and tie in the hall, kicked off his shoes and dumped his briefcase where he stood.

"Hey," Jasper called from the door of the movie room. He had a whiskey in his hand and popcorn crumbs on his shirt. "Rough day?"

"You could say that," he said as he made for the kitchen.

"Can I help?" Jasper's voice was low as he stepped up behind Hilary and slid his hands around his hips. He brushed his lips against the nape of his neck and Hilary could smell the alcohol on his breath.

"Jazz," he said wearily as he got a tumbler and the vodka out of the cupboard, "I'm tired."

"I've been thinking about what you said," Jasper murmured against his skin, sliding a hand into the front of his trousers. "About us both being so wrapped up right now. I think I need to make it up to you. Remind you what you mean to me."

Hilary opened his mouth to protest but then Jasper grasped his cock. Hilary gasped and dropped his head back against his fiancé's shoulder.

"It's been too long," Jasper whispered as he stroked him. "I need you, Hil. Let me do this."

Hilary clenched his eyes shut, the waves of sensation rolling out from his crotch momentarily chasing everything away.

"Jazz, I..." He inhaled as Jasper increased his pace and began licking and nipping at his neck.

"Let it go, babe," Jasper whispered, thrusting his hard cock against Hilary's arse. "Whatever it is, just let it go."

Hilary turned and kissed his fiancé hungrily, grabbing a handful of his T-shirt and pulling him close. Jasper moaned and Hilary breathed in his smell, swallowed his taste, sank into the familiarity that for so long had felt like home.

"Hil," Jasper panted breathlessly as Hilary kneaded his hardening cock through his jeans. "Jesus, Hil..."

"Fuck me, Jazz," Hilary moaned into Jasper's open mouth. "I need you to fuck me. Hard. Like you used to."

Jasper groaned and thrust against Hilary's hand. "The stuff's in the bedroom."

"No," Hilary said, biting his earlobe and undoing his fly. "Here. Right here."

"Okay." Japer nodded feverishly, kissing him and sighing as Hilary freed his erection. "Fuck. Yeah. Here's good. Just hang on..."

He hurried from the kitchen, pulling his T-shirt over his head as he went. He returned, naked, with a bottle of lube. Hilary yanked him close and kissed him, running his hands over the toned torso, up the muscled back, over the firm arse. He pushed his straining erection against Jasper's crotch, earning a strangled cry from his fiancé. Jasper tugging at Hilary's belt, swearing. Hilary undid it, shoving his trousers down and stepping out of them without breaking the heated kiss.

Hilary took their quivering cocks in hand and began pumping them. Sparks fired up Hilary's limbs. Jasper's breathing was ragged against his mouth as he fumbled with Hilary's shirt buttons.

"Leave it," he breathed. "Do it now."

Jasper let out a low growl, spun him around and shoved him against the counter, parting his legs with his foot. Hilary heard the lube bottle click then Jasper was pressing two slick fingers into him.

Hilary stifled a moan and clutched at the counter, crushing his eyes shut. Jasper shoved and fumbled, finding the spot inside him that made white fire flare behind his eyes. He cried out, the sound distant in his own ears.

"Fuck, Hil," Jasper panted into his hair. His whole body was trembling. "I'm not gonna last. Are you ready?"

He slid a third finger in, stretching clumsily, and Hilary grabbed a cupboard handle, the ache under his belly tightening and starting to glow.

"Do it *now*."

Jasper seized his hips and Hilary felt the blunt end of his cock pushing against his entrance. He took a breath, making himself relax, and Jasper pushed all the way in.

"Fuck," Jasper swore, shaking against Hilary's back. "Fuck, that's good."

"Move," Hilary begged, gripping the handle and the counter harder. "Jazz, please."

Jasper grunted, tightened his grip on Hilary's hips, pulled almost all the way out and thrust in again. Hilary let out a strangled noise, leaning over the counter, sending the vodka bottle rolling toward the stove. Jasper thrust faster and heat flamed under Hilary's belly. He barely heard his own voice begging Jasper to go harder, faster over the thunder of his heart.

Jasper made a desperate noise, bending him over and grabbing his weeping cock, pumping it mercilessly.

"I'm…Christ, Hil, I'm close. Fuck…*fuck*."

Hilary closed his ears and clenched his teeth, focused on the hand on his cock and the familiar hardness plumbing his depths as the glitter of climax began to quiver behind his balls. But then Jasper was moaning, high and loud, thrusting deep and holding himself there, shuddering with release. Hilary felt the heat of his fiancé's seed spill into him. He took Jasper's hand, which shook on his own cock, and pumped it vigorously until heat surged up his belly into his chest, his legs shaking as the orgasm came over him in waves.

They sagged, panting, against the counter. Sweat stuck their skin together. Jasper pulled himself out and laid a series of tired kisses across Hilary's neck and shoulders.

"Fuck. I needed that," he whispered, running his fingers through Hilary's hair as he straightened up. "Gonna go shower, babe. Clean this up, will you?"

He left and Hilary heard the shower start.

Hilary stared at the soiled kitchen counter and wondering at the emptiness stealing through him in the wake of the warmth that was fading even faster than usual.

Chapter Six

The day of the trial dawned dry, with the first real blue sky of the year. The sun warmed the London air to an unseasonal balminess, and not a single cloud marred the sky as Hilary crossed the courthouse carpark.

"Bloody weather," Beck muttered as she hurried along next to him, pulling at the collar of her tight dress.

"At least you don't have to wear a tie," Hilary said, earning a sharp look.

"Let's not do the tights-versus-ties thing, boss," she said. "You'll lose."

He smiled but then swore under his breath as they came to the edge of the crowd of reporters and gawkers that filled the courthouse steps.

"Crap," Beck muttered. "As if I wasn't hot enough. *Excuse me.*"

Hilary followed his researcher as she elbowed her way through to the front row of onlookers, just as the Hart-Gosfords' limousine drew up at the curb. Cameras immediately started flashing and microphones were brandished. Hilary hurried forward when the door opened and out stepped Merriweather, his sharp eyes scanning the crowd. He opened the back door wider and out climbed Dominic.

His suit was impeccable, the cloth the dark, somber gray of storm clouds. The look on his face was set and grave. His hair was styled, his eyebrows drawn low over his eyes. The crowd surged forward, firing questions, but he ignored them all as he locked eyes with Hilary. Hilary tugged at the jacket of his own suit, even though it was already straight, and resisted the urge to fiddle with his tie.

Dominic's eyebrow twitched as if sensing his thoughts but then he was turning back to the car to hand Eloise out of it. She straightened with dignity, looking taller than anyone there, despite not even coming to Dominic's shoulder. She wore a maroon dress with a high neckline, a ruby pendant glowing like blood against the dark fabric. She stepped aside, sparing the crowd not so much as a glance as her son-in-law turned to help his wife out of the car.

Amelia emerged into the sunlight with her head held high but her eyes cast down. She wore a navy suit, elegantly tailored but conservative, over a hot-pink silk blouse. The colors set off her white-blonde hair. Her minimal makeup brought out the deep silver of her eyes and the determined set of her lips. A modest diamond in each ear and her platinum wedding band were the only jewelry she wore.

Hilary suddenly realized how beautiful she was. His stomach flopped over, and he bit the inside of his cheek, hoping nothing would show on his face.

Amelia took her husband's arm and Eloise fell into step at Dominic's other side. Merriweather preceded them up the steps, shouting commands as he parted the crowd. Hilary and Beck followed a half-pace behind.

Not a single member of their party said a word until they were safely inside the air-conditioned interior of the courthouse. Amelia let out a shaking breath and Eloise peered down her nose at the crowd outside the glass doors, but Dominic didn't move or speak. He was staring down the marble hallway to the courtrooms.

"Okay, everyone," Hilary said, checking that both his phones were on silent. "Just remember what I said. Try not to react to anything anyone says. Don't look at the jury. Amelia?" She met his eye and tilted her chin. "If you and Mrs. Hart could sit directly behind us, that would be best. The show of support will be helpful. Merriweather, you, too."

"I need to stand at the door, sir. Watch everything at once."

"The court has its own security," Hilary said. "And they are more than capable. Please sit with the family and keep your personal comms off."

Merriweather muttered but switched his own phone to silent.

"Try not to worry too much when you hear the prosecution's case," Hilary went on, meeting each of their gazes in turn. "It's their job to frame everything in the worst possible way. Just remember we get to present our own case next, and the defense always gets the last word."

The women nodded. Dominic gazed at him, the shadows in his eyes and the tightness of his jaw unfamiliar on his usually stalwart face.

Beck plucked at Hilary's elbow as they turned to make their way down the hall. "He's scared," she murmured in an undertone.

Hilary didn't answer.

Whispering broke out on all sides as the party filed into the courtroom. It was considerably busier than it had been for the plea hearing. Hilary stood to one side to let Dominic sit first. Dominic leaned in to give Amelia a kiss on the cheek before she and Eloise took their seats in the front row.

"Shame they don't let cameras in here," Beck muttered. "That's a photo opportunity that might have done him some good."

Hilary didn't reply, but before he could sit down, Laurette Augustine strode over, gave Dominic a withering glance and drew Hilary aside.

"It's not too late, you know."

"I think it is," Hilary said ruefully.

"You're really doing this yourself?"

Hilary nodded without comment.

"I can't ask Jabal to go easy on you," she said with a glance back at the white-wigged barrister sat at the prosecution's table, laying out papers with the precision of a surgeon.

"I didn't ask you to."

Augustine sighed then nodded. "Okay, then. Good luck, Hilary."

He inclined his head then a door opened and the jury filed in.

"All stand for the Honorable Ms. Justice Fotheringham."

As Judge Fotheringham approached the bench, Hilary tugged at his collar and flattened his tie, the air suddenly stifling, despite the air conditioning.

"You got this, boss," Beck murmured. Then Dominic caught his eye. He gave Hilary a nod. The air suddenly didn't feel quite so charged.

"Please, sit," Fotheringham said as she took her seat and pulled out her glasses. The room hushed as the judge read out the case details.

"Would the prosecution like to make its opening statement?"

"We would, my lady," Amir Jabal said, standing and squaring his shoulders.

"Proceed."

Jabal swept to the front of the room and bowed to the jury. He was a small man, but the barrister's robe gave him breadth, and his expression radiated cool control. Hilary took a steadying breath and resisted fiddling with his pen with a considerable effort.

"Ladies and gentlemen, I would first off like to thank you for your service. Cases like this one are never simple, and the responsibility can be intimidating. So, I would like to make this as easy for you as possible. To begin, I would like to spend a moment establishing the facts."

Jabal tucked his thumbs into his lapels and his expression darkened.

"Around eleven p.m. on Saturday the twenty-second of November last year, someone entered 4 Kensington Gardens, North Acton, a property rented by Elizabeth Mary Wood. This person then shot both Elizabeth, known as Lizzie, and her twin brother, Dean, who was visiting. Their bodies were found in the early hours of November twenty-third by a postal worker."

Jabal produced a remote from his robes and turned on the widescreen TV set next to the witness box. He clicked another button, and a photo of Lizzie's corpse came up on the screen. He'd chosen the picture where she appeared to be staring right at the camera, her bloodied lips parted, eyes wide and staring and unquestionably dead. A small susurration went around the room.

"Lizzie was found in the living room," Jabal went on. "She had been shot seven times with a nine-millimeter handgun. The final, fatal shot went through her temple. Dean was on the stairs." Jabal clicked again to display the photo of the young man's body sprawled on the staircase, his head twisted to the side, blood smeared all around. "He had been shot twice in the back."

Jabal clicked again and the screen went black. Hilary examined the jury, nervousness creeping through him at the looks on their faces.

"No murder weapon has so far been identified and no witnesses saw anyone come or go from the property after Dean had arrived at approximately six p.m. that evening. There were no foreign fingerprints found at the scene and very little forensic evidence except" — Jabal thrust his hands into his pockets and examined the jury from under his heavy eyebrows — "except a hair. One single hair. DNA analysis of that hair has proved that it belongs to the defendant, Mr. Dominic Hart-Gosford." Jabal cast a glance toward the defense table. Hilary held the look and resisted looking back at his client.

"Lizzie Wood had worked at Homes with Hart, a charity funded and run by Amelia Hart-Gosford, the defendant's wife, until a few weeks before she died. She was fired for 'financial irregularities'." Jabal raised an eyebrow. "Now it's true that Lizzie Wood wasn't the best with money. She consistently spent more than she earned and had run up some considerable debt. The defense will no doubt present evidence that she occasionally sought illegal means to assuage her financial burdens. But whatever corner she'd been backed into, I think we can all agree that neither Lizzie nor her brother Dean deserved to die."

A few members shook their heads. Hilary kept his face blank.

"These are the facts of the case," Jabal stated. "They are undisputed. However"—he stepped closer, displaying his palms to the jury—"what *I* intend to prove is that the defendant here today murdered both victims. I will demonstrate that he had motive, means and opportunity and that, combined with the fact that his DNA was found at the scene, should be more than enough to prove beyond all doubt that this man committed this despicable act." He made a show of gathering his emotions, pressing the pads of his fingers together as he took a breath and let it out slowly again through his nose.

"Putting this man in prison will not bring Dean and Lizzie back. It will not restore Mr. and Mrs. Wood their children, the twins' friends their companions. But it will, at least, give their loved ones some desperately needed closure. And it will also ensure that this man is held to account for his actions and ensure he cannot hurt anyone else. That, ladies and gentlemen, is our task here. To atone for the past...and protect the future."

He bowed and made his way back to his seat. He met Hilary's eyes as he passed. Hilary returned the look coolly.

"Mr. Whyte?" prompted Fotheringham.

Hilary stood, taking a moment to tap his notes together in the thick, echoing silence that filled the room. He could feel everyone's eyes on him, including Dom Gosford's.

He approached the jury with his pulse pounding his wrists and temples. He reached deep inside for the part of him that remained stolid, no matter what—the part of him that had kept him afloat at St. Edmund's and the dark times that had followed. It was the part him that had survived, that had driven him to fight—that would always fight.

He met the eyes of all the men and women of the jury one by one. He opened his mouth. He heard himself start to speak in a level, controlled tone, quickly burying his astonishment at just how calm he sounded and focusing on the members and not on the sensation of Dominic's eyes burning into his back.

"Ladies and gentlemen. The defense does not dispute any of the facts of this case," he began. "It's perfectly true that forensic evidence suggests that my client's hair was found at the scene. It is also true that he had both access to and experience of handling the kind of weapon that killed these two young people. He has no alibi for the night of the murders. And, most importantly, as my esteemed colleague stressed, Lizzie and Dean Wood are dead, and they shouldn't be."

The eyes fixed on him did not blink. He didn't either.

"What the defense intends to show you is that, whilst this is a terrible crime, there is no proof of my client's involvement. He may not have the best reputation or the best personal history, but there's no proof he even knew Lizzie. There's no proof he accessed a gun that night and certainly no proof he came to 4 Kensington Gardens with the premeditated intention to kill." Hilary pressed his palms together to hide the fact that they were sweating. "Whatever the prosecution shows you, it won't be proof. There *is* no proof. And no one, not even someone as objectionable as my client" — surprise slackened the expressions of some of the jury, followed by tightness as they suppressed smiles, and Hilary's heart lifted — "should be convicted of any crime, especially one such as this, without proof."

Hilary returned to his seat feeling slightly dizzy but, somehow, managed to lower himself into it without knocking anything over. Eloise and Amelia wore twin expressions of wariness mixed with disapproval, but Beck slid him a sly grin. Dominic sat rigid, his gaze fixed ahead as Judge Fotheringham scribbled more of her innumerable notes.

"Would the prosecution like to call its first witness?"

"We would, my lady," Jabal said, standing. "We call Alan Brockle to the stand."

"Sure you're not gonna bring up his drinking?" Beck murmured as the middle-aged postal worker, crushed into an ill-fitting suit, made his way, sweating, to the witness box. "Or the fact that he was late for work that day? Or that he should never have opened the door in the first place?"

"He saw what he saw," Hilary murmured. "It's not the poor bastard's fault he found the bodies. Making him look bad will only make us look worse."

Beck handed him the witness profile without further comment as Brockle swore his oath.

"So, Mr. Brockle," Jabal began, his swarthy face set in deep, sympathetic lines. "I know it's upsetting, but do you mind if we go through the events of the morning of November twenty-third?"

"Uh…sure," Brockle said then, blinking and shooting a rabbit-in-headlights look at Dominic. "I mean, yes. Yes, sir."

"You don't have to call me sir," Jabal said with a tight smile. "Now, what time, to the best of your recollection, did you arrive at Lizzie Wood's home that morning?"

Jabal led Brockle through his quavering account of arriving at the house, noticing that the door was open, not getting any answer to the bell. The jury watched him intently, apart from the occasional glance sent Dominic's way. Hilary was relieved to note that Dominic remained focused on the witness and kept his face blank but not hard. Fear had changed it — softened his jaw, deepened the lines in his forehead and around his mouth. Hilary could never remember seeing vulnerability in his expression before. He looked older and almost impossibly beautiful.

Hilary hurriedly returned his attention to the witness.

"Is it normal protocol to open a door and leave a parcel inside an unresponsive property, Mr. Brockle?" Brockle started to sweat even more. "You're not in any trouble," Jabal added. "We're just establishing something for the jury in case the defense wants to pick up on it. They need to know it's not of any significance."

"Objection," Hilary called, getting to his feet. "Leading the witness."

"Sustained," said Fotheringham without looking up.

"I'll rephrase," Jabal said patiently. "Were you afraid you would get into trouble for delivering a parcel in this way, Mr. Brockle?"

"N...no, not really," Brockle managed. "We ain't supposed to do it, but I just... I know it's a pain for folks to come to the depot and I was already running late.

Figured if I dropped it on the mat and shut the door, it would be safe enough…"

"So you pushed the door open?"

"Yeah."

"And what did you find?"

Brockle's pallid features flooded with color. He sipped at the glass of water provided and stared at the floor.

"It's okay. Take your time."

Brockle described the silence. The blood. The smell. The way Dean had been so pale and so motionless. The way he'd known instantly how wrong it all was. He didn't look at Jabal or the jury as he spoke. He stared at the glass of water, and it was clear he was reliving every terrible second of that morning.

"Thank you, Mr. Brockle," Jabal said gently. "I know that was hard. But you did very well. Mr. Whyte is going to just ask you a couple of questions now, all right?"

Brockle nodded stiffly, still staring blindly ahead.

"Mr. Brockle," Hilary said with a warm smile as he approached the witness box, hoping the sweat standing out on his own back wasn't evident through his jacket. "I want to repeat what my esteemed colleague said. As hard as it must be for you, he is right when he says it's vitally important that the jury have as much information as possible in a case like this."

"I understand that, sir," Brockle said, raising his eyes to meet Hilary's.

"Please, you can call me Hilary," he said with his most disarming smile. The large man let out a shaking breath and appeared to relax. "I only have two questions for you, Mr. Brockle. The first one… Do you regularly deliver to 4 Kensington Gardens?"

"Yes, sir. I mean…" He smiled nervously. "It's my regular route, yeah."

"So you know the area well?"

"That I do. I live just a few streets back. My kids go to school just around the corner. Nice area." He froze. "Least, I thought it was."

"Thank you, Mr. Brockle. I know this is difficult. My second and last question, then you should be able to go." Hilary paused then indicated Dominic. "Have you ever seen my client either at Lizzie Wood's address or in the local area?"

"Objection," Jabal barked, standing. "The witness has already stated there was no one else at the property on the morning of the twenty-third of November."

"I'm not asking about that morning," Hilary said easily. "I'm trying to establish if there is any evidence that my client knew where Lizzie Wood lived."

"Overruled," Fotheringham said. "Mr. Brockle? Please answer the question."

Brockle swallowed, nervous again. "No. No, I ain't never seen him before."

"Thank you, Mr. Brockle."

The witness was shown out by the usher and a gentle murmuring started up amongst the onlookers.

"Adeel Bukhari next?" Hilary murmured as he resumed his seat. Beck nodded and handed him the profile. Dominic clasped his hands together on the table and continued to stare straight ahead. The usher showed the young man to the witness box. He glared daggers at Dominic until his attention was summoned by the court official for his oath.

"Mr. Bukhari. Thanks for joining us," Jabal began. "You were Lizzie Wood's supervisor at Homes with Hart, is that correct?"

"Nominally, yes. But we were just colleagues, really. Friends."

"How would you describe Lizzie?"

Bukhari said that Lizzie was a good worker and a fun colleague, always well-dressed and stylish. She was generous with her money when they went out as a team, even though they all had an idea she couldn't afford it. She had never mentioned any specific debts to him, certainly nothing about loan sharks or blackmail. She was upbeat, ambitious but, Bukhari mused, there had definitely been something upsetting her recently. She had been acting distant and seemed to be constantly glued to her phone.

"Were you surprised when she was fired?"

"I was shocked," Bukhari said, his expression tight. "We all guessed she had money trouble, but none of us could believe she'd steal from the charity."

"Did she? Steal from the charity, I mean?"

"Objection," Hilary called. "The witness did not hold a position within the company to know this as a fact either way."

"Sustained."

Jabal looked thoughtful. "Very well. Do you think she was capable of such a thing, then?"

"No," Bukhari stated vehemently. "No, she wasn't. She was a good person. A kind person."

"Then why would Mrs. Hart-Gosford fire her?"

"Objection!"

"Sustained. Let's stop this now, Mr. Jabal." Fotheringham looked at the barrister over her glasses. Hilary suppressed a smile as color flooded Jabal's face. "You've established that the witness worked with the victim and his personal opinion of her. He is not in a position to state his employer's motives for firing her unless she told him. Did she, Mr. Bukhari?"

Bukhari frowned. "Uh..."

"Did Mrs. Hart-Gosford tell you why Miss Wood lost her job?" Fotheringham stated levelly.

"No, your honor."

Fotheringham's mouth pursed. "You address a High Court judge as my lord or lady, Mr. Bukhari. But never mind. Continue, counsel."

"Apologies, Judge," Jabal said, not meeting her eye. "Why do you *think* Lizzie was fired, Adeel?"

"I think it was because *she* wanted her out of the way," the witness said, jabbing a finger at Amelia. She stiffened but her expression never faltered. Eloise's eyes glinted with gray fire. Dominic's hands curled into fists under the table. Hilary gave him a warning look before forcing his attention back to the witness.

"Let the record state that the witness gestured to Mrs. Amelia Hart-Gosford with his last statement," Jabal said. "And what makes you think this, Adeel?"

"The last couple of times I've seen them together, they were arguing."

"Do you know what about?"

"No."

"Lizzie never talked to you about it?"

Bukhari pursed his lips again. "No. But she started avoiding meetings Mrs. Hart-Gosford was due to attend. Then she started calling in sick. Then she just never came in at all and we were told she'd resigned."

"Resigned?"

Bukhari nodded. "That's what our team leader told us."

"I see. Mr. Bukhari, would you mind telling us if you recognize the defendant?"

The witness's intense gaze swung Dominic's way. "Yes."

"How do you know him?"

"I've met him."

"More than once?"

"Yes. At charity fundraisers. And he came to the office sometimes."

"Have you ever conversed with him?"

"Yes."

Jabal took a moment to look heavily at Dominic. "What is your impression of Mr. Hart-Gosford, Mr. Bukhari?"

"He's a psychotic murdering asshole."

"Objection!"

"Sustained," Fotheringham said, sending a sharp look at the witness. "I understand emotions are running high today, but such language will not be tolerated. Mr. Jabal, please control your witness or we will have to dismiss him."

Bukhari shifted in his seat as Jabal visibly reined in his patience. "Apologies, my lady, ladies and gentlemen of the jury. As Judge Fotheringham says, this is an emotional case. It is understandable that the victims' friends and family would find it hard to remain objective. But for the sake of the case, Mr. Bukhari, would you mind describing to us, as calmly as you can, why you have formed this opinion of the defendant?"

Bukhari did just that. He described the level of drink Dominic consumed at the fundraisers, the contempt with which he treated the other guests, the rudeness he displayed when Amelia's employees tried to talk to him. He described the way Dominic looked around any room he was in with disdain in his eyes, like he hated the world and everyone in it. He described a particular conversation with Dominic he'd had as they were all leaving a charity auction in which he implied that his wife's charity work was a waste of time and just a rich woman's way of assuaging a guilty conscience.

"He said that?" Jabal said.

"He did."

"Did he say anything else?"

"He stopped talking when Lizzie joined us," Bukhari said, still glaring at Dominic. "She tried to ask him if he'd had a good evening, but he slammed his glass down and turned away. It was like he was afraid to be near her, like he was afraid of what he might do."

"Objection," Hilary said. "Witness is speculating."

"Sustained. Mr. Jabal, any more questions for this witness?"

"None, my lady," Jabal said, bowing his head. "Thank you, Mr. Bukhari. Mr. Whyte. Your witness."

"Go get him, sir," Beck whispered as Hilary strode to the witness box.

"Mr. Bukhari," Hilary started, smiling pleasantly, "are you still employed by Homes with Hart?"

Bukhari glared. "No."

"No?"

"No, I am not. I resigned."

"You resigned? You weren't fired?"

"Objection," Jabal said, standing. "Relevance?"

"My lady, the prosecution has gone to some lengths to establish the witness's opinion of the victim, his employer and my client. I'm just trying to establish some much-needed context to these opinions."

Fotheringham examined Bukhari then Jabal. "Overruled."

Jabal sat, pursing his lips.

"Mr. Bukhari?" Hilary prompted.

"What?"

Hilary raised his eyebrows and was gratified to see some of the jurors shifting in their seats. "Would you answer the question please? And remember, you're under oath."

Bukhari's jaw worked. "I resigned."

"Why?"

"I didn't want to work for that family anymore."

"Were you asked to resign?" The witness glared out at the audience. "Mr. Bukhari—"

"Yes," he snapped. "My team leader said if I didn't leave, she'd make me. But I wanted to go, so I went."

"When was this?"

"About a week after Lizzie died."

"Why did your team leader ask you to resign?"

"Objection," Jabal interjected. "If the witness couldn't speculate why Lizzie was fired, surely he can't speculate about his own being asked to leave?"

"Sustained. Be careful, Mr. Whyte."

Hilary cursed inwardly but made sure his face was neutral. "I'll rephrase. Did your team leader explain to you why she wanted you to leave?"

Bukhari leveled a black glare at Hilary. He didn't answer. Hilary nodded to Beck, who got the iPad ready, then withdrew his own remote and turned on the TV. The tablet synced and a long list of numbers and dates appeared on the screen.

"These are your phone records for September, October and November of last year. Do you recognize the highlighted number?"

"No," the witness snapped. "Who memorizes phone numbers anymore?"

"Very well, I'll tell you. It's Lizzie Wood's phone number." Hilary tilted his head. "You contacted Lizzie Wood every day, sometimes two or three times, either by text or phone call, right up to and including the day she died."

"We were friends."

Hilary nodded to Beck who swiped the iPad. A list of text messages filled the screen.

07 November, 15:11: *Liz, please. Just fucking call me back already. We can sort this out.*

07 November, 17:35: *FFS, Liz. You enjoying this or something? Grow TF up.*

15 November, 02:31: *U fkin bitch*

22 November, 11:54: *I could have helped you. I hope you know that.*

"Objection," hollered Jabal. "The defense is attempting to undermine the integrity of the witness by displaying these messages out of context. Just because they had disagreements doesn't mean his recollections of Lizzie or Dominic Hart-Gosford are discountable."

"Not discountable," Hilary said. "Just not objective, my lady."

Fotheringham looked at the screen. "Overruled. Continue, counsel."

"Thank you, my lady. Mr. Bukhari, do you want to add context to these messages for the jury?"

Bukhari ground his teeth. "Lizzie and I were close, you know? Good friends." He stared at the screen, sweat shining on his face. "But she wouldn't level with me, let me in on what was going on, with the money and everything."

"Could these disagreements explain why she began to distance herself from you?"

"No."

"No?"

Bukhari shook his head. "It wasn't like that. She was getting all secretive. Taking phone calls in other rooms. Texting all day."

"Lizzie and her best friend did a lot of texting during this period," Hilary said smoothly. "We have those phone records, too. Her friend was concerned about someone in Lizzie's life."

"It wasn't me."

Hilary paused. "So you don't you think it's possible that your behavior could have unnerved Lizzie, and that's why she drew away? And that maybe she was talking to her friend regularly, for support?"

"No," Bukhari stated. "We were *friends*. I sent her those messages because I cared about her. And something was wrong. I could tell. And she wouldn't tell me anything."

"Mr. Bukhari. Did your team leader ask you to resign because you had grown obsessive about Lizzie? And that after she died you became irrational, accusatory, disrupting meetings and taking to social media to accuse the Hart-Gosfords of foul play, even though she only lost her job because she was stealing?"

"You're twisting it all up. I knew something was wrong. And I knew it was that bastard" —he jabbed a finger at Dominic—"that was freaking her out."

"How do you know that? Did she tell you?"

"She didn't have to."

"I would like to spend a moment focusing on this last message, Mr. Bukhari," Hilary said, nodding to Beck, who swiped to the next slide, which displayed the last message by itself.

22 November, 10:54: *I could have helped you. I hope you know that.*

"Can you explain what you meant in this message?"

The witness stared at it, his expression dark.

"Mr. Bukhari?"

"No."

"You can't explain it?"

"I don't remember it."

Hilary raised his eyebrows. "You've shifted to past tense in this message. Was that a conscious decision?"

"I don't remember."

"It was the day she died," Hilary put in. "I would have thought you would remember very well."

"Objection," Jabal glared. "Inflammatory."

"Sustained." Fotheringham peered at Hilary over her glasses. "Again. Careful, counsel."

Hilary nodded understandingly. "I apologize, Mr. Bukhari. It was almost five months ago. It's understandable you don't remember, even though this was the last text you ever sent her."

"That's not..." Bukhari floundered. "It's in past tense because I decided to stop talking to her. I knew it was best. It was over. I realized it that day. That's the only reason I didn't message again. Then the next day I heard..." He choked.

"Do you need a moment, Mr. Bukhari?" Judge Fotheringham said.

"No," he growled, swiping at his eyes. "Let's get this over with."

"I think that would be best," Hilary replied. "So, my final questions. First, did Lizzie Wood ever state outright to you that she was afraid of Mr. Hart-Gosford?"

Bukhari glared. "Not in so many words. But—"

"Just yes or no, please."

He looked away. "No."

"Did she ever tell you she had made any sort of financial arrangement with Mr. Hart-Gosford? Again, yes or no only, please."

"No."

"Did she ever tell you that he had threatened her, directly or indirectly? Or that she had grounds to blackmail him?"

Bukhari's face filled with color. "No."

"No more questions, my lady," Hilary said and returned to his seat. Beck gave him a grin.

"Thank you, Mr. Bukhari. You can stand down. And I think it's time we break for lunch," the judge said, consulting her watch. "Prosecution will call its next witness when we return." She hit her gavel and the jury were led out of the room. Fotheringham followed them. Excited chatter burst out on all sides the second the door shut behind them.

"She *was* stealing, Mr. Whyte," Amelia said, looking searchingly at Hilary. "That's the reason I was seen arguing with her. That's why she lost her position."

"The accountants have provided me with all that, Mrs. Hart-Gosford," Hilary said levelly. "I didn't use it because it doesn't make Lizzie's position any less sympathetic."

Amelia's face fell. "And it's Frank next? From the gun club?"

"That's right," Hilary said.

"He's going to say Dominic could have taken my gun?"

"We think so," Hilary said, glancing at Beck. "But we'll be able to demonstrate that just because it's possible doesn't mean it happened."

Amelia nodded, raising her hand to Eloise, who was beckoning to her from the door. "I just wish it was over."

"Soon, Mel," Dominic murmured. "It'll all be over soon."

"Go get something to eat," Hilary said, turning away to help Beck pack up their folders and tablets. "See you back here at two."

Amelia went to join her mother. Dominic turned sideways to slide his broad frame behind Hilary. As he passed, he laid a hand on Hilary's back. Hilary looked up and caught Dominic's eyes and the softest suggestion of a smile on his lips before he moved away.

"What the hell?" Beck whispered.

Hilary blinked and thrust the rest of the files into his briefcase. "What?"

Beck was staring. "Did he just feel you up?"

Heat flooded Hilary's face. "Of course not."

"That looked deliberate, boss. Is he being a creep? If he is, this is done. I'll file that motion myself—"

"No, no," Hilary said hurriedly, his earnestness surprising himself. "No, it's not that. I just... I think he has a hard time saying things out load."

"And what was *that* saying, exactly?"

Hilary snapped his briefcase shut. "I think he's just grateful."

"Well, he'd better not thank me in that way," Beck said, shoving the iPad in her bag. "I'll snap his hand off."

Hilary followed her out of the room with his head down so she couldn't see him smile.

Chapter Seven

Frank Hermann wasn't much older than Hilary, but the lines of worry in his high forehead plus the broken capillaries around his bulbous nose, made him look considerably older.

He answered Jabal's questions mechanically, making it obvious that he'd rehearsed them. Hilary watched impatience growing in the tightness around Jabal's eyes with some satisfaction but had to fight not to clutch his hands together too tightly as Hermann confirmed that not only had Dominic attended the range with his wife a number of times but he was also an excellent shot. They displayed some of the targets from his practices, the holes all concentrated around the heart and head.

"So the cameras weren't functioning on the twenty-second of November last year?" Jabal stated, pinning the witness down after he'd started rambling about the service contract they'd been struggling to find the funding for.

"No...I mean, yes, they were but...not great."

Jabal took a moment. "Could you tell us exactly what you mean by '*not great*'?"

"Uh...sorry. I'm not sure what you're asking? They worked a bit...but...like I said, not great."

Jabal pursed his lips. "Did the cameras capture all twenty-four hours of November twenty-second, Mr. Hermann?"

"No..." Hermann said carefully. "We got some of the morning and a little of the lunchtime rush...but they started messing up from about two. The security system people couldn't get anyone out until the next day. I tried to fix 'em, but I'm not much of a tech whiz, see?"

"The police checked the footage and found this to be correct," Jabal said, glancing at the jury. "In fact, the cameras were functioning fine until about twelve-thirty, then the feed became intermittent until two p.m., after which they captured nothing at all. Is the reception manned twenty-four hours, Mr. Hermann?"

"Uh, it's supposed to be, but the girls need a break sometimes, you know. Make a brew or whatever."

"Was the desk manned twenty-four hours on the day of November the twenty-second?"

"I couldn't tell you, sir."

"Is there any way to know definitively either way? A badge swipe system? Or a computer system reception use?"

Hermann shook his head. "No. The girls just sign in and out on the wall chart, like the rest of us. But they don't bother if they're just nipping out for a fag."

"So is it possible for someone to have come into the club, accessed the armory and left without being caught on tape or seen by the reception staff?"

"Oh yeah, sure. It's possible."

"Is it also possible that that same someone could have returned later that night, or even in the early hours of the following morning, without being seen or taped?"

Hermann winced. "Yeah. It is. The bosses are in a right spin about it. Clients are suing. And the council's up in arms—"

"Objection," Hilary said in a bored tone. "Irrelevant."

"Sustained."

Jabal sent Hilary a look he could have sworn was grateful. "One last thing before I hand over to the defense counsel, Mr. Hermann. Now, I apologize in advance, because I know this is a delicate matter, but the defense will only bring it up if I don't..."

Hermann fiddled with his tie. "You're gonna ask about my, um...my tips?"

Jabal raised an eyebrow. "'Tips', Mr. Hermann?"

The security man winced.

"Would it be fair to say that you have accepted some very generous *tips* in exchange for letting non-members have use of the gun club?"

Hermann raised his watery gaze to meet Jabal's. "Yeah. It's true. I'm sorry..." He glanced at the blank-faced judge and quickly away. "I'm sorry for it, that I can tell you. I'm facing disciplinary. But I swear, *everyone* does it. Have for as long as I've worked there. The owners, they pay us pennies, really. The members know that. They—"

"Objection," Hilary said again, sending a pleading look Jabal's way.

"Sustained," Fotheringham said, peering down at the witness. "Mr. Hermann, please only answer the question directed at you and try to refrain from supposition, if you can."

"Yes, ma'am. Sorry, ma'am."

"That's all right. Mr. Jabal?"

Jabal took a breath. "Thank you, my lady. Mr. Hermann, taking into account the malfunctioning security system and the susceptibility of you and your fellow staff to bribery...would you say it's fair to state that anyone wishing to access guns would find it all too easy to do so?"

Hermann had gone pale. He said something, his voice choking and squeaking.

"Sorry, Mr. Hermann. Can you repeat that so the jury can hear?"

He cleared his throat. "Yes, Mr. Jabal. I think he'd be able to swipe the guns, that's for sure. And get them back without no one seeing or saying nothing."

"Thank you. Your witness, Mr. Whyte."

Hilary stood. He buttoned his suit jacket and strolled over to the witness box.

"Mr. Hermann, the cameras weren't working on the night of the twenty-second. We've established that. You've also established that staff aren't around twenty-four hours like they are supposed to be."

"Yes, sir," Hermann said nervously. "That's what I said, sir."

"Mr. Whyte is fine," he said. "Or Hilary, if you prefer."

Hermann frowned. "Hilary?"

"That's right."

"I thought... Ain't that a girl's name? Are you...?" He looked at Jabal helplessly. "Are you tran... transexual...or something? I'm sorry. I'm not very good at these things, I dunno how I... What do I call you?"

A shocked murmur went around the court. The color bled from Hermann's face. Judge Fotheringham banged her gavel.

"Quiet," she ordered and banged again until the murmurs finally fell into shocked silence. The jury exchanged glances. "Mr. Hermann, perhaps it's best if you just stick to 'Mr. Whyte'."

"I'm sorry," Hermann stammered, clutching his hands in his lap. He looked like he was about to cry. "I'm sorry, Mr....Mr. Whyte."

Hilary smiled reassuringly. "Don't worry about it, Frank. I've confused lots of men before now." An uneasy titter went through the room and Hermann gave him a grateful look, wiping his glistening forehead with his sleeve. "Now I just have two questions," Hilary went on, hands behind his back, "and if you could just answer yes or no to those, then you can go."

"Sure...course."

"First question," Hilary said, glancing back at Dominic, meeting his heavy gaze. "Did you see my client at the gun club at any time on the twenty-second of November or in the early hours of the twenty-third?"

"No."

"Have any of your colleagues told you *they* saw him that night?"

Hermann shook his head.

"Out loud, if you could...for the transcript."

Hermann leaned forward and stated, "No," into the microphone.

"Mr. Jabal has established that it's possible that staff at the gun club might have been bribed to say they didn't see him, even if they did. You still agree with that statement?"

"I…" Hermann fidgeted then caught Hilary's eye. "Yes, sir."

"But either way, no one is prepared to testify that they *did* see him? And no cameras can prove he was there?"

"Yes, I mean no…" He blinked. "I mean…yes, no one is admitting they saw him. And, no, the cameras didn't tape nothing after two p.m., like Mr. Jabal says."

"So there's no proof at all?"

"No," Hermann sagged, as he caught Jabal's piercing eye. "No proof, Mr. Whyte."

"Okay. That's great. Thanks, Mr. Hermann. No more questions."

* * * *

"Jesus Christ, boss," Beck muttered as they left the room after the crowds had spilled away. "You couldn't write this stuff, could you?"

"No," Hilary said, taking off his glasses and rubbing his eyes. "Thankfully. Not sure I'd want to read it. Mr. Hart-Gosford…" Hilary straightened his spine as Dominic joined him in the corridor, Amelia and Eloise conversing together in low tones off to the side, Merriweather a step behind them, scanning the passersby. "How are you holding up?"

"They made me sound like a monster."

"We'll get our chance to counter," Hilary said, looking at his watch, suddenly unable to meet his client's eye. "And, if it's any comfort, none of those people today particularly impressed the jury. But there's a few more witnesses for the prosecution before we get to call our own."

"The victims' neighbors?" Dominic said.

Hilary nodded. "And some friends. Family. Character witnesses, mainly. No one knows anything that can prove your involvement, but I want you to prepare for more of what Bukhari started today."

"I'm prepared," Dominic said.

"Good. Go home. Try to get some sleep. It all starts again tomorrow."

* * * *

Two more days and five more witnesses came and went—Lizzie's friends and neighbors, Dean's co-workers and housemates. Then, finally, after lunch on the fourth day, Amir Jabal called Karen Wood to the stand.

The victims' mother cried so much that she couldn't answer Jabal's questions about Lizzie's character, career path or her increasingly desperate requests for loans. After almost an hour of the woman's agony, Judge Fotheringham called an early finish.

"We'll pick your testimony up tomorrow, Mrs. Wood," Fotheringham said quietly as people began standing from their seats. "But only if you feel up to it."

The woman covered her face with her hands and gave herself up to convulsive sobbing as her husband helped her down from the witness box. He gathered her to him, his thin face tight with pain, and she sobbed into his chest. An usher stepped forward to show them into a side room as the jury were led out. The people filing from the main doors were silent and somber.

"Mr. Jabal, Ms. Augustine." Fotheringham beckoned to the prosecution. They hurried to the bench where Fotheringham began to converse with them in low tones.

"She'd better be giving them a bollocking for calling a mother as a fucking character witness at her own kids' murder trial," Beck muttered, and they packed up their files.

"I'd say that's exactly what she's doing," Hilary replied, examining the judge's expression. It was only then that Hilary noticed the look on Dominic's face.

"Dominic?" Hilary said quietly.

"This isn't right," Dominic murmured.

"It's hard to listen to. But the prosecution's job is to garner sympathy."

"That woman's grief should not be part of this," he said, his voice like thunder in distant hills.

"I agree," Hilary said. "But it was Augustine's decision, not ours."

"Don't think about them," Amelia said, squeezing Dominic's arm. "You didn't hurt them."

"Someone did."

"Yes, but it wasn't you. We'll show them it wasn't you."

"But they're out there. Whoever did this is still out there, while we're here torturing what's left of the family."

"We just need to focus on you," Amelia urged.

"Those parents need the truth," Dominic snapped. He sent Hilary a pained look then stormed away. Amelia went after him. Eloise leveled an assessing look at Hilary and Beck, then followed at a more sedate pace, Merriweather at her heels.

"Bugger me," Beck murmured. "He was almost human for a moment there."

Hilary didn't answer.

"Cheer up, boss," Beck said, patting his shoulder. "We've just gained a whole afternoon of prep-time."

"No." Hilary shook his head, pocketing his phones and retrieving his case. "Take the rest of the day off, Beck. This case is weighing on all of us. No research, no prep. That's an order."

She raised her eyebrows, but she was smiling. "An order, sir?"

"A…strong request," he moderated. "We all need a break."

"I will if you will," she said as they made for the door.

Hilary smiled. "Agreed."

"I mean it," she said, giving him a look. "Turn that work phone off. Netflix and chill with Jazz, you hear?"

"I hear." Hilary nodded.

"You swear?"

"I swear," Hilary said, laying his hand on his heart. "I'll head right home. And you'll do the same?"

"I will," Beck said, looking suddenly very tired. "No fight from me, sir. Not this time."

"Good. See you tomorrow."

Court finished early. Heading home. Watch a film?

Hilary sent the text and started the car, a confused mix of emotions tightening his chest.

"Those parents need the truth."

Dominic's words echoed in his head. He saw again the pain that had darkened his black eyes as he'd watched Karen Wood being led from the room by her distraught husband. He shook his head to try to clear it. Beck was right. He needed a break. Some distance. Getting emotionally involved in any case was bad news, even when staying objective felt like the most inhuman thing you could do.

Then there was the memory of the kiss throwing everything even more off-balance.

He took a breath. An afternoon off. That was all he needed. A chance to reconnect with Jazz a little. Figure out what he wanted. What was going on between them.

By the time he was letting himself into the flat, he was almost looking forward to it. It was only as he realized the flat was empty that Jasper's reply pinged back.

Sorry, babe. Heading out. Marcia's arranged a meeting with some YouTuber. Don't wait up.

He stared at the message until it blurred. A dull ache he was becoming all too familiar with blossomed behind his ribs. He left the flat again, suddenly unable to stand the silence, returned to his car and started driving, telling himself it would help him think.

An hour passed…then another. He wove through London's choked roads, stopping, starting, willing his mind to settle, but it wasn't listening to him. Darkness fell and he realized he was parked outside the Hart-Gosford townhouse. He gazed up at the walls towering above the gate. There were lights on upstairs — one turned off, then another.

All at once he could taste Dominic again, smell his skin, feel the checked power in the grip of his strong hands — hands that had hurt him in the past, a mouth that had mocked him now rendering him helpless in a completely different way. He was drowning in the realization that a man so much stronger than himself, had been trying to speak to him through one desperate, drunken kiss that had sparked more desire in Hilary than in the last year of his relationship with his fiancé.

Emotion filled him like boiling water. Raw, red anger for Dominic, but a more acidic, bitter wave for himself. He tightened his fingers on the wheel until his knuckles ached.

"What are you doing to me?" he said out loud, voice quavering.

When the front door opened and the broad silhouette of Merriweather appeared, Hilary turned the key in the ignition and drove away.

* * * *

Beck's face slackened as Hilary joined her outside the courtroom the next day.

"Bloody hell, boss," she murmured, looking him up and down. "What happened? You look like you slept in your car."

"Did you bring it?" Hilary said, downing the rest of the double espresso that was doing little more than making him feel nauseated.

Beck held out the garment hanger bag with a heavy frown. "What happened to Netflix and chill?"

"I won't be long," he said, taking the bag and making for the men's.

He shaved in the bathroom sink, earning a sympathetic look from the court clerk who came in to use the urinal before the session started. Hilary tried not to look at the dark circles under his pale eyes, the haggard tightness of his jaw as he scraped away the last of the stubble. He splashed his face with cold water, willing his brain to engage. But it seemed all he could think about was the hard ache, like concrete, in his gut.

He changed in a cubicle and pulled his hair back into a tight tail. A text message popped up on his screen.

Hey, babe. Sorry I never made it home last night. Turned into a bit of a booze-up. Hope court goes well. See ya later x

He put the phone away again.

He was tying his tie with four minutes to spare when Dominic Hart-Gosford pushed open the door.

Their eyes met in the mirror. For a second Hilary was certain he'd looked into his face and knew everything. He felt cold and hot at the same time and was unnerved to see Dominic's expression shift. A darkness came into it that, somehow Hilary knew, wasn't directed at him.

"Miss Donavan said you were in here."

"I'm nearly done."

Dominic's eyes roamed over him as he finished tying his tie. "Late night?"

"Something like that."

"Merriweather said you came to the house last night."

"No, I didn't."

"He said he saw your car."

"He's mistaken."

Dominic looked at him appraisingly as he buttoned his jacket and retrieved his briefcase. "You can be human, you know, Hilary. It is allowed."

Hilary tightened his grip. "We're going to be late."

"Are you sure you feel up to it?"

"I'm fine."

Dominic regarded him a moment longer, appearing to consider something. But then he stepped aside and followed him out of the bathroom without speaking.

The court was already full by the time they entered. The announcer stepped in just as Hilary and Dominic reached their table and commanded everyone to stand. The jury filed in, followed by Judge Fotheringham. But instead of taking her seat at her bench, the judge remained by the door.

"I would like to see defense counsel in my chambers for a moment, please," she stated.

Augustine did not look up from her iPad. Jabal rummaged in his briefcase and did not meet Hilary's eyes, either. He exchanged a glance with Beck, who raised her eyebrows then stood with him.

"What is this?" Eloise Hart demanded with a frown. Dominic watched Hilary, his hands in his lap, his face unreadable.

"We won't be long," he said, then followed Beck to the judge's chambers.

Judge Fotheringham's face was grave as she sat at her desk.

"Mr. Whyte. Miss Donovan. This is to let you know that the prosecution has made an application to me to read out a statement from Mrs. Woods this morning instead of having her give any more live testimony." She regarded them over her glasses. "I'm willing to grant the application but only on approval from you, as it means you won't get to cross."

Hilary sensed Beck stiffen but kept his attention on the judge.

"If you refuse consent, which is well within your right, the prosecution will have to either make Mrs. Woods appear" — the tone of the judge's voice made it clear what she thought of that idea — "or strike her off their witness list."

Hilary looked to Beck, who raised one eyebrow questioningly. Butterflies had started flapping through the hard fog in his belly as he tried to read her expression.

"We're happy to allow the prosecution's application," Hilary said, keeping his hands pressed to his thighs to make sure they stayed still.

Fotheringham nodded in approval, and they filed back into the buzzing courtroom.

"Without that cross we can't draw attention to Lizzie borrowing all that money from her folks and never paying it back," Beck murmured as they returned to their table. "Or the fact that she has applied for credit cards in her mum's name."

"I know. But getting the victim's mother taken off the witness list or forcing her to testify both just make us look heartless," he said as he took the day's papers out of his case. "With reason."

"Well, I'm not sure Ms. Tarrant QC would approve," Beck said with a soft smile. "But I do. And, more importantly, so does the judge."

Judge Fotheringham was calling for quiet as Hilary took his seat and leaned in to murmur into Dominic's ear to explain what had happened. He fought back the reactions in his body as the light, fresh smells of his skin and hair threaded themselves through his consciousness. For a split second, the pain in his chest eased and he could breathe again. But when the black eyes gazed into his, Hilary was again eerily certain that Dominic was reading his mind and turned away.

"Ladies and gentlemen of the jury," Judge Fotheringham stated over the dying chatter. "Mrs.

Karen Wood will no longer be appearing in person to deliver her testimony. I'm sure you can understand and make allowances for this. Instead, the prosecution will read out a statement. However, I would also like you to consider in your deliberations that, as the witness is no longer appearing in person, the defense will not get a chance to offer counter-questions. It is important you consider Mrs. Wood's words...but it is also important that you consider them in light of this."

The judge examined the jury over her glasses as Jabal stood with a tight expression next to Augustine, whose attention was still fixed on her iPad. After a moment of tense silence, Fotheringham nodded.

"Go ahead, Mr. Jabal."

"Thank you, my lady," Jabal said and turned on the television.

"Oh fuck," Beck muttered as a picture of a smiling, happy boy and girl, grinning gap-toothed over a birthday cake with seven candles, appeared on the screen.

"Just relax," Hilary murmured. "Don't react."

Dominic stared as the picture changed to one of Lizzie in a mortarboard and gown, flanked by her parents and brother, all holding flutes of champagne, squinting in bright summer sunshine.

"Now follows Mrs. Wood's statement for the jury." Jabal cleared his throat. "I am sorry for not being there again today," he began, face grave as more pictures of Lizzie and Dean faded in and out on screen. "It hurts me deeply that I cannot speak at the trial of the man that killed my children. It was the only thing left I could do for them, but it is simply beyond me." Jabal looked up. All the jury's eyes were on him, as were the eyes of everyone else in the room. "There are literally no words for a mother who has lost a child," Jabal continued. "Let alone for one who has lost two. Lizzie and Dean were my and their father's world. They were our reason for being alive, even the hard times. And there were some, no parent can pretend it's all easy. It's true Lizzie struggled with money…"

Hilary watched the jury intently but none of them seemed to even blink.

"And being honest about it, perhaps I didn't set the best of examples for her. Our house has two mortgages. Our car was repossessed last year, too. But Lizzie was simply a bright girl who loved life and seized everything it had to offer, even when it was beyond her reach. We did not begrudge her her mistakes. That's how we learn. And we know, given the chance, she would have worked it all out. But, honestly" — Jabal paused and Hilary was certain the gathering of himself was only partially for show — "even if she never could, she still deserved the chance to try."

Hilary snuck a glance to his left. Dominic sat very still. The dark of his eyes was stormy, the full mouth set in hard lines. There was anger there, anyone could see that, and Hilary prayed the jury wouldn't glance over — not least because he also knew that they weren't close enough to see something else burning in the back of his eyes. A dark flame of pain had lit there that, despite everything, somehow managed to warm the cold cavity in Hilary's chest.

"That chance has been taken from her," Jabal continued, turning the page of the statement, "just like it's been taken from her brother. Dean was her rock, her confidant and her friend in everything. He was loyal and kind and he loved his sister. They were both good people. They both died terrified and in agony."

Jabal paused. Hilary was sure his face had softened. "I now have to live the rest of my life knowing their last moments on this earth were filled with suffering. No one should have to live with something like this. *No one*. And whoever has inflicted this pain on those I love the most needs to be punished. Not for my sake. Not even for Lizzie and Dean's sake. But for the sake of all parents, all loved ones. Because whoever did this has no love in their life, no notion of happiness or care for the pain of others. And, for that reason, they need to be denied the chance of ever inflicting that heartlessness on anyone else again."

The TV screen faded to the last and most famous set of pictures of Lizzie and Dean, the ones on all the news sites, selfies taken with some friends at a bar a week before they died. Their eyes were bright, and their matching smiles were wide. Jabal let the image stay on the screen for a long moment then turned the TV off. Utter silence filled the room.

"I think we will take a break," Judge Fotheringham said. "Fifteen minutes, everyone. Then the prosecution can call their final witness."

Chapter Eight

"What a load of sentimental nonsense," Eloise muttered as they filed into an anteroom. "No facts presented. Not a single scrap of evidence. It was manipulation, plain and simple. I'm astonished the judge allowed it. Even more astonished you did, Mr. Whyte."

"Allowing the statement was the best option available," Hilary stated. Amelia had drawn Dominic into a corner and was engaging him in hushed conversation. His face was grim, his shoulders slumped. Something tightened in Hilary at the sight, and he stepped to the door. "Try to relax. Court reconvenes in ten."

"Sara Holden," Beck murmured as they left the antechamber and made for the courthouse café.

Hilary nodded. His personal phone was buzzing. He felt sick and tired. He withdrew his phone and saw a missed call notification from Jasper. Something sharp went through his chest. Beck glanced at it then her expression changed.

"I'll get the coffees, boss," she murmured. "You call him back."

He tried for a grateful smile, stepped out of earshot, took a breath and called Jasper.

"Hil, glad I caught you. Doorman said you went out and never came home last night?"

"I'm in court, Jazz."

"Hil," he said firmly, "where did you go?"

"Where did *you*?"

Jasper made an impatient noise. "I told you. I was at some event with a YouTube personality at The Lansbury. It went on late, and they gave me a room."

Hilary swallowed, unable to think of anything to say.

"Where did you go, Hilary? What's happening with you?"

Hilary looked at his watch. "I've got to go."

"Don't hang up on me, Hil. This is serious. You've been weird and distant for weeks. You should at least be honest with me."

"We should both be honest with each other, shouldn't we?" Hilary heard the words leave his mouth like someone in a dream. The echoing silence on the end of the line made the pounding in his head louder than thunder.

"Can we please talk about this, whatever this is?" Jasper said, quietly.

Hilary stared at the wall.

"Hilary" — Jasper's voice had risen — "we have to sort this. We have to. Tell me we'll talk tonight."

"Yes, fine," Hilary snapped, something ugly uncoiling in his chest. "We'll talk."

"Thank you," Jasper said, voice tight, and guilt prickled up Hilary's spine. "Good luck in court."

Beck handed over his coffee in silence and they returned to the courtroom. Hilary took a moment outside to breathe deep until he was sure his face was blank then pushed open the doors.

Dominic's eyes locked on him as he approached and didn't look away when he sat and began leafing through his papers.

"Prosecution calls Miss Sara Holden."

"Last chance for you to tell me anything I should know," Hilary murmured as the young woman approached the witness stand.

Dominic didn't reply.

Sara wore a simple black dress and no makeup. Her expression was grave, her brown eyes heavy with sorrow and anger, and Hilary's heart sank as she watched the jury drink in her intense earnestness.

"Miss Holden, thank you for joining us today. We know this must be hard," Jabal began.

"I'm here for Lizzie and Dean," she said. Her voice was firm. Her coffee-colored eyes landed on Dominic and burned. "It was the least I could do."

"That's very good of you," Jabal continued. "Could you start off by stating for the jury what your relationship to the victims was?"

"I'd been friends with the Wood twins for years. I went to uni with Lizzie. Dean used to visit a lot. They were close. *We* were close."

"Being close to Lizzie, perhaps she confided things to you? Things she didn't to anyone else?"

"Objection," Hilary stood. "Calling on the witness to speculate."

"I believe, as Lizzie's best friend, Sara's speculation is relevant, my lady," Jabal replied smoothly.

"I agree with Mr. Jabal, Mr. Whyte. Objection overruled. Answer the question, please, Miss Holden."

"She told me everything," Sara said. "Things she didn't tell no one else, not even Dean."

"Things about her love life? Work? Money?"

"Yeah. All those things."

"So I'd like to ask if you had cause to be concerned for your friend in the weeks running up to her murder?"

"I did," Sara said, holding Jabal's gaze steadily.

"In what way?"

"I knew she was in deep. Cash problems, you know?"

"What do you know, exactly?" Jabal said, clasping his hands behind his back. "And how do you know it?"

"She told me she was panicking about her rent," Sara said. "She was behind already. And the dealership was gonna take her car off her. And, on top of it all, she'd just lost her job."

"She told you these things?"

"Yes."

"When?"

"That night," she said, nodding at the blank TV screen. "That night when we were all out at the pub together. Dean had gone to the loo. She didn't want him to know how bad it had got. And she didn't want him to hear about her plan to get out of it all."

Jabal raised his eyebrows. "And what plan was that?"

"She said she had something worked out," Sarah said, voice hardening. "That she had figured out how to get all the cash she needed and to teach someone a lesson while she was at it."

"'Teach someone a lesson'? Those were her words?"

"Yeah."

"Did you get an idea about what exactly she was planning? Or who she was talking about?"

"She said she knew something bad about someone she had worked for, something they'd pay to keep quiet."

"Objection," Hilary said, skin going cold. "Vague."

"Sustained."

"Yes, sorry, Miss Holden. This is important information—so important we need it to be as accurate as possible. So Lizzie stated to you that she'd planned to blackmail someone? Someone she used to work for?"

Sarah shifted in her seat, glancing at Dominic and away again. His expression was carved from granite.

"Please. You can speak freely," Jabal urged.

Sara sighed. "Lizzie was great. You have to understand that. She was fun and honest and she really wanted to do right by everyone. But money... Money was a big deal to her. She liked nice things. We all like nice things. But she didn't want to work for no bank or poncey marketing company. So she...yeah, she spent more than she earned. A lot more. But we're all human, right?"

"Of course," Jabal said, spreading his hands.

"She needed a way out." Sara took a deep breath, lowering her eyes. "She said this man she knew stuff about wasn't a good man, but that he was rich enough to buy himself out of any trouble he got into. She was going to hit him where it hurt...his money."

Hilary's throat closed over. He resisted looking at Dominic or Beck with an effort so great that his shoulders ached.

"And she didn't tell you who this person was?"

Sara shook her head sadly. "No. She never named him. Said it wasn't safe for me to know. But she definitely said it was someone who she used to work for. Not *with*. *For*." Her eyes slid to Amelia and her expression chilled. "She said it was her chance to get back at all of them. So it wasn't hard to guess that it involved that family somehow."

"Objection," Hilary said. "My lady, this has gone beyond speculation and hearsay."

"I have to agree with Mr. Whyte now, Mr. Jabal," Fotheringham said heavily. "Please, can you restrict your questions to obtaining facts from the witness."

"Of course, my lady," Jabal said with a smile that unnerved Hilary. "Miss Holden, I will then ask you this. What was it exactly that made you think that the Hart-Gosfords were the targets of Lizzie's blackmail?"

Sara's eyes sharpened. "Whoever it was, he was rich, and he was linked to Homes with Hart. She said so."

"How do you know it was a male?"

"Because Lizzie was sleeping with him."

The courtroom hushed. Amelia went stiff in her seat. Eloise's face was pinched. Dominic's face hadn't changed, but his hands were clasped tightly together in his lap. Hilary fought the feeling of falling and locked his eyes on Sara.

"Forgive me, Miss Holden. How do you know this? Did she tell you?"

"Not outright," Sara said, glaring at Dominic again. "But it was obvious. She had that look, you know? When you've met someone, when you're doing it with someone you shouldn't be." She frowned. "She enjoyed it. Enjoyed the rush."

"So there were past examples of this?"

"Yeah," Sara said. "I'll say again, she was a good person. You need to know that. But she liked…married men. The ones in unhappy marriages." Hilary dared a glance over his shoulder. All the color had drained from Amelia's face. Members of the audience slid glances her way. Dominic's eyes remained fixed ahead. "It sounds so much worse than it is. But she liked them because she thought… She thought she could help them. She felt she could offer them something different…better. But it never worked out. She never learned."

"And she had told you that this man, he was a bad man?"

"That's what she said."

"Why would she sleep with him if she thought he was a bad man?"

"Objection—" Hilary started, but Jabal waved an impatient hand.

"Miss Holden, did Lizzie tell you *why* she thought he was a bad man?"

"Yes." Sara sent Hilary a sharp look. "She did. She said he was manipulative and sadistic. She wouldn't be involved with him if she'd known that to start with, so I'm guessing she only realized it later."

"But she never explicitly told you she was sleeping with him?"

"No." Sara tilted her chin. "But I could tell she was."

"How?"

"She was acting weird. Tense. Texting lots and not telling me who it was."

"How many times, to your knowledge, had she had affairs like this?"

"At least twice," Sara said. "She showed me pictures. But it always ended because they never left their wives, no matter how unhappy they were." She glared at Dominic again. "They never do."

"So, forgive me, Miss Holden. Just to make things clear for the jury... If she told you about these affairs in the past, showed you pictures even, why didn't she name this mystery lover? This same man who she stated she was going to blackmail? Why didn't she confide more details to you?"

"I don't know," Sara admitted. "I think... I got the impression that under it all, under all the excitement and the anger...she was scared of him."

Hilary's stomach dipped. Sara glared at the floor, her jaw set, her hands clasped together in her lap. Jabal smiled over at him.

"Your witness, Mr. Whyte."

Hilary stood. He prayed his voice would be steady. He didn't look at Dominic as he moved to the witness box.

"Thank you, Mr. Jabal. Miss Holden, I really do just have one question for you. Do you have any evidence, any evidence at all, about anything you've said today?"

"Beyond what she told me, you mean?" Sara said acidly.

"Yes."

She blinked.

"Maybe I can help. She never showed you any pictures or named this mystery lover. Did she show you any text conversations with him? Or take calls with him whilst in your presence?"

"No, but—"

"We've heard testimony from her supervisor, Adeel Bukhari, earlier in the case. It was clear they had a...difficult relationship. Couldn't it have been him that Lizzie was talking about?"

"No," Sara stated firmly, though she had hesitated before answering. "She mentioned Adeel once or twice," she went on, scanning the crowd and eventually picking out the sour-faced young man who was seated near the back, his eyes burning and jaw clenched. "She said he'd got clingy, annoying, but she could handle it, she said. She definitely wasn't scared of him."

"So you're saying it couldn't possibly have been him she was referring to when she talked about blackmailing someone, about getting someone back?"

"She specifically said this guy was rich. There wouldn't be any point in blackmailing Adeel. Lizzie knew he was almost as broke as she was."

Hilary cursed silently. "Did Dean ever express any concerns?"

"No, no, he didn't. But, Mr. Whyte, Lizzie was my best friend. Have you ever had a best friend?"

Hilary hesitated. "No. I must confess that I've never been lucky enough for that."

"Well then, I feel sorry for you," she said, and she only sounded half-angry. "Lizzie and I knew each other better than we knew ourselves. And I knew she was scared."

"Okay," Hilary said gently, "I believe you. But can you tell me what, exactly, makes you think it was my client she was scared of?"

"She named his company —"

"His wife's company. Not his."

"Just look at him," she cried, gesturing at Dominic. "Just look at the bastard. Have you ever seen anyone who looks more like a murderer in your life?"

"Miss Holden," the judge cut in.

"You killed my friend," Sara cried. "You killed Lizzie! And yet *I'm* up here. *I'm* the one trying to make everyone believe you're the evil one, while you just *sit* there—"

"Miss Holden." Fotheringham's voice rose as the jury stared, shifting in their seats. Dominic didn't look away. "I understand this is hard. But you only risk compromising the trial if you don't stick to the facts."

Sara closed her eyes and crushed the back of her hand to her mouth.

"Take a moment," Hilary said softly. "Do you want some water?"

Sara nodded. Hilary moved the glass within reach for her and she sipped. He could feel Jabal's consternation and Beck's approval from across the room.

"Okay. Thank you for everything, Miss Holden. I only have one more question."

"What?" she snapped as she put the glass back down with a shaking hand.

"How do you know she was sleeping with this person?"

"I told you—"

"Not a gut feeling this time, please, Miss Holden," Hilary said gently, laying his hand on the side of the witness box. "As valuable as a gut feeling can be between close friends, in a murder trial the jury need facts. Evidence. Neither we nor the prosecution have found anything to suggest that Lizzie was seeing someone. Do you have anything at all beyond what you *feel* to suggest otherwise?"

Say no, Hilary silently begged, clutching the side of the witness box to make sure his hand didn't shake. *Please say no.*

Sara took a shaking breath and appeared to calm. She met Hilary's eyes. "How about condoms?"

Hilary blinked. "Sorry?"

"Used condoms. In her bathroom bin."

Hilary took a breath. "The police did not find—"

"It was about two weeks before she died," Sara said levelly. "They were long gone by then."

Hilary fought the sensation of falling and gripped the witness box tighter. "No physical evidence that my client had entered that house was found beyond a single hair."

"That's not my problem, is it?" Sara said coolly. "She was sleeping with someone all right, Mr. Whyte. She also told me that she planned to beat a rich arsehole at his own game by taking his money. And I know she liked married men. I really don't think anyone needs any more facts than those, do they?"

* * * *

"You *were* sleeping with her?" Hilary kept his voice low with a gargantuan effort.

"Hilary, this isn't—"

"Jesus fucking *Christ*—"

"Uh, boss?" Beck tapped her knuckle on the frame of the open anteroom door, looking between Hilary and Dominic nervously. "Mrs. Hart and Hart-Gosford are both out here…"

"Keep them back a moment," Dominic said, "please?"

Beck nodded and pulled the door shut.

"I don't believe this," Hilary said, shaking his head.

"Hilary, please," Dominic said. "Come home with me so I can explain."

"It's too late," Hilary said, heading for the door. "Don't you see? It's too late, Dominic. If you'd told me the truth, I could have prepared. It was my question that made her remember those condoms. Do you realize that?" Hilary fumed. "The prosecution didn't know about them, or it would be in the statements. It was because *I* was certain she had nothing beyond a suspicion that I pressed her. Because *you* didn't tell me, I blundered right in—"

"Hilary." Dominic stepped up, voice low and hard. "This is not the place. Come to the house."

"No," Hilary said, turning the handle to open the door. "We meet in my office from now on. Now go home. I've got to go try to get ahead of this before Monday…"

Dominic put his hand on the door and shut it, standing between Hilary and the exit. "I want you to come to the house."

"So your wife and mother-in-law can spend an hour tearing chunks off me when I could be trying to fix this mess? I don't think so."

"They're going to meet with the company lawyers," Dominic said. "They need to try to shield the charity as much as they can. They'll be gone all night. It'll just be us. Please."

Hilary met his eyes. They burned into his own. The rolling nausea that had been swaying like seawater in his guts for days threatened to spill up his throat. But he tightened his grip on the door handle and fought it all back down.

"This had better be good," he muttered and pulled open the door.

He soon lost Dominic's limousine in the traffic between the courthouse and Mayfair. He concentrated on the robotic voice of the satnav and not the setting cement weighing down his limbs. He stopped at a red light just as his phone started to ring. He looked at the screen, sighed then answered through Bluetooth.

"Beck."

"Jesus, Mary and Joseph," she said. "What a shit-show. Where are you?"

"I'm off for a meeting with our client. He insists he can explain everything."

"It's a bit late for that."

"I have pointed that out to him. Can you get to the office and look into all this? See if there's anything out there that supports any of what she said?"

"We already looked," Beck protested, "and the police did. There's nothing, boss. No johnnies. No physical evidence or any other witness. And, really, Holden never really said anything that proves—"

"She's got the jury convinced," Hilary said bitterly. "Did you see their faces?"

Beck sighed. "So what's the plan?"

"Honestly…I don't know."

"Perhaps we reorder our witnesses?" Beck hedged. "Put McGarry on first? Or Dominic even. Perhaps he can be convincing enough—"

"No, no," Hilary said, rubbing his aching head as the light turned green and he moved back into the traffic. "No changing anything now. It'll just look like they've rattled us."

"They have."

Hilary let out a noisy sigh. "Let me see what he has to say for himself. If you and Simon could just double-check there's no proof of an affair, that's something we could work into McGarry's questioning."

"Right. Good plan. Remember, it's not over until the Judge Lady sings. Good luck, boss."

Hilary pulled up outside the townhouse with his stomach tying itself in knots. Merriweather was just climbing back into the limousine as Hilary got out of the car. The man's grim stare was fixed on him, and Hilary was sure there was warning in the narrowed eyes before he shut the door. The limo pulled away as Hilary approached the house. Dominic stood in the open doorway, watching him.

"No watchdog, Dominic?"

"I said we'd be alone. I keep my word."

Hilary passed him into the hall. Dominic clicked the front door shut. Silence fell between them.

"Well?"

"We should have a drink," Dominic said, moving down the hall.

"I don't want a drink."

Dominic didn't answer and moved into an airy dining room, making for a dresser laden with decanters. Hilary stood in the doorway, clutching his briefcase and grinding his teeth.

"I suggest you tell me whatever it is you want to tell me so I can get on with trying to save this case."

Dominic poured himself a measure of whiskey, swallowed it and refilled the glass.

"Fine," Hilary said, turning to go. "You had your chance. Enjoy the single malt. You won't be getting that in prison."

"You really don't know what I'm going to say?" he said, finally turning to face him. Hilary paused in the doorway. A dark heat had lit Dominic's eyes. The fingers that gripped the tumbler were white at the knuckles.

Hilary shook his head. "I'm done with this."

"What?"

"Done with these mind games," Hilary said. "I don't know what you're getting out of all this, but I'm not going to be part of it anymore."

"What do you mean?" Dominic said, following him as he made for the front door.

"I'm filing that motion for change of counsel first thing Monday morning," Hilary said, opening the door. "Happy? You got what you want."

Dominic slammed the door shut again. "That's not what I want."

"Then what *do* you want?"

Dominic's pupils dilated. His lips parted. A tremor went through Hilary. He tried to open the door again, but Dominic grabbed the front of his suit and thrust him against the wall.

Before he could even draw breath to protest, Dominic was covering his mouth with his own. Hilary was vaguely aware of his glasses and briefcase falling to the floor, of the blood rushing through his veins, of the feeling of the solid body crushed against his, but none of it was making a whole lot of sense. Dominic slid his tongue into his mouth, deep, devouring, demanding.

Hilary shuddered. His strength left him in waves. His knees weakened and Dominic tightened his grip, holding him up. He weaved his fingers into Hilary's hair and pulled his head back so he could deepen the kiss. Dominic tasted like whiskey and sweetness, smelled like herbal shampoo and male skin. It filled and overwhelmed Hilary until he didn't know where he was or even who he was.

Dominic let out a low moan and pushed his hardening erection against Hilary's hip. Hilary snapped back to reality with a jerk.

He shoved Dominic back. "No."

"Hilary."

"Stop this—"

Dominic pinned him in place, brushed his lips over his ear, ran his hands up his arms, breathed hot breath over his neck. "Let me show you, Hilary," he panted, sliding a hand inside Hilary's jacket. "Let me show you how good this could be."

Hilary let out a low, desperate noise, clung onto Dominic's lapels like a drowning man and kissed him again. He thrust his tongue into his mouth, drinking him in, sinking into the warmth of his large, strong body. Dominic slid his hand to the small of his back and drew him close, his other hand gripping his wrist. He pulled Hilary toward the stairs. Hilary went, vaguely aware of Dominic pushing his jacket off his shoulders and tugging at his tie. His own hands were frenzied, pulling Dominic's shirt out of his trousers and fumbling at buttons and belt buckles.

Suddenly Hilary was tumbling onto a bed, Dominic's shirt was open and his sculpted chest and hard abdominals were exposed. Hilary climbed on top, burying his face in the hot skin of his firm neck, breathing those intoxicating scents deep, shaking at the feel of the firm muscles under his hands. Dominic let out a moan, low and almost animal, that had Hilary's rational mind spinning away.

Hilary grazed a hard, brown nipple with his teeth and Dominic growled, rolled Hilary under him and kissed him so deeply that Hilary could barely breathe. Dominic tore his shirt open then that hot mouth was trailing down Hilary's neck to lick and suck at the tattoos across his chest. Dominic brushed fingers over his abdomen and down his thigh. He gasped as Dominic took his nipple into his mouth. He arched up off the bed, fire coursing through him and pooling in his groin. He couldn't remember the last time he'd been touched like this—so possessively, so urgently—or the last time he'd reacted so strongly and instantly.

As if sensing his thoughts, Dominic slid a hand down his belly and cupped his straining cock through his trousers.

Hilary gasped, desperate for air.

"Tell me what you want, Hilary," Dominic whispered in his ear, his own hardness pushing into Hilary's leg. "Tell me exactly what you need."

"I..." Hilary managed before cutting off another strangled cry as Dominic thrust his hand inside his underwear. The unfamiliar hold was broad and strong and determined, pumping his length with such precise skill that the glittering storm of his orgasm began to spike and twinkle in his pelvis.

"Jesus," he panted, crushing his eyes shut. "Christ, fuck, I... Please..."

Dominic let out a shuddering breath against Hilary's jaw, like the words alone were sending him over the edge, then Dominic yanked Hilary's trousers down and the bed shifted as he knelt over him, kissed him deeply and took both their cocks in his hand. Dominic stroked them together, fast, hard, fisting his free hand in Hilary's hair. Hilary cried into Dominic's wet, searching mouth and dug his fingers into the hard, muscled back.

"Look at me, Hilary," Dominic breathed against his lips. "Let me watch you come."

Hilary forced his eyes open. He didn't recognize the face above his own. Dominic's hair was mussed, his mouth open and bruised-looking, his skin flushed and damp. The dark eyes that burned into his were like openings onto a night sky, one aflame with stars and mystery and...something else.

Dominic worked their cocks faster, sending sparks dancing up through Hilary's chest. Hilary opened his mouth, to beg him either to stop or to go faster, he didn't know which, but then white light was exploding under his belly and pouring into his legs, chest and arms. He arched into Dominic's hold and the world fell away in ripples of fire and electricity. He felt the heat of his seed splash on his belly and thighs. He heard Dominic groan, a deep, helpless, bestial sound then the stickiness of his cum spattered across Hilary's skin and slicked his grip on their cocks. He gave them both a few more lazy tugs, sending embers sparking up Hilary's nerves, then released his hold.

He hung over Hilary, his weight on his elbows, gazing down into his face with a generous warmth softening the hard lines of his face.

Hilary's pulse calmed. His breathing slowed. He could smell their cum and sweat. Ice water flooded his belly.

He pushed Dominic back. He sat on the edge of the bed, willing his legs to work but struggling to stand.

"Not regretting it already, surely, Mr. Whyte?"

Dominic sprawled across the pillows looking sinfully alluring, his hair disheveled, his shirt open, gazing at Hilary with sharp, watchful eyes.

Hilary managed to stand. He pulled up his underwear and trousers and began casting about for his tie.

"You're not seriously thinking about leaving?"

Hilary retrieved the tie and attempted to button his shirt with shaking hands.

Dominic raised his eyebrows. "You really think you should leave looking like that? They've got people watching the house, you know."

Hilary caught sight of his reflection in the mirror. His hair was loose, sticking up at the back where it was tangled from Dominic's fierce grip. His shirt was rumpled and stained and there were damp patches on his trousers.

"It'll look worse if I stay."

"Nonsense," Dominic said. "You came home to discuss the case. You stayed later than you meant to, had one drink too many and decided to stay in the guest room. What's more innocent than that?"

Hilary put his hand out to steady himself against the wardrobe. His brain rioted, trying to make sense of it all. Dominic's touch was still hot on his skin. He could still taste him in his mouth, feel the dampness across his thighs, still smell the musk of sex in the air.

"Seriously, Hilary," Dominic said, shifting across the bed. "You can't leave now. Stay. Besides, I'm just getting started..." He reached for the tail of Hilary's shirt, but Hilary stepped out of reach.

"Where's that guest room?"

Dominic's face darkened. A hundred unknowable things passed through his eyes then he cast his eyes up at the ceiling. "There are several. Next floor up. Take your pick."

Hilary made for the next floor so fast he almost stumbled on the stairs. He opened the first door he came to. Finding an empty bedroom, he hurried in, slammed the door, locked it and leaned against it.

When his trembling limbs would obey him, he staggered into the en suite and turned on the shower, blasting the water on its highest setting and climbing in.

He didn't know how long he stayed in the shower but when he finally emerged the en suite and bedroom were both filled with steam, his pale skin was burned pink and yet he could still feel and smell Dominic. He padded to the bed, his hair dripping. It was so large and looked so soft with crisp, white bedding.

He crawled into the clean sheets, giving himself up to their welcoming coolness and, slowly, his head stopped spinning. Darkness was only just starting to gather outside, but the adrenaline was draining away and that, combined with the sleepless night before, stole him away before he could have another thought about what he'd done.

Chapter Nine

Hilary woke to silence, the feel of unfamiliar sheets and a confusing sense of contentment mixed with dread in his belly. When he opened his eyes and took in the Hart-Gosfords' guest bedroom, still shadowy in the pre-dawn light, the dread swamped all. He scrabbled for the alarm clock on the bedside table, bringing it close to his face.

It was a little after six a.m. He threw the covers back and hunted through his discarded clothing for his phones. Both his work and his personal phone were dead. He swore, searching the room for his glasses. The memory of strong hands shoving him against the wall, a determined mouth covering his own then the distant sound of his glasses falling to the floor rose in his mind.

He swore again, pulled on his clothes and opened the door a crack. The house was silent. Ice crawled up his spine. What if Amelia had returned home? What if she was downstairs right now, waiting to confront him? Or, worse, asleep, oblivious, in the bed in which her husband had jerked him off the night before?

He took a breath, trying to get his thoughts in order. The silence stretched on, and he made himself move. He crept down the stairs, the thick carpet muffling his footsteps. All was quiet and still. The door to the master bedroom stood open. He held his breath and stepped closer.

The room was empty, the curtains drawn back, letting in the start of the dawn. The huge, wooden-framed bed was neatly made, the duvet and pillows tugged straight, betraying no sign of what had happened. But Hilary didn't even try to convince himself that it had been a dream. Every time he thought about it, he felt Dominic's touch, smelled his hot skin, felt their warm seed spatter across his belly and thighs as they came together.

He turned and hurried down the hall.

He paused at the top of the stairs. Another door stood open on his left. Through the gap he caught sight of yet another bedroom. But this one was filled with furniture and possessions. Not a guest room...

Hilary listened intently then, when the silence continued, took a breath and pushed the door wider.

The bed was made up with sky-blue covers. Indigo curtains draped the engraved headboard. A bedside table held a lamp, a stack of books, a photo in a silver frame. There was a dressing table against the wall, laden with jewelry and makeup boxes. Strands of necklaces hung from a statue of Venus set on a table next to it. There were framed prints on the walls, Impressionist like the ones downstairs but warmer, softer somehow, all in deep blues and purples that brought to mind summer skies and flowing rivers.

The air smelled of hair products and the light, floral scent of Amelia's perfume. He drifted farther in, until the framed photo next to the bed came into focus. It was Amelia with her arm around the shoulders of another woman. They were both smiling, flushed with happiness, their hair whipping about in a strong wind, a mountain landscape in the background.

Hilary looked around the room for another long moment, something tickling at the edges of his mind, but then a phone ringing somewhere downstairs shattered the silence. Adrenaline spiked through his chest, and he hurried from the room. He hovered on the landing, listening for the sound of anyone moving. But the phone continued to ring unanswered and, eventually, stopped.

He found his suit jacket hanging on the end of the banister at the bottom of the stairs. He pulled it on and fastened it, hoping it covered the worst of the stains, then cast around for his glasses. He finally spotted them on the floor under a table, the frames snapped, the lenses crushed. He cursed yet again, pocketed them and went in search of a mirror to tie his tie. He found one near the kitchen door and peered at his blurry reflection. His hair had curled after going to bed with it damp from the shower. His shirt was rumpled and mis-buttoned. He tied his tie and did his best to straighten himself up then became aware of the tantalizing smell of fresh coffee.

He glanced at the front door but inhaled the smell deeper and his mouth dried out. He followed it down the hall to the kitchen and peered in. The vast, airy room was empty. The fittings were chrome, the surfaces black marble. Skylights overhead let in the gray morning light, bathing everything in silver. A coffee machine burbled in a corner and, as Hilary got closer, he spotted a note set on the counter.

Gone for a run. Back soon. Help yourself. D.

Hilary had taken a mug out of the cupboard before he checked himself, slammed the cupboard door and hurried down the hall. He pulled open the front door, resisted looking around for anyone who might be watching and made for his car.

He turned the ignition on, plugged in his phone then searched in the glove compartment for some spare glasses. The only ones he found were an old prescription pair, but they were better than nothing. When the world was almost in focus again, the previous day came screaming back, and all he could do was sit there, clutching the wheel and trying not to panic. Black spots danced in front of his eyes, his chest burned and his breathing rasped in his throat. He closed his eyes, reached inside, made himself take long, slow breaths until the panic passed.

He opened his eyes just as a tall, broad figure in sweat-soaked jogging gear turned the corner into the private street. Dominic stopped in his tracks, his eyes locked on Hilary's car, his face unreadable. Hilary pressed the accelerator and raced away, not looking back.

His skin felt tight and raw. He drove without really thinking about where he was going. Finally, his phone turned on and all the missed calls, texts and WhatsApp messages from Jasper began to pour in. He gritted his teeth and queued up the voicemail.

Hil, where are you? Why didn't you come home? Please, call me and let me know you're okay.

Hilary pulled over into a lay-by and closed his eyes until his pulse steadied. Three more breaths and he felt calm enough to press the call button.

Jasper answered after one ring.

"Hilary? Thank fuck. Where the hell are you?"

"Uh…nowhere."

"What?"

Hilary willed his voice to be level. "I had a late night. I stayed at the office."

"I called Beck. She said you weren't there."

"Checking up on me now?"

It was a moment before Jasper replied. "I've got ten minutes before I have to head out to another promo, Hilary. I want you to tell me what's going on."

Hilary took a shaking breath. "Sorry. I'm sorry. It's just this case…"

"I knew it. It's that man. He's got you all tied in knots—"

"No," Hilary said, a little too vehemently. "No, I can… I can handle it." He cursed the wobble in his tone. "Look… I'm sorry, Jazz. I am. But court did not go well yesterday. I'm up to my ears. We'll talk later, okay?"

"At the restaurant, right?"

Hilary blinked.

"Vincenzo's, Hil," Jasper said, his voice sharpening when Hilary didn't answer. "I go away tomorrow for three weeks. Tell me you're coming to dinner so we can work out…whatever this is."

Hilary bit his lip.

"Hilary…" The annoyance in Jasper didn't quite hide his hurt. The claw of guilt twisted in Hilary's belly.

"I'll be there."

"Thank you," Jasper said. An uncomfortable silence followed until Jasper added, "Love you," before hanging up.

Hilary rubbed his aching temples, attempting to get a handle on his rioting thoughts. By the time he pulled back out into the traffic, he had only partially succeeded.

He deliberately took longer than he needed to picking out the frames for his new glasses to make sure Jasper had left by the time he got home. He stripped out of his stained and rumpled clothes, shoved them in a garment bag and hung them in the hall with the rest of the dry cleaning, glad to get them off his skin. He pulled on a faded hoodie and put a Limp Bizkit album on the turntable in the music room, cranked up the volume and sat at the desk, opened his laptop and plugged his work phone in to charge.

There were dozens of missed calls, messages and emails from Beck and Simon, from Augustine and, of course, from Amelia. He sent up a silent prayer of thanks that there was at least nothing from Eloise, but it was the text message from Dominic that forced itself to the center of his attention.

Don't you think we should talk?

He gritted his teeth, deleted the text and went to make coffee. Once he'd downed half the cup, he braced himself and called Amelia. The discussion lasted almost an hour. Sara's testimony had rattled her, Hilary could tell. He tried to reassure her, but it was all he could do just to stop his voice from catching.

"My husband was not having an affair with that woman," Amelia ended firmly.

Hilary clutched the edge of the desk and poured all his strength into sounding neutral when all he could think of was her husband's mouth on his skin. "There's no proof, Mrs. Hart-Gosford. That's what's important."

He hung up feeling cold and ill and like he needed another shower. Instead, he made himself read through the emails from his researchers. Beck and Simon confirmed that there was no physical or photographic evidence of Lizzie having any sort of affair, least of all one with Dominic. He tried to feel relieved.

He was just forcing down a piece of toast when Dominic called. He ignored it. Seconds after it stopped ringing, another text flashed in.

Hilary. Please. We need to talk about this.

Hilary swore viciously, turned the music down and snatched up the phone.

"Hilary. Finally."

"Will you stop texting my work phone?"

"So give me your personal number."

Hilary hung up.

He turned the volume back up, pulled his files over and buried himself in the work — the witness testimony, the evidence lists, the ballistics reports. He went through everything twice, fielding calls as he went, knowing he could not afford to let anything else slip through. Augustine called again mid-afternoon just as he'd moved one file aside and uncovered the change of counsel motion.

He stared at it several moments before answering.

"Laurette."

"Hilary. Hi."

"What can I do for you?"

"Has your client decided to see sense yet?"

Hilary lifted his coffee cup, found it was empty, slammed it down again. "My client is innocent. Some used johnnies in a bathroom bin don't change that."

"Come on, Whyte. Holden nailed him to the cross. That and the mum's testimony... You'll be lucky if the jury doesn't lynch him themselves."

"Are you threatening bodily harm, counsel? Pretty sure that's illegal."

"Five years."

"What?"

"Get him to plead guilty and he'll get five years. He'll be out in three."

Hilary took his new glasses off and laid them carefully on the desk on top of the change of counsel motion. He pinched the bridge of his nose, attempting to drive his headache away so his thoughts could order themselves.

"Anyone would think you were scared of our witnesses, counsel."

"We just want this over. You saw Karen Wood and her husband. You heard her statement. This needs to end."

"I couldn't agree more. So perhaps you should be out there trying to find the real culprit?"

A heavy pause. "He got to you, didn't he?"

"What?"

"At the beginning you were defending him because it's your job. Now you believe him. What changed?"

Hilary felt sick. He took a deep breath, replaced his glasses and straightened his spine. "He didn't do it, Laurette."

Augustine paused. "This is his last chance. You owe it to your client to at least let him know about the offer."

Hilary stared at the phone screen for a long time after she hung up. He tried to ring Dominic three times. Three times, he couldn't bring himself to press Call. If he heard his voice again, now, he…he didn't know what he'd do, what he'd say.

He returned to his files, shoving the change of counsel motion to the bottom of the pile.

Korn's *See You on the Other Side* album was spinning silently on the needle when Hilary finally registered that night had fallen. He checked the time. Less than an hour until he was supposed to meet Jasper. Hilary bit his lip and checked his personal phone, but his fiancé hadn't tried to call. He hadn't texted.

He made himself move to the bedroom and changed in a daze. He chose black trousers and the salmon shirt he knew Jasper liked, the one he said went with his hair. He put silver rings in each ear and brushed out his hair. He stood in front of the mirror, spinning his engagement ring and staring at his reflection. There was something different about his face, a look he didn't recognize. He told himself it must be the new glasses.

He was ten minutes late getting to the restaurant. When he finally arrived, he pushed the swinging doors open, no more certain of what he was going to say than when he'd left the flat.

A waiter led him past the tables at the windows overlooking the Strand and up to the gallery. Jasper stood from a table in one of the screened booths.

"This isn't your usual table."

"No," Jasper said as he sat. "I…I thought we should have some privacy."

"You're not tweeting this, then? Shocker." Hilary sat and pulled the menu over.

"Hil…"

"I want some wine. Please."

Jasper pursued his lips, nodded and lifted his hand. The waiter was there in an instant and soon returned with a bottle of sauvignon blanc. Jasper poured it himself. Hilary drained his glass and held it out for a refill.

Jasper met his eyes as he filled it up again. "Are we going to talk?"

Hilary downed another mouthful then lowered the glass and stared into the golden liquid, the fuzz of the alcohol burning in his empty belly. He dared to raise his eyes to meet his fiancé's. Jasper had the most beautiful blue eyes, clear and bright as a tropical sea. The light in them, as well as the way they had looked at Hilary when they first met, used to set his heart fluttering in his chest. Now it was fluttering for very different reasons, and Jasper's usual sparkle was absent, leaving a dour, questioning look in its place.

Hilary opened his mouth to tell him everything, but instead heard himself saying, "I'm sorry if you think I've been acting strange, but it really is just the trial."

Jasper's fine brows drew together. "You've never acted this way during a trial before."

"What way?" Hilary demanded.

"Like you're angry with me all the time. Like you don't want to be around me."

"I can't understand how you've got that idea when you've not been around enough for me to act in any particular way around you."

"So that's really what all this is about?" Jasper said. "My *schedule*?"

Hilary's throat closed over. "We're both busy. I'm just as bad, I know, but…"

"But?"

Hilary stared at his wine. "Neither of us seem to be making the effort to make time for each other anymore. Don't you think that's...worrying?"

Jasper watched him for a long moment in silence, emotions rolling through his eyes. Then he reached out and took Hilary's hand. "I knew when we got together that sometimes our jobs would have to come first...but my feelings toward you haven't changed."

Hilary gripped his glass. "You spend more time talking to people online than me. It's been that way for a while."

"My media profile needs constant maintenance," Jasper insisted, his hand still on Hilary's. "Marcia and the publicity company do most of it. But I have to do my bit, too."

Hilary took a breath and met Jasper's penetrating look. An icy calm stole through him. "Do you really want to marry me, Jasper?"

Jasper looked shocked. "What?"

"It's a simple question."

"Why would you ask that?"

"I'm not sure of the answer anymore."

Jasper's jaw tightened. "Hilary, I know you have this drive, this *need* for success. I'm glad you think I'm part of that. But I'm not perfect—"

"I don't need perfect," Hilary said levelly, pulling his hand away and resting it in his lap. "I just want you to answer."

"Of course I want to marry you. Would I have asked you if I didn't?"

"If it would be good for your image? Maybe."

Jasper paled under his tan. Regret began to claw across Hilary's skin, but he didn't look away.

"I asked you to marry me because I want to be your husband," Jasper said after the silence had stretched on a moment too long. "And I want you to be mine. I want a life with you."

"So cancel the wedding. Let's go to the register office. Now. Tonight."

"Hil, we can't. The money we've paid alone…"

"Who cares about money?"

"We've signed contracts," Jasper insisted. "Pulling out of them now would be bad news for both our careers. And what would our families say? Everyone's invested in this, Hilary. I thought you were, too."

Hilary refilled his glass while struggling to think of a response.

Jasper leaned back in his chair. "So is this really just about the wedding? We've talked about this, Hil…"

"*You* talked. I just went along with it."

Jasper's face softened. "You're right. I thought I was prepared for the circus, and I thought you were, too…but I think the truth is, it's freaking us both out."

Hilary drank more wine.

"It's true, though, isn't it? You're freaked. It's okay. You can tell me."

Hilary lowered the glass. The waiter tried to return to take their order, took one look at Jasper's expression and scurried away.

"The size of the wedding freaked me out from the start," Hilary stated. "The engagement photoshoot was sleazy bullshit. The fact that you tweet our relationship to the world like it's just *content*…" Hilary tightened his hand on his glass as it poured out of him, like an old dam finally bursting. "It just doesn't feel like any part of this is real anymore."

"It is," Jasper said, shifting still closer. "I promise it is, Hil. Sure, it's buried under some crap at the moment. And perhaps some of that is my fault..."

"Perhaps?"

"You wanted to date a film star, Hil. I promised I would try to protect us from the worst of it. But you knew I was never going to be able to control it all."

"I didn't want to date a film star. I wanted to date *you*, Jazz—the guy who likes shit music and cheap beer."

"Hey," Jasper said with a weak smile, "attacking my music taste is below the belt, isn't it?"

"But I *believed* in that," Hilary said. "I believed in you liking Arctic Monkeys and Coldplay and Heineken. It was honest. It was real. It's who you really are." Hilary took another breath, willing his voice not to shake. "I know your life demands a lot from you. I was willing to go along with it. To be with you. But you show so little of your real self to me these days..."

"That's not true, Hil."

"When was the last time we stayed up all night listening to records? Getting pissed and stoned and just having a laugh? The only time we stay up now is to watch movies you're going to be in the remake of."

Jasper's face tightened. "I thought you liked watching movies with me."

"I did when you enjoyed the movies," Hilary said quietly. "Not when you were researching them."

Jasper released his hand.

"I knew there'd be a lot to cope with," Hilary murmured. "I was happy to do it when I thought it was all a show and *we* were the real part. Now it feels like the show is becoming who you are—and that being with me...marrying me is part of that."

"How is marrying you part of a *show*?"

Hilary shrugged and drained his wine. "It plays well with your demographic. Marcia said so. And what did your dad say at that food tasting? '*Good-looking lawyer ticks the boxes*'?"

"He didn't say that."

"He bloody did, Jazz."

"Well, so what if he did? Fuck him. And fuck Marcia. So they're glad I'm marrying you because they think it's good for my image. Let them think it. I'm marrying you because I want to be with you for the rest of my life."

"And because splitting up now would effectively be career suicide."

Jasper's face hardened. "If I thought you'd said that for any other reason than to hurt me right now, I'd be out of the door. And I get you're under a lot of stress. But if you really believe that's the only reason I'm with you, you need to tell me. Because there's no coming back from this if it's the truth."

Hilary's palms tingled. His chest tightened. His throat closed over. The pain in Jasper's eyes was sharp and clear. Hilary thought of the Maldives, the trip where they'd had sex in the sea, a fortnight where they'd done nothing but eat and drink and fuck and laugh and no one knew or cared who they were. They'd been *together*. Really together.

And on the last night, Jasper had pulled out the ring. They'd just shared a joint and he'd not been able to stop giggling. Hilary could still smell the weed and taste the vodka, remembered the night that had followed when they'd fucked until dawn.

Then he thought about how it had all changed the minute they'd landed back in England. Jasper was on the phone to his agent the second they got off the plane, working out the engagement announcement, the photoshoots and initial plans for the wedding before they'd even retrieved their luggage.

He looked down at the pristine tablecloth with his vision blurring.

"I guess…" Hilary took a breath and closed his eyes. "I guess I'm just scared."

Jasper leaned into his side and threaded his fingers through his own. "That's fine. I'm scared, too. And, yeah, maybe I've been burying myself in work to get away from that. And I'm sorry. I'll try harder, I will." He put a finger under Hilary's chin and raised his eyes to meet his. "But we both have to accept we have careers that take a lot from us and always will. Mine is no less important than yours."

Hilary felt heat flood his face. "I never said it was."

Jasper raised an eyebrow but then dropped his gaze to their joined hands. "I need you, Hilary." He squeezed his hand. "I fell in love with you because you made me feel normal."

"Whereas I fell in love with you because you made me feel special," Hilary breathed. Jasper opened his mouth, but Hilary plowed on. "But either way I don't think you *are* normal anymore, Jazz. And perhaps I'm not…or never was—" He made a frustrated noise. "Maybe I'm not who you thought I was, either." Jasper stared at him. Hilary drew a breath. "The point is things have changed—or maybe reality has finally come knocking. Either way, I think we need to be honest about it."

Jasper looked uncertain. The moment in which nothing but doubt could be read in his fiancé's eyes was long enough to fill Hilary's stomach with certainty as cold and suffocating as ice water. But then he took Hilary's other hand. "You *are* special. And that's nothing to do with me. You need to start believing in yourself. Believing you deserve to be happy."

Hilary's throat closed over. He felt Dominic's mouth on him—smelled his skin, his herbal shampoo, felt the gentle touch of his large hands, remembering his strength as he stopped him from falling.

He crushed his eyes shut. Jasper pressed his lips to Hilary's cheek. He smelled like lemongrass and seawater, so different, so fresh, so familiar.

"Marry me, Hilary. Please. I need you."

* * * *

Jasper spent an hour bringing Hilary off that night. He was attentive and tender, gentle and warm, touching, caressing. He spent twenty minutes preparing him with lube and gentle, slow, probing fingers. Hilary's breath caught in his throat and his body responded, even though his alcohol-fogged mind still rioted in his skull. He sank himself into it, willing the sensations to banish the gray ghosts in his mind.

"I love you, Hilary," Jasper whispered in his ear over and over as he fucked him, slowly, gently, rubbing against that spot inside Hilary that made his muscles clench and his vision blur. "I love you."

Hilary crushed his eyes shut and tried not to think— not to think about the fact that Jasper had turned the light off before they'd started, about the fact that he was fucking him from behind and sounded like he was reading lines from one of his films.

They came at the same time, Jasper's face buried in Hilary's neck, his fingers interlaced with his own, hanging on like a man about to fall off a cliff.

* * * *

Jasper forgot to set an alarm and the morning dawned in chaos. Hilary watched from the kitchen doorway, his hands curled around his mug as Jasper tore around the flat, grabbing his cases and ski goggles before planting a bruising kiss on Hilary's cheek and hurrying for the door. Marcia and the driver stood by the lifts, Jasper's agent managing to look both impatient and relieved at the same time.

"Sure we can't convince you to come, Hilary?" Marcia beamed as she hustled Jasper into the lift.

"It's all a bit too late for that." His tone prompted a quizzical look. He gestured at his bare feet, shorts and washed-out Linkin Park T-shirt. She smiled after a moment then joined the party in the lift.

"Speak later, Hil," Jasper said. "Love you."

The doors slid shut before Hilary could reply.

Chapter Ten

Hilary smoked an entire pack of cigarettes as he worked that afternoon. He opened all the windows but was relieved to know that it wouldn't matter if the smell lingered. Jasper was gone for weeks. He told himself he was only relieved because the less distraction he had from the trial, the better.

He lit another cigarette as he re-read Eloise's witness statement, despite already knowing it by heart.

My son-in-law had decided not to attend the banquet that day. That's why he came to see me at the gallery, to let me know. It was a brief discussion. No, he didn't elucidate why. I couldn't possibly comment on whether Clarence Lavelle's presence was a factor. You would have to ask Dominic. And, no, I don't know where he went after that. Amicable? Of course, it was amicable…

Hilary emptied the fruit bowl and consumed an entire multipack of crisps as the day wore on, spreading peanut butter on a bagel when that wasn't enough. He ordered pizza as the evening drew in, and when he finally looked up from his laptop with an uncomfortable fullness in his stomach, he was shocked to find the pizza box empty. He couldn't remember the last time he'd such an appetite and didn't know whether to attribute it to stress, the late night with Jasper or the relief that he was gone.

He pushed that thought away and opened the forensics file.

* * * *

Monday was overcast and cool, even for April. Hilary cursed the chill as he entered the courthouse. At least if it had been warm, he could have blamed his sweaty palms on the heat.

Dominic was waiting outside the courtroom. Hilary had spent all morning preparing himself for seeing him again, but as he took him in—his tall frame, his broad shoulders, the dark eyes that went right through him— his stomach bunched. He cast his eyes down and made to pass.

"Hilary—" Dominic started, stepping in his path.

"We should go in," Hilary said, trying to move around him, but Dominic grabbed his elbow.

"Hilary, you can't avoid me like this."

Hilary clenched his jaw. "We're presenting your defense today. We can't be late."

Dominic's gaze lingered on the new glasses, then released him. Hilary straightened his suit and strode into the courtroom. He didn't meet Beck's concerned look as he laid the files out on the table.

"Everything all right, boss? You look...tense."

"All good," he said, taking his seat as Dominic leaned over to murmur into Amelia's ear. Hilary shifted his chair to face away from them and, finally, the jury filed in.

"Did you work all weekend?" Beck murmured, still watching him as they all stood.

"You telling me you didn't?"

Beck gave him a baleful look and he attempted an encouraging smile in return as Judge Fotheringham took her seat.

"Would the defense like to call its first witness?"

Hilary stood. The room hushed. He felt Dominic's eyes on him and sipped from his glass of water to unstick his tongue. "Defense calls Rabbie Gowan."

The forensic analyst was a small man with a lined face, glasses and a benign expression. He swore his oath and took his seat, apparently unruffled by the thickness of the air that was making it hard for Hilary to breathe.

"Good morning, Mr. Gowan. Thank you for joining us today. Would you mind stating your occupation for the court?"

"I am Chief Analyst at the Metropolitan Police Forensic Investigative Service."

"And you oversaw the analysis of the forensic evidence collected at Lizzie Wood's flat, is that right?"

"That's right, yes." He smiled, his eyes steady.

"The prosecution has outlined the forensic evidence in this case in some detail," Hilary said, hoping he didn't sound as harried as he felt, "so we needn't go over that again. Today I'm more interested in your personal observations on the findings."

"My observations are all in the reports, Mr. Whyte. I sign them off before they get submitted to the police."

"You've worked in forensics a long time, is that right?"

"Nearly thirty years now."

"I suppose in that time you've worked on a lot of murder scenes?"

"Unfortunately, yes."

"Would you say it's unusual to find a murder scene where the perpetrator has left so little physical evidence?"

Gowan glanced at Jabal then back at Hilary. "It has been known."

"How usual or unusual is it, would you say?"

"Objection," Jabal put in. "Asking the witness to speculate."

"Sustained," Fotheringham said without looking up from her notes.

"I'll rephrase. In your personal experience, have you ever had so little to work with?"

"On occasion," Gowan replied. "Usually when the perpetrator knows how to avoid leaving trace evidence."

"So says your report," Hilary said, clicking the TV on to display the document. "Leading to the prosecution's opinion that this was a carefully planned, premeditated crime."

"The evidence would support that, yes."

"Does the evidence support my client being at the scene, Mr. Gowan?"

"His DNA was found."

"One hair, yes?"

"That's right."

"No skin cells? No fingerprints? And no other hair, just that one?"

"That's correct."

"In which case, is there any chance that this could have been a lab error?"

Gowan blinked. "Our preservation of evidence methods are extremely rigorous—"

"So, it's impossible? There couldn't possibly have been a mistake?"

"Well, no," Gowan said, interlacing his fingers in his lap. "There's always the capacity for human error. But—"

"Wouldn't you say, if the killer really had been careful enough to leave virtually no trace evidence behind, that it would be more likely that the one piece that *was* found could have been due to, I don't know, evidence contamination?"

Gowan frowned. "What exactly are you implying, Mr. Whyte?"

"I'm not implying anything," Hilary said simply. "I'm simply asking if it's possible. A yes or no will do."

"Objection," Jabal said, frowning. "My lady, Mr. Whyte is simply baiting an expert witness in a desperate attempt to undermine the jury's faith in the forensics of this case."

Fotheringham was looking at Gowan, tapping her pen. "Overruled."

"My lady—"

"The jury needs to understand the evidence in context. The witness is an expert, as you say, so I think his opinion is relevant. Mr. Gowan, if you could answer Mr. Whyte's question?"

A line had appeared between Gowan's graying eyebrows. "I would be happy to, my lady. Yes, it's possible that the hair ended up in evidence by accident. Possible...but not likely. It's also possible that the DNA analysis was incorrect. Again, possible...but not likely.

There is also the chance, as I think you were implying, that it was planted." A murmur went through the courtroom and the jury exchanged glances. "All these things are possible. But, in my experience, the highly unlikely rarely happens—and science does not lie."

"Though it can be…presented in a certain light?"

"Facts are always facts, no matter how you present them."

"Were any condoms found at the crime scene?"

"Objection," Jabal cut in. "The jury has the evidence lists. We already know no prophylactics were found at the scene. That does not make Sara Holden's account any less relevant."

"Sustained," Fotheringham said looking over the top of her glasses. "Let's not go over points we don't need to, Mr. Whyte."

"No, my lady," Hilary said, ducking his head. "I apologize. I just wanted to remind the jury that no such items were submitted to evidence."

"Consider them reminded," Fotheringham said, turning back to her papers. "Continue."

Hilary turned back to the witness with his own banal smile. "Mr. Gowan, no used prophylactics were submitted to evidence. Was the bathroom bin?"

A pause. "Yes. Yes, it was."

"And Miss Wood's bedlinen?"

"That's right."

"Was any of my client's DNA found at either of those places?"

Augustine's face darkened and Jabal stared hard at his notes.

"No, it wasn't," Gowan stated flatly.

"If the victim was in a sexual relationship with my client, in your expert opinion, would you think there would be *some* physical evidence of it, of his presence, somewhere in her home? Even if she'd cleaned the bin and washed her sheets since?"

Gowan gave Jabal a sympathetic look. "I would expect to find something, yes. But only if that was the location where they chose to meet, of course."

Hilary swore internally as Jabal's mouth twitched. "Of course," he said quickly. "It's just Miss Holden specifically said that she'd seen the evidence of their sexual relationship in her bathroom bin, so it seemed an important fact to establish either way. Was any other DNA found in that bin?"

"Yes," Gowan said, pushing his glasses up his face. "From both the victims and perhaps two other unidentified persons."

"But nothing of my client's, apart from that hair?"

"Correct."

"And that hair was found *under* Dean Wood's body, on the stairs?"

"Again. Correct."

"What would you say that implies, Mr. Gowan?"

"Mr. Whyte," Gowan said, frowning, "I am not a detective. I'm a scientist. I analyze the evidence provided and report on my conclusions. The police examine my conclusions and fit them within the frame of their investigation. I can only tell you how and when the victims died, and who the evidence suggests was present at the time."

"'Suggests' being the key word, I think?"

Gowan shrugged. "What was found at the scene and who it belongs to is fact. The only ambiguity comes from the fact that we can't prove how or when it ended up there. But your DNA does not usually end up somewhere you've never been."

Hilary cursed silently once more as the man's calm, unblinking gaze held his own.

"One final question from me then, sir. If the forensic evidence really is that conclusive, why don't you think the prosecution called you as a witness?"

"Objection." Jabal shot to his feet. "My lady, Mr. Whyte is asking the witness to speculate yet again."

"Sustained," Fotheringham said a little impatiently. "Mr. Whyte, you know very well that Mr. Gowan can't possibly guess as to the prosecution's motivations when drawing up a witness list."

"Perhaps Mr. Jabal can answer the question then?" Hilary said smoothly, turning to face the barrister. "Is it perhaps because the evidence is so sparse that it doesn't really prove anything?"

"Mr. Gowan's report was ample for our purposes," Jabal replied. "We saw no need to drag him in here to defend his findings."

"I haven't asked him to defend them...only to put them into context. And I believe he's done that. Thank you, Mr. Gowan. No more questions from me, my lady."

Hilary returned to his seat with the courtroom bubbling like a pot on a stove. The smallest of smiles turned up the corner of Beck's mouth as he sat and sipped water, hoping his hands weren't shaking enough to spill. Dominic was watching him, but he didn't turn his head to meet his look.

"Mr. Jabal, would you like to cross?" Fotheringham prompted. Jabal and Augustine broke off their whispered conference and the barrister stood.

"I only have one question for Mr. Gowan," Jabal said. "Does the evidence prove that Mr. Hart-Gosford is innocent of this crime?"

"No," Gowan responded. "No, it doesn't." He glanced at Dominic. "But I'm afraid it doesn't prove his guilt, either."

More excited murmuring broke out and Fotheringham banged her gavel for silence. "Thank you, Mr. Gowan. You may stand down. We will break for lunch. Mr. Whyte, you can call your next witness when we reconvene."

"Did that go well?" Amelia asked, watching the jury file from the room.

"It's laid more groundwork for reasonable doubt," Beck said, gathering her papers, "which is just what we need."

"Who is next?" Eloise said as she scrolled through emails on her phone, tight mouth pinched.

"Francis Meek," Hilary said, opening his briefcase.

"Who?"

"The accountant," Dominic said in a low voice, dark eyes scanning the thinning crowd.

Eloise shot him a look. "I don't know that name."

"One of the underlings," Hilary said grimly. "Your personal accountant is in Dubai. But Mr. Hart-Gosford is confident Meek will be able to present evidence that the money didn't come from him."

Eloise pursed her lips further. "Well, you'll have to forgive me if I don't attend this afternoon. I have several meetings I've been putting off—"

"Mother," Amelia said, "we need to show our support—"

"You show your support, dear," she said, sweeping up the aisle to where Merriweather was waiting at the door. "I'll be back tomorrow for my testimony. In the meantime, the world goes on, and there are matters that really do require my attention. Merriweather? Ask Harold to bring the car around, please."

"At once, ma'am," Merriweather said, holding the door open, glancing once at Dominic then following his mistress from the room.

"Mr. Whyte, a word?" Amelia asked.

The look on her face set Hilary's skin crawling. He glanced at Dominic, who was staring at the door, then followed Amelia out of earshot with his blood throbbing in his temples.

Amelia lowered her voice and looked him in the eye. "My husband tells me you've been avoiding him."

Hilary tried to swallow, but his mouth was too dry. "That's not true. I've just been working—"

"It's important that you agree to meet with him. He has things he needs to tell you."

Hilary's skin rippled into goosebumps. "Your husband has insisted on many occasions that he has told me all I need to know."

"He thought he had. But now..." Her glance slid to Beck, watching with a line between her eyebrows, then she took his elbow and drew them farther away. "We had hoped it would never become relevant. But perhaps it has."

"What's become relevant, Mrs. Hart-Gosford?"

Her blush-painted lips pressed together. "Just meet him tonight. We've got somewhere...discreet, where you won't be overheard. He'll explain everything. He had hoped to talk to you over the weekend, but it sounds like he failed."

Hilary's throat threatened to close. Dominic's black gaze was fixed on him, making his stomach flop over.

"Please, Mr. Whyte."

The earnestness of her tone caught him under the ribs. Her eyes were shining with urgency.

"If your husband has something so important to say, he should tell me now."

"No," Amelia said, glancing at the empty jury box. "Not here. Just agree to meet him and we'll arrange everything."

Hilary searched her eyes and found himself nodding, even though his stomach was jerking around like a stranded fish. "If you insist."

Amelia didn't smile but her eyes brightened, and she sent Dominic a relieved glance. "Thank you, Mr. Whyte. You won't regret it."

"I hope you're right," said Hilary with feeling and left the room without meeting Dominic's eye.

* * * *

"Think this'll be straightforward," Beck said, sipping her iced coffee and leafing through their list of questions for Meek as they sat in their window seat at the courtroom café. "Only thing we need to worry about is putting the jury to sleep."

Hilary nodded distractedly, staring out of the window.

"So what did the missus want?"

"What?"

"Amelia," Beck said, putting her elbows on the table and looking him in the eye. "What was all that about?"

Hilary pushed his pasta round his plate and didn't meet her eye. "Nothing."

Beck raised her eyebrows then returned her attention to her food. "I like the new glasses, by the way," she added, opening the accountant's file.

Hilary laid his fork down. "I'll see you in there."

"You don't want that?" she said, nodding at the half-eaten lunch.

"Help yourself. I'm not hungry," he said and left.

Francis Meek wore an Armani suit and a lemon-yellow power tie, but that was where his noteworthiness ended. He was submissive and crawling, shy and flinched at every question, both from Hilary and even more during Jabal's cross, managing to answer without answering every time. Hilary fumed silently at the defense table.

"Never met a money man so unsure of himself," Beck muttered in an undertone as Jabal attempted to pin him down on their audit procedures. "You usually can't shut 'em up."

"Maybe this was a mistake," Hilary replied.

"It's fine. The jury isn't listening," Dominic murmured.

Hilary saw Dominic was right. The court members were staring at the floor, the ceiling, their watches.

"We might as well have not called him," Beck muttered.

"No," Hilary said. "This is good. It's establishing that there's nothing interesting in the accounts."

"Maybe," Beck said, scribbling a note on her pad. "Now if Jabal could just draw his cross out long enough for them to forget everything he's actually said, more to the good."

Hilary silently agreed, not least because the longer this continued, the longer it would be before he would have to be alone with Dominic.

Even Hilary was fighting to keep from fidgeting as Jabal's cross finally drew to a close, Meek having successfully spent almost three hours not saying anything of significance either way and the judge calling an end to the day.

However, Hilary's malaise evaporated the minute Beck lifted a hand in goodbye and left him standing outside the courthouse doors with Dominic.

"Amelia says you've finally agreed to talk to me."

Hilary looked anywhere but at his client. "She said it had to be somewhere…private?"

"It's for the best."

"You should tell me now…here."

Dominic lifted an eyebrow as he watched the people file in and out through the doors. "Believe me. You don't want that."

Hilary shifted his briefcase from one hand to another, cursing his thumping heart. "Fine. I'll drive."

Dominic didn't speak on the slow, traffic-choked journey, apart from to give Hilary directions. Part of Hilary was grateful, while the other half raged for him to spit out whatever he was going to say and get it over with. But Dominic navigated in a flat, toneless voice and the air in the car seemed to thicken to the point where Hilary began to see black spots dance in front of his eyes.

He blinked them away and saw they were headed in the opposite direction to Mayfair, taking the Blackwall Tunnel under the river and making for Greenwich. Residential apartment blocks glinted in the evening sun. As they turned off the main road, Dominic tapped something on his phone and the gates of a private underground car park swung open ahead.

They rode the lift up from the car park in silence. Hilary pretended to be reading emails and willed his breathing to stay calm until, finally, the lift opened into a luxurious, open-plan studio apartment. Floor-to-ceiling windows looked out over the jumble of north London across the sluggish glimmer of the Thames. The furniture was simple, in creams and browns, leather and wood and wool. Hilary was instantly reminded of the bedroom at the townhouse. He cleared his throat to attempt to dispel the memory and finally turned to face Dominic.

"You've got five minutes."

Dominic shrugged off his suit jacket, loosened his tie and made for the oak sideboard laden with bottles and crystal. "Drink?"

"No, thank you."

"Come on, Hilary," he said. "Vodka, is it?"

"I'm driving," he said firmly.

Dominic sighed, poured a measure of whiskey, sipped it. He looked tired, the lines in the corners of his eyes even deeper than before.

"Amelia and I have had a long talk. I've realized I need to be honest with you."

Hilary hoped the needle of nervousness lancing through his gut didn't show in his face. "So you admit you've been lying?"

"I never wanted to hide things from you, Hilary. But old habits die hard."

"What do you want to tell me?" Hilary demanded. "Bearing in mind it's probably already too late."

"I wasn't sleeping with Lizzie Wood," he said after a pause.

"So why did Holden think you were?"

"I don't know. But I couldn't have been. I swear, I didn't know Lizzie. And even if I did, well..." He raised his eyebrows. "She's not my type. Understand?"

Something clicked into place in Hilary's brain. Something he'd been resisting fitting together but now he let it, everything seemed much clearer. "You're gay…"

He sipped his drink.

"But you're married."

Dominic gave him a level look. "Amelia and I have an…understanding."

Hilary raised an eyebrow. "You expect me to believe this is a mutual thing?"

"It is. Mutual…in every way."

Hilary hesitated. "Amelia's gay, too?"

Dominic nodded, coming forward, sipping his drink but not taking his eyes off Hilary. "We met at university. Debate club. We took opposing sides on purpose, just to pit ourselves against each other. Then we started getting drunk together at the college bar and found we could pour out everything we were angry about and that we both…understood. The next thing we knew, we were friends." He gazed at the wall, a line between his eyebrows. "I'd never had friends before."

"You had friends," Hilary said. "Michaels, Finley?"

Dominic's frown deepened. "They weren't friends. They were followers." He met Hilary's look. "They were scared of me."

Hilary looked away.

"Amelia was never scared of me. She understood me. We have a lot in common—more than we could admit to in public, in fact." He topped up his glass. His voice had changed, lowered, and his cut-glass accent had softened. Hilary got the impression that he was hearing things Dominic didn't usually say out loud. "One of those things was both having nightmare families breathing down our necks to play the game. So we came to an arrangement."

"What sort of arrangement?"

"We agreed to get married, so we could live our real lives in private."

Hilary took a moment to process this. "You expect me to believe you thought that was necessary? In this day and age?"

"You don't know our families."

"But they *must* know," Hilary said. "If they've ever been to your house, they'll have seen…"

"Having separate rooms isn't that unusual."

"But Amelia has that picture by her bed…" Hilary clamped his mouth shut but Dominic smiled.

"So you knew."

"No," he said, turning away. "No, I didn't know. And I shouldn't know now. You should either have told me at the start or not at all."

Dominic stepped up so close behind Hilary that he could feel on his breath on his neck. "That was the original plan. We agreed our arrangement wasn't relevant, that we should keep it from you. But then you walked into my house, so ready to do battle again after all these years. Christ, you were beautiful…and I wanted…"

Hilary spun around. "Stop. Just stop."

"I tried, Hilary," Dominic said slowly. "I did try to resist. But being around you…I fell into those old habits. Bad habits. But it's only because…" Light danced at the back of his black eyes. He laid his glass down on the side. "I know I haven't handled this…well."

"You fucking *think*?" Hilary rubbed his hand over his face. "You know this means that you really are a blackmailer's wet dream, right? My Christ, Dom. No fucking wonder—"

"No one was blackmailing me. I swear. No one has ever approached me about the arrangement."

"What about the rest of the family? Eloise?"

He snorted. "Eloise would never stoop to something so vulgar as murdering a blackmailer. Besides, whatever impression she gives, this trial is torture for her. The shame of it all. She would never tolerate such a thing."

"So what would she do?"

"She'd make it go away...quietly, like she has before. Not like this."

A chill rode up Hilary's spine. "And what about Amelia?"

Dominic looked into his glass. "She would have told me if anyone had threatened her."

"You're certain of that?"

"We're partners...in everything." Hilary gave him a questioning look. Dominic's face hardened. "We've been married over ten years. So we're not in love in *that* way. But we trust each other. Both our survivals depend on it."

"That's a bit extreme."

"No, it's not," Dominic said. "You can have your *People* magazine wedding to another man in front of the whole world. And that's a good thing, whatever I think about it. But it's a luxury, Hilary."

"Excuse me?"

Dominic raised an eyebrow. "I'm simply saying that none of the freedoms you enjoy are ones that apply to us. Our families... They're old—old-fashioned, old names, old grudges. We can do whatever we want behind closed doors. Hell, they probably know we do it. But if any of it ever came out, both our families would have a lot to lose."

"So you'd both rather live a lie than get cut out of the will?"

"It's not about money," Dominic said. "It's about belonging somewhere—amongst people who will protect you, even when they don't approve."

"At what cost?"

Dominic looked away. "It's worked for us. Amelia's been with her girlfriend for years. Fatima's from a conservative family, too. But they've found a way to be together that doesn't involve sacrificing their place in their families. They're happy."

"And you? Are you happy?"

Dominic threw back his whiskey. "I'm…content. Or, at least, I thought I was." He gave Hilary another heated look. "The other night…that—"

"Enough," Hilary snapped. "We're not talking about that."

"Why not?"

"I was tired, stressed. We were…" He made an impatient noise. "It was a mistake. And if you don't want to have your entire defense chucked out of court, I suggest you work on forgetting it ever happened."

"But I don't want to forget."

They stood toe-to-toe, staring at each other. Hilary's breath deepened. "I don't understand. I don't understand any of this."

"I think you do."

"But in school…" Hilary's jaw ached with how hard he was clenching his teeth to stop everything spilling out like gore from a lanced wound. "You hated me."

"I never hated you."

"But you bullied me, called me names, beat me up…"

"I never hated you," Dominic repeated, his voice tighter than before.

"Then…*why*…?"

Dominic's eyes flashed with pain. He lifted a hand. Hilary froze. Dominic paused, like Hilary was a wild animal that might turn and bite. But when he didn't move away, Dominic brushed Hilary's hair out of his eyes, gentle as a breath of wind. The touch sent electricity dancing over Hilary's skin at the same time as a black hole opened in his gut, threatening to swallow everything he thought he knew.

"I'm sorry," Dominic said, the words sounding like they were being torn out of him. "I'm so sorry, Hilary."

He leaned forward, and before Hilary could clear the fog in his brain, Dominic was brushing his lips over his. Hilary's breath caught in his throat. Dominic took his lower lip between his own. He rested his fingers on Hilary's arms, a light touch, loose enough to let him pull away if he tried.

"Let me show you…" His breath was warm and smelled of whiskey. The fragrance from his hair filled Hilary's head and dizzied him. His lips were tender as they mouthed at his, coaxing, encouraging. "Let me show you how I really feel."

Hilary let out a shuddering breath, feeling part of himself go with it, shut his eyes and found himself kissing back. Dominic slid his tongue over Hilary's mouth. He was gentle, questing, seeking permission. Hilary opened his mouth and Dominic slid his tongue inside. He tasted like alcohol and fire and Hilary felt his knees threaten to go and clung on tighter.

Dominic let out a low, helpless noise that had the blood surging through Hilary's body. Nothing existed but this powerful frame, the intoxicating mouth, the large, strong hands pushing his coat from his shoulders with such tenderness that it was like they had never known violence or anger.

Hilary allowed Dominic to rid him of his coat and suit jacket then slipped both his hands up inside Dominic's shirt to knead his muscled back. He quivered to feel it, feel his strength as the muscles bunched and slid beneath the silk of his skin. The sound Dominic made in response, like someone in pain, unmanned Hilary further and he arched his hips, desperate for friction on his swelling cock.

Dominic broke the kiss with a gasp and mouthed at Hilary's neck. "God, Hilary," he panted, "I want you."

Hilary's blood ran cold. He could feel the large erection against his leg, the broad, unfamiliar hands working at his buttons. He broke away, casting around half-dazed for his coat.

"Hilary—"

"No," Hilary forced out as he stooped to retrieve the coat. "I won't let you do this."

"Hilary, please—"

"It's over, Dom," Hilary said, jabbing the button for the lift. "I'll try to prove you're innocent. Maybe you are. Either way, I want this over, then I never want to see you again."

"I don't believe you mean that," Dominic said, kissing the back of his neck.

Hilary shivered and clenched his eyes shut as the lift pinged and the doors slid open. "In what universe would I not mean it?"

"One where you need something. Need me. Need me to mend everything I broke."

Hilary turned. Dominic gazed down into his eyes. The face was all too familiar but the look in his eyes was one he'd never seen in them before.

"I'm engaged."

"He doesn't make you happy."

Hilary flushed. "You don't know anything about us."

"I recognize heartache when I see it."

Hilary stepped into the lift. He hit the button for the ground floor but Dom grabbed the door.

"You're so critical of mine and Amelia's arrangement. But if you marry Jasper Prince, you're doing the same thing — worse, because you're not being honest about it, even to yourself."

"It is nothing like the same thing. We love each other."

"We can't ignore this."

"I won't do this, Dom."

"Why not?"

"Let go of the door," Hilary said, stabbing the button again.

"Not until you tell me why."

"There's a million reasons," Hilary snapped.

"Give me one you actually care about."

"I'm your *lawyer*, for fuck's sake."

"True," Dominic said calmly. "But not relevant."

Hilary gripped his coat so tight that his fingers ached. "It's wrong."

"It doesn't feel wrong, does it?" Dom stepped into the lift. He ran his hands up Hilary's arms, never taking his eyes from his face. Hilary tried to speak but his mouth was dry. He felt as if his strength were pouring out of him and that this man was offering him his. He closed his eyes, groping after cold reality, but it was like trying to grasp falling rain. He found himself being drawn against that firm body and was no more able to resist than a blade of grass could resist the pull of a hurricane.

Dom drew him back into the apartment and lowered his mouth to Hilary's jaw, brushing kisses over the sensitive skin under his ear. Hilary shivered, arousal pooling in his belly. Dom pulled off his tie, unfastened his collar, pulled it aside. He kissed the inked skin of Hilary's collarbone, his tongue, lips and hot breath lighting fires under his skin. Hilary's body clenched and he groaned, suddenly unable to bring to mind any of the reasons why he wasn't supposed to be enjoying this.

Dom undid his remaining buttons one by one, kissing and licking the skin as he went.

"When was the last time your fiancé showed you how beautiful you are?" he murmured against Hilary's breastbone. "When was the last time he made you come so hard you forgot the world around you?"

Hilary opened his mouth to protest but then Dom took his nipple between his lips. Hilary let out a noise he'd never heard from himself before. He grabbed at Dom's shoulders to keep himself upright. Dom backed him against a leather sofa. Hilary panted, his cock straining against his trousers as Dom switched to the other nipple while ridding him of his shirt.

He sucked and nibbled until all the tattered remnants of Hilary's reason melted away. He pawed at Dom's clothing until he straightened, locked eyes with him and unfastened his shirt. Hilary gripped the sofa to stop himself from batting Dominic's hands away and yanking it off him. Finally, the shirt was undone, and Dom was shouldering out of it. Hilary had to fight for breath. Dom was even more heavily muscled than the tailored lines of his suits would suggest. His shoulders sloped like a mountain range. His arms were heavy and thick with toned flesh. The wide planes of his chest, dusted with dark hair, looked harder than steel and his abdomen was a rippling mass of muscle. His skin was the warm tan of rich coffee. He looked like he'd been sculpted rather than born.

Hilary's mouth dried out. Dom watched his face and smiled. "Glad you approve."

Hilary fished for a smart response, but his brain wouldn't engage. Dom stepped close so Hilary had to crane his neck to look into his face. He ran his hands down Hilary's chest and belly, chasing the tribal ink, the red roses, the blue diamonds and the feathered birds gliding around his navel.

"They really are amazing, you know," Dominic said huskily. "Do you have any idea how distracting this is going to be in court, knowing you have all this under your suit?"

"Speak for yourself," Hilary managed and pulled Dominic's head down for another kiss.

Dominic moaned and maneuvered himself between Hilary's legs, drawing him in with a hand at the small of his back. When their erections thrust against each other Hilary gasped, feeling like every inch of his skin was strung with charged wire.

"Jesus," Hilary said, fumbling at Dominic's belt. "Get this off."

Dom chuckled against his lips and obliged, undoing his belt and the top button of his fly, but then pushed Hilary's impatient hands aside to begin undoing his. As Dom's fingertips grazed the flesh of his lower belly Hilary quivered, clenching his eyes shut to avoid looking at anything, anything that might remind him of the reality of the situation, instead allowing himself to be consumed by the taste of his kiss, the feeling of the strong thighs between his legs and the skillful fingers undoing the zip of his fly.

Dom hovered his fingers just under Hilary' belly button, rubbing in slow circles until Hilary made a strained noise. Dom smiled against his lips, slid the hand into his underwear and took his cock in a firm, possessive grip.

Hilary gasped again, fisting his hands in Dom's hair, and Dom took the opportunity to thrust his tongue even deeper into his mouth. He pressed his whole body forward, grasping Hilary's thigh with one hand as he started to pump his cock with the other. Hilary broke the kiss to swear, clutching the strong shoulders, digging his fingers in hard enough to bruise.

"Christ," he cried as Dom worked him, slow and steady, his large hand all too knowing on his aching length. "God, Dom..."

"You have no idea how amazing that sounds," Dom panted in his ear, "to hear you say my name like that. This stuff you do to me, Hilary. You will never know..."

Hilary cried out again as Dom brushed his palm up and over the sensitive head of his dick, sliding his other hand up his thigh to cup his arse whilst sucking his earlobe.

"Tell me, Hilary," he breathed throatily in his ear, "tell me what you want the most."

Hilary let out a strangled cry, trying his best to regain his power of speech as the fire flared under his belly.

"Go down on me," he panted. "Please, Dom. *Now.*"

Dom's moan rumbled deep in him like an earthquake. He dropped to his knees, yanked Hilary's trousers down and took his length all the way in. Hilary clung to the sofa, crying out and almost suffocating in the sensation of the warm, wet heat. Dom used one hand to knead at his balls whilst drawing back to the tip, running his tongue all along the underside then around the head then taking it all the way into his throat again. Golden flames flared in Hilary's pelvis, and he could no longer feel his aching knuckles, his thighs straining to keep him upright or the hammering of his heart. He forced his eyes open.

The sight of Dom Gosford, on his knees, his own large, thick cock in his hand as he mouthed and sucked at Hilary's, was all it took to bring Hilary crashing into orgasm like a raft swept over a waterfall.

"Jesus, fuck I'm... Dom...I'm gonna—"

Dom took him into his throat and the world fell away into shadow and light, sparks and heat and the sensation of molten gold flooding his body.

Chapter Eleven

"This was a mistake."

"One of our better ones," Dom murmured as he got to his feet, his voice slurry with sex.

Hilary turned his face away, heat flooding his cheeks.

"How about that drink?" Dom said after the silence had stretched into awkwardness.

Hilary nodded, not making eye contact as he pulled his trousers back up. He heard the sound of ice dropped in a glass then the glug of liquid. He retrieved his rumpled shirt from the floor and pulled it on as Dominic held out a glass filled with ice and a clear fluid.

"I have no idea if it's good," he said as Hilary took the glass. "I just know it's from Russia."

Hilary had glimpsed the bottle of single variety Belvedere vodka when he'd come into the room and sipped the fiery liquid appreciatively. "It's good," he said.

Dom smiled a half-smile and gestured at the sofa. Hilary glanced at the lift door but, suddenly tired beyond all reason, sat. Dom shrugged his own shirt back on and sat a careful distance away, sipping his whiskey in the silence.

"You never answered my question," Hilary said quietly.

"Which one?"

"If you didn't hate me...why..."

"Why was I such a cunt?"

Hilary looked at him. He sat with his arm along the back of the sofa, close to but not touching Hilary's shoulder, regarding him with a sad smile. "Well...yeah."

"I've spent a long time trying to answer that question," he murmured, "as have various therapists. All I know for sure is that back then I was...angry. All the time."

"Why?"

"Lots of reasons," he said with a wry smile. "And no reason at all. My dad was..." He hesitated. "I had what my therapist calls a 'troubled upbringing'. But I know now that you can only blame your parents for your shit for so long. I know myself better now. And one thing I did figure out was why you wound me up so much back then."

Hilary stared at him. Dom's full mouth was unsmiling, but his eyes were warm. Hilary fought the sensation of double vision, this face he knew so well wearing an expression he never knew it was capable of, let alone would ever be directed at him.

"You...you *liked* me?" he said, voice barely above a whisper.

"You never guessed? Even now?" Dom asked gently.

Hilary glanced at his discarded tie, the briefcase lying where he'd dropped it, felt the ghost of that hot touch across his skin. "Honestly? I thought you'd taken your mind games to a new level—and that I was falling for it all over again."

Dom's face darkened. "Then you really must think I'm evil." Hilary didn't answer. Dom's heavy gaze slid away. "I fought it. Fought you. It confused and angered me. But...yes. It was all because I liked you—more than liked."

Hilary slumped into the sofa cushions, staring into his drink as hard thoughts shifted position in his head, clunking into place to make a clear but grim picture.

"I'm sorry. It's not enough. But I wanted to say it, anyway."

A knot in Hilary's chest, one that had been there for years, unacknowledged, suddenly loosened. "Why me?"

Dom raised an eyebrow. "You're joking, right?"

"There were prettier guys at that school. Ones that were out, even. And less awkward." He shrugged. "They were popular enough that being gay didn't matter. I was the freak with dyed hair and piercings."

Dom drifted back to the drinks counter. He topped up his whiskey then held out the silver vodka bottle. Hilary held out his glass for more. He downed a mouthful as Dom resumed his seat, unnerved at how relaxed he seemed to be for the first time in days—weeks, even.

"They were the same as everyone I'd never known my whole life. You were extraordinary," he said softly, gazing at the wall. "And not just because of the lip ring and the eyeliner. I mean, don't get me wrong" — Dom gave him a smirk — "to someone that far back in the closet, that was all confusing enough. But it was the way you carried yourself. You never let me just deal it out. You fought back." He shook his head. "And the more you took, the more I wanted to push you, to see what you'd do. I was...fascinated. I wanted to *be* like you...but I couldn't be." He frowned into his glass. "And it made me angry."

"So that's why you called me 'Lilywhite'? 'Fairy'? That's why you started that fight in the changing rooms?"

"Yes...that's why." He lifted his gaze. "It's not a good reason. Quite the opposite. But it *is* the reason."

Hilary sipped his drink, staring out of the window as thousands of lights winked into life in the gathering night.

"I still don't think I can forgive you."

"I never asked you to."

"That's not what this is all about?" Hilary asked, running his finger round the vodka glass so it sang. "Redemption?"

Dominic shook his head and shifted along the couch. "I wanted to show you now what I should have shown you then. But it's too little too late. I know that."

Hilary swallowed. Dominic's skin was so warm, even through their shirts. The dark fire of his eyes was so deep and intense that Hilary felt it sizzle over his skin. He was being pulled in, like water down a plug hole, and struggling to swim against the current.

"Don't you feel something, too, Hilary?" Dom said softly, lowering his voice.

"Dom..."

"I'm not asking you to forgive me—just to be honest about how you feel now."

Hilary met his eye. "You made my life hell. A living hell. For years."

Dom's eyes darkened. "I know. And I can never fix that." He rested his hand on Hilary's knee. "But that night, when I kissed you…if you'd yelled or taken a swing or filed that change of counsel, I swear I would have disappeared from your life forever and never looked back. But you didn't, Hilary. You kissed me back. I never dared hope…" He took a breath. Hilary's heart jerked about behind his ribs. "I don't deserve anything from you. But I still think you feel it, too."

His hand was hot. Hilary's body trembled.

"Did you kill those kids, Dom?" The question came out raw, the words hardly above a whisper.

"No," he responded instantly, not blinking.

"You really didn't know them?"

"I didn't know *her*." The darkness in his eyes had shifted, like clouds moving in a night sky.

Hilary stared. "Dean?"

Dom nodded stiffly. "That's what I brought you here to tell you."

Icy waves spilled down Hilary's neck. "For how long?"

"Not long," Dom said, setting his glass aside. "Three months, maybe?"

"The hair…"

Dom stared at the wall. "It was probably on his clothes from the last time he'd come here."

"You met…here?" Hilary looked around the apartment, which seemed to have more shadows than before.

"It's the safest place we could be together."

"How did you meet?"

Dom didn't answer immediately. When he did, his voice was hard, like scar tissue over an old wound. "It was one of Amelia's events…a particularly tedious one. Everyone seemed to want pictures. I'd gone out on fire escape for a break." He stared at nothing, gaze far away. "Dean was in the alley having a smoke. He was part of the catering team that night. He nodded and smiled at me and…it just happened."

"What happened?"

Dom shrugged. "We talked. He was just…easy. He must have known who I was. But he didn't ask about Amelia or the family. He didn't seem to care. And he seemed to know, instantly know, just by looking at me, that I was gay." He stared at his wedding ring. "But he didn't judge me for that, either."

Hilary spun his glass around in his hands. "He sounds nice."

"He was." For the first time, Hilary heard regret in his tone. "He was nothing exceptional. Just…nice."

"What happened then?"

"Nothing, that night," Dom said quietly. "We just talked—about food, wine, traveling. He wanted to move to Paris and train under a Michelin chef." Dom clenched his jaw. Hilary waited for him to continue, resisted pushing even though it felt like a nest of snakes had hatched in his belly. Eventually, Dom took a breath and continued. "I said I employed a Michelin star chef at The Salisbury, and if he wanted to come over some time, I could have her cater for us. He said yes."

"So you started sleeping together?"

Dom nodded. "I have to make sure my partners are agreeable to keeping things…discreet." He glanced at Hilary and away again. "And he was. I could tell I was just a distraction for him, as he was for me. Looking back with what I know now, I think it was because he was worried about his sister...her money troubles. He just wanted something separate from that."

"Did he talk to you about her?" Hilary said, sitting up straighter.

Dom shook his head. "We didn't talk about personal things. I never knew he had a sister, let alone a twin. I could just tell he needed an escape...like me." He looked out of the window. "He was a good kid, Hilary."

"Dom," Hilary said gravely, "did he tell Lizzie about you?"

"He knew he couldn't tell anyone."

"That doesn't mean he didn't," Hilary went on. "Twins are close, even more than normal siblings." Hilary took a moment to marshal his emotion. "Everyone else is on the outside of their world, even if they don't mean them to be."

Dom looked at him then away. "He wouldn't have told her."

"Dom, think about it. Lizzie told Sara Holden about someone in her life she disapproved of. Someone rich. Someone she saw as manipulative who had done something blackmail-worthy and she intended to make him pay. Could she have known about you and Dean and thought you were abusing him?"

"I wasn't abusing him," Dom said, his face darkening. "We were both aware and consenting. He understood how careful we needed to be. He agreed to everything."

"Do you know, as a fact, that he never mentioned you to his sister?"

Dom clenched his jaw. "No. Of course I can't know that. But Lizzie didn't blackmail me, Hilary," he insisted. "I was telling the truth about that. No one has approached me about Dean or any of my partners."

"They're both dead, Dom. It can't be a coincidence."

Dom's face crumpled. "I've tried to figure it out but I can't. No one has made any demands for money. No one told me they knew. And Dean never mentioned anything. The first thing I knew about what had happened was when the police were hammering on my door and arresting me for his murder."

Hilary tapped his glass with his finger. "The condoms?"

"Not mine," he said. "We met here, like I said. This place is safe. One of Amelia's companies owns the deeds, not me, so my name isn't even attached to it. And the security cameras are run by another of her companies."

"So Amelia knows everything? About this place, about your affairs?"

"Of course she does," Dom said. "Like I said, we're partners. There are no secrets between us."

"Does she know about me?" Hilary asked, not liking how his voice had changed.

"I've not told her, but I think she guessed."

Hilary put the glass down with shaking hands.

"It's okay, Hilary. She won't tell anyone."

"This is such a mess," Hilary said, running his hands through his hair. "You swore there was nothing to blackmail you over. Now there's a sham marriage, gay affairs and you were sleeping with one of the victims."

"No one knows."

"Amelia does."

"She wouldn't hurt anyone," Dom said darkly.

"You know that for sure, do you?"

"Yes."

Hilary raised his eyebrows.

"If you don't believe me, perhaps your cynical lawyer's soul will understand that none of this is in her interests. She depends on our arrangement just as much as I do. And she wouldn't need to frame me for murder if she wanted rid of me."

"It sounds more like the Cold War than a marriage."

"We can count on each other. Can you say the same about your relationship?"

Hilary scowled. "We are *not* discussing my relationship. We're discussing yours. Plural. And the fact that *someone* must have known about them if Lizzie found out."

"Wouldn't the prosecution have brought it up if they had any suspicions?"

"True," Hilary admitted. "Christ, I don't know how you've hidden all this so well."

"Practice," Dominic said with a sardonic smile. "And I need you to know I'll protect you too, Hilary," he said, suddenly earnest. "No one will know about this…not from me."

"Is that for my benefit or yours?"

Dom regarded him coolly. "Both."

"Augustine's offering five years," Hilary said after a strained pause.

"What?"

"Plead guilty and you'll be charged with manslaughter with diminished responsibility. You'll get five years. You'll be out in three."

Dom stared at him. "You think I should take it."

"I think it's the only way you can be certain of having any kind of future."

"And what about Dean's future? And Lizzie's?" Hilary looked at him. His face was grave. "If I admit to this crime, the person who did it will never be found. I can't let that happen."

Hilary gazed at him. It was now so easy to look into his face—the face that had once come to him in night terrors, the face that he'd scrolled hurriedly away from whenever it appeared on news websites or social media, the face that had almost had him regretting all his career decisions when Gunnerson had told him he'd have to defend this man on a double murder charge which, at the time, Hilary had been thoroughly convinced was justified.

And now, instead of the familiar rush of fear and hate, Hilary wanted to sink into him, to let him shoulder his burdens, at least for a while. Dom was the only person Hilary had ever known who he thought capable of it. Perhaps had always been.

"What are you doing to me, Dom?"

Dom brushed his knuckles across Hilary's jaw. "Helping you see the real me? At least…that's what I'm trying to do."

Hilary kissed him. Dom sighed and shuddered. Hilary had never induced such instant desire in Jasper or anyone. The thought of it intoxicated him. The scent and taste of his hot, sweet mouth only fanned the flames.

He thrust his hands into the open shirt and allowed them to roam, drinking in the feel of the powerful body—the body of someone so large and strong that Hilary knew he could overpower him but was choosing not to. A flash of excitement went up his spine.

"Hilary," Dom gasped, pushing him down into the sofa, stripping off his shirt again and pushing Hilary's off so they were skin on skin. "God, you're amazing."

Dom was hard again. Hilary could feel it against his leg and felt his own sated member stirring. His breathing hitched and his whole body sang as Dom lowered his full weight onto him, pinning him to the couch, running his hands down his sides and legs. He hooked them under Hilary's knees and pulled them up and apart so he could settle himself more fully between Hilary's legs. Hilary moaned to feel Dom's restrained erection pushing against him and yanked both their flies open as quickly as he could.

Dom let out a long, low moan as he rid them both of their remaining clothing and thrust lazily against Hilary's arse. Their skin heated where it touched. Dom's kiss was breathy and hungry, deep and intense even as his languid grip on Hilary's hardening cock was gentle and teasing.

He ran his free hand down Hilary's thigh and continued to rock against him, his hardness feeling almost alarmingly large and unfamiliar against that sensitive, vulnerable place. But anticipation tightened Hilary's belly and he moaned, running his hand down the powerful back and over the taut arse, drawing him close.

"Tell me you've got some stuff somewhere close," Hilary panted, tilting his hips to better feel the friction of that large member rocking against him.

"You…you like it this way?"

"Christ," Hilary breathed between clenched teeth, crushing Dom into him. "Yes, I like it that way. I like to be fucked…hard."

"Oh, God," Dom moaned. "You have no idea how much I want to." He cut off with a groan as he pressed his cock forward, crushing it against Hilary and making him whimper. "But not tonight. Not tonight."

"Why?"

Dom shook his head, almost pained. "It's too soon," he whispered, mouthing his ear. "When you're ready."

"I'm ready now."

"Another time," he whispered. "If you ask for it again, if you still want it, then…yes. But not tonight."

Dom kissed him, deep and long, and pumped his cock with slow, skilled strokes until the sparking warmth began to gather again, lower and slower than last time, but warmer, like a long summer evening. Desperate to hear his voice again, Hilary fumbled between them for Dom's own member, inhaled sharply to finally feel how large it was. Dom gasped against his mouth as Hilary started to stroke it.

Very soon they were shuddering together with liquid heat spurting over both their hands. Dom kissed him deeply as they came, swallowing his cries like he would consume him whole. As their breathing slowed and their skin cooled, so did the intensity of Dom's kiss until finally he lifted his head and gazed into his eyes.

"Would you sleep with me, Hilary?"

Hilary lifted his eyebrows. "I'm not sure I could manage a third time."

"I mean sleep." Dom smiled softly. "Stay with me tonight. I'll order some food. Then we can sleep, just sleep."

Hilary wasn't prepared for the tenderness of the request or his reaction to it. He opened his mouth to say no, that he should really go, that they had court the next day and he needed a change of clothes. But, instead, he heard himself say, "All right."

Dom smiled.

They ate red curry and drank the Thai beer Dom had ordered with it. They talked about food and theater, cars and music. The avoided the case, their past…Jasper. It was like reality wasn't allowed to intrude by mutual unspoken agreement. Dom smiled and teased but the acid malice that had always tinged his humor was gone. Hilary smiled, ate and, eventually, yawned.

Dom steered him to a bedroom containing a king-sized bed with cool, cream covers. They stripped to their underwear and crawled in. Dom tucked his tall frame up behind Hilary and draped an arm over his waist.

Hilary reached for his work phone to start going through his emails, convinced he would never sleep with all the clamoring thoughts and swirling guilt competing for attention in his brain. But the next thing he knew he was drifting back to consciousness in the dim light of dawn. His arms were wrapped around a firm body and there was a sleepy, peaceful feeling in his chest. Gentle breaths ruffled the hair at his temple and the hardness of a large, unfamiliar cock pressed into his thigh.

The night before rushed back, bringing with it the black fog of shame. His stomach tightened. He checked his phone. It wasn't even six, but he knew he couldn't lie there any longer. He extricated himself from the warm embrace then padded around the room, dressing quietly, and made for the door.

"Leaving so soon?"

Hilary turned back. Dom stretched languidly, his muscles bunching and sliding under his skin. His hair was mussed, his eyes dark with drowsy desire. Hilary's mouth dried out but he cleared his throat and looked away.

"I have to go home to get ready. Big day today."

Dom sighed and sat up, the cover falling from the sculpted planes of his chest. "Eloise."

"Eloise," Hilary said with a half-smile and opened the door.

"Hilary…" Hilary looked back. Dom looked like he was searching for words. "Thank you," he eventually said, "for staying."

Hilary nodded and left.

* * * *

"Defense calls Mrs. Eloise Hart."

Eloise had worn a somber, conservatively cut trouser suit in ivory silk for her court appearance. The porcelain effect was enhanced by the pearls at her neck and the blood-red manicure. Hilary spotted this last as she took her oath and exchanged glances with Beck.

"I told her no bold colors," Beck murmured as Eloise took her seat, her sharp gaze sweeping the room like an eagle from an eyrie.

"Mrs. Hart," Hilary began, being sure to smile, "would you please state your relationship with the defendant for the court."

"Dominic is my son-in-law. His wife, Amelia, is my only daughter."

"Are you a close family, would you say?"

Eloise raised an eyebrow. "My daughter is the most important thing in the world to me."

"And my client?" Hilary kept his breathing measured, fighting a flush. He'd struggled to meet Amelia's eyes when he'd arrived that morning. Luckily, she seemed happy to avoid meeting his and they'd taken their seats quickly, if a little awkwardly. Beck was engrossed reviewing her notes and hadn't seemed to notice none of them speaking to each other.

Eloise now glanced at Dom who sat, well-groomed and blank-faced, at the defense table, her own expression masked. "Dominic is a fine man from a good family. He and Amelia are happy together. That's all that matters."

"So would you say you get on?"

Her eyebrow lifted again. "Most of the time, yes."

"Just 'most of the time'?"

"We don't always see eye-to-eye on the best way to do things, like any business partners. But overall, yes, we have a good relationship."

"So any disagreements, they were largely about business matters?"

"Yes."

"Nothing personal? I only ask because Mr. Jabal will no doubt be citing articles and reports of public arguments between the two of you."

Eloise folded her hands in her lap. "Dominic and I are very different people, but he is my family. Whatever disagreements we have, personal or professional, that will never change."

"You said he was a *fine man*," Hilary said, glancing back at Dom, who sat with his eyes on Hilary and not his mother-in-law. Hilary suddenly wished more than ever that he knew what he was thinking, what was in the air between them, so strongly that it took him a moment to recall his question. "Could you expand on that?"

"He is hard-working, when he cares to work. He sticks to his principles. And he respects Amelia and his place in this family. I couldn't ask for more."

"You say he 'sticks to his principles'," Hilary said, again fighting a blush. "For the jury, could you explain how you've formed this opinion of him, despite his very public record of being anything but principled?"

Eloise looked right at him. He had the unnerving sensation of those gray eyes looking right into the deepest, darkest secrets of his mind. For a terrifying second, he was certain she knew everything. He forced himself not to blink.

"Where do you come from, young man?"

"Me?"

"Yes, Mr. Whyte. I'm addressing you, aren't I?"

Hilary glanced at Beck. She gave a tiny helpless shrug. Hilary turned back to Eloise.

"London, ma'am."

"It's a big place, Mr. Whyte. Where exactly?"

Hilary resisted clenching his teeth. "Watford, originally."

"Good. And what do your parents do?"

"My dad is a retired solicitor."

"And your mother?"

"A housewife."

Eloise inclined her head. "People who knew their roles, knew what their family needed from them, yes?"

"Yes. I would say so."

"Well. My family are from Westminster. Dominic's the same. The names of Hart and Gosford can be traced back to the War of the Roses. On opposing sides, as it happens, but even people with long memories like ours have moved on from that."

"Mrs. Hart—"

"Dominic's father was Deputy Prime Minster. Mine was Cabinet Secretary. They, too, knew what was needed of them and gave it freely. That is having principles—principles as old as England itself. It's no secret that Dominic and his father clashed growing up. It's no secret we've clashed ourselves. But whatever our personal battles, the war is greater than the individuals involved. Dominic understands that. That is why, even if we do not always agree, we have the mutual respect of soldiers fighting the same fight."

The jury was staring. The court audience was utterly silent. Jabal's and Augustine's faces were unreadable. Hilary felt a flush of anticipation as he tried to figure out if the attention was good or bad.

"A principled man, then. Would you say he was capable of violence?" Hilary held his breath.

"Capable, yes. His arrest record is evidence enough of that. But he wouldn't kill anyone."

"No?"

"No."

"What makes you say that?" Hilary hoped the question didn't sound like he wanted to know for himself as much as for the jury.

"People kill out of desperation," Eloise said. "Dominic is now part of a family that would ensure he was never driven to such extremes."

Hilary prayed that he'd imagined her hesitation and that, if not, no one else had noticed it. "You were the last person to see him that day…at your art gallery?"

"That's right. We'd met to discuss the banquet I was hosting that night."

"There were rumors of a disagreement at this meeting. Are they accurate?"

"No," Eloise said firmly. "He told me he could no longer attend. I was displeased but he's a grown man. I can't make him attend functions he doesn't want to."

"Did he tell you why he wouldn't be attending?"

"No. I did not ask."

"Did he mention to you where he planned to go after he left the gallery?"

Her face pinched again. "No. We do not have that sort of relationship."

"Can you describe his mood when he left?"

This time Eloise's pause was unmistakable, and Hilary cursed her under his breath. "He seemed much his usual self."

"Not preoccupied? Anxious? Angry?"

"No more than usual."

The jury exchanged glances. Hilary fought to find a way to bring it back. "I just want to make this absolutely clear for the court, Mrs. Hart. You said my client knows what's expected of him. That belonging to your family is like being a soldier fighting a war. If he was being blackmailed, if the security of the family was being threatened, do you think he might—"

"He didn't kill those people."

"How do you know?"

"Dominic is many things, Mr. Whyte, but stupid, he is not. Perhaps some would consider killing a blackmailer well within the principles that this country was built on"—a susurration went through the air as people shifted in their seats. Jabal straightened and Hilary's heart clenched in his chest. Eloise didn't even pause—"but to kill one yourself? And leave evidence behind? Even so little?" She shook her head. "No, Mr. Whyte. Dominic is not that stupid."

"No more questions, my lady," Hilary said faintly and returned to his seat. Beck looked dumbstruck. Amelia was white as a sheet. Dom's jaw was set. His eyes were fixed on Eloise, who stared right back, her gray eyes calm, hands neatly folded in her lap.

Jabal stood. The faintest suggestion of a smile played on his lips. "No questions, my lady," he said.

"He doesn't fucking need any," Beck muttered. "Boss, honestly. This is not what we rehearsed. I told her specifically—"

"I know you did," Hilary murmured.

"What the hell was she playing at?" Beck whispered as Fotheringham excused Eloise. "She doesn't want the scandal, so why deliberately act like a tyrannical sociopath?"

Dom was grim and silent as his mother-in-law left the courtroom without looking back. His hand was curled into a fist on the desk in front of him. Amelia sat rigid behind him, not meeting anyone's eye.

"I guess some things are just too engrained," Hilary said, "even when it's in your best interest to try to shake them." Dom caught his eye. Hilary looked away.

"Next witness, Mr. Whyte?"

Hilary stood and sent up a prayer. "Defense calls Bruce Merriweather."

Chapter Twelve

"Mr. Merriweather, you've been employed by the Hart-Gosfords for how long, exactly?"

"Getting on twelve years," Merriweather said, meeting Hilary's eye squarely and speaking levelly. "Ever since Mistress Amelia and Master Dominic married."

"And you were employed by the Hart family before that?"

"Yes, sir. Seven years."

"That's nineteen years, all told. A long time. So would you say you know the family well?"

"Very well, sir."

"And Dominic Hart-Gosford in particular?"

Merriweather glanced at Dominic, and he nodded. "Yes, sir. We've spent a lot of time together over the years."

"And how would you describe him?"

"Master Dominic's a good man."

"Would you expand on that?"

"He's a good employer. Pays me well. Appreciates my work and my advice. Treats me like an equal."

"Do you think he is guilty of the crime he is accused of?"

"No, sir. Absolutely not."

"Why not?"

"I know him, sir. Like, *know him* know him. Sure, he's been in a few scraps in his time. What man hasn't? But killin' two kids like that? No way. It's beneath him, that is."

"Even if, as the prosecution has implied, he were being blackmailed?"

Merriweather snorted. "Not seen no evidence of that, sir. But even if he was…he's got enough money, you know? And good lawyers, too."

"So you're saying even if Lizzie Wood was blackmailing him, there would be no need for him to kill her?"

"Course not," he said, curling his lip. "There are much quieter ways to deal with a mess like that. But, as I say, I certainly seen nothin' to suggest anyone were being blackmailed."

"You worked at the banquet the night of the murders, is that right?"

"That's right, sir."

"Do you know why Mr. Hart-Gosford didn't attend?"

"No, I don't, sir."

"Do you know where he went instead?"

"No."

"Is it unusual for you to not know where he is?"

Merriweather glanced at Beck who offered him the slightest incline of her head. "It is, I have to say, sir. Unusual…but not unknown."

"So he's vanished like this before?"

"Once or twice, sir, yes."

"Do you know where he goes or what he does?"

"No, sir," Merriweather said, folding his arms. "Sometimes a bloke just needs space, you know? And I'm pretty sure no one fucking died every time."

Hilary suppressed a smile as Jabal glared and a murmur of shocked amusement rippled through the audience.

"Thank you, Mr. Merriweather, no more questions."

"Mr. Jabal, do you wish to cross?" Fotheringham said.

"I just have one thing to check with Mr. Merriweather, my lady," Jabal said. "There is CCTV evidence of you arriving at Brentwold Hall a little after three p.m. that day, Mr. Merriweather."

"That sounds about right."

"Oh, it's very right," Jabal said, turning on the TV. Footage from the cameras in front of the towering Georgian hall began to play. Merriweather could be seen climbing out of a car and making for a side entrance. The time stamp read 15:06. "Cameras don't lie."

"Okay then," Merriweather said, small eyes narrowing. "So I arrived just after three. So?"

"Your employer left Mrs. Hart's art gallery at 16:03. You were already at Brentwold. So there really is no way for you to know where he went and what he did."

"I already said so, sir," Merriweather drawled.

"I know you did," Jabal said smoothly. "I just wanted to show the jury the proof that, whatever you say your personal opinion of your employer is, you really have no idea what happened that day."

Merriweather's jaw worked. Hilary's skin prickled. He kept his attention fixed on Merriweather and didn't dare glance at the jury.

"No, sir. I don't. But I know he didn't kill no one."

"How can you be so certain?"

Merriweather glanced at Dom, then glared at Jabal. "I just know, all right?"

"No more questions, my lady," Jabal said and resumed his seat.

* * * *

"Christ on a bike," Beck muttered as they left the courtroom when the judge called an end to the day. "I hope Merriweather's as tough as he looks, because I'll be amazed if someone doesn't have a go at Hart-Gosford tonight."

"You were right," Hilary said defeatedly. "I should never have put them on the stand."

"You couldn't have known Eloise would go off-script, boss," Beck said. "Or that she'd sound so fucking bats if she did."

Hilary rubbed his forehead as the headache threatened to return. "He needed a barrister today."

"Nah," Beck said, with a half-smile. "A barrister would have pushed her into being even more inhuman. You acted like you knew it was gonna happen and didn't make it any worse that it was bound to be." She frowned. "*Did* you know it was gonna happen?"

"No. But I guess I knew, deep down, that people like her just don't see, or don't care, how they come across when asked to justify themselves. I just hoped she'd hold it together for Dominic's sake."

"Mr. Whyte. A word?" Dom had appeared at his elbow.

Amelia watched them from by the door. Beck glanced between them, but Hilary raised a reassuring hand and allowed himself to be drawn aside. He took a moment to push away the sudden rush of blood his client's proximity caused in his body and schooled his face. "It's not as bad as it seemed."

"Isn't it?"

Hilary winced. "You should know Beck coached Eloise on a whole different set of responses."

"I know she did."

"We've still sewn a fair amount of reasonable doubt. Once we've—"

"Hilary," Dom said softly, "come back to mine."

Hilary blinked. "What?"

"You're tired. You need to relax."

Hilary's skin rippled. He glanced to Beck, but she was now talking to Amelia.

"I can't," he said.

"You don't want to?"

Hilary opened his mouth, closed it again. He looked away. "It's DI McGarry tomorrow. Beck and I have to prepare—"

"You need to eat," Dominic murmured, still in that soft undertone that was like feathers brushing over Hilary's skin. "And sleep. And, well..." He lifted the corner of his mouth. "Sometimes distraction can be a useful aid to productivity."

"We can't do it again, Dom," he whispered.

"Why not?"

Yearning woke in the pit of Hilary's stomach, but he shook his head. "This is serious."

"Oh, I know," Dom muttered. "But if my days as a free man really are numbered, I'd rather make the most of what I've got left."

"I won't let you go to prison," Hilary said.

Dom paused. "If it were up to you alone, I wouldn't doubt it."

"I really have to work."

"Work at mine. I promise I'll only distract you when you want me to."

He looked at Beck and Amelia, who were now hovering farther down the hall, eyes turned their way.

"What if they figure it out?"

"Amelia doesn't care. And Miss Donavan would never believe it, even if you straddled me right here."

Hilary pushed his glasses up into his hair and rubbed his eyes.

"Come on, Hilary. I'll order Mexican. It's your favorite, right?"

Hilary blinked. "How do you know that?"

"At school you were always early to lunch on Fridays. They did those awful fajitas, remember?"

Hilary felt all at once unnerved and strangely touched. "I remember."

"I know a place that does them a lot better."

Hilary teetered, fighting the sensation that he was stood on the edge of a cliff. But when he looked into Dom Gosford's eyes, he realized he'd already jumped.

"Okay," he said softly. "Thank you."

* * * *

The fajitas really were excellent, the tequila-flavored beer even better, and Dom was as good as his word, eating silently at one end of the Greenwich flat dining table while Hilary ate amongst a spread of files and paper at the other. He talked to Beck through his headphones as he ate.

"We're not beaten yet," she said. "If you get McGarry on the hop, they'll quickly lose sympathy for her. Just…"

"What?"

"Be careful, boss."

"Yeah, I will. I am. I'm gonna go. Try to get some sleep."

He hung up and turned more pages over, swallowing the last of his beer and realizing with surprise that he'd cleared his plate.

"Better?" Dom sat with his legs crossed, a glass of whiskey in his hands.

"I think so," Hilary said distractedly, searching for the ballistics report. He was skimming it as a text message pinged on the screen of his personal phone.

Hey, babe, how's the case going? Missing you xx

Hilary stared at the text. He felt cold. He jumped when Dom put a hand on his shoulder.

"It's okay, Hilary," he said in a low voice, trailing his fingers up his neck. Dom leaned in and kissed the back of his neck, his lips gentle. Hilary's breath caught and the blood rushed down his body. Dom slid his fingers between the buttons on his shirt to rub soft circles on his chest.

"Dom, I…"

"Shh," Dom said, taking his earlobe into his mouth and tonguing the soft flesh. Hilary shivered.

"Jazz just texted. I…"

"Tell me to stop and I'll stop," Dom said, unbuttoning Hilary's shirt and slipping his hand inside. Hilary inhaled deeply, closing his eyes and leaning his head back as Dominic lavished attention on his neck while brushing his nipple tenderly with his fingertips. His cock jerked and Dom reached lower to fondle it through his trousers.

"You want this, Hilary," he whispered. "You need it, just as much as I do."

Hilary turned in the chair, grabbed Dom's shirt front and pulled him in for a savage kiss before his brain could take over. Dom rumbled deep in his chest and lifted him from the chair. He rid him of his shirt and trousers as he backed him toward the bedroom, but they only made it as far as the living room.

The next thing Hilary knew he was naked on the rug and Dom was on top of him, stripped to his underwear, kissing his way down his body with his fingers brushing fire up his thighs.

"Tell me again, Hilary," Dom whispered against his quivering abdomen. "I want to hear what you want."

"Jesus, Dom," Hilary panted, threading his fingers through the dark hair, unable to think or reason. "Just make me feel good again. Please."

He felt Dom smile against his skin then he took the head of Hilary's weeping cock into his mouth. Hilary cried out. The slick heat of Dom's mouth, the greedy way he took him all the way in and growled deep in his chest, like just the taste was driving him to distraction, made Hilary's head spin and his fingers tingle. The heat and wet and the feel of the large, muscled body between his legs took him somewhere far away, where he was still himself but not someone he recognized. Hilary allowed the awakening fire to burn all remaining fragments of thoughts away and harnessed all his strength to stop himself from coming right there. He wanted it to last...wanted to feel this way forever.

When he heard the click of a lube bottle and felt a slick finger rub around his tight entrance, he forced his eyes open, fighting for breath.

Dom was watching his face. The look in his eyes felt like it would burn the skin from Hilary's bones. He took Hilary in deep into his throat again and pushed a finger in, maddeningly slow.

Hilary made a helpless noise, grabbing handfuls of the rug, the world suspended on a thread of quivering gold. Dom pushed his finger farther in, found Hilary's most sensitive and intimate of places and rolled his finger over it. Hilary came in a flash flood of fire and ice and helpless cries.

When he could see straight again, Dom was bent over him, working himself and kissing him deep, sighing and moaning. Hilary could taste himself on Dom's tongue and shivered all over again. He groped for Dom's hot, heavy cock, stilled his hand and pushed him back.

Dom made a questioning noise but didn't break the kiss. Hilary continued to guide him back until he was sitting against the sofa then bent his face to Dom's chest. Hilary kissed the hot, firm skin, shivering at the salty sweet flavor and the answering tremble in Dom's flesh. He made his way down his body, hungry for the smells, the tastes, the feel of all of him.

"Hilary," Dom breathed. "You don't have to —"

His words were cut off by a strangled groan as Hilary took the large, wide length into his mouth. The taste and smell were alien and intoxicating, the feel of its heaviness in his mouth almost overwhelming. His sated cock twitched at the thought of what it might feel like inside him, stretching and plundering him, but he concentrated on working the sensitive flesh, sucking and licking until Dom's moans gained pitch and his hard abdominals tensed under Hilary's fingers.

"I'm... I'm going to... Hilary...*fuck*."

Then he was moaning, low and long and coming in hot, thick waves in Hilary's throat, his fingers tightening in his hair and his powerful thighs bunching.

Several dreamy minutes later Hilary lay sprawled along the sofa, Dom against his back, his heavy arm laid along his side as his breathing leveled in sleep, brushing the back of his neck. He almost followed Dom into oblivion but then caught sight of the files littering the dining table. He moved Dom's arm off him, retrieved his glasses from the floor and a dressing gown from the bedroom and returned to the table.

He rooted through the papers until he found DI Sharon McGarry's background check and opened it to the first page. It was only as he was reading the opening sentence for the third time that he realized he was thinking about Jasper's text.

He glanced up. Dom's eyes were closed, his large chest rising and falling steadily. Hilary took up his phone and read Jazz's message again with the chill of shame crawling over his skin. His thumb hovered over the keyboard as he tried to think of a reply. Nothing came. He made a frustrated noise and opened Instagram to search Jasper's feed. Maybe if he saw his face, he'd know what to say...how to feel.

There were dozens of pictures. Dozens. He'd been gone two days. The most recent one was of him and his family, all kitted out in snow gear, grinning for the camera in front of a handsome log cabin with the caption *Wholesome times with the fam. @quinnlyalpineresort is the absolute best. Highly recommend. #goodtimes*

He scrolled on…and froze. His fiancé sat in a hot tub, one hand in his hair, the other on his sculpted abdomen. The drops of water on his skin glowed with whatever filter he'd used. He looked up through his eyelashes, his eyes the hot blue of a summer sky. Hilary recognized the look, one that usually made his pulse quicken, but seeing it like that, directed at the entire world, made him feel like the floor was rocking under him.

Hilary's throat ached as he swiped. There were more pictures—Jasper in the tub, perched on the side, laughing, smiling, always that suggestion in his eyes, the swimsuit plastered to his toned thighs, looking out at him like he was ready to reach out and ravage him.

Hilary told himself, as he always did, that this wasn't the real Jasper Prince. This was the brand…Marcia's creation. He had always known this. But somehow, this time, he wasn't quite able to believe it.

Before he was able to take control, his eye was dragged to the comments.

Fuckin hot flame emoji

You could ruin me, Jasper, and I'd just ask you back for more.

Let's see one without the pants!!!!!!

DM me, plz. xxxxxx

Hilary felt more and more unwell but couldn't look away.

See the fuckable lawyer finally dumped you. Does this mean he's single?

Admit your engagement's a lie, Jasper. You're happier without him.

Don't get married, Jasper. We all know you don't love him.

Bloody fag couldn't hack the publicity.

Jasper had replied to every single comment...except the ones about him.

"Everything okay?"

Hilary looked up. Dom stood at the sideboard, pouring drinks.

"Fine," Hilary said, putting the phone face down on the table. "I just need to be ready for tomorrow."

"You look upset."

"I'm not."

"What happened?"

Hilary schooled his face and met his penetrating gaze. "Nothing. Just wishing a barrister was questioning McGarry tomorrow." He took the drink Dom offered and saw amusement lighting his eyes.

"You're a hundred times more convincing than any barrister would be."

"I'm glad you think so," Hilary said, sipping the vodka and searching the papers for evidence reports, even though his brain was spinning so fast that the text was blurring before his eyes.

"Let me testify."

Hilary looked up. "What?"

"I know you don't think it's a good idea," Dom said as he pulled out the chair next to Hilary. "Miss Donovan explained I'm only on the list for appearances' sake. But I think you should let me do it."

"I don't think it would work in our favor, Dom," he said carefully.

"I convinced you, didn't I?"

Hilary blushed and drank more vodka.

"I'm an innocent man, Hilary, accused of killing someone I cared about."

"They don't know that," Hilary cut in. "And they're not going to."

"I know that," Dom said. "But surely I deserve the chance to tell my side? I owe Dean that much."

Hilary met the earnest, heavy gaze with a penetrating one of his own. "Are you still not going to tell me where you were that night?"

Dom's face hardened. For a moment he looked exactly as unyielding as he had when Hilary had first walked into the townhouse living room. But then his gaze slid away, and the illusion was gone. "It's not relevant."

"You still don't trust me?"

"I trust you," Dominic said. "But you don't need to know." Hilary stared at him, trying to untangle the confusion that was warring with his newly acquired understanding and not sure which was winning. "Put me on the stand, Hilary," Dom said softly. "Let me show the world who I really am."

"That's not a good idea."

"I'm not a good man," he said. "There's no point in pretending otherwise. But I'm not a killer. I believe the jury will see that."

Hilary stared at the papers, his fingertips itching.

"Are you sure you're feeling okay?"

"Fine. I could just murder a cigarette."

"You smoke?" Dom said, surprise smoothing his face.

"Not officially."

"I see," he said, the amused look back on his face. "Well, I'm sorry, I can't help with that," he said. "That's one particular vice I never got drawn into."

Hilary took a large swallow of his drink, grateful for the warmth that burned down his throat and went some way to swamping the nervous tingling in his belly.

"And the others?" he heard himself asking as he turned a page.

"Others?"

Hilary met his gaze. "The drinking. The gambling. Crashing the cars, picking fights. All the reasons I shouldn't put you on the stand?"

Dom stared into his glass. "Sometimes the old Dom comes back."

Hilary looked at him hard. "Why did you punch that gay man, Dom?"

Dom met his look. "Is that worse than punching a straight man?"

"It looks worse."

"Even now that you know the truth?"

"Even more now that I know the truth."

Dom held his look for a long time then stared at the wall. Hilary sipped his drink and made himself wait, never taking his eyes from Dom's face.

"Jack Hadnall was a member of a club I frequent," Dom said quietly. "A discreet club. Private. I go there sometimes to…meet people."

"Men?"

Dom nodded. "Not often. I don't let myself get involved with anyone often — not unless they're worth the risk." He glanced at Hilary and away. "Hadnall…propositioned me there a few times. I turned him down."

"Why?"

"I didn't like him. Didn't trust him. But he was…persistent."

"He must have really liked you, then. That's not making the story sound any better."

"I didn't say it would," Dom said darkly, sipping his whiskey. "But I don't think he liked me, not the real me. He just had this idea of me." Dom gave Hilary a significant look. "From the press and so on. Other people at the club said that Hadnall liked it…rough in the bedroom. He obviously thought I could give him what he wanted. But that really isn't what I'm into, whatever you might think." He searched Hilary's eyes a long moment. Hilary tried to decide what he was feeling but couldn't. "So I steered well clear. But one night I was leaving the club with someone else and Hadnall followed us out. He was drunk…high. He threatened me and the man I was with."

"Why didn't you just leave?"

"I tried. But then he threatened Amelia."

Hilary blinked. "What did he say?"

"Called her 'fag-hag', of all the vile expressions," Dom said, curling his lip, "and many other, even less savory things. Said that she was to blame for my behavior, that she was making me suppress who I really was." He shook his head. "My partner, sensibly, had left by this point, but Hadnall wouldn't let me pass. I told him to move out of the way. He wouldn't. Said he would make me face up to the truth of myself. That if it took getting Amelia out of the way, he'd do it."

"So you hit him?"

Dom looked at the table. "I…snapped. One minute I was seeing red, the next thing I knew, Merriweather was pulling me off him."

"Merriweather was there?"

"Merriweather is always there," Dom said significantly.

"So he knows you're gay?"

Dom shrugged. "He doesn't ask questions. But he's the only person I trust as much as Amelia."

"It was too late, though…"

"Yes," Dom said quietly, eyes far away. "I looked down. Hadnall's face was broken and bloody and so were my hands. I don't remember it happening…but I know it did."

Silence stretched between them, deep and dark. Hilary knew a nervous tickling around his belly, the black fog threatening to steal up and into his mind. But he focused on Dom's face, on the pain he could see in the back of his eyes, and didn't let himself look away.

"Anger issues, they used to call it. But my current therapist calls it 'unresolved childhood trauma'."

Hilary swallowed. "What did he do, Dom? Your dad?"

Dom looked at him. "Are you asking if he abused me?"

"Yes. I am."

"That's the excuse abusive people use to justify their actions. I refuse to do it."

"It's not an excuse. It's a reason. A real reason."

Dom sighed. "My father didn't abuse me, Hilary. Not in the way you're thinking."

"What's the way I'm thinking?"

He gave him a frank look. "You think he touched me. Raped me?" Hilary held himself very still, kept his face neutral and nonjudgmental. "No. He would never do such a thing. Nor would he tolerate it being done to me, either."

"Abuse isn't always sexual."

Dom was quiet a long moment and Hilary wondered if he'd pushed too far. But Hilary kept himself still, quiet, waiting and, eventually, Dom's face softened. "He knew the truth about me before I did. He tried to…correct it."

Hilary swallowed his shock. "Physically?"

"Sometimes," Dom said, without intonation. "More often verbally."

"Why?"

"He perceived 'giving in' to such things as weak. Perverse. Thought that being straight was a matter of willpower." Dom met his eyes. "He never said as much, of course, but I know, now. Now I belong to a family that understands."

Hilary stared at the table a long time. "Hadnall's threats didn't make it into the arrest report."

"We struck a deal." Dom stared out of the window at the glinting night. "But you can't keep the truth buried forever."

"Merriweather… Hadnall… The people at this club… More people who know the truth… People that you haven't told me about…"

Dom gave him an apologetic look. "I'm so used to keeping these secrets it's become instinct." He sighed and looked away. "Yes, they all know. But all of them, even Hadnall, want it private just as much as I do. He was a member of that club for a reason, just like me. None of them told Lizzie. None of them told anyone. Otherwise, the prosecution would know, wouldn't they?"

Hilary rubbed his aching eyes. Silence descended for a moment.

"Does he still make you angry? Your dad?" Hilary asked once he couldn't keep the question in any longer.

"We don't speak anymore."

"What about your mum? Your brothers?"

"They all sided with him."

"That must be tough."

"It was when I needed them. I don't anymore." Dom raised his eyes to his. "You have a brother and sister, right? Twins?"

Hilary nodded.

"This case must be hard for you."

"Finding the truth is usually hard," Hilary said, glancing at his phone. "But it's always worth it, no matter how much it hurts."

Dom was quiet a moment. He gazed at Hilary, his eyes contemplative. "I said you'd changed since school...and yet in some ways you haven't," he said softly. "I still see that old shadow in your eyes sometimes."

Hilary attempted to open his throat with another large swallow of vodka. "Some things just become part of you, I guess."

"Does Jasper know that part of you?"

Hilary put the glass down firmly. "I'm not talking to you about him."

"Why not?"

"Because…" Hilary fought for words then gave up. "Just because."

Dom nodded, agreeing if not accepting. He stood. "I'm going to bed," he said, brushing a knuckle over Hilary's cheek. "Could I tempt you to join me?"

Hilary let out a shuddering breath, pain lancing his chest anew. "What are we doing, Dom?"

Dom looked surprised. Then his expression softened. "We're making up for lost time."

"But…I don't understand what's happening here."

Dom leaned down and kissed him gently, barely a touch, tender, reassuring. "It's hard when you feel things you think you shouldn't," he whispered against his lips. "I understand that. But I want to help you feel good, Hilary. That's all I've wanted for a long time." He pulled away and looked into his eyes. "Come to bed?"

Hilary took a steadying breath and turned back to the table. "Soon," he said, opening another file. He waited until he heard the bedroom door click shut before he opened up Jasper's text message to reply.

It's time to be honest, Jazz…

He stared at the message, then he remembered Jasper's face at the restaurant, his pained, hurt words. He thought about how it felt, knowing he went home to a movie star every night. A movie star who loved him, he was sure. Well, almost sure…

Then he remembered the guest list for the wedding, the attention on social media every time it got mentioned, the hundreds of notifications he got every day of people liking or commenting on photos of him and Jasper or articles about their relationship. He tried to imagine how he could face DI McGarry the next day if he brought this up with Jasper now over text message. He deleted the message and retyped it.

All fine here. See you soon x

He sent it before he could think any more about it and turned back to the case files.

* * * *

He pulled himself from Dom's sleeping embrace before dawn the following morning.

"You should leave some clothes here," Dom said sleepily, managing to ripple Hilary's skin with the hungry look in his half-open eyes. "Then you wouldn't have to rush off every morning."

Hilary set aside the prickly feeling that generated in his belly and left before the sight of the toned, naked body could derail his focus any further. When he arrived at the courthouse a few hours later, feeling physically better for a hot shower and a fresh suit, even if his mind refused to settle, he found he was able to meet Dom's and Amelia's eyes with a bland smile and a reassuring nod. Eloise did not look up from her phone when they reached the courtroom door.

"Wonderful that you could join us again, Mrs. Hart," Hilary said as he held the door open.

"We all need to know what this policewoman has to say," she said, tucking her phone away in her handbag as she followed her daughter to the front row. "Since you see her as fit to testify in Dominic's defense."

Hilary held his tongue with an effort but forgot all about her when he noticed Beck's expression. Her face was strained, and she was staring at Augustine and Jabal as they murmured urgently to each other.

"What is it?" Hilary said, lowering his voice.

"Dunno," Beck murmured. "But something's up."

A court clerk appeared at their table. "Judge Fotheringham wants to see all counsel in chambers."

"What is it?" Dom asked as the clerk hurried away.

"I don't know," Hilary said. "Stay here."

Judge Fotheringham was sat at her desk with a file open in front of her and a pinched look on her face.

"Good morning, counsel." They all murmured a greeting and she looked up. "New evidence has turned up," she said, holding out the file. Hilary took it and Beck leaned in to read over his shoulder. His blood chilled as he read and turned the page to see the photo of a metal cylinder.

"The silencer?" Beck asked.

"*A* silencer," Augustine corrected.

"Though ballistics have confirmed it is a fit for a nine-millimeter," the judge went on.

"Where was it found?" Hilary said, skin prickling.

"In a drain," Augustine said, glancing at Jabal. "In an alley behind Curzon Street in Hammersmith."

Beck stared. "That's Adeel Bukhari's street..."

"Yes, but—" Augustine started.

"My lady, I want this submitted as evidence for the defense," Hilary cut in, placing the file back on the desk.

"I thought you might," the judge said, pulling the file toward her.

"My lady, there is nothing to say that this silencer was used in this crime," Augustine went on. "There is no DNA, no forensic evidence on the device at all. And, from what they can tell, it has only been in the drain a few days."

"What are you suggesting, counsel?" Hilary asked.

"I'm not suggesting anything," Augustine replied, her voice flat. "But it's our considered opinion that this finding is not significant to this trial."

"My lady, it has to be," Hilary insisted. "Bukhari had a personal relationship with the victim, a tempestuous one at that. And now, just a few days after his testimony—"

"Bukhari has an alibi," Augustine put in. "And we only found the silencer because of an anonymous tip. It's not enough to warrant—"

"This is not the place for a case review, counsel," Fotheringham interrupted. "If the defense wants to submit it as evidence, that is their prerogative. It's up to them to try to establish its significance, just as it's up to you to establish the lack of it, if that's your position."

Augustine folded her arms. Jabal watched her with his hands behind his back.

"DI McGarry is our first witness this morning," Beck said with a half-smile. "Let's ask her if it's significant."

Augustine glared.

"The defense's request is granted," the judge said, holding out the file to a court clerk. "The silencer is hereby submitted as evidence. The details will be emailed to you and hard copies made for your files. Then we can start."

"This is it, boss," Beck murmured, scrolling on her phone as they re-entered the courtroom. "The break we've been waiting for. Got the files. I'll add them to our slides."

"Do you really think Bukhari did it?" Hilary asked quietly, trying not to stare at the grim-faced young man who again sat near the back, staring at nothing.

"Dunno," Beck said, following his gaze. "But we don't have to know, do we? Just make the jury think it's possible."

"What's happened?" Amelia asked, standing with Dom as they returned to the table. Eloise was talking on the phone and turned away.

"Some new evidence," Hilary said as the clerk brought him their paper copies. He explained in an undertone. A light lit in Amelia's pale eyes. Dom clenched his jaw.

"This is it," Amelia said. "This is what proves he didn't do it."

"It's a good start," Hilary said. "We just need to get McGarry to admit it's significant."

"She won't do that," Dom said. He was staring at Bukhari. As if sensing the look, the young man returned his gaze. The hatred that twisted his face was intense. "He did it?" Dom's voice was low, his expression tight. "It was him? He killed them?"

"We don't know," Hilary said. "And neither do the police. It's circumstantial evidence at best. But anything that points the focus away from you is good."

Dom met his eyes. Pain darkened them to jet. Hilary's heart clenched. But then the judge was announced, and the jury filed in.

"Defense counsel, if you'd like to call your next witness?"

"Defense calls Detective Inspector Sharon McGarry."

McGarry strode to the witness box with her back straight and her head held high. Her graying hair was tied in a tight bun and her round face was calm, her mouth a thin line as she took her oath and sat, contemplating Hilary with keen, amber eyes.

"DI McGarry, thank you for joining us today. You oversaw the investigation into the murders of Lizzie and Dean Wood, is that correct?"

"It is."

"How much involvement would you say you had in the case?"

"I coordinated the investigation, analyzed the forensic reports and conducted the bulk of the interviews."

"Including those with my client, is that right?"

The hard eyes slid past Hilary to Dom. "That's correct."

"What was the first thing that made you suspect Mr. Hart-Gosford?"

"When we discovered Lizzie Wood's former employment at Homes with Hart."

Hilary raised his eyebrows. "So you began to suspect my client purely on the basis that one of the victims had, up until a few weeks before her death, been employed by his wife's company?"

"Yes."

"A bit tenuous, don't you think?"

McGarry regarded him levelly. "Not when we considered his criminal record...his violent past."

Hilary took a breath, resisting glancing at the jury. "Yes, let's talk about that a bit more. You were the arresting officer in how many of my client's previous offenses?"

"Three."

"So three out of the five times my client has been arrested prior to this crime, you made the arrest?"

"That's what I said, yes."

"Why is that?"

She folded her hands in her lap. "The crimes were committed within my jurisdiction."

"Would you say, Detective Inspector, that your history with my client has biased you against him?"

"No."

"No?"

"Absolutely not. I deal with the evidence presented to me and make a judgment based on the facts. Nothing more."

"But there are so few facts in this case," Hilary went on, not breaking eye contact. "So little actual evidence."

"We have your client's DNA at the scene. We have witness testimony stating that your client was in a sexual relationship with one of the victims—"

"Miss Holden's testimony was hardly conclusive. Her revelation about the condoms wasn't in her initial statement. And she didn't even know the name of the person she claims Lizzie planned to blackmail."

"Objection," Jabal said, standing. "Attempting to antagonize the witness, my lady."

"Sustained."

"I'll rephrase," Hilary said. "So, you are stating before this court that you believe the evidence presented to this court is utterly conclusive? That it's not possible for anyone else to have committed this crime?"

"I am."

"Even though it is a matter of public record that you've arrested him three times in the past, including once for drink driving, even though, on that particular occasion, he passed the breathalyzer test?"

McGarry's eyes glinted. "Your client was drunk, Mr. Whyte. There's CCTV footage of him unable to keep in his lane. He nearly knocked over a cyclist."

"But he passed the breathalyzer, correct?"

"He did," McGarry added after a pause.

"A fact that meant he was never charged?"

"I know the law, counselor. I also know that your client is a violent criminal who was being threatened with blackmail by Lizzie Wood, and we have built a very strong case to prove as such."

"You are using words like 'know' and 'prove'. But you don't know, do you? And you haven't proved anything."

"I have been a serving police office for almost twenty years," McGarry stated. "My experience has taught me that unfortunately people who are either desperate or evil are capable of pretty much anything."

Hilary raised his eyebrows, even as his blood cooled in his veins. "Evil's a strong word, Detective Inspector."

"I don't use it lightly," she said. "But to answer your question, counsel, it's important the court understands that the evidence against your client is highly suggestive, even if you want to spin it as *inconclusive*. They also need to understand that in cases without hard evidence, which do happen, we look at everything else."

"Everything?"

"*Everything.* Your client has a violent criminal past. He has no alibi. He had access to the sort of weapon used, and there is evidence that he had a motive." She transferred her hard stare to Dom. Dom held it steadily, his hands folded on the table in front of him, not moving, his face unreadable. "You say my personal history with your client is an obstacle to my judgment. I and any other police officer would say it's exactly the opposite. I know what that man is capable of, and I know he killed those people. I just can't prove it."

A murmur went through the court. Augustine was staring at the jury, and he knew she was trying to work out, just like him, which part of the arresting officer's statement had hit home the most.

Hilary pulled out the TV remote and clicked the display on. Beck swiped on her iPad until the file photograph of the silencer came up.

"Can you tell us what this is, DI McGarry?"

McGarry paused. "It's a silencer."

"This turned up just this morning," Hilary said to the jury. "The defense has attained permission from Judge Fotheringham to submit it as evidence. Can you tell me where this was found, Detective Inspector?"

"It was found in the drain of an alley in Hammersmith."

"Whereabouts in Hammersmith, exactly?"

McGarry met his eye with a sharp look. "Behind Curzon Street."

"This is *bullshit*." All eyes turned toward Bukhari, who was now on his feet, red-faced, stabbing his finger at the screen. "I've never seen that fucking thing before. You're setting me up! You—"

"Mr. Bukhari," Judge Fotheringham attempted to interrupt, but the young man raved on, weaving between the chairs toward Hilary.

"*You* put that there! You fuckers are trying—"

Security intercepted him and tried to steer him toward the doors. He shouted louder, pulling at the guards' grip, ignoring Fotheringham's warnings of arrest.

He only shouted louder as he was dragged toward the exit, gesturing wildly at Dominic. "*You* did this.

You fucking killed her, you bastard, murdering asshole. I *loved* her. *You—*"

The doors shut behind them and an eerie hush fell. All eyes turned toward Hilary. McGarry sat ramrod-straight in the witness box, her face set.

"For those of the court who don't know, Mr. Bukhari lives on Curzon Street—"

"Objection," Jabal stood. "My lady, the defense is making accusations he neither has the evidence or the authority to make—"

"My lady agreed to me submitting the silencer as evidence," Hilary cut him off, "along with the fact that it was found this morning in a drain almost directly behind Mr. Bukhari's house—"

"My *lady*," Jabal protested again as chatter broke out on all sides. "This is simply unacceptable—"

Fotheringham banged her gavel until quiet was restored.

"Your objection is overruled, Mr. Jabal," Fotheringham said evenly. "You will have your chance to question the significance of this evidence in cross. Until then, you should allow the defense to finish its questions."

"Yes, my lady," Jabal said grimly, resuming his seat.

Beck was fighting a smile. Dom was staring at the courtroom door. Amelia was looking quietly triumphant. Next to her, Eloise sat bolt upright in her seat, her eyes on the screen, her phone forgotten in her hand. Hilary frowned at her but then the judge called for him to continue.

"Detective Inspector," he said, "we haven't yet had your opinion on this finding."

"No forensic evidence was found on the silencer," she said. "There is nothing to link it to the crime under discussion."

"Apart from the fact that it is a fit for a nine-millimeter handgun? And found in close proximity to an associate of Miss Wood?"

"Environmental forensics suggest it was only put in the drain within the last few days," McGarry went on, giving him a level look. "I fail to see why Mr. Bukhari would dispose of evidence so clumsily at this particular time."

Hilary shrugged. "You said yourself that desperate people do desperate things."

"There is currently no evidence to implicate Mr. Bukhari in this crime."

"But you have to admit, it's possible?"

"Mr. Bukhari was cleared. He has an alibi —"

"Provided by his family," Hilary cut in. "Not exactly objective witnesses, even by your standards, surely?"

McGarry's jaw tightened. "There is no proof of Mr. Bukhari's involvement."

"There's no proof of my client's, either," Hilary said. "One hair, Detective Inspector. One hair...that's all you have."

"And the defendant's link to the victim —"

"What about Mr. Bukhari's link?"

"Objection." Jabal stood. "My lady, Mr. Bukhari is not on trial here."

"Sustained. Mr. Whyte, please withdraw that question."

"I withdraw it," Hilary said levelly. "I don't think the jury needs an answer to appreciate there is just as much, or as little, evidence against Mr. Bukhari as there is against my client, and that the only reason Mr. Hart-

Gosford is sitting in this courtroom is because of DI McGarry's personal—"

"*Objection.*"

"I resent your implication, Mr. Whyte—"

"Quiet." Fotheringham banged her gavel and both Jabal and McGarry fell silent. "Mr. Whyte, are you done?"

"No more questions, my lady."

Hilary returned to his chair. Beck's eyes glittered with triumph. Amelia gave a tiny nod as he resumed his seat. Eloise was again typing on her phone and didn't look up. Dom's gaze remained on McGarry as Jabal rose from his seat.

"Detective Inspector," he said, "you've been a serving police officer for almost twenty years, you said?"

"That's correct."

"Have there ever been any formal disciplinary proceedings taken out against you?"

"No."

"Have there ever been any complaints?"

"Yes," McGarry said carefully. "Families of perpetrators often complain. They don't like to believe their loved ones are capable of the things they've done."

"Have any of these complaints been upheld? Or taken to the Independent Police Commission?"

"No."

"Haven't you, in fact, received several commendations for your service?"

"I have." Her eyes slid to Hilary.

"So would you agree that you have a wealth of experience behind your professional judgment?"

"I would."

"Good," Jabal said, stepping out from behind his desk. "I would say so, too. This silencer the defense has pinned so much hope on," he said, gesturing at the screen. "What is your explanation for its being found now?"

"I don't have one," McGarry said smoothly. "As there is nothing to prove it is linked to this case."

"Do you at least have an opinion?"

"My opinion?"

"Yes. Your considered, expert opinion. What does your experience as a police officer tell you about this silencer turning up at this location at this time?"

"Objection," Hilary said, standing. "Calling to speculate."

"I understand that, my lady," Jabal went on smoothly. "But we've established the witness is an experienced police officer and a commended, acclaimed investigator. I think her speculation, just like Mr. Gowan's, is worth consideration."

Fotheringham examined McGarry for a moment. "Overruled."

"My lady—"

"Mr. Jabal is right," Fotheringham went on. "DI McGarry's opinion has weight. Detective Inspector, please answer the question."

Hilary sat, heat flooding his face.

McGarry's eyes swung to Dom. "I would never pursue this as a line of inquiry with so little to go on. But my personal opinion is that it has been planted there to mislead the court and muddy the waters of this trial."

Hushed chatter went through the audience. Augustine sent Hilary a level look. Jabal smiled.

"No more questions, my lady."

"Mr. Whyte?"

Hilary's heart was thumping in his chest. His palms itched.

"Mr. Whyte?" Fotheringham prompted. "Any further questions?"

"No, my lady."

Ripples of conversation filled the room as McGarry departed the witness stand. She did not look back.

"We shall have a break," Fotheringham announced, banging the gavel. "Five minutes, counsel, to get yourselves in order. Then the defense can call its next witness."

"It's okay, boss," Beck started. "We can work with this. We—"

Hilary didn't hear the rest. He made for the door in a daze, trying not to hurry. The doors seemed heavier than lead. He stepped into the corridor, slipped behind a marble column and leaned against it, loosening his tie and taking deep breaths until the world stopped spinning. He took his glasses off and cleaned them, willing the familiar action to calm his nerves. But then he remembered his old pair breaking, Dom's touch burning on his skin, him crying out as they came together. He remembered the faces of the jury as the Detective Inspector accused them of planting evidence and Dom's black, hard stare as he listened and grew angry.

He shook his head and put his glasses on, willing his throat to loosen so he could breathe again.

It was then that he spotted Eloise, phone to her ear, her kitten heels clicking on the marble as she hurried from the courtroom. Her face was set, lips pinched.

"—did you think you were doing? Of all the utterly stupid..." She stopped, glaring at the wall, color flooding her pale cheeks. "I don't care what you thought. This wasn't... That's not what I told you to do. We had a *plan*. I don't *care*. Just fix it. I don't care how..." Eloise froze, spotting Hilary. "I'll call you back," she said and hung up, folding her hands in front of her and sending Hilary a narrow look. "Mr. Whyte. Are you well?"

"Quite well, thank you. Everything all right with you?"

"Apart from the jury thinking Dominic has planted evidence now on top of everything else, you mean?"

"Who was on the phone, Mrs. Hart?"

Eloise shoved the phone in her bag. "And how is that remotely your business?"

"If it's involved with Dominic's case, it's my business."

She raised her eyebrows. "So it's 'Dominic' now, is it?"

"Boss?" Hilary swallowed his response as Beck joined them. "Everything okay?"

"Yes, fine," Hilary said.

"We should get back in."

"Yes, you should," Eloise said, tugging her handbag higher up on her arm. "It seems Dominic's case hangs in the balance. I suggest you pull yourself together...and fast."

"What was all that about?" Beck murmured as Eloise swept away, back to the courtroom.

"I don't know," Hilary said as he watched her go. "She was arguing with someone on the phone. Something about a plan."

Beck frowned. "What plan?"

"I don't know. But someone didn't stick to it."

Beck stared after the retreating figure. "Do you think it's connected?"

"I…don't know."

"Boss, we gotta act fast. I don't know if McGarry helped us or screwed us, but whatever she did, we need to undo some of it for sure."

"I know," Hilary said, making for the doors, his mind starting to spin again as he returned to the defense table just as the judge and jury resumed their seats. Dom was staring straight ahead whilst Amelia muttered in his ear, holding his shoulder. Hilary looked away as he sat, pretended to rifle through papers as he tried to think. Beck was whispering urgently, suggesting they bring Bukhari back.

"Or the gun club guy," Beck went on. "We can re-establish Amelia never even owned a silencer—"

"Does the defense have another witness?"

"It won't take much, boss," Beck went on. "We just need to shake what she said, let them see it's just McGarry's speculation. We—"

"Mr. Whyte?" Fotheringham's voice held a note of impatience.

"Call on me."

Hilary's head was pounding so hard that he barely heard Dom. The papers blurred on the desk in front of him. The black spots started dancing.

"Hilary."

Hilary raised his head. Dom's face was close to his. Hilary could suddenly taste him and smell his hair. He remembered the gentle touch of his strong hands, the tenderness with which he coaxed him out of himself.

A roaring started up in his ears. He closed his eyes against it all. When he opened them again, he was standing with everyone looking at him, silence all around.

"Defense calls Dominic Hart-Gosford."

Chapter Thirteen

Silence fell as Dom took the stand. Augustine's eyes were narrow. Jabal's were filled with a grim satisfaction. But Hilary barely registered any of it. His pulse was fluttering in his wrists. The pounding in his temples was getting stronger.

The roaring in his ears gained volume as Dom took his oath and sat, calm and collected, crossing his long legs and meeting Hilary's look without expression. Dom gave him an infinitesimal, reassuring nod. Hilary pulled in a deep breath and willed his trembling nerves to still.

"I will start by saying that I advised my client against taking the stand in his defense," Hilary said, meeting the eyes of the jury. "I know the members of the court will have endeavored to remain objective in the face of media speculation, but we're all human." Hilary pressed his fingertips together. "But Mr. Hart-Gosford is taking the stand today not for himself but for Lizzie and Dean. He wants to tell the truth, whatever the cost to him, because the real perpetrator of this crime is still out there and he wants them punished just as much as the rest of us do."

"My lady, please," Jabal drawled, getting to his feet. "Does the defense have any questions to actually ask?"

"I beg your pardon, my lady, and the pardon of the court members, too," Hilary said. "I just wanted my client's reasoning established before we began. Mr. Hart-Gosford" — Dom's eyes were steady — "did you know Lizzie Wood?"

"No."

"Despite there being photographic evidence of you attending the same events together on more than one occasion?" Hilary clicked the clicker and the photograph of Dom at the event with Amelia and Lizzie appeared on the screen.

"I attend many events for my wife," Dom said. "But they are *her* events, not mine. I don't socialize at them."

"You didn't have a personal relationship with Lizzie of any kind?"

"I did not."

"You didn't speak to her, or to Adeel Bukhari, at any of these events?"

"Not to my recollection. That's not to say it didn't happen," he said with a keen glance at the prosecutor's table. "But as Mr. Bukhari's own testimony established, I do not enjoy talking to people at these events."

Hilary swallowed. "Did Lizzie Wood ever approach you outside of work, try to blackmail you at any time?"

"Certainly not."

Hilary winced. Dom's face was cold. Beck watched with a grim expression, her hands tight around the iPad. Hilary looked away before she could meet his gaze.

"Why do you think Lizzie told her friend Sara that she did, then?"

"I don't know," Dom said. "But, as Miss Holden herself admitted, Miss Wood never named me — never showed her any evidence of the identity of whoever she claimed to be angry with."

"She did state it was someone linked to her old job."

"I can't explain that. I only know it wasn't me."

"Can you offer any reason why you have been implicated in this crime?"

Dom glanced at the jury. "It seems the entirety of the case against me is the hair they found at the scene."

"Your hair."

"So the tests say."

"Can you offer an explanation as to how it ended up at the crime scene?" Hilary held his breath.

"I was never at that house."

"Can you see why the police arrested you, though, Mr. Hart-Gosford?" Hilary said, keeping his voice level with an effort. "Like DI McGarry said, your arrest record, the lack of alibi, your link to one of the victims —"

"My link to Miss Wood is tenuous," Dom stated, and Hilary tried to tell him with his eyes to soften his tone, prayed for him to stop sitting so casually in the chair, but Dom was talking to the jury and not to him. "As to my personal history…" He took a breath. "I have made mistakes over the course of my life. Many people do, when they find it hard to see a good road open to them, when they're unsure whether love really exists in the world, when they suspect they will never be worthy of it even if it does."

He finally looked back. His eyes burned into Hilary's. It seemed like the whole room held its breath.

"It's not an excuse for the way I've lived," he said quietly. "Just an explanation."

"Do you regret the things you've done?" Hilary asked, trying to sound dispassionate. Trying not to sound like he was desperate for the answer for himself.

"Yes, I do. Every day."

"Why now?"

Dom's jaw tightened. He glanced at Amelia, who inclined her head. The jury watched, breathless. Dom sat straighter in his seat.

"Because I've recently learned what it feels like to have people believe in me," he said. "I've learned, perhaps, that I'm worthy of some people's good opinion—people who are important to me." Glances slid to Amelia. She stayed very still, her eyes on her husband.

"It has allowed me to hope that I may be given the chance to make amends for some of the hurt I've caused." Dom looked at the jury. "I have spent a great deal of my life being selfish. Angry. Violent, on occasion, it's true. But whatever chance I do or don't deserve, these two young people..." He paused. Hilary watched him swallow and saw a very real pain brighten his eyes. He snuck a glance at the jury. They were focused on Dom, but each expression was guarded. "These two young people are dead, and the trail to their killer is getting colder by the day. Lizzie and Dean's parents deserve to know what happened to their children. I want to tell the truth here today because I want them to get their answers."

Hilary took a breath. "The prosecution will cross-examine you shortly. They are going to point out that you had the motive, the means and the opportunity to commit this crime. They are going to try to make the jury believe that that is all they need to judge you guilty. What can you give them that will help them see beyond these circumstances?"

"Just what you've spent this entire trial demonstrating, Mr. Whyte," he said softly. "That there is no proof I did any of these things. And you can only convict someone if you consider them guilty beyond all reasonable doubt." He looked at Augustine again. "Of course I'm going to say I'm innocent. Who wouldn't when charged with such a horrible crime? But, frankly, what I say or don't say doesn't change the fact that they cannot prove anything beyond all reasonable doubt."

"You admit you may have met Adeel Bukhari at some events but have no recollection of it. Did you know where he lived?"

"No."

"Could you have found out?"

Dom looked at him closely.

"I'm only asking because the prosecution will. They are going to ask you if you could have found Mr. Bukhari's address through your wife's employment records. They're going to make it look like you planted that silencer to incriminate Mr. Bukhari after his impassioned testimony here, to distract attention from yourself."

"It's all possible. I could have done such a thing — but I didn't."

Hilary inclined his head. "Mr. Jabal is going to ask you some questions now," Hilary said, trying to speak to him with his eyes. *Don't fuck this up.* Dom nodded.

Jabal stood and Hilary returned to his seat.

"Fuck me, boss," Beck whispered as he sat. "Talk about skating a bloody knife edge."

"He did well," Hilary murmured as he tapped files together.

"Yeah, talking to *you*…"

Hilary watched Jabal approach the witness box, his heart fluttering like a caged bird as he took in the grim set to Dom's face.

"Mr. Hart-Gosford," Jabal started, an expression just short of a sneer twisting his face. "You have admitted yourself that you are a violent person. Is that right?"

"That's not what I said."

"I think it is," Jabal said. "Would you like the court reporter to read it back?"

"I said I have a violent past."

"So wouldn't you say that makes you a violent person?"

"No."

"Then what does it make you?"

Dom's expression didn't flicker, but Hilary saw the dark fire light in his eyes and bit the inside of his lip. "It makes me someone who has made mistakes."

"Mistakes that have ended with injuries grave enough to land people in hospital, isn't that right?"

Hilary suppressed a groan.

"I believe there were some bruised ribs involved after one fight, yes."

Jabal took a paper handed to him by Augustine. "Jack Hadnall. Forty-one. Admitted to the Royal London Hospital on the twenty-second of April last year. Two broken ribs, a black eye. Sprained wrist. Split lip."

"He broke my nose, too," Dom said levelly. "Though you won't have a record of that as I had it treated privately at home."

"What did Mr. Hadnall do to earn your ire, Mr. Hart-Gosford?"

"Objection," Hilary called. "Relevance?"

Jabal raised his eyebrows. "Your client is the one who is suggesting his violent past should be discounted. I'm merely trying to establish if that's the case, my lady."

"Overruled."

Hilary swore under his breath as he sat down.

"Mr. Hart-Gosford?" Jabal prompted. "Why did you attack this man?"

"He threatened me."

Jabal visibly gathered his patience. "Okay, why?"

"I don't know."

"You don't know?"

"That's what I said."

Jabal raised his eyebrows. "So he just cornered you on the street, unprovoked?" Dom didn't answer. Hilary clenched his hands together. "Witnesses say they heard Mr. Hadnall taunting you," Jabal went on, referring to his paper. "Taunting your integrity. Your wife. Any of this sounding familiar?"

"That wasn't in the witness reports."

"Not at the time," Jabal replied. "But the witnesses have recently been re-interviewed. Funny how their recollections seem to be clearer now than at the time. Why do you think that is?"

Dom didn't answer.

"Okay then, how about this one?" Jabal said turning the page. "George Fletcher. October 2020. Admitted to University College Hospital with a fractured wrist and concussion. What did this man say to you, Mr. Hart-Gosford?"

"It was a drunken fight after a card game turned sour. I was injured, too."

"As badly as Mr. Fletcher?"

"None of this is relevant, Mr. Jabal."

"I'm afraid I beg to differ."

"I've already said I've made mistakes...that I regret them."

"Oh, I'm sure you do, now that they've landed you with a double murder charge."

"*Objection.*"

"Sustained. Careful, Mr. Jabal."

"Apologies, my lady. I withdraw the statement. I'm just finding it hard to believe Mr. Hart-Gosford has had any reason to change."

"I already said—"

"Yes, that you found someone who makes you feel worthy," Jabal mocked. "Who is that someone, Mr. Hart-Gosford? What miracle worker has made you understand the worst of yourself and convinced you to make amends, when even your marriage hasn't been enough to rid you of your violent tendencies?"

"That's not relevant either."

Jabal's gaze slid to Hilary. He went cold.

"Is it true, Mr. Hart-Gosford, that you went to the same school as your solicitor, Mr. Whyte?"

"*Objection.*" The word came out high and tight and Hilary fought to keep control. "My lady, that *really* is not relevant."

"Are you sure about that, Mr. Whyte?"

"I must say, Mr. Jabal," the judge said, "I'm struggling to see the significance."

"Surely a childhood association with his client must be significant, my lady."

"Well, it depends on the extent of the relationship, which I would hope has already been examined and deemed within reasonable parameters."

"Yes, but, my lady—"

"Mr. Hart-Gosford," Fotheringham went on with a sigh, "were you friends with Mr. Whyte at school?"

"No, my lady."

"Have you had any association since?"

Hilary felt sick. Dom shook his head. "No, my lady. I haven't seen him even once since I left school."

"I don't think there is any conflict of interest here, Mr. Jabal."

"I wasn't worried about conflict of interest in that way, my lady," Jabal said, his eyes gimlet-sharp. "I was just wondering if Mr. Whyte, someone who knew Mr. Hart-Gosford in his formative years and who has recently re-entered his life, might be the person who has suddenly and very conveniently inspired Mr. Hart-Gosford to mend his wicked ways?"

"My lady," Hilary started but Dom spoke.

"Yes," he stated. "Yes, he is, as it happens. He is an excellent lawyer and a good man. He would inspire anyone to be a better person."

Jabal blinked. Fotheringham frowned. Beck looked between them, bewildered. Hilary lowered himself back into his seat, feeling the blood drain from his face.

"So now we have an explanation," Jabal said calmly. "And yes, I believe your schoolfriend lawyer could very easily persuade you to take such a stance in court, Mr. Hart-Gosford, when the case hinges upon it."

"The case hinges on your proving I killed two people," Dom returned. "You can't."

"This is the misapprehension you and Mr. Whyte have been laboring under this whole time, Mr. Hart-

Gosford. I don't need to prove it," Jabal said with a small smile. "I just need to show the jury the sort of man you really are. Then the truth will be evident." Hilary resisted clutching at the table as Jabal flipped through his files. "The school you went to with Mr. Whyte. What school was that?"

Dom's jaw clenched. "St. Edmund's Academy for Boys."

"That's the one," Jabal said, peering at his papers. "Did you graduate from that school?"

"I graduated from Munroe-Robert's Sixth Form College."

"By the skin of your teeth," Jabal said, his finger marking a place on the paper.

"Objection," Hilary snapped.

"I withdraw," Jabal said, waving a hand. "Why the change in schools, Mr. Hart-Gosford?"

"It was over a decade ago, Mr. Jabal."

"You must remember, surely?"

Dom glared. Hilary shut his eyes. "I was expelled from St. Edmund's."

A murmur went around the room.

"What for?"

Dom didn't reply. Hilary opened his eyes. Dom's black gaze burned into Jabal, but the barrister remained unfazed.

"Why were you expelled?" Jabal prompted. Still Dom didn't speak. "Fine. I'll tell the court if you won't. You threatened a teacher, isn't that right? A female teacher, yes?"

Disapproval rippled through the audience.

"That's correct," Dom said flatly.

"Witnesses state you were heard to say, *'I'll fucking kill you, you sadistic bitch. Just see that I don't.'*"

Hilary stared at his hands. The roaring had returned to his ears. He swallowed bile.

"I said that. It's true."

Jabal blinked. "Why? What could this sixty-year-old woman have possibly done to make you threaten her like that?"

"I don't recall."

"Perhaps Mr. Whyte remembers?"

"Objection," Hilary snarled. "My lady, we've already established my attendance at my client's school is not relevant to this case. And I'm sure it's quite clear in the school records that my client and I were in different years, and I wasn't present at this scene."

"Yes, I think you had better leave that particular line of questioning alone, Mr. Jabal," Fotheringham stated with a look over her glasses.

"My apologies, my lady, Mr. Whyte. We'll move on." Jabal clicked the remote. The photo of Dom leaving Eloise's gallery appeared on the screen. "This is the last time you were seen on the day of the murders. Neither you nor your car appear on any more CCTV until eight the following morning. Nothing was charged to any of your credit or debit cards and your phone was turned off the whole time."

"That's not a question, Mr. Jabal," Dom said.

"Here's my question. Where did you go?"

Hilary's heart sank. *I told you so* was written on Beck's face. He looked away.

"Where I went that night is not relevant."

"If you are innocent as you suggest," Jabal went on, "it is more than relevant."

"It's not my job to prove my innocence," Dom said. "It's your job to prove my guilt. You're still not doing that."

Jabal hesitated and Hilary's heart fluttered. Jabal clicked the remote. Footage from the banquet started playing on the screen. Finely dressed people sat around the huge table, sipping wine and eating from silver and china, their jewelry glinting in the candlelight. Amelia sat on her mother's right-hand side. Merriweather made his way down the line of guests, pouring wine. Eloise was smiling and graceful as she chatted to her guests. Amelia's gaze was fixed on the empty chair beside her.

"Why didn't you go to your family's dinner that night, Mr. Hart-Gosford?"

"I didn't want to."

"Your mother-in-law was entertaining some very distinguished guests." He paused the video just as Merriweather was bringing a dish to the table and Eloise had stood, her glass raised in a toast to the well-dressed man on her left. "Isn't it rather significant that you didn't go?"

"I didn't want to," he repeated.

"But you won't tell the court what you were doing instead?"

"No."

Jabal nodded thoughtfully. Hilary stared at the screen, the rest of the room starting to blur.

"If you won't tell us where you were when Lizzie and Dean died, perhaps you will tell us where you were the night before last?"

"Excuse me?"

"Where were you? On Tuesday night?"

"Why?"

"Please just answer the question."

Dom's gaze flicked to Hilary then away. Hilary's skin started to crawl. "I was at home."

"Not in Mayfair, you weren't," Jabal said, tilting his chin. "The police obtained a warrant for your house's security cameras. You did not return home after court."

"I have more than one home, Mr. Jabal."

"I see. So, where's this other home?"

Hilary clenched his hands together under the table.

"I have a flat. I don't think its exact location is anyone's business."

Hilary winced. Beck groaned.

"And that's where you spent Tuesday night?"

"Yes."

"Can anyone confirm that?"

Hilary prayed with every ounce of internal strength that Dom wouldn't look at him. An agonizing time later, Dom shook his head. "No. I was alone."

"That's your statement?"

"Objection, my lady," Hilary said, getting to his feet and willing his legs to hold him. "How is Tuesday night relevant to anything?"

"The police believe that the silencer ended up in Mr. Bukhari's drain that night."

"My lady, my client has not been arrested or charged for this offense."

"Sustained. Mr. Jabal, would you like to ask the defendant a direct question about the silencer?"

"Of course. Mr. Hart-Gosford, did you drop the silencer used in the murder of Lizzie and Dean Wood in the drain behind Mr. Bukhari's house the night before last?"

"No, I didn't."

"But you have no alibi for the time it was put there, just like you have no alibi for the night of the murders?"

Dom's face was hard. "I've never owned a silencer. I've never owned a gun. And if I was going to attempt to frame someone else for a crime I committed" — his eyes went straight to Augustine — "I would have done it right. Frankly, I'm offended you think I would be stupid enough to kill someone, not arrange an alibi, then plant evidence and make the same mistake."

Hilary stared at him. Dom's face was set. Augustine's was flushed. Beck clenched her jaw and Hilary fought harder than he'd fought anything in his life to stay quiet.

"Is that so?" Jabal said with a note of triumph.

"It is so. And while you're wasting time and resources here, the real killer is out there…"

Hilary didn't hear what else Dom said. His head was spinning. He stared at the banquet scene without seeing it, without hearing what Jabal said next or Beck's urgent suggestions. It was over. Dom was going to prison. He would never see him again. Never get to ask him about what he'd said today. Never find out if what was between them was anything more than two outcasts desperate for comfort.

He blinked at the screen. He frowned at the image, suddenly in sharp focus. The blood rushed around his body and his mind cleared like a blind being lifted.

"No more questions, my lady."

"Mr. Whyte?"

"Boss?" Beck hissed.

Hilary's blood pounded in his ears.

"Mr. Whyte? Any more questions for your witness?"

Hilary pulled one of the stills from the banquet out of his file, the same frame as the one on the TV. He pushed his glasses up and brought it to his face to stare at it hard.

"Mr. Whyte?" the judge prompted sharply.

"My lady," Hilary said, standing. "The defense would like to call on Mr. Merriweather one more time."

"My lady," Jabal implored. "Defense has already questioned that witness."

"Some new information has come to my attention," Hilary said, clutching the picture. Fotheringham looked first at him, at the image he held, then frowned at the TV screen. She sighed and scribbled on her pad.

"Very well, Mr. Whyte, if you insist. But this really will have to be your last witness."

The judge excused Dom whilst Jabal started to protest. The room broke out in excited muttering until Fotheringham had to call for quiet again.

Hilary turned to Amelia who sat staring at him with wide eyes. "Where's Merriweather? Is he here?"

"He's out with the car."

"Can you call him, please? Tell him we need him urgently."

"Of course," she said, searching her bag for her phone.

"What exactly is your thinking, Mr. Whyte?" Eloise demanded, face pinched.

"What is this?" Dom asked as he rejoined them.

Hilary tried to find words and couldn't. Dom searched his face then glanced down at the image in his hands. His expression changed.

"Hilary, wait—"

"I have to."

"I… You're wrong. It's not possible."

"Look at it, Dom," he said, aware of Beck's bewildered frown. "What else could it mean?"

Dom stared at the picture, the lines around his mouth deepening. Eloise was demanding explanations. Dom opened his mouth to speak, but then the doors opened and Merriweather strode in, his scarred face grim.

"Mr. Whyte? What's this? Mistress Amelia said —"

"Can you take the stand again, please?" Hilary said, keeping his voice toneless.

Merriweather's small eyes narrowed. "I already answered me questions. You haven't prepped me for no more."

"Please, Mr. Merriweather. The court is waiting."

Merriweather looked to Dom. Dom was staring at him, a darkness in his eyes blacker than anything Hilary had seen before. Merriweather paled.

"Yes, sir. Whatever you say, sir."

The courtroom bubbled as Merriweather took the witness stand, straightening his coat and tie and sitting stiffly on the edge of the seat.

"Boss," Beck started. "What the hell?"

Hilary handed the picture over, pointing to the image of the butler bent over the banquet table, placing a silver dish in front of the African ambassador. Beck's eyes widened. Hilary took a deep breath, wiped his palms on his coat and stepped toward the witness box.

"Mr. Merriweather. Thank you so much for rejoining us on such short notice."

"Course," Merriweather said, looking round uneasily. "What d'you need?"

Hilary attempted to smile. He gestured at the banquet image still on the TV screen.

"We've been through this once already," Hilary said. "But would you just remind the court of what we're looking at here?"

"Sure. It's the banquet on the night of the killings."

"And what was your role at this banquet, exactly?"

Merriweather was staring at the screen. Hilary tried to decide if his lip was twitching. "Well, you can see 'ere," he said, nodding.

"I see you serving food."

"That's right," Merriweather said. "Serving food, wine. Making sure all the staff knew what they was doing and where to get everything."

"A vital role, especially at an event such as this."

"That's right."

"Can you tell the court precisely what you're doing in this image, Mr. Merriweather?"

"Serving, ain't I? Like I said."

"Yes, but *what* are you serving?"

"Objection." Jabal stood. "Relevance?"

"The relevance will become clear very soon, my lady," Hilary went on.

"Overruled," Fotheringham said, peering at the TV. "Just make sure it is very soon, counsel."

"Thank you, my lady. Mr. Merriweather. What are you serving in this image?"

"I dunno," Merriweather said, face filling with color. "Could have been anything."

"This is the second course. Does that help?"

Merriweather shot him a look. "No. It don't."

"Okay, let's put that aside for now. Perhaps you can just explain to us the odd thing about the way you are serving this dish?"

"I don't get you."

"Look hard, Mr. Merriweather. I'm sure it'll become clear."

Merriweather peered at the image, at the figure in the smart black suit and white gloves bending over a guest's shoulder to place the dish on the table.

Hilary raised his eyebrows. "Anything?"

"No."

Hilary paused. "Are you right or left-handed, Mr. Merriweather?"

Merriweather's jaw bulged but he did not look away from the screen.

"Mr. Merriweather?"

"Right. I'm right-handed."

"And yet you're serving with your left hand here," Hilary said, pressing play on the remote. The figure in the white gloves returned to the sideboard, selected another of the silver dishes with his left hand and moved farther down the table to place it before the next group of diners.

"It was probably easier to reach into the table with me left," Merriweather said with a shrug.

"I don't think it was," Hilary said, nodding as the server knocked against the shoulder of one of the diners as he lowered the dish, ducking his head in apology. "And I must say this makes it look like you've never waited at a big occasion in your life."

"My lady," Jabal barked, "I have no idea where Mr. Whyte is going with this, but it is clearly a last desperate attempt to sow doubts in the mind of the jury. I repeat that it is irrelevant and purposeful misdirection. Mr. Merriweather should be dismissed with the court's apologies, and we should move to closing statements."

Fotheringham was watching the footage and glancing at Merriweather who sat, red-faced and sweating, in the witness box.

"My lady," Hilary said quietly. "Would you be willing for me to just ask one more question before sustaining Mr. Jabal's objection?"

Fotheringham tapped her pencil, weighing up Merriweather, who glanced at her nervously then away.

"Very well. But Mr. Jabal is right, counsel. I won't have this drawn out any longer than is necessary. So if there is something of significance in this footage that Mr. Merriweather can help us with, I suggest you get to it."

"Of course," Hilary said, rewinding to where the server set down the first silver dish. "I just want to ask you again, one more time, Mr. Merriweather. What dish are you serving here?"

Merriweather squirmed in his seat. He glanced back to Dom, who sat with a face like thunder, his eyes locked on the TV screen. Amelia, pale and wide-eyed, sat stiffly in her seat behind him. Eloise was stony-faced, her back rigid, her hard gaze locked on Merriweather.

"I told you already. I don't remember."

"Mrs. Hart provided us with a copy of the menu from that night," Hilary said. "So I can tell the court, if you want me to. Unless you'd rather have a quiet word with the prosecution in private?"

Merriweather's cheeks puffed. His hands were curled into fists. He breathed heavily through his nose but didn't reply.

"Okay, Mr. Merriweather. You had your chance. It's Maafe, a West African stew made from peanuts." Hilary gestured at Merriweather's wrist. "You wear a medic alert bracelet. It is for your severe peanut allergy, isn't that right?"

"Yeah, I'm allergic," Merriweather snapped. "I can still... I mean... I ain't eating it, am I?"

"You went into anaphylactic shock in my office just because you were in the same room as a peanut butter sandwich. You," he said, pointing at the screen, "would never have been able to go anywhere near this dish."

"Objection," Jabal stammered, his own face red. "Is Mr. Whyte really implying that the man in this video is not Mr. Merriweather?"

"You worked as a stunt double before you worked for the Hart family, isn't that right?" Hilary went on without pausing. "I'm sure you met many men with builds and looks similar to your own who all knew a thing or two about mimicking body language. Too bad your friend didn't remember about the peanuts."

"You're talking bollocks," Merriweather snapped. "Don't you think someone would have noticed if it weren't me?"

"Perhaps they did, perhaps they didn't," Hilary said, resisting a glance at Amelia. "It was a busy night, a very important night for your employers. You are a valued employee, but do you really think the Harts would note the serving staff closely on an occasion like this?"

"This is fucking ridiculous."

"Mr. Merriweather," Fotheringham warned, "if you could watch your language."

"Sorry," he growled. "But the man's off his rocker."

"Am I?"

"Why the fu... Why would I send a *double* to do me job for me, huh?"

"Because at the time this footage was taken, you were in London killing Lizzie and Dean Wood."

All the color drained from Merriweather's face. Jabal was shouting more objections, but Fotheringham's replies and the shocked babble from the audience were all drowned out by the pulsing in Hilary's temples. He held Merriweather's look and didn't blink.

"Admit it," Hilary called over the noise. Fotheringham banged her gavel with more force and the hubbub died to an uneasy murmur. Jabal was still petitioning the judge to put an end to it, but Hilary raised his voice and kept his eyes on Merriweather. "You told me how protective you are of your master. Perhaps you learned of Lizzie's plans to blackmail him. Perhaps it was you she approached, knowing you would never let any scandal come to the family. You chose a busy night — one when even people who know you well might not notice if you weren't quite acting yourself — and took care of it. Took care of *him* — like you always have."

"*My lady —* "

"If I did it to protect him," Merriweather growled, "why would I do it on a night he weren't about, a night that might get *him* in trouble?"

"His decision not to attend the banquet was last-minute," Hilary said calmly. "Perhaps the event was to be both your alibis. But my client's change of plans ruined everything."

"This really has gone far enough — " Jabal shouted above the tumult. Fotheringham banged her gavel until silence fell.

"Overruled, Mr. Jabal," she said with a keen look at Merriweather. "Mr. Merriweather, if you have an explanation for this, now is the time to give it."

"I'm telling you, it's bollocks," Merriweather insisted. "If I thought Master Dominic were gonna end up in prison for something I did, I would've said, wouldn't I?"

"Unless you, like the rest of us, were gambling that he'd never be convicted on so little proof?"

"You're wrong—"

"Then, when it looked like the trial might be going the wrong way, you planted the silencer behind Mr. Bukhari's house and tipped off the police—"

"*No*—"

"We don't know the whole truth. Not yet. But I can think of no other reason why this man," Hilary said, pointing at the screen, "appeared at the banquet that night pretending to be Mr. Merriweather."

"That's *me*," Merriweather persisted.

"It's not, sir," Hilary said. "We can adjourn and subpoena your GP if necessary—"

"You're wrong. You're all *wrong*."

"Mr. Merriweather," Hilary said with finality, "whatever you've done, or why, you did it for my client. If he's convicted of this crime, he goes to prison. Are you really going to let him pay for your actions with his life?"

"Objection, my lady," Jabal's voice was edged in ice. "Manipulative."

"Sustained," Fotheringham said, and Hilary wondered if her implacable face had tightened. "I think you've made your point, Mr. Whyte."

Hilary inclined his head. "Just one more question, my lady?"

Fotheringham peered at Merriweather then at Jabal. "One more."

"My lady—" Jabal protested.

"Make it count, Mr. Whyte," the judge said, speaking volumes with her eyes.

Hilary met Merriweather's eye, his pulse pounding in his neck. Merriweather's jaw bulged. His collar looked too tight. Fire was burning in his mud-brown eyes.

"Mr. Merriweather," Hilary said calmly, "did you kill Lizzie and Dean Wood?"

It seemed everyone in the room held their breath. Hilary's palms itched. He watched the emotions chase each other through the man's eyes. Finally, they slid to Dom. Dom met his servant's gaze, his eyes dark with anger and pain. Amelia's lips were pressed together. Eloise stared hard enough that Hilary expected Merriweather to erupt into flame. Beck's face was carefully schooled but Hilary knew her well enough to recognize the mix of excitement and terror brightening her eyes.

The man dragged his gaze back to Hilary. He took a shaking breath.

"Yes," he said. "Yes, I did."

Chapter Fourteen

The audience and jury were hustled from the room amidst much chatter and disruption. As soon as the room was emptied of public, Merriweather was arrested and escorted out of the room by security and Fotheringham called all counsel into her chambers.

"Hilary." Dom grabbed his elbow, but the usher called him again.

"Boss…" Beck prompted.

Dom's eyes were bright with a thousand unsaid things, his grip on Hilary's elbow tight.

"Go," Hilary said, nodding to the exit. "We'll talk later."

Hilary felt Dom's eyes on him until the judge's door closed between them.

"If this witness is telling the truth," Fotheringham began, "then this trial needs to be adjourned and the case reopened."

"Merriweather is lying. He was manipulated into confessing by the defense, my lady," Augustine said, giving Hilary a look.

"That's not true, my lady," Hilary said. "Have the footage of the banquet looked at again. Question the attendees, the other serving staff—"

"What I want to know is why this hasn't been looked into already," Fotheringham demanded, glaring at the prosecution. "Here we are, weeks into this trial, with those poor parents desperate for a result. And only *now* do we know a key associate of the accused has lied about his alibi."

"We don't know he lied, my lady," Augustine tried, but Fotheringham cut her off with a look.

"The man's allergy is so severe that it's in the risk assessment for this trial," she said. "And I have checked that menu myself. The second course was peanut stew. There is no way Bruce Merriweather is the man in that video."

"With all due respect, my lady," Jabal said, steepling his fingers, "it is surely up to the jury to decide whether that has any impact on this case."

"How could it *not*?" Hilary said.

"Even if he really is the killer," Augustine stated, "and that's a big 'if', I'd bet my life he did it on your client's orders. It doesn't mean the defendant's innocent, just because he didn't pull the trigger himself."

"You're wrong," Hilary snapped. Augustine's surprise flattened her face and Jabal gave him a sharp look.

"That's not what our client's on trial for, and you know it," Beck said with a warning look at Hilary "If that's the case you want to make, we need a mistrial and the case reopening."

"We can't," Augustine snapped back. "Not now. We're too close."

"Don't you think you should at least look into it?" Beck said with a helpless gesture.

"We followed the evidence," Augustine argued. "This turn of events doesn't prove —"

"He *confessed*," Beck said, her control finally slipping. "You can see it in his face. The man bloody did it."

"Please," Fotheringham said raising a hand. "I understand this is tense, but we are professionals here. And justice for the victims and their family is what's important."

"We wholeheartedly agree," Augustine stated. "So let us deliver our closing statements and let the jury decide."

"You're really going to let this go on? When another man has confessed —?" Hilary started.

"There's nothing to link Merriweather to the victims, apart from your client—" Augustine snapped back.

"Only because you haven't looked," Hilary replied.

"My lady," Jabal objected plaintively.

"Enough," Fotheringham said, standing. "Mr. Whyte, I'm sorry, but the confession is not enough to adjourn the trial if the prosecution doesn't want to change the angle of its inquiry. And that's your final decision, is it, Miss Augustine?"

Hilary watched the prosecutor narrowly. Her arms were folded, her eyes hard. Jabal looked doubtful. Finally, Augustine looked at Hilary. "We go on."

Jabal's face fell and Beck's tightened. Hilary struggled to decide how to feel, hope chasing doubt around his head like storm debris washing down a drain.

"As if the bloody *butler* did it," Beck whispered furiously, making a noise that was half-laugh, half-scoff as they walked down the corridor. "You really couldn't write it. And I'm more bloody confused now than I was at the start of this mess."

Hilary was unable to find his voice to answer.

Dom was stricken and pale when Hilary entered the anteroom they'd been allocated. Amelia was sat next to him, holding his hand. Hilary fought a stab of jealousy.

"Where's Eloise?" Hilary asked, looking round the otherwise empty room.

"She left to meet the other lawyers," Amelia said. "To get ahead of this before the story breaks."

Hilary nodded, aware of Beck standing at the door and Amelia's eyes on him, even as Dom's remained fixed on the floor.

"You really think he did it?" Amelia said softly.

"Yes. I think he did."

"But...why?"

"I don't know. Maybe Lizzie really was planning something against Dominic, and Merriweather found out."

"But how? Merriweather never met Lizzie. I doubt he even knew who she was. And he couldn't have paid her that ten thousand—"

"I don't know," Hilary repeated. "I'm not a detective. The police may get to the bottom of it, if he talks..."

Amelia shook her head, gazing at her pale-faced husband. Hilary looked away.

"So what happens now?" she asked.

"Closing statements," Hilary said. "Then the jury will deliberate."

Amelia stared. "The trial's continuing?"

"The prosecution wants to carry on," Hilary stated. "The judge has agreed."

"But Merriweather confessed —"

"Augustine is not convinced," Hilary said dourly.

"She saw that man on the tape," Amelia said. "What other explanation can there be?"

"The tape is tenuous," Hilary said. "I made it sound convincing because it convinced me, but it's not proof. No one has mentioned Merriweather not being at the banquet before now. You were there, Mrs. Hart-Gosford, and you never mentioned —"

"I didn't notice," Amelia cut him off, her face pained. "I was too busy worrying where Dominic was to notice anything. But seeing the tape back... I can't believe I didn't see it at the time."

Hilary shrugged helplessly. "None of us did. And Jabal is right. We've noticed it so late that it comes across as desperate."

"So Dominic could still go to prison?" Amelia asked disbelievingly.

"It comes down to the case we've made," Hilary said gently. "And the case they've made. But I hope, now, the jury will doubt your husband's guilt as much as we do."

"Hope isn't much to go on," Amelia said.

"It's all we have," Dom said. He finally raised his head. "It's all we ever had. Mr. Whyte, could we speak in private?"

"Dominic..." Amelia started but he stood and put a hand on her arm. She seemed to read something in his face because she nodded and left the room, sending Hilary an unreadable look over her shoulder as she did so. Beck lingered in the doorway until Hilary sent her a reassuring smile, then she, too, stepped out, closing the door behind her.

Hilary met Dom's solemn look with unease prickling up his spine.

"You should have asked me first."

"I'm sorry?"

"Before you went after Merriweather. You should have asked me."

Hilary frowned. "I was doing my job."

"I know," Dom said. "But—"

"He killed them, Dom."

"Merriweather is a good man."

"He's a murderer."

"We don't know that."

Hilary took a moment to measure his response.

"You're fond of the man. I get that…I think. But can't you see it's affecting your judgment?"

"You stated your personal connection to me didn't affect yours."

"I was lying."

Dom's eyebrows drew together. Hilary felt warmth flood his face.

"I thought you did it, Dom." Dom's face shifted. Hilary made himself continue. "I told myself I wasn't judging you. I was taking you at your word. Doing my job. But, looking back…"

Dom began to turn away. Hilary grabbed his arm. "But now I know I was wrong," he said. "My point is you can't always tell when your feelings are getting in the way."

"Merriweather has always been there for me," Dom breathed. "Took me home when I was too drunk to see. Broke up the fights. Listened to me when I was raving." He winced. "I just can't believe he would do this to protect me, when it's landed me here" — he looked around the chamber — "at the mercy of twelve strangers who will judge me just like you did."

"We've done a lot of good work here today," Hilary said, but Dom shook his head.

"Perhaps this is right," Dom whispered. "Perhaps this is justice."

"You don't mean that."

"I didn't kill anyone, Hilary, but I've hurt people. Hurt you. And it looks like Lizzie and Dean were hurt because of me, too. Perhaps it's right that I've ended up here. Perhaps I deserve this —"

"You're innocent, Dom. You shouldn't go to prison for this."

"But perhaps I should go for everything else."

Hilary's heart ached. He couldn't see any trace of the malicious, mocking boy that had teased and bullied him, knocked him to the ground in the changing rooms to stop him from biting his arm after he'd called him one name too many. There was no trace of the person who had lurked in his nightmares and twisted the knife of insecurity in his guts for most of his life.

This man was lost, broken. The owner of a past he was so thoroughly ashamed of that it haunted his every waking moment.

Before he had time to think about what he was doing, Hilary had put his hand on his jaw, drawn his face down and kissed him. Dom stood unmoving for a breath then sighed, opened his mouth and stepped into Hilary's embrace. Hilary slid his arms around him and held him close, felt him lean in. Hilary held him, kissed him, breathed deep the heady, bittersweet scents of his vulnerability and fear.

Dom broke away, breathless, and pressed his forehead to Hilary's.

"At least it's over," he whispered.

Hilary couldn't find any more words. He took a deep breath, holding tight onto Dom's arms. He opened his mouth to try to say something but started when someone knocked on the door. They stepped away from each other as the door opened. Beck's expression tightened as she glanced between them. Hilary resisted straightening his suit.

"They're waiting, boss," she said.

Hilary nodded. Dom left the room without looking back. Beck put a hand on his arm as Hilary tried to pass. Her face was unusually serious.

"Boss…"

"Not now, Beck," he said, fighting a blush with all his might.

"No, now, Hilary."

Hilary stiffened but allowed himself to be pulled back into the room. She shut the door. She stood with her arms folded, face intent. "Your private life is far beyond my business," she said. "But—"

"Beck—"

"Just let me say this," she said, raising a hand, "then I promise I'll never bring it up again. Okay?"

Hilary took in her expression then nodded.

She sighed, face softening. "Just be careful, boss. I mean…really careful."

Hilary fought the emotion that threatened to come through in his voice. "I'm always careful."

She seemed about to say something else but instead nodded and opened the door. "Oh, the twins are here."

Hilary blinked. "Where?"

Beck pointed. Maxwell and Minnie stood in the corridor, scanning the crowd filtering back into court.

They both brightened as Hilary approached.

"What are you doing here?" Hilary asked.

"It's all over Twitter," Maxwell said as Minnie pulled him into a tight hug. She stepped back, her small mouth pinched, and Maxwell held out his phone.

Hilary scanned the list of Internet articles and posts about Merriweather's arrest.

"Jesus," he swore, shaking his head. "Someone's leaked it."

"Someone confessed?" Minnie pressed. "Someone else?"

"I can't talk about it," Hilary said, glancing up as the usher appeared at the courtroom doors, gesturing at him. "Guys, it's great of you to come, but—"

"We're staying," Maxwell said firmly.

Hilary managed a smile. "Thanks."

They followed Hilary in and took seats near the back. The room was more crowded than ever. The usher, seeing Hilary return, opened the inner door and the jury filed in, followed by the judge.

"And we are back in session," Fotheringham said, raising her voice to be heard. "If the prosecution would like to give their closing statement?"

"Thank you, my lady," Jabal said, standing. Augustine sat stiff in her seat and didn't meet Hilary's eyes as Jabal made his way to the jury box. Hilary looked to Dom. He looked drawn but oddly calm, the storm settled in his eyes.

"Ladies and gentlemen," the barrister started, his hands behind his back and his face set in solemn lines. "This has been an emotionally draining few weeks for all involved—for yourselves, for the witnesses and most of all for the victims' family," he said, offering a nod to the Woods who sat, looking small and tired, in the front row. "The prosecution has laid before you everything the police turned up in their investigation. The defense has gone to great pains to make a point of the lack of evidence and the nature of DI McGarry's personal judgment of his client. But, as she said, when your judgment is backed up by years of experience and the expertise of scientists and forensic analysts, it is just as important as hard proof." Jabal glanced back at Dom.

"Don't react," Hilary breathed, but Dom appeared to be in a dream state, staring ahead without reaction.

"Whatever the defense has said about the evidence," the barrister continued. "Whatever they have claimed about body-doubles…even considering Mr. Merriweather's confession…" Jabal raised an eyebrow. "Remember that man's loyalty. His position. The fact that this is far from the first time Mr. Hart-Gosford's trusty servant has cleaned up his mess." He scanned the faces of the jury, his frown deepening. "And remember that hair, ladies and gentlemen. Mr. Hart-Gosford's hair. It's been proved to be his, whatever the defense has implied about lab errors or tampering. It was his and it was at the crime scene." Jabal raised his hands. "If everything the defendant claimed is true, how did it get there?"

Jabal began to pace, his expression thoughtful. "What this comes down to is that Mr. Hart-Gosford had the motive, the means and the opportunity. His DNA was found at the scene. He has a history of violence and problems with alcohol and drug abuse." Jabal stopped and raised his head. "I trust the police. I trust their work. Their belief that the defendant committed this crime is anchored in a foundation of evidence and experience. They believe he deserves to be punished for what he has done. For the victims' sake. For their parents' sakes." He spread his hands. "For all our sakes."

He paced again. "I'll close with this. Be confident in your judgment. Be confident in what you've been shown, in what you believe. Then you can be confident that justice for Lizzie and Dean will be done." Jabal bowed to the jury and returned to his seat.

Hilary's mouth was dry. His limbs wouldn't work. He looked to his brother and sister, pale and earnest, at the back of the room. He saw reassurance in their eyes but still couldn't move.

Then he felt a hand on his arm. He looked around. Dom was gazing at him, his mouth soft, eyes earnest.

"I believe in you," he breathed.

The roaring in his ears died away. His pulse calmed. He drew in a deep breath. He stood. He strode to the jury box, a new warmth chasing the chills of uncertainty from his limbs.

"Ladies and gentlemen," he began, gratified that his voice carried. "Mr. Jabal is absolutely correct when he talks about the emotional toll the last few weeks must have taken on everyone here." He met the eyes of each jury member in turn as he spoke. "These young people have had their lives brutally taken, leaving a shattered family behind. That is tragic. That is wrong. And punishing the person responsible is not only just but necessary." His expression softened. "But the fact of the matter is, my client is not the responsible party."

He spent a moment listening to the expectant silence and scanning the faces of the men and women in the jury box, all focused on him.

"I'm not going to say the police's charges were based on nothing. The prosecution is right when he talks about my client's troubled history, his controversial public persona, his violent past. But who we really are is so much more than who we have been." He paused, probing for the old uncertainty, the ghost of hurt, but found only a curious, steady glow. "If you condemn him for his past…that's this case closed. That's Lizzie's and Dean's names filed away in some police archive, never to be looked at again, whilst their killer, a man who has admitted to this crime in front of all of you, goes free. Because make no mistake, if Mr. Hart-Gosford is convicted of this murder, the police will not and cannot look at Mr. Merriweather's confession in any more detail." Hilary lifted his arms. "Seems crazy I know…but the confession is not enough at this stage."

He looked at the floor, took a breath and raised his eyes again. "My client's reputation is what decided his guilt for the police and the prosecution. If you take that same tactic, the killer will go free. Lizzie and Dean's parents will have to live knowing he's still out there." Hilary stepped forward and lowered his voice. "I'll repeat Mr. Jabal's last words. Be confident in your judgment. Just make sure you're judging the right person."

He was shaking as he returned to his seat. The air was thick with silence.

"The jury may now retire to consider their verdict," Fotheringham said and banged her gavel.

"Blimey," Beck murmured as she gathered papers together without meeting his eye. "Well…you have me convinced, boss."

Hilary started to collect his own things without answering.

"Thank you, Hilary," Dom murmured, leaning close.

"Just doing my job," Hilary said without looking up. He turned to Amelia and saw uncertainty glinting in her gray eyes. "The court officials will find you somewhere to wait. Do you want anything? Coffee?"

"No, thank you. How long do you think it will be?"

"There's no way to know," Hilary said. He felt drained. A pit had opened up in his stomach and he was suddenly more desperate for a cigarette than he had been in years. "Could well be several hours...or days. Just try your best to relax as much as possible."

"Will you wait with us?" Dom asked.

Hilary swallowed. "Of course. We both will," he said. "We'll just get some coffee first. Beck?"

"Sounds good, boss," she said and made for the door. An official led Amelia and Dom away then Hilary followed, slower, aware of all the eyes fixed on his client.

Maxwell and Minnie were waiting just outside the door.

"Jesus, Hil," Maxwell said in a slightly breathless voice, "that was amazing. I really believed you."

"It was the truth."

"He really didn't do it?" Maxwell asked carefully.

"He really didn't."

Minnie smiled. "Told you, Max. People can change."

Maxwell raised his russet eyebrows. "Well then, I owe the bench nurses a drink."

"Oh, Max," Minnie scolded.

"What? The man's a psycho. I thought it was a safe bet."

"He's not a psycho," Hilary said. "He's... complicated."

They both looked at him.

"Has something happened, Hil?" Minnie asked, eyeing him warily.

"Happened?"

"You just... Something's different..." Minnie said, fiddling with her necklace, troubled eyes fixed on his face.

"He's not been fucking you about, has he?" Maxwell said, freckled face flushing with anger.

"No," Hilary said hurriedly then, more firmly, "No. He hasn't."

Minnie looked thoughtful whilst Maxwell looked doubtful.

"Mum and Dad have been worried, you know," Maxwell went on, his tone softer. "They'd never say so, but they remember that summer. They remember you not leaving your room for days, barely eating —"

"I didn't know who I was," Hilary said, "what I wanted to be. But I'm not that kid anymore."

"We know, Hil," Minnie said, squeezing his arm. "But you'll always be our little brother, see?"

"I know," Hilary said, warmth stealing through him. "Thank you."

"Well, I never thought I'd say this, but rooting for Dom Gosford, mate," Maxwell said, smile thin but eyes friendly.

Hilary managed a smile. "Thanks."

"Hil, you look done in. Can't you go home?" Minnie asked.

Hilary shook his head. "I need to be here at least until they reach a verdict, unless they retire for the night first."

"Well, you'd better get that coffee," Maxwell said, checking his phone. "And I'd better get to my shift. But call if you need us, yeah?"

"I will," Hilary said. "Thanks, guys."

"Any time, Hilary," Minnie said with a smile. "I need to rush, too. The Madagascan vanilla shipment is arriving at the bakery tonight. Jasper's going to love the crème brûlée cups." She beamed.

It took Hilary a fraction of a second too long to smile. Thankfully, Maxwell was asking Minnie for a lift and neither of them seemed to notice.

He walked with them to the exit, kissed Minnie's cheek, accepted a shoulder-squeeze off his brother then waved them into the afternoon rain. They left with their heads bent together, faces intent, back in their own private world, and Hilary tried to ignore the clench in his chest.

Beck waved from her table in the courtroom café when he appeared in the doorway. "I thought you might want to sit here for a bit," she said, pushing a pudding-bowl-sized cup of black coffee toward him.

"Thanks," he said, sitting and sipping the hot, bitter liquid, willing it to douse his craving for nicotine.

"You've given him the best chance possible," she said, sipping her own drink and staring out into the rain. "It's in the lap of the gods now."

"Don't remind me," he said, putting his cup down in the saucer with care.

Beck sighed and leaned her elbows on the table. "I'm sorry…about before."

He shook his head. "It's fine…"

"No, it wasn't my place. I'm sorry. I just give a shit, that's all." Hilary looked up. The unfamiliar serious look was back on her face. "You know that, right? That I give a shit?"

"I…yeah," Hilary fumbled. "I do. I owe you, Beck." She shook her head, but Hilary carried on before she could protest. "No, I do. You're the one who has done the grunt work here. And you were right…about Eloise, about putting Dom — Mr. Hart-Gosford — on the stand." One of her eyebrows lifted but she didn't comment. "You should seriously look at becoming a barrister, you know."

She laughed. "What? With the wig and gown malarkey? Not while I still draw breath. Besides…" She grinned. "Perhaps I like working with you. You ever consider that?"

Hilary stared at her.

"You told Sara Holden you don't have a best friend," she said, the spark returning to her eye. "That pissed me off, you know."

"Sorry. I am. I just…" He looked out into the rain, feeling raw. "I don't always read people very well."

"I think you read them far too well," Beck said, draining her cup. "But you have no idea how to handle it when they care." She put the cup down and gazed into it. "It happens, you know. Especially if things have been…hard, in the past. I know. I do." She lifted her gaze. "You just gotta be willing to re-learn some stuff. To see when things aren't good for you. And to see when they *are* and have the guts to hang on to it."

Hilary stirred his coffee, discomfort unfolding in his stomach. "Where's this coming from, Beck?"

"Shit, I dunno," she said with a nervous laugh. "We're both sleep-deprived, I guess? And I need a fucking drink." She stared around the busy café with a frown. "Promise me we can go for a pint after all this, whatever the verdict."

Hilary smiled. "Yeah, sure. Sounds good."

Beck nodded decisively and stood. "I'll go see if Morticia and Gomez need anything. You take your time with that, you hear? Get some headspace."

"Thanks," Hilary said. "I really mean it."

She returned his smile and left.

Hilary leaned back into the chair and sipped the strong coffee. Waiting for a verdict still knotted his insides, but now, for some reason, his mind felt clear. Calm.

He jumped when his personal phone buzzed in his pocket.

Jazz calling…

A rush went up his spine. He stared at the screen then, finally, hung up and returned the phone to his pocket. He drained his cup and stood. The phone buzzed again with the short burst of an incoming message, but he didn't look.

Dom was standing at the window of the anteroom when Hilary entered. Amelia sat with Beck on the sofa, engaged in quiet conversation. Hilary settled at a table, making an attempt at reviewing his notes. He stole glances at Dom, but he never looked up from his somber examination of the rain-washed car park. Hilary was overcome with an almost painful desire to touch him, hold him, find out what he was thinking, to tell him he'd tried. *Really* tried. He willed him to at least look at him, but he remained transfixed.

The minutes crawled into hours. Beck went for more coffee, bottles of water and sandwiches. They drank the coffee in silence, ignoring the food and not making eye contact.

"They must be calling it a night soon," Beck said as the hands on the wall clock crept toward nine p.m. Darkness had fallen outside. Amelia was talking to her mother on the phone. Dom sat staring blankly at the wall.

Hilary was drawing breath to say something, anything, to get Dom to look at him when a court official opened the door.

"The jury has reached a verdict."

Silence flooded the room like icy water.

"That's…good, isn't it?" Amelia ventured, putting her phone back in her bag. "That they've decided already?"

Hilary and Beck exchanged glances.

"Let's find out," Dom said, standing and buttoning his jacket. He held the door for Beck and Amelia but Hilary put a hand on his arm before he could follow them.

"Dom," he breathed, his tongue heavy in his mouth. "Whatever happens, whatever they decided, I want you to know…"

"It's okay, Hilary…"

"No," Hilary said. "Let me say this." He took a breath. "Whatever the outcome of this is, I want you to know…I believe in you."

A smile turned up one corner of Dom's full lips. "Then it was all worth it," he murmured and kissed Hilary's forehead. Hilary fought for more words, but none came.

They returned to the courtroom in silence.

Chapter Fifteen

Hilary's nerves buzzed as the jury resumed their seats. It seemed everyone in the room held their breath as Fotheringham examined them over her glasses.

"Has the jury reached a verdict?"

"We have, my lady," the spokeswoman said, standing and offering a piece of paper to the usher.

"Would the defendant please stand?"

Dom and Beck both stood. Hilary somehow managed to do the same, though he had to steady himself with a hand on the table.

The usher unfolded the paper. "On the two charges of first-degree murder, the jury finds the defendant Dominic Hart-Gosford...not guilty on either count."

Hilary clutched the table. The audience bubbled with shock. Beck inhaled sharply. The prosecution sat rigid in their seats, Augustine's fists clenched in front of her.

Hilary was vaguely aware of Fotheringham banging her gavel for order as he turned to face Dom. The color had drained from his face but he looked younger, the lines smoothed away and eyes wide, lips parted in shock. His gaze fell on Hilary and swam, but then Amelia was pulling him into an embrace. Dom took his wife in his arms and buried his face in her neck and Hilary blinked, his face heating, and turned his back.

The commotion continued to swell as Fotheringham followed the jury from the room. The audience began to file out in ones and twos, chattering, pointing, their attention divided between Dom and the Woods still sitting in the front row. Hilary's stomach clenched when he took in the bewildered-looking couple staring up at Augustine as she spoke to them, her face tight with regret.

Dom straightened and followed his gaze. He drew breath to speak but Amelia took his arm and guided him toward the doors.

"We should catch up," Beck said, shouldering her bag. "There'll be press…" She looked over to where Augustine was helping Karen Wood to her feet. The woman's face was white as a sheet. Her husband sat staring at nothing, looking thin and hollow. "They'll get their closure, boss," she whispered. "Just not today."

Hilary nodded and allowed Beck to lead him out of the courtroom.

Augustine caught up to them in the corridor. Her face was grim, but she held out her hand. "I guess I should say well done, Whyte," she said stiffly. "That was quite the piece of theater."

"It was the truth," he said, shaking her hand.

She grimaced. "A version of it, maybe."

Hilary watched as two security guards led the bent figures of the Woods to a side entrance. "Put

Merriweather away, Laurette," Hilary said in a low voice. "Whatever it takes."

She narrowed her eyes. "Even if it means re-arresting your client for joint enterprise?"

"He acted alone."

"Even if he did, he did it for your client…to keep his secrets hidden." Her eyes glinted and Hilary went cold under her penetrating gaze. "Can you really say Gosford's blameless?"

"Blameless? No." Hilary glanced at Dom standing at the glass courthouse doors with his wife, camera flashes lighting up the night and washing his tired face white. Their eyes met down the busy corridor. "But who is?"

Augustine gave him a keen look, shook Beck's hand and left.

"Ready?" Beck said as they reached the doors and saw the crowds of press waiting on the steps, jostling with their umbrellas for space near the front.

"Ready as I'll ever be," he said, managing a reassuring smile for Dom and Amelia. "How are you doing?"

"Thank you, Mr. Whyte," Amelia said, emotion tightening her voice and silver eyes bright with unshed tears. "For everything. You've saved us both."

"Just doing my job," Hilary said. Dom was gazing at him with a hundred unknowable things storming in his eyes and Hilary fervently wished they were alone. He looked away, out of the doors to the assembled crowds. "Let's get this done, shall we? I have a statement drafted—"

"Let me speak to them," Dom said.

Beck looked at Hilary, and Hilary, after a moment examining Dom's face, nodded.

"Boss—"

"He knows what to say," Hilary murmured, earning a nod from Dom, and opened the door.

The Hart-Gosfords stood with their backs straight, their eyes clear. Something sharp dug into Hilary's stomach at the sight of them standing arm in arm, presenting a united front to the surging throng of reporters. Dom started speaking in a strong, firm voice. Silence rippled through the crowd as the reporters stretched their microphones and dictaphones forward.

He thanked the jury for their decision. He stated that he was glad the Ministry of Justice was now on the right path for securing closure for the Wood family. He wanted to again thank his wife and his family for their support. He paused, blinking the rain from his eyelashes as the reporters crushed closer.

"I also want to thank my legal team for their tireless work and unwavering belief in me. I owe them my life…my future. And I intend to continue to prove myself worthy of the verdict they helped secure today."

The shouted questions commenced as soon as he'd finished, but Dom looked back at Hilary and, for a moment, it was like they were the only two people in the universe. But then Amelia was urging him through the crowd toward a waiting limousine.

The car pulled away and the reporters began to disperse. Soon all Hilary could hear were the screech and honk of traffic and the rain hammering on his umbrella.

"So," Beck said eventually, "how about that pint?"

* * * *

Hilary downed the vodka soda and ordered another whilst the barman was still pulling Beck's lager. They took the drinks to a table and Hilary sighed as he sat, feeling a weight roll off him, even though his chest hadn't stopped aching.

Beck raised her pint. "To innocent arseholes."

Hilary smiled and clinked his glass off hers. They both drank and Beck grinned.

"You did it, boss."

"*We* did it."

"Yeah, fine," she said. "*We* did it."

They drank quietly, Beck scrolling through her phone and shaking her head. "My Christ," she said. "You wouldn't believe we'd won, reading some of this."

"Don't look at it," Hilary said, swirling the ice in his drink. "There'll be something else for them to be outraged about tomorrow."

"Hopefully charges against Bruce Merriweather." She shook her head and put her phone aside. "Do you really think he was acting alone, boss?" she added quietly, not meeting Hilary's eyes.

"Yes. I do."

Beck shook her head again. "What makes someone take it into their head to do something that extreme?"

"Loyalty. Love. Protectiveness." He shrugged. "Stupidly powerful sometimes, that stuff."

"You can say that again," Beck said as she watched Hilary over the rim of her glass.

Hilary lifted his drink again as his phone began buzzing on the table.

Jazz calling....

Beck glanced at the phone then at Hilary's face. "I'll call him tomorrow," he muttered, disconnecting the call.

"None of my business, boss," Beck said quietly. "Never was."

Hilary tried to unpack that but then sighed when his work phone pinged.

"Never ends, does it?" Beck muttered as her own started ringing. She moved off to a quiet corner to answer and Hilary opened his text.

I need to thank you properly. Come to the flat. D.

Hilary's skin tingled in anticipation, sudden, hot desire scorching the fatigue right out of his body. He started as Beck returned to her seat and hurriedly pocketed the phone.

"Janice," she said as she finished her drink. "Gunnerson wants a meeting. Probably the next bloody case already. Another?" she said, nodding at his empty glass.

"You have another," he said, fishing the company credit card from his wallet. "Or several. You've earned it. But I've got to go."

She took the card and lifted an eyebrow. "You sure?"

"Definitely. And take tomorrow off. I'll see you Monday."

He left without processing whether or not she replied.

It was only as he climbed out of the Uber outside the Greenwich apartment building that Hilary realized he'd left his umbrella behind, but the freezing rain didn't dampen the fire burning under his skin.

Dom was waiting for the lift doors to open. He'd shed his jacket and tie. His shirt was open at the collar. His hair was disheveled, like he'd run a hand through it. The color had returned to his face, but the darkness swimming in the depths of his eyes was more tumultuous than ever. He took in the sight of Hilary dripping on his carpet with something heated stealing through his face.

Everything Hilary had planned to say skimmed out of his head like a stone bouncing over the water.

"Hilary —"

Hearing his name spoken in that deep, throaty voice, tight with desire, snapped the last threads of Hilary's control. He shoved Dom against the wall, pressing his body against him and claiming his mouth. He thrust his fingers into his hair, pulling his head down and plunging his tongue deep.

A low sound, almost helpless, escaped Dom, and he tugged at Hilary's sodden coat. Hilary let it and his suit jacket fall to the floor then fumbled at Dom's shirt buttons as Dom unknotted his tie.

It dropped to the floor along with Dom's shirt, then Dom was urging him back, never breaking the desperate, clumsy kiss, all teeth and tongue, or his systematic removal of Hilary's clothing.

Somehow they made it to the bedroom and Hilary was sinking into the vast, soft duvet, pulling Dom with him. Dom moaned deep in his throat as his hands ran down Hilary's sides to cup his arse. Hilary gasped and thrust upward, his cock already hard and aching. Dom's large, thick length was rigid and pulsing against his stomach. Hilary shifted, parting his legs so Dom lay between them, and arched against him, reveling in the hot skin grazing the sensitive flesh.

Dom let out a shuddering breath, dug his fingers into Hilary's hips and trailed heated kisses along his jaw to his ear.

"You saved me," he panted. "You saved me, Hilary."

"God, Dom," Hilary breathed, closing his eyes, running his hands down the hard, muscled back, trembling to feel his powerful body weighing him down, surrounding and embracing his own.

Dom mouthed his earlobe and slid a hand between their bodies to grasp their cocks. Hilary whimpered, tilting his head so Dom could suck on his neck while he worked them together.

"I'm going to show you everything," Dom purred against his skin. "I'm going to show you just how fucking amazing you are."

"Dom," he started but then Dom was taking his nipple in his mouth and the power of speech abandoned him.

He felt loose and raw, exposed but wonderfully free. Dom moved down the bed, his mouth burning on his belly. Golden fire surged in Hilary's abdomen, and he heard the noises he was making as if from a great distance.

Dom's lips left his stomach, and he felt his hot breath against his cock. He opened his eyes and stopped Dom with a hand on his shoulder.

"Wait," he forced out of his tight throat. Dom paused, gazing at him through his eyelashes. His thick, weeping cock was flushed and hard in one hand. The other was tense on Hilary's thigh and his open mouth, red and wet with kissing, hovered over Hilary's erection. The sight alone almost brought him to the edge, but he clutched Dom's shoulder and the sheets and fought for control. "Please, Dom…"

"Tell me, Hilary," he said huskily.

"I want you to fuck me," he rasped, his blood pounding in his wrists, neck, temples and groin. Color filled Dom's face and he clutched Hilary's thigh tighter.

"Are you sure?"

"Yes," Hilary said firmly. "I want it. Want you. *Now.*"

Dom let out a low, animalistic groan and climbed back up the bed and thrust his tongue into Hilary's mouth. Hilary whimpered and opened himself to him, digging his fingers into his arms. Dom crooked his knee and thrust against him and they both gasped.

"Ask me," Dom growled, grasping Hilary's cock and pumping it. "Ask me again."

"Fuck me, Dom," Hilary cried. "Now. *Please.*"

Dom dragged his teeth over his shoulder as he reached for the bedside cabinet. Hilary closed his eyes and buried himself in the bubbling sensations — the smell and weight of Dom, the powerful hand stroking him and that large, hard length pressing between his legs, trembling, tantalizing him.

A lube bottle clicked and the next thing he knew, Dom was pushing two fingers in at once.

Hilary cried out and his spine curled off the bed. It was sudden and Dom's fingers were large, but the urgency and desperation in the movements and the hot breaths against his neck chased heat through his veins and he gave himself up to the invasion, made himself relax and take the digits in.

"Tell me," Dom rasped in his ear. "Tell me when it's good."

"Deeper…" Hilary muttered, pushing against the fingers. Dom reached farther in, stretching and rubbing. "Ah, fuck," Hilary cried as Dom brushed against the sweet, sensitive spot deep within him that sent stars dancing across his vision. "There…"

"Here?" Dom breathed, nipping his earlobe as he repeated the motion.

Fire and lightning exploded in Hilary's belly. He grabbed the headboard with both hands and cried out.

"Fuck, Hilary," Dom rumbled in his ear, easing a third finger in. "You have no idea…no fucking idea how good you feel."

"Fuck, Dom," Hilary whimpered as Dom stretched and worked him with meticulous, gentle fingers. "Jesus. Hurry."

Dom grunted and took his weight onto his elbows as he reached in deep one more time. "Tell me how you want it."

"Face to face," Hilary begged before his brain had caught up. "Let me see you."

Dom kissed him, making nonsense sounds in his throat as he withdrew his fingers and tore open a condom packet. Then Hilary felt the blunt, lubricated head of Dom's sheathed cock pushing against his entrance.

Dom broke the kiss to suck in a deep breath as he began to push in. Hilary stopped breathing entirely.

"Christ," Dom gasped. "You… Jesus…it's so good. You must…tell me if I hurt you."

"Just do it."

"You must tell me," he said, his voice raspy with arousal, stopping with just the head inside Hilary, his whole body trembling. "Promise?"

"I promise," Hilary growled, grabbing Dom's arse and pulling him forward. "I will, I promise. I…"

His words trailed away into incoherence as the broad length slid into him, deeper, stretching, until Dom was all the way in. He stayed there, frozen, breathing hard as Hilary lay, dizzy with pleasure and the unfamiliar sensation. He felt so full, stretched and complete, and he wondered if anything would ever feel good in comparison again. But then Dom was rocking back on his knees, pulling partway out and pushing back in.

Hilary threw his head back and keened high in his throat. Dom kissed him, swallowing his cries as he pulled back, then pushed forward, sliding his hard, thick length even deeper. Hilary lifted his knees and groaned and again, Dom repeated the motion, pulling out then sliding back, painfully slowly, pushing hard, far, until Hilary's hips lifted off the bed and he was deeper inside Hilary than anyone had ever been before. Dom held himself there, quivering, clutching onto Hilary's wrists and pressing his forehead to his.

"I can't believe this," he breathed, almost completely withdrawing. "You're here, you're…ah…" He thrust in again, faster this time, dragging another strangled cry from Hilary.

"My God," Hilary panted, threading his hands through Dom's hair and planting kisses all over his face. "Don't stop."

Dom smiled, showing canines, his eyes burning into Hilary's, and thrust again, faster. "I'm not gonna be able to stop," he panted. "You must…please tell me…"

"It doesn't hurt," Hilary said through clenched teeth. "I swear. Harder."

Dom groaned and buried his face in Hilary's neck. He shifted his weight onto one elbow, lifted Hilary's leg, adjusted his angle and pulled back only to plunge deep again and again and again. He increased his pace and thrust harder, his powerful frame bunching and sweat breaking out on his skin. Hilary clutched the headboard tighter with one hand and dug his fingers into the small of Dom's back with the other, feeling the mass of his body moving above him, around him, in him.

A fire hotter than Hilary could ever remember lit inside him like a furnace. It spread, white and burning, up through his chest and along his arms. It flooded his head so he couldn't see or hear. He knew he was shouting—Dom's name, nonsense sounds, anything and everything in between—but he couldn't hear any of it. He was consumed by the blinding ecstasy that exploded inside him every time Dom pounded into him.

Time, fatigue, pain and worry lost all meaning. All that existed was pleasure, heat, the salty, intoxicating smell of Dom's skin and the sensation of his thick, hard flesh penetrating him over and over again, reaching parts of him that no one, not even himself, had ever explored before.

The world vanished behind a curtain of sparks. Dom cried his name and the storm that had swollen in Hilary's abdomen broke. Liquid fire and blinding light poured through him, and he let it sweep him away, drowning him in boiling starlight.

* * * *

Hilary accepted the glass of vodka from Dom without looking up. He'd lit the living room fire, and Hilary gazed into the flames, holding the tumbler of vodka but not drinking, the softness of Dom's dressing gown gentle against his skin. The delicate sensation of contentment was like a soap bubble around him. He kept very still, not even daring to taste the drink, knowing as soon as he allowed himself to think, it would burst.

"I don't know how to feel," Dom said softly.

The bubble popped. Hilary downed a large mouthful of burning vodka. "I don't either."

"I meant about the verdict," Dom said. "Not about you."

Hilary finally looked up. Dom's eyes were tired but still. His hair was damp from the shower and Hilary could smell that maddening shampoo he used. His dressing gown hung open over the firm, muscled chest, the dark hair tempting as Hilary remembered what it felt like between his fingers. He lifted his gaze with an effort.

"The verdict was a good thing. The right thing."

"It wasn't what those parents needed."

Hilary sipped his drink, the coldness chasing away the last of the heat lingering under his skin. "The police are on the right track now." Dom didn't speak. When Hilary looked up, he was staring into his whiskey. "What is it?"

"It just feels like we're missing something."

"Just because you want Merriweather to be innocent doesn't mean he is."

Dom gave him a heavy look. "That's not what I meant."

Hilary sighed, downed his drink and moved to the counter to pour himself another. "I'm afraid real life is rarely like the legal fiction. You never get all the answers."

"I'd like to meet them…"

"Who?"

"The parents."

Hilary turned to face him. "That is *not* a good idea."

"I need to see them. To apologize —"

"You didn't kill their children."

"It was still my fault."

"How?"

Dom's face was grave. "Merriweather did it for me. He said so."

Hilary sat on the coffee table and put his hand on Dom's knee. "You mustn't think like that."

"It's the truth."

"Even if it is, do you really think meeting with the Woods would make them feel better?"

"They need to know I'm sorry," Dom said. "That I never asked for this… It's better than them thinking I don't care."

"Better for them, or better for you?"

Dom's gaze slid to the floor. Hilary sighed and sat next to him. "It's okay to not know what to do with yourself. To want to do something to fix it all, even when it can't be fixed."

"So what do I do?"

"Nothing," Hilary said softly. "You'll come out the other side. But you can't force it better or to be over any quicker."

Dom's eye flickered. "When did you have to learn this?"

"We all have to learn it at some point."

Dom's face fell. "I'm sorry, Hilary," he said, voice hoarse.

"I know," Hilary said, squeezing his arm.

"I want to fix it," Dom said, staring into the fire. "But I only break things."

Hilary tapped his finger off the side of his glass. "Dom, there's something you should know…"

"What?"

"The reason I was like I was…why I am like I am. It wasn't you. Or…it wasn't *all* you."

Dom lifted his gaze, a questioning line between his brows.

"Don't get me wrong," he went on. "You were a five-star arsehole. You made me miserable…for years." Dom winced and Hilary looked away. "But then you left and…it didn't go away."

"What didn't?"

"The darkness. The fear." Hilary stared into the fire. His breathing was shallow. He felt cold but he didn't want to move, either closer to the fire or into Dom's warm arms, fearing either way he would get burned. "That summer after you left school…I sank low. Real low. I felt like everything was going to be dark forever. I had thought you were the problem. But you were gone, and everything was still…shit. Worse, even, because I couldn't just blame you anymore."

Dom rested his hand on his, but he didn't speak. Hilary felt like he was balanced on a cliff edge, gazing down into a dark, swirling sea below, and if he took one wrong step, he'd plummet down and never resurface.

"But," he continued, "eventually I realized that I hadn't just been fighting you. I was fighting everything, fighting the world. I stopped fighting. That's when I won."

Dom pressed a chaste, tender kiss to Hilary's lips. Hilary sighed and sank himself into it, wrapping his arms around the solid, reassuring weight of his lover. Dom held him close and pressed his lips to his cheek, his eyebrow, his forehead.

"You took the fight out of me years ago, Hilary Whyte," he whispered into Hilary's hair. "Before I even realized there was no point fighting anyway."

"Have you ever realized that?" Hilary said, only partly joking.

Dom smiled a half-smile. "I'll get there…one day."

They drank in companionable silence for a while. Then Dom propped his head up on the heel of his palm and gazed into Hilary's face, his expression turning solemn.

"Do you know why I got expelled?"

"You threatened Madame Forbé."

"Yes, but do you know why?"

Hilary looked away. "Honestly, I didn't think you needed a reason."

It was a moment before he continued. "She hit kids. Did you know that?"

The vodka suddenly tasted bitter. "There were rumors. I never saw anything, though."

"She picked the young ones. The vulnerable ones. The ones who wouldn't say anything. The meter-rule she kept behind her desk…" Dom's eyes darkened. A stab of old fear went through Hilary's chest but then Dom blinked, and the look was gone. "She broke Ashley Jones' knuckles that year. You didn't hear about that?"

Hilary went cold. "No. No, I didn't. That school was good at covering things up. But still, Dom. She was an old woman. A cruel one maybe, but still...an old woman."

Dom gazed into his empty glass. "The main reason I did it was because I knew I had to get away."

"What?"

"After that fight in the changing room...when I saw the darkness in your eyes, the hatred in your face, I finally realized..." He took a breath, gazing into the fire. "I realized I was destroying you. Destroying us both. I knew I had to get away from you as quickly as I could."

Hilary took a moment to find his voice. "And getting expelled was the only way you could think of to do that?"

"The way my mind worked then, yes."

"You're a fucking idiot, Dom Gosford," Hilary breathed. "I told you then and I'm telling you now. You're a fucking idiot."

Dom smiled a sad smile. "That's putting it mildly."

Hilary's throat closed over. He stared at Dom, seeing a shadow of the boy behind the man's eyes. Then something shook loose inside him, and he went limp, settled against Dom's side. Dom put an arm around his shoulders. Hilary closed his eyes. It was so warm, so easy. But there was still one thing he couldn't let go, a needle pricking at the peace surrounding him.

"So, how's Amelia?"

A pause. "She's okay. She's with Fatima now, hopefully not thinking about me."

"I saw you both when the verdict came through. When you faced those reporters together." Dom brushed his fingers up and down Hilary's arm without responding. Hilary stared straight ahead, his throat aching. "You really do love each other, don't you?"

"Yes, we do." Dom sighed. "You have to understand, Hilary...for a long time we were the only people in each of our lives we could rely on. We've been through a lot together. We're not in love as man and wife, but we're partners...comrades. She has never abandoned me, even in my worst moments. And I..." He paused. When he continued his voice was raw. "I won't abandon her, either."

Hilary's eyes prickled. He blinked angrily.

"She really doesn't care?" he ventured, pushing the thoughts aside and wreathing his fingers with Dom's.

"She cares," Dom said softly. "Not about me sleeping with men. But about me being happy? Yes. She cares about that."

Hilary raised his head. Dom's face was close to his, his gaze warm and a soft smile on his lips. "Are you happy?"

He smiled wider. "I'm getting there."

They kissed, gently, tentatively. Hilary allowed himself to enjoy it for several minutes before pulling back.

"Dom...I... You were right...about me kissing you back." Dom waited, not speaking, and Hilary tried to fight his words and emotions into order, only having partial success with both. "This...didn't come from nowhere. I've hated you for most of my adult life. You represented—I dunno—everything I've left behind but still have in me, a part of me that's still hurting. But then, when you kissed me..." He swallowed, his throat tight. "In that moment you erased it all. For an instant you took it away." Dom's eyes on him were intent. Hilary made himself finish the thought. "This has been good for me. Really. I needed it, even. I think it was important we...found a way through everything."

Dom went very still. "Past tense, Hilary?"

"Tonight was..." Heat crept up Hilary's face. He could still taste Dom on his tongue, feel the pleasant burn of his large cock in his arse. He remembered the sensation of being washed away, taken somewhere where nothing else mattered but them, together and how good they made each other feel. A place where, somehow, everything made sense.

Hilary crushed the feelings hurriedly. "It was great. It really was. The perfect way to..." He took a breath, not looking away even though Dom's gaze was darkening by the second. "To end this. To say goodbye."

Dom didn't reply. His fingers were tight around the empty whiskey glass.

"I'm getting married, Dom."

"You don't have to."

"I *want* to."

"Make me believe that, and I won't say anything more about it."

Hilary frowned. "You want to do this, now?"

"I don't want to do it at all."

"Dom," Hilary said, pleadingly, "it has to end."

"Why?"

"We're both committed to other people..."

"Are we?"

Hilary flushed. "Even if we weren't...you're my client."

"Not anymore."

Hilary flinched at his tone. "You're still my firm's client. It was never going to last. It couldn't."

"I don't see it that way."

Hilary sighed. "You can't always get what you want."

"Do you still tell yourself that?"

Hilary stiffened. "I'm sorry, Dom. I'm sorry if I've misled you or this hurts. I've enjoyed our time together. It's been…" He searched for words. "Good. Very good. But I love Jasper. I'm going to marry him."

"Better the devil you know, is that it?"

Heat flared in his chest. "You don't know anything about us."

Dom leaned forward. "You have this need to overachieve, Hilary. Isn't dating a movie star just part of that?"

"You know nothing about it," Hilary bridled.

"Celebrities aren't normal people, Hilary," Dom said. "He'll mess it up. He'll hurt you."

"Well, you'd know all about that." Dom's face flattened and Hilary reached deep for patience. "He's good for me."

"Is that because of who he is? Or *what* he is?"

"You don't know him."

"The whole world knows him," Dom said mildly. "He tweets every thought that goes through his head."

Hilary looked away, his jaw aching with clenching it.

"You can't be happy, Hilary. Or why are you here?"

"That's not fair."

"Isn't it?"

Hilary glared. "Jazz and I…? Yes, we've got some things to work through. We'll do that once we're married. We promised each other we would."

"I think you're still scared." Dom put his hand on Hilary's arm. "Still scared of that darkness. Scared of taking risks."

"Look… I don't know what you thought was happening here, but it was never going to last."

"*Why*?"

Hilary made an impatient noise and stood, poured himself a triple vodka and downed it. "You mean *apart* from the fact that you're a client, you're married and I'm engaged?"

"Yes."

"Isn't that enough?"

"No," Dom said, coming over to him. "All those things can change or be lived with…"

"Would you divorce Amelia?" Hilary asked. He held his breath, pained by how much he needed an answer.

"No," Dom said after a long, aching pause.

"Well then."

"We can work around it…"

Hilary stared at him. "You expect me to be your shameful secret, your bit on the side? While you and Amelia attend balls and banquets together?"

"It's not like that…"

"It *is*. It would be."

"We'd know the truth," Dom insisted. "You and me. Isn't that enough?"

"No, Dom, it's not."

"Marry him if you need to," Dom said after a hard silence. "If you really feel like you can't back out right now. I understand the pressure of publicity—"

"That's not why I'm marrying him—" Hilary argued but stopped when he saw Dom's knowing expression.

"I'll share you, if I have to, for a while. I've waited this long, I can wait a bit longer. But at least acknowledge that we can try to see where this takes us."

"No," Hilary said, banging his glass down. "I won't do it. I can't."

Dom's face was blank. Hilary's chest was strung with hot wire, tight with everything he still wanted to say but couldn't.

"Fine," Dom said, his voice hoarse like he was accepting a prison sentence. "I've let you go once before. I can do it again. I think…"

"Dom," Hilary said softly, "we barely know each other."

"That's not true."

"We've just been caught up in…whatever this is. And, yes, maybe I needed a distraction from Jasper until I figured out what I wanted." Dom's face darkened and Hilary looked away. "But that's all it was."

"You don't mean that."

"I'm sorry you think I'm the answer, Dom," he replied. "I'm not. You really don't know me, not who I am now."

"And Jasper does?"

"Yes."

"This is real, Hilary—what's between us, what has been between us all along. I understand you don't want to accept it. Not yet. But I think you will." Dom raised his eyes. "And when you do, I'll be waiting."

"Real life doesn't work like that."

"It works however you want it to work," Dom responded. "If you're brave enough to make it happen. I know you're brave enough, Hilary. You're the bravest man I know."

Hilary gazed into his eyes, a thorn of doubt twisting in his belly. Then he made for the bedroom to find his clothes. Dom stopped him with a hand on his arm.

"I won't bring it up again," he said, stepping close and talking into his hair. "I want you to be happy. I'll let you go, if that's what it'll take. Just...please..."

"Please *what*?"

"Can I see you...until he gets back?"

Hilary didn't move, didn't speak. He felt rooted to the rug.

"Let me be your distraction a little bit longer, if that's really all I was. Then, I promise...if you still want to go, I'll let you go. You'll never hear from me again...if that's what you want."

I don't want that...

Hilary stopped the words before they left this mouth. He turned in Dom's arms. "We should say goodbye now," he whispered. "It will only be harder if we leave it any longer."

"Just tell me what you want."

Chapter Sixteen

"There you are." Jasper's voice through Hilary's car speakers was weighted equally with relief and annoyance. "I heard about the verdict. I tried to call — "

"Sorry," Hilary said, steering through the early morning drizzle, trying to focus, even though it felt like his mind was being torn in several directions at once. "I went out with Beck. Just needed to switch off for a bit."

"Sure, I understand. But, Jesus, what a result. Well done, Hil. Plenty of people think you've worked a miracle there."

"He didn't do it," Hilary said as he turned a corner and Greenwich fell behind the gauze of rain in the rear-view mirror. "The jury saw that in the end."

"That man walked because of you, not because he was innocent."

Hilary winced. "Whatever. It's done."

"I'm glad," Jasper replied, sounding relieved. "And not just because of the wedding…"

Hilary winced. His thoughts whirled like a plug had been pulled on his sense of security. He opened his mouth to say something—he wasn't sure what, only that he couldn't keep it in—but then Jasper was talking again.

"I just wanted to congratulate you, but I gotta go. We're live-streaming an interview in a sec. Just tell me you're okay?"

Hilary tried to answer the question himself, found he couldn't. "I'm fine," he lied.

"Great. Speak soon. Be good."

Jasper hung up. Hilary hesitated then dialed another number.

Dom picked up after one ring. "Hilary?"

Hilary let out a breath, his fingers going cold, even while a fire lit in his chest. "We've got two weeks. Make them count."

* * * *

Hilary never left anything at Dom's flat—not a change of clothes, not a phone charger, not a toothbrush—despite the fact that he had to be up before six every morning to get back to his own place to change before work.

He divided his brain down the middle. Dom existed in one part and the rest of his life existed in the other. He was scrupulously careful to never allow them to blend. It took almost constant vigilance, and he wondered more than once how Dom and Amelia could bear to live like this.

But as he worked, attended meetings, took lunches with clients, that small, private part of him continually glowed with anticipation, silently counting the minutes to when he'd next cross the threshold of the Greenwich flat, let the lift door shut on reality and give himself up to the world Dom made for him, filled with warm caresses, whispered confessions and seismic orgasms.

That part of him never looked at the calendar, never acknowledged that the days were ticking by and soon, Jasper would return. Reality had to return with him, and the wedding day was getting closer by the minute.

And so it was a few nights later that he woke to find himself alone in Dom's vast, pillow-strewn bed. He squinted at his phone screen to discover it was a little after two in the morning then noticed there was a light under the door. He emerged, blinking, into the sitting area, bathed sickly white by the light of Dom's large television. His broad back was silhouetted against the screen, and Hilary could see that his body was rigid as iron.

"Dom?" he murmured sleepily. "What is it?"

Dom didn't answer. Hilary put his glasses on, and the screen came into focus.

A serious-faced newsreader spoke into the camera, a picture of a hollow-faced, gray-haired man in a suit being hustled into a car by several armed police in the corner of the screen. Hilary took a step closer so he could read the subtitles.

...shocked this evening to learn of the arrest of Clarence Lavelle for child sex offenses. In a statement, the Crown Prosecution Service have revealed that the former Foreign Secretary has been under investigation for several months and that, after a warrant was issued to search Mr. Lavelle's property, they now have enough evidence to charge him with possession of indecent imagery and several counts of sexual assault of a minor. Mr. Lavelle has yet to make a statement, but it is believed...

The TV blurred before Hilary's eyes. "Jesus, Dom," he breathed. "You knew him, didn't you?"

"My father knew him," Dom said, his voice so low it was barely audible. "Worked with him. Had him over to the house."

Hilary swallowed. "Did he ever…?"

"No," Dom said quickly.

"You said your father would never allow anything like that to happen to you," Hilary said, unable to look away from the screen. "You were talking about Lavelle?"

It was a long time before Dom answered. "My parents sent us to our rooms whenever he was visiting. He had this way of looking at me and my brothers…"

Hilary went cold. He tried to take Dom's hand but was overwhelmed with the futility of the gesture, so kept still.

Dom sipped whiskey as they showed the footage of Lavelle being escorted from his mansion, camera flashes bleaching the scene white every few seconds, the man's jowly face blank, devoid of emotion.

"But one time," Dom spoke quietly, without turning, "he was drunk, upstairs, searching for the bathroom. I was on the landing, seeing what the noise was…"

"How old were you?"

"Twelve." He downed his drink and glared at the screen. "He tried to touch me. I broke his nose."

They stared at the screen in silence as a DCI addressed questions from a crowded pressroom, the subtitles flashing the shocking revelations in bold white script making Hilary's stomach churn.

"I'm sorry."

"Nothing for you to be sorry for."

"I'm sorry I never knew."

Dom finally looked at him. His face looked unfamiliar in low light. "No one knew. He told my family he'd walked into a door."

"People did know, though," Hilary said as the subtitles listed high-profile names connected with the cover-up. "Too many people."

"Pretty much anyone with influence enough to help him cover it up...including my parents. It wasn't unusual. It just wasn't talked about."

"And yet Eloise invited him to that banquet?"

Dom's grip tightened on the glass.

"Did she know? About his connection to you?"

"She knew."

Hilary felt sick. "Then why—?"

"Eloise would do almost anything for appearances. And the Lavelle family are influential, even now. But I have a line."

Hilary held himself very still. "Where did you go, Dom? That night?" Dom gazed at him, his eyes reflecting the light from the TV. "It's over. You don't have to hide anything anymore."

Dom set his glass down, took Hilary's hand and drew him close. He kissed his jaw, the hollow under his chin, then his lips.

"Let's not talk about it anymore," he whispered, brushing his tongue over Hilary's lips until he sighed and opened his mouth to him. Dom slid his tongue in, holding him tight, and didn't stop until Hilary had forgotten all about his question.

* * * *

Almost a week after the trial, Hilary was startled out of a reverie when Janice opened his office door with an earnest expression on her face.

"Your meeting with Mr. Gunnerson, sir."

"Yes, of course," Hilary said, tucking his phone and the WhatsApp conversation with Dom hurriedly out of sight. "Is Beck ready?"

"He just wants you."

Hilary fought the sinking feeling as he left the office. The old lawyer wore his usual inscrutable expression as Hilary took his seat in front of his boat-sized desk, but Hilary had worked with him long enough to recognize the look in his eyes.

"Something wrong, sir?" Hilary said, fighting a blush as the one hundred and one possible things that could be wrong rose in his mind.

"Yes and no," Gunnerson said, interlacing his fingers on the desk. "It's not been publicly announced yet, but I thought you should know... Bruce Merriweather has finally been charged — two counts of murder, one of obstruction of justice."

Hilary held himself very still.

"He has pleaded guilty to all charges and been sentenced to life."

"I..." Hilary started, cleared his throat and tried again. "Good. Some answers for the parents, at last."

"Some," Gunnerson said, "but not all."

"How do you mean, sir?"

Gunnerson extracted a piece of paper from the file on the desk and held it out. "Merriweather's confession."

Hilary's skin tingled as he read.

"He knew too much about the crime to leave the police in any doubt as to his being the culprit. He knew more about the holes in the gun club's security than the prosecution. He has also volunteered the location of a private security camera on which the police found footage of him planting the silencer. So he's told them everything...apart from *why*."

Hilary focused on the typed script rather than meet his boss's eye. "The police and the CPS still saw it as enough to charge him."

"They did," Gunnerson inclined his head. "And rightly so. The man did it. There's no question about that. However..." Gunnerson straightened in his seat. "It's clear that he did it—did all of it—because of his obsessive devotion to that family. Which makes me question—"

"Dominic Hart-Gosford knew nothing about this," Hilary said, fighting to keep his face blank. "*Nothing*."

Gunnerson was quiet a long time. "As it stands, there are no legal ramifications that can be leveled at our client, and that's all that matters. But I won't be the only one looking at this matter and thinking there are pieces missing."

Hilary swallowed. "You don't think this is over?"

"I'm saying that unless something distracts the media soon, there's a chance they could get hold of a thread and pull. And we need to do what we can to stop that happening."

"Merriweather acted alone," Hilary said. "He has said as much. The family is not culpable for his actions."

"Yes, I am aware. But we need to keep our eyes and ears open."

Hilary frowned. "In what way?"

Gunnerson looked him in the eye. "I think the trial has given you and Mr. Dominic a...shall we say, renewed connection?"

Hilary's stomach lurched as he tried desperately to read any potential implication behind his employer's words. "I'm not sure what you mean, sir."

One bushy eyebrow twitched. "I have read the transcripts of the trial. Your closing statement makes it clear that you care about the man's welfare. And the company phone records show he's been in contact with you regularly since."

Hilary clenched his teeth.

"And there is nothing inherently unusual about that," Gunnerson went on airily, though there was no mistaking the knowing look in his eyes. "Plenty of clients are...grateful...to their solicitors after such a near miss. But the best solicitors use every situation purely for the benefit of their clients."

"What exactly are you asking me to do, sir?"

Gunnerson turned his fountain pen over in his hands. "I feel it would be to our advantage if you could use your connection to keep your ears open for anything further that might...complicate things. So that if anything more does come out of any of this, we'll be prepared."

"Are you asking me to spy on my client?"

Gunnerson's lip turned up. "Not spy, my boy. Just...stay focused on them all. And if you find anything of concern, anything that leaves them potentially vulnerable to further legal consequences, you come to me immediately."

Hilary held his tongue with an effort.

Gunnerson tilted his chin. "We have a duty to protect our clients, Hilary. And you've done a tremendous job with this case, as I expected. But if this really isn't over" —he laid his hand on the file containing Merriweather's confession — "we need to be prepared…for our client's sake. Understand?"

Hilary hesitated then nodded. "I understand, sir."

"I knew you would, my boy. Oh, incidentally, you should know that the partners are meeting next week about the junior partnership. I know you'll be off on your honeymoon soon," he said, pulling more files across the desk and opening them, "but I have a feeling you'll be returning home to some very welcome news indeed."

Heat battled cold through Hilary's insides as he left. Beck was on the phone and Simon staring at his iPad as he passed through their office. Beck was laughing. He suddenly wished he could talk to her. But between the new cases piled on his desk and heading straight to Greenwich from work every day since the trial, they'd barely exchanged ten words since the week before.

He shut his office door, sank into his chair and put his head into his hands. The wall between the divisions in his mind was quivering. He took a swallow of his lukewarm coffee then retrieved his personal phone from his coat pocket.

He took a breath, then typed.

Use this number from now on. Hil.

He manually typed in Dom's number and sent the text. Seconds later a reply came in.

So I finally have your personal number. What's happened?

Explain later.

He sent the reply then put the phone in his drawer, ignoring the buzz of another incoming reply. He turned to his pile of case reviews, resolved to bury himself in paperwork until he had the mental willpower to rebuild his wall.

When lunch came, he accepted the coffee and wrap Janice brought him with a smile.

"Thanks," he said as he closed down one case review and opened the next.

"Mr. Hart-Gosford is here, sir," Janice said.

Hilary paused with his wrap partway to his mouth. "What?"

Janice's eyebrow twitched at his tone. "He's in the waiting room. I told him you were on lunch. He said he'd wait."

"No," Hilary said, laying the food down and standing. "No, send him in."

"Sir, he's not alone."

Hilary frowned. "Who's with him?"

Janice's face was grave. "Mr. and Mrs. Wood."

Hilary chilled. "What?"

"The client says he has a proposition for them, and he wants you there when he delivers it."

Hilary attempted to gather his scattered thoughts, but it was like trying to catch falling sand on a windy day. "Could you put the Woods in the conference room?" he managed, swallowing half the scolding hot coffee in one go. "See if they want tea or anything?"

"Yes, sir. And Mr. Hart-Gosford?"

"I'll deal with him."

Dom stood languidly from his seat as Hilary entered the waiting room. He looked impossibly delectable in his charcoal suit, blood-red tie and heavy wool overcoat, the shoulders bejeweled with rain drops. He held a thin plastic file in one hand.

"Hilary, you look unwell."

"What's going on, Dom?" Hilary said, reaching for the file.

Dom pulled it out of reach. "I have something I would like to discuss with the Woods. I want my solicitor present when I do."

"What is it?"

"I want to explain everything with them present. Shall we join them?"

"Dom," Hilary said, lowering his voice, "we've been through this. I know you feel guilty, but—"

"I have to do this," Dom insisted. "I have to. And I'll do it with or without your approval, Hilary. But I'd prefer to do it with."

Hilary swallowed. Dom's full lips were turned down, his eyes deep and dark as wells. Hilary took a shaking breath. "If you insist, I can't stop you. But I want it on record that I've advised you against this."

Dom's mouth twitched. "I do love it when you're authoritative," he whispered. "Though you really should know how distracting it is."

Hilary fought a blush and stepped toward the door. "Let's get this over with."

Hilary led the way to the conference room. Karen and Terry Wood sat at the farthest end of the large table, looking small and rumpled against the backdrop of the elegant, high-ceilinged room. They were gazing at their untouched cups of coffee in silence but stood as Hilary and Dom entered, holding hands and staring at Dom like he was an animal about to pounce.

"Sit," Hilary ordered Dom in an undertone, indicating a chair at the other end of the table. Dom sent him an inscrutable look but obeyed. Hilary pulled out a chair next to the Woods and sat, shifting close as the couple lowered themselves into their own, looking at him with wide, watery eyes.

"Mr. and Mrs. Wood," Hilary started, making sure to look them both in the eye, even though the pain glinting there lanced through him like a knife. "Mr. Hart-Gosford has informed me that he has a proposition for you. Both he and I know that nothing he can do now can ease the trauma of what has happened to your family, but my client feels obligated to at least try."

"He said he wants to help," Terry said, his voice creaking like an old oak in the wind. "Karen wanted to at least see what he has to say for himself. But if he thinks for one second he can buy himself out of this—"

"I'm not offering you money," Dom cut in smoothly. "I would never be so revoltingly insensitive."

Karen looked at her husband, her lips pale and trembling. Terry hesitated then nodded stiffly. "At least you've got that much sense. Spit it out, then."

Dom slid the plastic folder down the table. Hilary opened it, skimmed the summary sheet at the top and felt his pulse quicken. He passed the folder to the Woods, who took it gingerly, like it might burn their fingers.

"I first and foremost want to say that I know Mr. Whyte is right," Dom started, his voice heavy with controlled emotion. "I can't make right what happened to your family. But I hoped you might be able to draw some small comfort from knowing that something positive could come out of all this."

"I don't understand," Karen Wood said in a small, thin voice. "You want to set up a charity?"

"A foundation...funded from the profits of one of my companies. But only with your permission."

"The Elizabeth Wood Foundation?" Karen's voice wobbled more than ever.

"It would offer financial advice and support to those struggling with debt. It would be staffed by qualified counselors and financial advisors. It would be completely free, and I have plans to set up bursaries to help with any public transport costs needed to access the service."

"Lizzie's debt didn't get her and Dean killed, Mr. Hart-Gosford," Terry Wood stated stiffly.

"I know that," Dom replied. Hilary fought to keep his face blank, the emotion storming in his lover's face threatening to wash his internal walls away. "But it's maybe the reason she felt backed into a corner, possibly the reason she felt extorting money was the only way to fight back."

Karen Wood blinked back tears. She clutched the folder with shaking hands. "Did you really pay off our daughter?" she asked, the words coming out in a harsh whisper. "Is that why you're doing this?"

"No," Dom said. "No, I didn't."

"Someone did," Terry said, shoving the folder back across the table. "Someone put that money in her account. And you can't tell me your bloody butler had that kind of cash to hand—"

"Mr. Wood—"

"It's okay, Hilary," Dom said, taking the folder back. "I know answers would help so much more than anything I can do." He paused. "Which is why I also want you to know I have a visit to Wandsworth arranged…"

The Woods blinked, what color remained in their lined faces draining away.

"Mr. Hart-Gosford," Hilary murmured, but Dom cut him off.

"I'm going to see Bruce to try to persuade him to answer our questions, to get him to explain—"

"What good will that do?" Terry Wood interrupted. "They're dead. They're bloody *dead*."

Karen pressed a hand over her mouth, stifling hitched sobs. Her husband pressed her hand but never took his eyes off Dom.

"Okay, I think this meeting is over—"

"Would you think about it?" Dom cut Hilary off gently, pushing the folder back toward the Woods. "Take as much time as you need. And if you decide no, I will go no further with it. But if you say yes, you will be giving vulnerable people someone to turn to, someone qualified and caring who will have their best interests at heart, no matter their situation or their past." Dom sent Hilary a significant look. Hilary's chest swelled, but he made himself focus on the Woods.

"If you would like me to look over the fine print and discuss the proposition in more detail, I'd be happy to do that," Hilary said. "Equally, if you would like to leave now and forget all about this, I can facilitate that, too."

Karen Wood's ragged breathing calmed. Terry glared at the folder, clutching his wife's hand tight. He eventually opened his mouth to speak, but Karen got in first.

"We'll read it."

"Karen, love…"

"It won't help us," Karen said, her voice catching as she took up the folder. "But it might help someone else. Please, Terry."

Terry's jaw clenched. He glanced at Hilary, then Dom, then nodded, closing his eyes.

"Thank you," Dom said. The words were so heartfelt that Hilary's chest ached.

The Woods stood, clutching the folder, and Hilary showed them to the door and called to Janice.

"Let Mr. and Mrs. Wood wait in the private waiting room until they feel ready to leave," Hilary instructed. "And arrange a car for them so they don't have to drive. Perhaps some fresh tea, too?"

"Of course," Janice said with her warmest smile as she led the couple away. Hilary didn't dare to hope that perhaps they stood a little straighter.

"Hilary," Dom began.

"Not here," Hilary said, glancing at the camera in the corner. "My office."

As soon as they were alone, Hilary turned on him.

"Dom," he said, exasperatedly, "what part of your brain didn't think to ask me about any of this before calling them here?"

"I appreciate you fighting for me, Hilary," Dom said, "but some things are down to me."

"Are you really going to Wandsworth?"

"Yes. Next week."

Hilary took his glasses off and rubbed his eyes. "I'm guessing there's no point in my telling you it's a terrible idea."

"None whatsoever."

Hilary sighed. "You're impossible, you know that?"

"More than you can ever know," Dom said in a low voice, his smile turning suggestive, making Hilary's skin prickle, but then he sobered. "What was that text about?"

Hilary blinked. The morning already seemed so long ago. "It was nothing. I just..." Hilary hesitated, went to the door, opened it a crack and confirmed that both Beck and Simon were gone for lunch and shut the door again. "They've noticed we've been calling. Texting."

"They?"

"Work," Hilary said, lowering himself into his chair. "They have access to all our work phone records."

Dom raised an eyebrow. "We've been...discreet."

"Thank God," Hilary said vehemently, pushing his food away, his appetite gone. "But I guess the number of calls caught Gunnerson's attention."

Dom's face was serious. "What did he say?"

"Nothing, really. Just enough to let me know he'd noticed. We just have to be more careful, that's all."

"That was it?"

Hilary hesitated, remembering Gunnerson's words. "Yes. That was it."

Dom narrowed his eyes. "I know when you're lying, Hilary."

Hilary made sure his face was blank. "I'm not under any obligation to share professional matters with you."

"No, you're not—not if you don't want to."

"Just use my personal number for now."

"Until Jasper comes back, you mean?"

Hilary frowned. "Dom..."

"Never mind..." Dom said, a forced smile smoothing his face. "I'll take what I can get. I'm used to that." He looked him in the eye. "What do you think about the foundation?"

Hilary raised an eyebrow. "Personally or professionally?"

"Both."

Hilary pushed a pen around his desk with his finger. "Professionally, I would call it an excellent PR exercise." Dom frowned and Hilary drew a deep breath. "Personally, I think it's wonderful you're trying to make it right—so long as you prepare yourself for the fact that some things just can't be fixed."

"Can't they?"

Hilary didn't answer.

Dom looked thoughtful for a long moment, then came around the desk, towering over him. Hilary stood awkwardly.

"What are you doing?"

"Taking what I can get," Dom murmured, snaking his fingers around Hilary's wrist and leaning in to kiss under his ear.

"Are you mad?" Hilary stammered, trying to push him away.

"Oh yes," Dom said, nipping his ear. "You've driven me quite to distraction."

"Dom, I..." He gasped as Dom kneaded the rapidly swelling bulge in the front of his trousers. "We can't..." Hilary breathed, even as he tilted his head back to allow Dom to trail kisses down his neck. "Not here..."

"You know the drill," Dom murmured against his skin as he undid Hilary's belt. "Tell me to stop and I'll stop."

"Christ," was all Hilary managed as the remains of the mental wall between his worlds crumbled to dust and Dom slipped his large hand into his trousers. "They'll be back any minute..."

"I'd better get to work then." Dom grinned against his neck then dropped to his knees.

"Dom, your suit…ah." Hilary clamped his mouth shut as Dom took him into his mouth. He shut his eyes and clutched at the edge of the desk as Dom worked him with his tongue, swallowing against the sensitive flesh. He clenched his teeth over the noises threatening to escape his throat, clinging to the desk so hard his fingers hurt.

Dom made a low noise in his throat and Hilary drew in a sharp breath. He looked down. The sight of Dom in his immaculate suit, kneeling on his office floor and sucking him off, was enough to send Hilary avalanching over the cliff and he came, pouring into Dom's hot, wet throat. He bit off the cry that climbed up from his chest, his knees buckling as he scrambled to stay upright.

When his vision cleared, Dom was brushing off his knees and straightening his tie.

"Until tonight," he said, buttoning his coat and kissing Hilary's cheek.

Hilary tried to reply when he heard Beck's voice through the door. He swore and tucked his softening cock back into his trousers.

"Get outta here," he said, zipping his fly just as Beck knocked and pushed the door open.

Hilary sat heavily to hide his untucked shirt behind the desk. Beck halted in the doorway, glancing between them.

"Sorry, boss… Your sister caught me on the street," she said, lifting the paper bag. "Scones. I didn't know you had a meeting."

"I don't," Hilary said, cursing his fair skin as it heated. "I mean…we don't. We just had a…something to discuss…"

Dom's eyes glinted. Beck's burned.

"Thank you for clearing that little matter up for me, Mr. Whyte," Dom said smoothly, then, nodding to Beck, "Miss Donavan," he said and left.

Beck put the scones on the desk. "I think there's cream and jam in there, too."

"Thanks," Hilary said, tucking himself into the desk so she couldn't see his unfastened belt. "You and Simon should have one, too."

"We already have," she said then, glancing back at the door, she leaned over and spoke in a low voice. "You're being sensible, boss, right?"

Hilary unstuck his mouth with the cooling coffee. "I don't know what you mean."

"I'm saying again, watch your back," Beck said, leaning closer. "What rich family is ever all they seem?"

* * * *

"I still don't think you should come," Dom said, staring out of the car window. "He's more likely to talk to me alone."

"You should have legal representation," Hilary said, not looking up from his phone.

Dom turned his head on the headrest. "Merriweather needs that more than me."

"He has it," Hilary said, putting the phone away. "One of the junior associates."

"They didn't fight very hard at his sentencing."

"Neither did Merriweather," Hilary said, looking out of the window as the car drew up to the iron gates of Wandsworth Prison. "Do you really think he'll tell you anything?"

"I won't know unless I try."

Merriweather's prison over-suit was at least two sizes too big. Hilary tried to decide if it was that which made him look smaller or if he'd also lost weight. His skin had a gray tinge and his eyes were hollow, but they lit up as Dominic followed Hilary into the room. Hilary took a seat in the corner, exchanging a nod with Merriweather's solicitor who sat, notepad ready, in the other corner as Dom took the other seat at the table.

"Master Dominic," the ex-butler said, smiling. "Kind of you to come, sir."

"You don't look well, Merriweather. Are they treating you fairly?"

"As fairly as the bastards can, sir."

Dominic continued to examine him. "You've had a reaction?"

Merriweather rubbed his mouth. "Yesterday. They forgot to tell me there were nuts in the cereal."

"I will make sure they are more careful in the future."

"It's all right, sir. What don't kill ya and all…"

Silence fell between them. Dom looked like he was searching for words. Hilary fought the impulse to intervene.

"You must know why I'm here," Dom said softly.

"I got a fair idea, sir, yeah."

"Tell me, Bruce. Tell me why you did it."

"I said already…to protect you."

"Why did I need protecting?"

Merriweather sent a penetrating glance at Hilary then leaned forward, looking Dominic right in the eye. "She *knew*, sir."

"Knew what?"

"Everything. About you. About Mistress Amelia. And she were gonna tell everyone."

"She told you this?"

Merriweather glanced at his solicitor then down at the table. "Yeah."

Dom paused. "She asked you for money?" Merriweather nodded. "But why you, Bruce? Why come to you?"

Merriweather's face screwed up. "She musta known I'd do anything for you, sir. And I would. I'd do it all again, too."

Dom examined him for several moments in silence. "Where did the money come from?"

"I have a bit put by in this...an account," he said, pulling at his ragged fingernails. "Hush-hush, you know." He gave Dom a crooked smile. "Always be prepared and that."

Dom held himself very still. "You paid Lizzie off?"

"Yeah. But then she came back. Said it weren't enough. Said she wanted to speak to you. Said if I didn't arrange it, she'd go to the papers." Merriweather shook his head. "She were a nasty piece of work, whatever the rest of 'em say. Pretending to be all high and mighty when she were just pissed off about being fired. That's all it was. I weren't gonna let no one go after you like that. *No one.*" Merriweather folded his large arms, meeting Dom's dark look without flinching.

"Why seven shots?"

"What?"

"You shot her seven times, Bruce. Why?"

Merriweather's face flattened. "Had to make sure the job was done, didn't I?"

"But only two for her brother?"

Merriweather bit his thumbnail, staring at the table. "He weren't supposed to be there. He surprised me. I'm sorry I...didn't want to hurt him. But it were too late.

355

He'd seen everything." He looked up again. "I am sorry you got arrested, sir. I am. I were so careful. How that hair got there, I swear, I don't know. But that bitch McGarry…" He clenched his fists on the table. "I really thought Mr. Whyte would get you off. When it looked like he might not, I fixed it."

"You planted the silencer?"

"That Bukhari bloke's a dodgy one." Merriweather narrowed his eyes. "Met him a couple of times with Mistress Amelia. Sleazy, that's what he were. Knew it wouldn't be hard to make it look like he'd done it, especially after that hoo-hah in court. And she'd given in, you know. Shagged him. Them johnnies? They'll have been his. His DNA will be in the bin, if they'd bothered to check it. I thought if they looked at him proper, it would be obvious he could have been the one that did her in."

Dom stared at him for a long time. "She told you all this? About Bukhari?"

"She liked to rant, that one," Merriweather said after a hesitation. "Men. Homes with Hart. All of it. Said we owed her — owed her and her brother, like their shitty life were all our fault."

"She was scared," Dom said softly. "She was in a place she couldn't see a way out of. Stuck. Lost."

"We've all felt that way, sir. We don't all choose to make it everyone else's problem, do we?"

Dominic stared at the wall.

"I did it for you, sir," Merriweather said earnestly. "To protect you. And I'd do it again."

"Okay, I think that's enough for one day," Merriweather's solicitor said, standing. "My client will be in touch if he needs anything, Mr. Hart-Gosford. But we'll have to leave it there for now."

They climbed into the car in silence. Hilary made sure the driver's attention was fixed ahead then took Dom's hand. "It's not your fault."

Dom stared out of the window. "If I'd been honest from the start, none of it would have happened."

"We can't stop ourselves from making mistakes," Hilary said, lacing their fingers together. "All we can do is try not to make the same ones over and over again."

Dom raised his eyes. They were heavy with pain. "How do I do it, Hilary?"

"I can't tell you that," Hilary said after a pause. "It's something we all have to figure out on our own." He paused. "Or try to, at least."

Dom raised Hilary's hand to his mouth and kissed his knuckles. "I intend to. I owe it to Dean. To Lizzie. To you."

"You owe it to yourself, Dom."

* * * *

Gunnerson assigned Hilary three more high-profile cases, one with another trial to prepare for. What time wasn't spent with the clients, writing up reports or on the phone to the CPS, was spent in meetings, lunches and dinners with the company partners. It meant he had little time to think about anything else, for which he was secretly grateful.

But then, at night, no matter how late he left the office, how wrung out he was, how much he knew he just needed to go home and sleep, he found himself driving to Greenwich, and, whatever time of the night it was, Dom was always there, waiting. They ate, they drank, they made love like nothing but the two of them existed in the world.

"Do you really want that partnership?" Dom asked softly as they lay in bed one night, the sheets tangled about them, the sweat still drying on their skin.

"What?" Hilary murmured sleepily.

"I think tonight is the latest you've ever got here," Dom said, rubbing lazy circles on Hilary's back. "Seems they're making you jump through a lot of hoops. And what will it really mean in the end? More work?"

"It'll mean I've made it—and that I have security. A future."

Dom's eyebrows rose. "You already have all those things."

"A partnership would mean I can influence company decisions," Hilary said. "Client lists. Case overviews. It'll help me help more people."

Dom smiled, his expression warm. "I love this about you. Criminal defense lawyers are usually far more jaded."

"With reason," Hilary said, staring at the ceiling. "But helping people in the darkest parts of their lives, it's important to me."

"Even the guilty ones?"

"Especially the guilty ones."

Dom ran his finger down Hilary's cheek. "How do you manage it? Seeing the very worst sides of people and still wanting to help them?"

Hilary took Dom's hand and examined the manicured fingernails, the strong knuckles, brushed his fingers over the skin to make the hairs stand up. "I have to believe there's hope for everyone."

"Does everyone deserve hope?" Dom asked after a pause.

He propped himself up on his elbow and gazed into his lover's face. "The Clarence Lavelles of this world? No," he said firmly. "But the job is to make sure they're punished in proportion to their crime." His gaze shifted to the wall. "Though I'm beginning to wonder if there is anything in proportion to what a man like that has done."

"I'm sorry I told you," Dom said after a pause.

"Don't be."

"You've been different since I did — staying at the office longer, working harder. What are you hiding from?"

Hilary tried to be annoyed but only smiled. "You've never tried to live with a solicitor before, have you?"

Dom's face was serious. "Tell me, Hilary."

Hilary sighed and settled himself back in the crook of Dom's arm so he didn't look at his face. "I've been thinking about the people that get away with things like that — and the fact that my firm and others like us help them do it." He swallowed. "I want to make sure that doesn't happen. That's why I want the partnership more than ever. To influence our case load, so we don't take on clients like that. But, somehow…"

"What is it?" Dom prompted when Hilary didn't go on.

Hilary sighed. "I don't know. I know getting that job is what I need to do to make a real difference. But I keep thinking the pro bono stuff I used to handle when I started out."

"Tell me about it," Dom murmured.

"I knew those people. I was one of them, really. The ones who took a wrong turn and were too angry to see it clearly. They were the ones who really deserved a second chance, the ones who would actually do something with it." He chewed on his lip a long moment. "But I can't turn back now."

"It's not your job to save everyone, you know," Dom said after another pause.

Hilary ran his fingers through Dom's soft chest hair. "Don't pretend you don't understand. You have ambition."

"Do I?"

"How many companies do you own?"

"I'd have to ask the accountant," Dom said with a tired smile. "But seriously. I only do what I do because it's just…how it worked out. I never really wanted this life."

"No one with the amount of money you have can say that and not sound conceited."

Dom turned onto his side and gazed down into Hilary's face. "I know that. It doesn't make it untrue."

"So why don't you give it all up?" Hilary said. "Divorce Amelia. Leave the money and position behind. Get a cottage somewhere remote and work in the local pub, date the postman."

Dom traced his fingers over the lettering tattooed into Hilary's chest. "That's what I should have done when I left that school. Run away. Been a nobody," he said, his gaze following the path of his fingers as goosebumps rippled over Hilary's skin. "Or, at least, only a somebody to those who mattered." He paused, his fingers stilling. "But I just know, given the chance, I would still make the same choices all over again." He raised his eyes to meet Hilary's. "Sometimes the ruts are already worn for us. You can't turn the wagon, even if you want to."

"You can't possibly believe that."

"I'd like not to. But your life, your family, your circumstances…they shape you, whether you realize it or not. If you ever do, it's usually too late. Just ask those pro bono cases who didn't take that second chance and ended up in prison or worse." Hilary opened his mouth to protest but Dom silenced him with a gentle kiss. "Some people…strong people," he said, running a thumb over Hilary's lower lip, "can buck the wagon into a different track. But most people aren't as strong as you."

Hilary's throat ached. He ran his fingers down the smooth jaw, up under the firm chin. He sighed.

"How are you feeling?" he murmured. "After Wandsworth?"

Dom sat up against the headboard with a sigh. "I've known and trusted Merriweather for years. He was part of my family." Dom shook his head sadly. "But that man today…? I didn't know who that man was."

Hilary squeezed his arm. "You never know anyone as well as you think you do."

Dom gazed down at him, pain sparking in his eyes. "You think so?"

Hilary kissed him, long and slow, drinking in the taste, smell and feel, pinning it down in his mind so he would remember it forever.

"You're a good man, Dom," he sighed against Dom's lips. "It's the world that's all wrong."

He felt Dom smile against his mouth. "I sometimes get things right," he said, kissing him back. Hilary let him, shivering as they ran their hands over each other. A frisson of desire glittered through him, but he made himself pull back.

"What is it?" Dom said, taking in the solemn expression on Hilary's face.

"You know Jasper's back tomorrow, right?"

Dom nodded. "I know."

Hilary blinked until the prickling in his eyes stopped. "Perhaps I should just go now…"

Dom brushed his hair back from his face. "Only if you want to."

"It would be easier."

Dom brushed his lips over his ear. "Easier doesn't mean better."

Hilary let out a shuddering breath, rolled Dom onto his back and climbed on top of him. Dom moaned and ran his hands down his back. Hilary dove his tongue deep into Dom's mouth, like he'd swallow him and keep him inside forever.

"Stay," Dom panted, raising his hips so his hardening cock pressed against Hilary's stomach.

Hilary nodded, kissing Dom's neck, his chest, his jaw, languidly rubbing his hardening length against his firm thigh.

"You know my offer still stands, don't you?" Dom whispered in his ear as Hilary grasped his large, swelling cock. He gasped and stilled Hilary's hand. "I'm serious. I don't want to lose you." Hilary met his eyes and fought the sensation of falling into them. "Just think about it."

"Don't talk about that now," Hilary said, resuming the task of pumping hardness back into Dom's thick member. Dom groaned, and when those large, strong hands dug into his back, holding them both together, Hilary allowed the world to melt away from his mind, for just a few more hours.

Chapter Seventeen

"Hil, baby," Jasper cried, shedding coats and travel bags and racing into the sitting room. Hilary almost had his breath knocked out of him as his fiancé seized him in a bear-like hug. Hilary was surrounded by the smells of expensive clothes and designer aftershave and something lurched sideways inside him. "God, I missed you," Jasper said, kissing him. He tasted of alcohol. Hilary pulled away.

"Are you drunk? It's not even noon."

"Gotta end the holiday on a high, right?" Jasper grinned. "Besides, you know the complimentary drink is the only thing that makes flying bearable for me. Come here." Hilary stiffened as Jasper thrust a questing tongue against his lips. When Jasper went still, Hilary kissed him back, putting his arms around him and holding on to the familiar, lithe shape, ignoring the chill of uncertainty that snaked through his body.

"All right, all right, break it up," Stewart Prince grumbled as he and Jasper's mother came into the room. "Gonna use your loo, lad," Jasper's dad continued. "Christ, the drive from Heathrow gets longer every time."

"John is bringing up the last of the bags in the lift, darling," Fernella said, pecking her son on both cheeks. "We really must dash once your father's done. Now, make sure you both rest up, boys. No more work now," she said, wagging a finger at Hilary's files littering the sofa and coffee table. "Three days to the wedding. You need to both look your best."

The Princes left, Fernella issuing more instructions as Stewart groused at her to hurry up. Then the door was shut and they were alone. Jasper was still beaming. His face was tanned, peeling a little in places from snow-burn and flushed from drink. His hair was stylishly mussed, his smile as wide and white as those in his social media pictures.

"Let's order takeaway," he said, pulling off his boots. "There's wine, right? I have so many photos. The chalet was fucking amazing. And the staff basically gave us the run of the place in exchange for a tag on Instagram. Seriously, Hil, you'd've loved it. We'll have to go back…"

Hilary accepted the glass of wine Jasper brought him and began tidying the case files on the coffee table.

"Oh and, my Christ, this was hilarious," Jasper said, swiping on his phone so the picture projected on the wall changed to another of a group of them in snowsuits, covered in snow, laughing raucously. "Jo fell off the ski-lift about four times in a row. Barely even got three feet off the ground. Seriously, she can ski like a demon, but the ski-lift? Forget it." He laughed, his eyes shining, draining another glass of wine.

"Looks like you had a great time."

Jasper looked at him. "Would have been better if you were there."

Hilary raised an eyebrow. "Sure about that?"

Jasper frowned. "Of course. I..." He made an impatient noise. "I missed you. I really did." He leaned forward and kissed Hilary clumsily, spilling wine.

"Fuck, Jazz," Hilary snapped as he pulled the case files away from the spill.

"Leave them," Jasper said, grabbing his shirt. "You're off work now, anyway." He slobbered against his jaw, grabbing his hand and pushing it against his groin.

"I'm really tired," Hilary said, without much hope, feeling Jasper's hard length through his track pants.

"Suck me off, Hil. Please... I've missed you so much. Please, quick..."

Hilary hesitated, but when Jasper pulled back with a puzzled look on his face, he got to his knees. Jasper shoved his trousers down, his eyes locked on Hilary's as he worked his cock feverishly. Hilary leaned forward, knowing at least Jasper would come in seconds then pass out.

Which he did.

Hilary existed in a cold, soundless bubble as the days passed in a flurry of beautician, hairdresser and tailor appointments, phone calls and pinging messages. He thought he was used to endless demands on his time and attention from work, but this was a whole new level. Marcia was with them for several hours each day, streaming and posting, fielding press and constantly briefing and re-briefing them on the schedule for the big day.

It seemed like it would never end but then, suddenly, Hilary was watching a gaggle of Prince women filling the flat, their arms full of clothes and cases, telling Jasper to hurry. Hilary blinked, watching it unfold in slow motion, wondering just where the time had gone.

"Night before the wedding, Jazz," Josephine twinkled. "You know the rules."

"Go," Hilary urged, pushing his fiancé toward his cousins. "I'll see you tomorrow."

"I love you," Jasper called as the gathering swarmed for the door with him in the midst. "See you at the altar!"

The door closed and silence filled the flat. Hilary looked at the clock. It was late, but the thought of going to bed made his adrenaline spike. The sooner he went to sleep, the sooner tomorrow would arrive.

He retrieved some vodka from the freezer and made for the music room.

He downed a shot, then another, then dug out *Mellon Collie and the Infinite Sadness*, placed the record on the turntable and turned the volume up.

He slumped in the armchair and let Billy Corgan's voice pour over him. He downed another shot and winced as the alcohol blazed through the protective walls in his mind. He stared out into the dark night then got up and opened the hidden drawer under the hi-fi and retrieved a box thrust right at the back.

The stale-sweet, earthy smell of marijuana filled his nostrils as he rolled a joint and lit it. He slumped in the armchair, inhaling deeply, tendrils of numbness threading through his veins. He closed his eyes and sank into the music, willing it to blot out reality the way it always used to.

The album finished. He put another on. He poured more vodka and rolled another joint.

It took several moments for him to hear the buzzing noise over the loud music, several more before his befuddled mind recognized it as the doorbell.

He padded to the front door in a daze, not even thinking to check the peephole before opening it.

Dom stood in the hall. He looked too large, too real, for that low-ceilinged, overly familiar space.

Hilary blinked. "What are you doing here?"

Dom's eyes trailed up and down him, taking in his bare feet, tracksuit bottoms, his oversized *My Chemical Romance* T-shirt, his unruly hair and, probably, very red eyes.

"I'm here to see you."

"You can't be here."

"And yet I am."

Hilary looked up and down the hall and stepped back. "Get in. Quick."

Dom followed Hilary to the music room in silence. Hilary turned the music down and picked the half-smoked joint back up, lighting it again. Dom scanned the band posters on the walls, the shelves of records. He flicked through them, his expression pensive.

"So you're really going through with it?"

Hilary downed his drink and poured another. "Don't."

Dom eyed him warily. "It doesn't look like you're looking forward to it."

"It's none of your business."

Dom moved to the turntable. "What are we listening to?"

Hilary held out the *See You on the Other Side* album sleeve. Dom took it, his eyebrows raising.

"Korn?" He glanced around the shelves. "Green Day. Limp Bizkit. Papa Roach. You still listen to all this stuff?"

"Not as often as I used to," Hilary said, stubbing out the joint.

"The embodiment of our generation's crisis," Dom said thoughtfully, examining the track list on the back of the album sleeve.

"Every generation has a crisis," Hilary said, retrieving another glass and pouring a measure into it.

"Is that right?"

"Course," Hilary slurred, holding out the vodka to Dom. He took it but didn't drink. "It's about trying to find certainty in a world where there isn't any. Once you accept that, you can move on. Just some people never do."

Dom watched Hilary drain his glass. He set his own aside.

"I'm sorry I don't have any single malt," Hilary said derisively as he slumped into the chair.

"It's not that," Dom said. "I'm trying to cut back."

"Fuck me. Miracles do happen."

Dom sat on the edge of the low table. "It's not too late, Hilary."

The record finished and spun on the needle with a soft crackling nose. Hilary sniffed, the numbness in his chest crumbling away. "It's almost fifteen years too late, Dom."

Dom took his hand. "It isn't. I won't let it be."

"If you'd just told me," Hilary said, banked emotion surging up his throat. "If you'd said *something* back then… If you'd just had the balls to admit what you wanted…" He broke off, choking.

"I can't change the past, but I can fix the future."

"How?"

"Come away with me. Tonight. You never have to say anything to him...to anyone."

"Are you serious?"

"Yes. Run away with me. Now. I'll take care of you, Hilary. I've got money put aside. We could just disappear—"

"What kind of arsehole do you think I am?" Hilary said, snatching his hand back.

"You're not an arsehole—just someone who doesn't think he deserves what he wants. You do, Hilary. I want to help you see—"

"You patronizing twat," Hilary snapped, standing.

"Hilary..."

"If I wanted to be with you, I would be," Hilary said, his voice rising. "I've made my choice, Dom. Accept it...or don't. That's up to you. But I won't be your crutch anymore. Grow the fuck up, already."

Dom's face flushed. The lines around his mouth deepened. Something dark swamped his eyes.

Guilt, pain and just a little fear swept up from Hilary's belly, but he held Dom's gaze and didn't flinch. He'd never flinched before, not even when Dom had had him pinned in the changing rooms, rage burning in his eyes, fist raised to strike. He wasn't going to start now.

"This is how you want to leave this?" Dom said. "You want these to be the last words we say to each other?"

"That's on you," Hilary said. "You shouldn't have come."

Dom clenched and unclenched his fists. Fear fizzed up Hilary's spine. But then he heard the front door slam, and he was again alone in the echoing silence.

* * * *

"Hilary? Hil?"

Hilary swore, groping for the cover that had been jerked off him.

"Jesus, Hil. Of all the nights to get wasted."

Hilary cracked an eye. Maxwell stood by his bed with the duvet in his arms, his face reproachful in the early morning light.

"Bugger off," he muttered, pulling the pillow over his head.

"I would, brother," Maxwell said, yanking the pillow away. "But you're late for the dresser. Lady Josephine is in a right tiz."

Hilary sat up, rubbing his temples. "Huh?"

"You were supposed to be with the dresser at eight," Maxwell said, drawing the curtains. Hilary cursed as the sunshine knifed through his skull. "It's nearly nine. Shows how desperate she was that she called me."

Hilary blinked and, finally, his brother's words began to register. He stared at the missed call notifications on his phone.

"Shit."

"Shit is right," Maxwell said throwing a towel at him. "But I explained to Cousin JoJo in very clear terms that you are perfectly capable of dressing yourself. Lucky for you," he said, eyeing Hilary as he fumbled for his glasses, "I'm good at lying."

"I'm sorry," Hilary said, rubbing his aching head.

"Don't be sorry. Min's making the coffee. Just get your arse into the shower."

Hilary showered then spent fifteen minutes trying to scrub the taste of booze and tobacco from his mouth. He drank the excellent coffee his sister brought to him and was relieved to feel it dulling the hard edges of his hangover as Maxwell moved around the bedroom, getting his wedding clothes ready.

Minnie brought him a bowl of her homemade granola then kissed him on the cheek. "I've got to go. The caterers need me. Good luck, little brother."

Hilary ate, pleased when he didn't immediately throw it all back up, then began to dress.

The suit was a custom from the Princes' tailor on Savile Row. It was a delicate ash gray that sat well against his milk-pale skin. The silk tie, a gift from Jasper, was a blushed apricot, which set off his hair. It had all looked great when he'd tried it on in the shop. Now he stared despairingly at his blotchy face and red eyes in the mirror, his damp hair starting to curl, the shadows under his eyes.

"Marcia's gonna kill me," he murmured, "if Fernella doesn't get to me first."

"You look great," Maxwell said, putting another cup of coffee on the dresser. He met Hilary's eyes in the mirror and winced. "Or, you will. You just haven't woken up yet, that's all. Here—" His brother spun him to face him so he could tie his tie.

Hilary searched his brother's face as he worked.

"Max…"

Maxwell frowned as he worked. "Everything all right?" Hilary swallowed at the coffee that threatened to return up his throat. Maxwell's expression tightened. "You know…it's not too late, Hil. If you, you know…"

Hilary willed him to say it, willed him to give him permission. But Maxwell never finished his sentence. He just squeezed Hilary's shoulders and planted a kiss on his head. "It's just pre-wedding jitters, little bro. It'll all be fine. You'll see."

One of the wedding planner's numerous assistants met them outside the building with a waiting car and a stern look.

Maxwell gave him a hug then the assistant was hustling him into the car before they could exchange another word.

"They've held the hair and makeup girls for you," the assistant said pointedly as she tapped at the screen of her iPad. "Once they've done their thing, it's champagne, canapés and photos in the courtyard with your family. The ceremony is at three. You are to be ready to enter the marquee at fourteen-forty-five. An assistant will fetch you at fourteen-thirty-five…"

Hilary stared out of the window and tuned out, watching the world go by from behind a fuzzy wall of unreality.

The bridal suite at Marlesborough Castle was, somehow, bigger than it looked in the pictures, even crammed as it was with people, portable makeup stations, clothes rails and his and Jasper's piles of honeymoon luggage. Hilary sat where he was told and stared at the reflection of the huge, canopied bed in the mirror with a sinking feeling. Women as fast and precise as hummingbirds flitted around him with brushes, hairdryers, straighteners and numerous bottles of sickly-sweet potions and unguents.

When someone offered him a glass of Buck's fizz, he clutched at it like a lifeline, draining it in one go and holding the glass out for a refill. His personal phone sat on the dresser. His heart leaped every time a notification lit the screen, sinking again just as rapidly when it wasn't a message from Dom.

By the time the crowd around the dresser stepped back, Hilary almost didn't recognize the man staring back at him. The shadows under his eyes were gone. His hair was neatly combed back from his face and tied at the nape of his neck with a silk ribbon in the same shade as his tie. A couple of artful strands had been teased free to fall into his face just so. Even his blue-green eyes looked brighter, and he wondered if the contacts they'd put in were colored.

"From your fiancé, Mr. Whyte..."

Hilary blinked at the small, velvet box the assistant set on the dresser. Inside was a pair of platinum hoop earrings, a single diamond set in each. They were simple and elegant, tiny enough to be tasteful, despite the winking gems. He took out his silver studs and put the hoops in with numb fingers. He blinked again at his reflection, suddenly sickeningly reminded of the face that had smiled benignly and without warmth out of their official engagement pictures.

"Oh, Hilary." His mother rushed forward in a flurry of perfume and chiffon as he stepped into the sunlit courtyard. She hugged him fiercely and planted a kiss on his cheek, stepping back to give him an admiring glance.

"Gosh, you look handsome." She beamed, wetness glittering in her eyes.

"The hair and makeup team are from Jasper's last film." Hilary smiled, accepting a glass of champagne offered by a server who had appeared at his elbow. "I would hope they know what they're doing. You look truly wonderful, though, Mum."

She blushed and tugged the wide brim of her hat. "Thank you, love. It's all new —"

"Hilary." His father beamed as he joined them, standing smart and straight in a new slate-gray suit and ocean-blue tie. "Looking very fine, I must say. And a beautiful day for it, too," he added, squinting up at the bright, warm sun set in a cloudless blue sky.

"It's all looking better than it did this morning for sure," Maxwell laughed as he came over from the bar with three glasses for him and their parents. He held Hilary's eye as they drank.

"Feeling better?" he asked as their parents turned their attention to the tray of canapés another member of the serving staff was offering.

"Yeah," Hilary said, somewhat truthfully. "Yeah, I just want this to be over."

"This way, please," called a photographer before Maxwell could answer. None of them had time to exchange another word as they were lined up against the water features and arches for photographs. Luckily, the champagne flowed as freely as the fountains and Hilary was able to maintain the numb shell around the ache in his chest as the morning wore on.

His heart lifted when Minnie was finally able to join them for the last round of photographs. She was resplendent in watered peach silk and simple silver jewelry, the vivid red of her hair ironed into flowing waves and glowing like fire in the sunshine. Her shy smile dimpled her cheeks and made her green eyes dance.

"You look amazing," Hilary said. "Ready to walk me down the aisle?"

"Think I need a little more champagne first," she murmured, glancing nervously at the bank of photographers hovering under the ivy-covered arch, checking light levels. Then she and Maxwell were herded to one side for shots of just the two of them.

"People just can't get enough of twins," his mother said, a small, proud smile on her face. "And they are a fine-looking pair, aren't they?"

"They are," Hilary said, a familiar twinge in his chest as he watched his siblings communicate with looks that didn't require words.

The sun gained height and heat as the day drew on. Hilary downed his last glass of champagne and set it aside, turning away more, the fuzziness in his brain threatening to spill into bleariness.

The next thing he knew he was standing outside a towering marquee and Minnie was looping her arm through his.

"Ready?" she smiled.

The music from the string quartet rose to a crescendo then a woman with a headset was giving them their queue to enter.

Hilary took a deep, steadying breath. "I'm ready."

Hilary now realized that, despite his caution, he had drunk more than was wise. The fizzing of the champagne mixed with the hangover and spiking adrenaline as he and Jasper said their vows combined to reduce the ceremony to a heart-thumping blur. He did remember that Jasper looked heart-achingly beautiful. His highlighted hair was the delicate gold of summer meadows. His tie matched Hilary's, but the suit was a shade darker, setting off his warm, rich tan. His smile was wide, and the way his bright, blue eyes gazed into Hilary's, he could almost believe he was falling in love all over again.

But when they kissed and the crowd erupted into cheers, he knew it was just another of his Oscar-worthy performances.

They barely had time to exchange a word as a married couple before they were whisked from the marquee for yet more photographs.

"You did great in there," Jasper whispered in his ear as the assistants fluttered around them, adjusting their clothing, the angle of the flowers and the positions of their hands on each other. "Just like a pro."

Hilary looked into his husband's eyes. They were sparkling. The smile was softer but more genuine than the one in the marquee. Hilary's heart clenched.

"It'll be okay, won't it?" he whispered as the photographers readied their equipment.

The faintest of lines appeared between Jasper's eyebrows. "Of course. Why? What's wrong?"

Alcohol was fuzzing away at the wall Hilary had tried to rebuild in his mind. Jasper's eyes were open and questioning—eyes Hilary knew so well and had loved very dearly, once. Felt sure he could love again, if only…

"Just a bit to the left, guys," said a photographer, gesturing. "Hold hands, please."

Hilary did as instructed, and when he looked back, Jasper had turned his face away, smiling for the camera, angling their joined hands between them so both wedding bands were on display.

There was food, more drink, endless speeches and, as always, the constant snap and flash of cameras. Someone had mercifully opened the sides of the marquee, allowing some breeze to flow, but it was still almost stiflingly warm under the gauze-draped ceiling. It seemed time was sluiced away by champagne and the ever-flowing torrent of uneasiness that poured through Hilary until it felt like he was smiling, talking and chatting to everyone from behind a wall of glass.

If Jasper noticed, he didn't let on. In fact, he only seemed to notice Hilary whenever a camera turned their way. Then he would murmur something Hilary didn't hear, take his hand and kiss it or kiss him full on the mouth, coaxing increasingly raucous cheers from the increasingly inebriated crowd.

Darkness fell and a forest of candles was lit. The golden light bathed everything in a fairytale-like glimmer. The tables were moved, and Ed Sheeran walked out onto the stage to a round of deafening applause. He perched on a stool, smiling shyly, adjusted his guitar and asked everyone to raise their glasses to the happy couple.

Hilary allowed himself to be led out onto the dance floor, feeling like he was wading through water, but pulled together enough focus to smile. He moved as Jasper moved, their bodies close, fitting together easily from long practice but without heat. The gentle notes of the guitar and the easy warmth of the singer's voice surrounded them. Cameras flashed. Phones filmed. Hilary's face warmed and he buried his face in Jasper's neck so he didn't have to see any of it, earning a chorus of admiring coos from the crowd. Jasper leaned his head into his but didn't speak.

Finally, the first dance was over. Jasper was whisked away to dance with his cousins as a band joined Sheeran on stage and launched into classic disco covers.

Hilary took the opportunity to steal away. He found his siblings just outside the marquee, sitting on an ornamental bench, smoking and smiling over glasses of champagne. Hilary hurried over to them, not caring this time if he was intruding, undoing his waistcoat as he went and taking the first real breath he'd taken in hours. The coolness of the night calmed his pulse, but his veins were singing out for nicotine.

"Please?"

Minnie held out her packet. "As it's your big day," she said with a wink. "But don't let the cameras catch you. I've already had one telling off."

Hilary took the lighter offered by Maxwell, lit the cigarette and breathed the smoke deep, sighing as it worked needles of calm into him.

"Jesus, fuck and Christ," he murmured, sighing smoke into the night.

"You did great," Maxwell said. He'd loosened his tie and run his hands through his red hair, the styled sweep now a mess of tumbling curls, but his eyes were as keen as ever. "Worst part's over, right?"

Hilary smiled but didn't answer. He looked around at the night-shrouded lawns spilling away on every side, the tempting dark solitude of the shadows. "I'm just gonna get some space for a bit."

Minnie nodded. "We're right here if you need us."

He drifted away, feeling lighter as he was swallowed by the darkness. He stepped around a hedge into a softly lit garden, all cool shadows and tinkling fountains, blissfully deserted.

Hilary leaned against a rose trellis and closed his eyes, drew deep on the cigarette and let the smoke out slowly. The music could just be heard. They'd switched to a slow number, the singer's voice gentle, tender as a caress. His nerves finally began to ease when the scrape of gravel made him jump.

He turned. A tall figure had stepped out from the shadow of the hedge. Hilary could just make out a dark suit, broad shoulders, a white shirt open at the collar. The face above it was masked in darkness but the black eyes looking out from under the sweep of dark hair made his heart stand still.

He tried to speak, tried to move, either away or closer, he wasn't sure. But he was frozen to the spot. Dom closed the space between them, silent as smoke, took Hilary's hand and drew him close.

"Christ, Dom," Hilary muttered, dropping the cigarette and hastily looking around to make sure they were definitely alone. "What are you doing here?"

"Shh," Dom said, slipping a hand around to the small of his back. Something inside Hilary shook loose. He leaned into that strength, clutching on, lowering his head to the broad shoulder, allowing himself to be held, supported.

Dom started to sway them to the smooth, gentle notes of the song. They moved in slow circles, shifting from one foot to the other, the music moving them like the waves of a gentle sea. He felt the swell of Dom's chest as he breathed, felt him exhale against his neck. He smelled like whiskey, herbs and good wool. He smelled like home.

The moment was like glass all around them. Hilary didn't dare speak in case it shattered. He clung on, moved as Dom moved, willing Dom's strength to sink into him.

All too soon, the song ended. Dom stilled. Hilary lifted his head. Dom was smiling but his eyes were dark. Hilary's chest clenched and he pressed his mouth to Dom's with a whimper, desire and desperation chasing away that last cloying fog of alcohol. Dom kissed him back, deep and languid, gentle but thorough. He made a noise low in his chest, somewhere between a sigh and a moan of pain. He broke away and pressed their foreheads together. His eyes were closed, his body shaking as his grip tightened.

"I couldn't leave it like that," he whispered.

"I'm sorry," Hilary replied, his voice choked. "I was upset. I—"

"You were right," Dom murmured. "It's too late. I wouldn't let myself see it, but now I do. You need him, need this life. I...I just have one thing I need to say, before we say goodbye."

Hilary couldn't speak but he managed a nod, holding Dom's hand tighter as the feeling of vertigo weakened his knees.

Dom was silent for a long time, his eyes closed, breath brushing Hilary's lips as he pressed their heads and bodies together. Another song started. The music and the scent of roses and grass threaded around them on the breeze. Hilary silently prayed that the moment would last forever, but then Dom opened his eyes.

"I love you, Hilary Whyte."

Hilary's throat closed. He tried to speak. Couldn't. Dom was smiling again. His eyes looked brighter. He pressed a chaste, tender kiss to Hilary's forehead. "Goodbye," he whispered.

He stepped away and cold rushed between them. Hilary blinked until he could focus. Dom was gone.

Chapter Eighteen

"Alone at last." Jasper beamed as he brought a tray out onto the *Empress'* sundeck. The yacht bobbed at anchor, the sun beating down from an azure sky, the Atlantic Ocean spreading in endless waves in all directions. Hilary sat up in his sun lounger to accept the glass his husband offered and dutifully clinked it off Jasper's.

Jasper sighed loudly as he settled himself into another chair, crossing his long legs and grinning. "Should be in the Caribbean in just over a week. Forecast is good so far. Until then, we've got all this."

"It's amazing," Hilary said, putting his phone back in his pocket. "And no phone signal, just like you promised."

Jasper examined him over his sunglasses. "Expecting a call, husband-mine?"

"Just wanted to check in with Beck," Hilary said, sipping his drink.

"They'll survive without you for a few weeks," Jasper chided, munching a strawberry from the bowl on the table between them.

"I know," Hilary said, topping up his glass.

"Where did you go after the first dance, by the way?"

"What?"

"I've been meaning to ask you," Jasper said, not looking at him, "but it's all been so hectic. After the first dance you disappeared. I tried to find you."

Hilary cleared his throat with more champagne and took a strawberry. "I just went for a walk."

Jasper raised his eyebrows. "You went for a walk?"

"It was all so mad," Hilary said. "I needed a break."

Jasper looked away. "It was a day and a half, wasn't it?" he said, fatigue seeping into his tone. But then he smiled, reached over and grabbed Hilary's hand. "But it's done now. And I'll keep my promise, Hil. It'll be all we ever talked about. Promise."

Hilary squeezed his hand back and smiled. "If you're sure that's what you want…"

Jasper frowned. "Of course it is."

Hilary swallowed, holding the hand still tighter. "You know you can be honest with me, don't you?"

"Honest about what?"

Hilary took a breath. "I want you to be happy, Jasper. But you have to be able to admit what you really want."

"I know that." He grinned, his smile only a touch brittle. "I want you. That's obvious, isn't it?" Hilary tried not to think about the fact that this was the longest conversation they'd had in days. "What's brought this on, Hil?"

"Nothing," Hilary replied, releasing his hand. "So long as you're sure."

"We've got the rings, haven't we? Can't get more sure than that."

* * * *

Sailing across the Atlantic on the luxury yacht could have been decidedly worse. The galley was well stocked, the weather glorious and Jasper was easy, laughing and attentive, more like the Jasper Hilary had known before they got engaged. They made love every night in the velvet-draped cabin and Hilary found he was able to enjoy it, to feel Jasper the way he used to and banish the ghost of a different pair of hands on his body.

The only time he found it hard was when Jasper asked him to turn over so he could take him from behind. Something changed when he did it. He held Hilary differently and his voice changed, like he was somewhere...or imagining someone...else.

Hilary put the idea in the part of his mind he'd closed off. But it became harder when they came within phone range of the first island. Their phones flashed and buzzed with notifications. When Jasper checked his, he smiled in a way he never smiled with Hilary.

Hilary was as unsure how to handle that as the fact that Dom had kept his promise. No texts, no emails. Nothing.

As Jasper piloted the yacht into a berth in the teeming marina, Hilary gave in to temptation and did a Google search. But the only new hits related to Merriweather's sentencing, and there was precious little of that. Lavelle now dominated the headlines. It seemed the world had moved on.

They ate, they drank, they had sex on the beach under the stars. Hilary found it easier and easier to ignore the doubt that had fogged so much of the last few months. Now it was just the two of them, uninterrupted, and he was sure he'd been right all along. Jasper was the right man for him. He'd wobbled, there was no doubt. Dom had represented…something. Something unresolved that now felt mended.

But this was Jasper Prince. He lit up the room when he smiled. Everyone they met wanted selfies with him. He'd stolen countless hearts around the world, Hilary's included. He laughed like he'd never known uncertainty or doubt in his life. It made it easier for Hilary to pretend he hadn't either.

It was when they were eating their final meal at a restaurant on the Guadeloupe shoreline, the sun sinking into the sea in a blaze of ambers and purples, that a text flashed on Hilary's screen that threatened to crack the barrier he'd built so meticulously around the uncertainty.

I miss you.

Hilary put his fork down. Jasper was chatting about desserts and examining the menu. Hilary drew his phone into his lap. He stared at the message with something curling soft fingers around his heart. He began to type a reply, looked up and saw Jasper across the table, now smiling at him as he held the menu out.

"Made your choice?"

Hilary deleted the message and put his phone in his pocket. "I'm guessing you've made it for me?"

Jasper smiled and ordered for both of them.

* * * *

By the time they were back at their flat in rainy London, they were both sunburned, fatigued and Jasper was already making excuses for a night away later in the week.

"After the thing with *Hello!* magazine, that is," Jasper murmured, staring at his phone as they rode the lift up to their flat. "They're doing a feature on gay marriage. Marcia wants us to do a follow-up in six months, too…"

Hilary nodded without speaking, thinking of pajamas, Grey Goose and a bed that didn't move.

"Oh," Jasper said, eyebrows drawing down as they stepped into the flat. "I see your mate's been up to his old tricks."

"What?"

Jasper held the phone out. Hilary's stomach dropped. It was a Buzzfeed article about Dom. There were pictures of a totaled Lamborghini, of him being breathalyzed then restrained from attacking people who were filming on their phones. One of the videos was included in the article. Dom's face was twisted with fury, the police barely able to hold him.

"Christ."

"I don't know why you're surprised," Jasper said as he stepped back to allow the porter to drop the last of their bags into the hall. "I'm going in the shower."

Hilary waited until he heard the water running before opening his laptop and searching the article.

…the family's high-paid legal team has ensured the worst punishment he will face is yet another fine, but this has once

again brought Dominic Hart-Gosford's recent murder charge to the forefront of everyone's attention. Of course, such examples of antisocial behavior are nothing new, as one of the pictures at the center of the Wood murder controversy testifies...

The picture of him storming out of the art gallery was featured, and a quick search of social media proved that it was doing the rounds again. Hilary propped his head in his hands and stared at it, the dark pain etched into Dom's face going right to his heart.

He blinked. He brought the laptop closer. The picture that had gone viral the first time had been cropped. This one was bigger. He could just make out Eloise Hart in the window of the gallery. She was smiling. Hilary frowned, first at her face, then at Dom's.

"Shit..."

"What is it?"

Hilary started. Jasper was in the doorway, rubbing his hair with a towel. He glowered at the screen. "You're not seriously getting involved already? We just got back."

"Something's wrong," Hilary said, searching the desk drawers for his work phone. "Very wrong."

"Your client's a prick," Jasper said, frowning as Hilary turned on the phone. "Hardly breaking news."

He scrolled through the dozens of notifications but there was nothing other than routine work messages. Nothing from Gunnerson. Nothing from Beck.

"They've not noticed..."

"Noticed what?"

His phone screen blurred as Gunnerson's words came back to him. He thought about the junior partnership, his as soon as he walked back into the office…if he did what was expected. He brought up the office number and stared at it.

"Hilary?" Jasper prompted.

"I gotta go," Hilary said, pocketing the phone and grabbing his keys.

"Now?"

"Yes, Jazz. *Now*."

"Are you serious? We were just starting to find our way back to each other—"

"I don't have time for this," Hilary said, moving for the door, but Jasper stepped in his way.

"You can't save him, Hilary. He's a lost cause."

"No one's a lost cause," Hilary said and left the flat before his husband could say another word.

He tried ringing as he raced toward Mayfair, but Dom's number rang out then went to answerphone. He tried again with the same result. He swore, tried a third time, only to have someone answer then cut the call.

He swore still more vehemently as he drove and hurriedly typed a text, one eye on the road.

I need to see you. It's important.

By the time he was pulling up outside Dom's townhouse, there was still no reply. He rang the buzzer several times, but no one answered. He cursed and ran his hands through his hair, making himself think calmly. He got back into the car and googled Dom's name.

His heart hammered as he scrolled through the lists of gossip articles until he found a tweet from a news network earlier that day.

Business as usual for the Hart-Gosford family as they throw a birthday dinner for the Finance Secretary today at Brentwold Hall...

It was over an hour's drive to the Harts' country mansion. A limousine was being waved through the gates when he arrived. He made to follow it, but the security guard held up a hand. Hilary muttered under his breath and lowered his window.

"Your name, sir?"

"Hilary Whyte to see Mr. Hart-Gosford."

The guard examined an iPad with a heavy frown. "I'm afraid you're not on the list, sir."

"I'm his solicitor."

"I'm afraid I can't admit you if you're not on the list."

Hilary watched the gates clank shut again with despair. "He'll see me. Just tell him I'm here."

"The family is entertaining—"

"Just *do* it."

The guard raised his eyebrows and retreated a couple of steps to talk into his walkie-talkie. After what seemed like an age, he finally activated the gate and waved Hilary through with a disgruntled expression.

Hilary parked crookedly next to the line of Rolls-Royces and Bentleys outside the towering porticoed entrance. Finely dressed people were climbing the stairs to the open front doors flanked by liveried footmen.

He was suddenly very conscious of his jeans and band T-shirt but hurried up the stairs without meeting any of the curious glances sent his way.

"Mr. Whyte?" A uniformed servant intercepted him before he reached the doors. "This way."

The servant led him away from the main entrance hall, down arched corridors, their feet echoing on the marble floors. He was shown into a high-ceilinged room with large windows, the walls filled floor-to-ceiling with bookshelves.

Dom stood at a drinks' sideboard, his back to the room, pouring whiskey from a crystal decanter.

"Dom—"

"What do you want, Hilary?"

Hilary blinked. "Are you drunk?"

Dom turned. His dark eyes were heavy. There were gray shadows under them. His dinner suit looked loose. He also seemed shorter, like he was slumped. "What do you want?"

"We need to get you away from here. *Now*."

He frowned. "What?"

"The minute Eloise realizes I'm here, she'll know why..."

"What are you talking about?"

Hilary lowered his voice. "It was her Dom. It was all her."

Dom downed the whiskey and shook his head. "Go away, Hilary."

"I'm not going anywhere," Hilary snapped. "Not without you."

"Oh, so you want me now?" Dom glowered, thudding the tumbler down with a crash.

"Dom, will you listen?"

"No," he said, moving to push past him.

"This isn't about you and me—"

"It could have been." Dom turned back, glaring. "It *should* have been. But you said yourself it's all too late."

"Dom—"

"You shouldn't have come, Hilary," he muttered. "You made your choice. Do me the courtesy of sticking to it."

"*Dom*," Hilary snapped, thrusting his phone into Dom's hand. "Eloise was the only person who knew you weren't going to be at the banquet that day — the only one who knew you weren't going to have an alibi."

Dom glared at the picture from the news article.

"What are you talking about?"

"Look at her," Hilary insisted. "She's smiling. Why would she be smiling if you'd just had a fight and you were set to publicly embarrass her?"

"Eloise is always happy when I'm not," Dom said, handing the phone back. "That's all."

"She invited Lavelle on purpose," Hilary said urgently. "She wanted you to duck out last-minute. She wanted you angry."

"You don't know what you're talking about..."

"You don't remember where you went after the gallery, do you?" Hilary said quietly. Dom stared at him. "You don't remember any of that evening. And you didn't want to tell me because you were afraid of what you might have done."

"No," Dom snapped. "I would never hurt Dean."

"But you blacked out?" Hilary insisted, stepping closer. "Assumed you'd got wasted but couldn't remember where you'd been or what you'd done?"

Dom's jaw worked. He looked away.

"Did Eloise give you anything to drink that day?"

"Hilary..."

"Think," Hilary snapped, grabbing his hand before he could turn away. "Did you eat or drink anything at the gallery that afternoon?"

"It doesn't matter…"

"It does. Think."

Dom's face tightened. "Whiskey."

"How many?"

"I don't know. Two?"

"She drugged you," Hilary murmured, holding the phone out again, making him look at the picture. "She knew after a fight like that you'd have one of your off-the-grid nights—turning your phone off, paying for everything in cash. And drugging you meant you wouldn't remember. Don't you see? She assured Merriweather you'd have an alibi, then engineered it so you would lose it at the last minute."

"You're saying she just *happened* to have drugged whiskey on hand?" Dom scoffed.

"She could have been planning it for months…years, waiting for the perfect opportunity."

Dom kneaded his forehead. "You're not making any sense."

"Think about it. Who had the power and the money to arrange all this? Who had the most to lose if whatever Lizzie knew came out?"

"Why would Lizzie go to Eloise and not me?"

"If she thought you were abusing her brother, what better way to hurt you than to go after the family that protected you?"

Dom lowered himself onto the edge of a damask sofa. "But Merriweather admitted…"

"He said himself he'd do anything for you, for this family. Eloise knew that, too. I bet there's no secret account. He didn't pay Lizzie that money. He probably never even met her before he killed her. Eloise just told him what he needed to hear about her to make him do what she wanted."

"Why pay at all?" Dom said, voice like gravel. "If Eloise planned to…do that. Why pay out in the first place?"

"To point the finger at you."

Dom blinked his bleary eyes. "But she was so adamant in defending me. She wanted the best lawyers…"

"She wanted rid of me because she'd read my trial record and was worried I might win. She didn't want someone better. She wanted someone worse. That performance on the stand? That was all on purpose. She wanted the jury to hate you. She wants you gone, Dom, don't you see? She'll try again."

Dom shook his head and shambled to the drinks counter. He poured and downed another drink.

"Stop drinking," Hilary said. "We have to go. Now, before she hears I'm here…"

"Too late for that, Mr. Whyte."

Hilary went cold. Eloise Hart closed the library door behind her. Her satin gown was the same shade of metallic silver as the Glock in her hand.

Dom's face darkened. His hand around his drink began to shake. "Eloise…"

"Let's not," Eloise said, coming farther into the room. "Confrontation is so tedious."

"Mrs. Hart—"

"Quiet," Eloise snapped, aiming the gun at Hilary.

"You won't get away with this," Hilary said, holding very still.

"I already have." Eloise's thin-lipped mouth turned up at the corners. "Merriweather has taken the fall for the removal of the Wood nuisance. And now you, Dominic," she said, then threw him the gun. He caught it clumsily and stared at it. "Now you are going to finish it."

"Dom—"

"Your life is over," Eloise said, eyes glinting. "Reputation in tatters. One lover dead. Another"—she leveled a glare at Hilary—"about to be disbarred and publicly disgraced."

"Don't listen," Hilary urged, stomach plunging as Dom stared at the gun in his hands.

"Do the only decent thing you can do with your life, Dominic," Eloise said. "End it. Free my daughter and yourself."

"Just let them divorce," Hilary said. "Let your daughter spend her life with who she wants."

Eloise's lip curled. "I know what's best for my family. And Dominic has left us no other way to end this cleanly."

"Dom, *don't listen*—"

"Enough from you, Mr. Whyte," Eloise snapped. "You think I haven't guessed what you've been up to? Utterly disgraceful. A married man, a client. And you married yourself?" She shook her head. "You'll be lucky if Mr. Gunnerson doesn't have you arrested."

"I'm sorry, Hilary," Dom murmured.

"No," Hilary said, lifting his hands as Dom raised the gun. "Dom, don't."

Dom pressed the barrel to his temple. "This is for the best," he said, voice thick. "I should have done it years ago."

"No, Dom," Hilary cried, reaching out. "Don't. *I love you.*"

Silence as suffocating as seawater flooded the room. Dom stared at him, the gun still to his head. Hilary's heart clamored in his chest. He begged him with his eyes.

"Lord above, I really do have to do everything myself, don't I?"

Eloise pulled another gun from her bag and aimed at Hilary. The shot split the air like thunder. A breathless second later, he forced his eyes open, not realizing he'd shut them. Eloise was on the floor, clutching her shoulder, her eyes wide, face gray. She gasped, pained, strangled breaths, too shocked to vocalize.

Dom lowered his gun. Hilary pulled breath into his aching lungs, staggered to Dom and pried the gun from his hands.

"It's okay," he murmured, over and over, touching his arm, his face, his hair. "I'll fix it, okay? I'll fix everything. It's okay. You're okay."

Dom raised his eyes. They were bleary and black with fear. Hilary put a hand to his cheek. "It's okay, Dom," he repeated. "I've got this. It's all going to be okay."

A clamor in the corridor broke the spell. Amelia hurried in, the dark-haired woman from the bedside photograph at her shoulder.

"Mother?" she said, looking around, then, spotting Eloise bleeding onto the Turkish rug, paled and clasped a hand to her mouth.

"Dom, sit." Hilary pushed him into a chair then hurried to the fallen Eloise, bunching her pashmina against the wound. "Amelia? *Amelia*," he said, raising his voice until Amelia focused on him. "Call an ambulance," he instructed. "Now."

"I'll do it," the other woman said, pulling out a phone. "Stay here, sweetheart. Don't move." Amelia knelt next to Hilary and helped him to crush the satin to her mother's shoulder, her face slack with shock.

"Mother, can you hear me?"

Dom stared at them all, unseeing. Hilary ached to go to him but then people were swarming into the room, servants and guests drawn by the noise. Exclamations, panicked questions and barked orders filled the air, which soon flashed blue with ambulance lights and screamed with sirens.

* * * *

Hilary had trouble recalling the days that followed in much detail. Everything merged into a mire of worry, fatigue and guilt-ridden relief. It seemed the police's questions would never be fully answered. McGarry stared hard at Hilary during their interviews, never wavering, even for a moment. But Hilary didn't either.

"It was self-defense," Hilary said. "She was going to shoot him."

"Mrs. Hart tells a very different story, Mr. Whyte," McGarry said, her eyes like cut glass.

"Of course she does," Hilary said. "She's a murderer."

Eloise was transferred from critical care to a regular ward just two days after surgery and was expected to make a full recovery. Hilary didn't know whether to be relieved or disappointed when McGarry shared the news.

Finally, the police got access to Eloise's phone and email records. That was when it all came out—Lizzie using an encrypted email account to contact Eloise, stating she knew Dom and Amelia's marriage was a sham, accusing Dom of gaslighting and abusing young men. She called him and the family that enabled his behavior monsters, parasites, and demanded they pay her enough so she could get her brother out of London, away from Dom, somewhere she could start a new life for both of them.

There was no evidence that she'd come back for more or ever demanded to see Dom in person. Hilary was certain that this was something Eloise had made up to persuade Merriweather to kill her.

Eloise had taken advantage of every error of judgment everyone involved had made with the cold precision of a surgeon removing shrapnel from a shooting victim, not caring that the patient was already beyond saving.

Finally, McGarry must have realized that she had all the answers she was going to get and, as much as she may have wanted to, realized she couldn't arrest Hilary for proving her wrong. He was released.

Gunnerson asked for his resignation within the week.

"I could very easily make a case for wrongful dismissal with all this, sir," he said, trying to stop the emotion shaking his voice.

"You could...but you won't."

"Why wouldn't I?"

Gunnerson lifted a bushy eyebrow. "Because you'd lose. And you know it."

Hilary dropped his resignation letter on his desk without breaking eye contact.

"You see me as the ogre," Gunnerson said as he tucked the letter in one of his innumerable files. "But we had a deal. When you realized it was Eloise, you should have come to me first. We could have avoided all this…unpleasantness."

"I made my choice, sir. I'll live with it."

Gunnerson gave him a keen look and the smallest of smiles. "Of that I have no doubt."

Jasper only knew what Hilary told him, but seemed to sense there were gaps Hilary refused to fill in. He had trouble meeting his husband's eyes, and when Jasper gave up telling Hilary when he was going to be away or how long for, Hilary barely noticed.

Beck came to the flat when he wouldn't answer any calls. She didn't say or ask anything. She brought takeaway and vodka and sat and listened to records with him and hugged him when he couldn't explain.

Max and Minnie both came to see him, too. Individually, this time, like the sensed he needed each of them to himself. He could tell by the way they both looked at him that they'd guessed everything, but they didn't press him. They gave him such loving smiles, telling him without words that, whatever happened, they knew he would get through this, that it allowed him to believe it that little bit more.

In that moment he wondered why he'd ever been jealous of their relationship. He saw now they'd always been a team. A family. And that it would never change.

That didn't stop him scouring the web all day and night for mentions of Dom, seeing what came out, what didn't. But the only thing that seemed to be certain was that, in the eyes of the world, the fact that his own mother-in-law had framed him for murder rather than face the shame of a divorce in the family seemed to somehow be his own fault.

Either way, whichever solicitor Gunnerson had sent to represent him knew their stuff and Dom had been released without charge. Hilary tried to get up the courage to contact him several times in the run-up to Eloise's trial. But he never felt brave enough to ring and deleted every message he typed before sending, no words seeming right.

Dom didn't contact him, either.

He was dreading their next meeting being in court, but Eloise's case never made it to trial. She pled guilty two days before it was due to start. Hilary would have given anything to know the terms of her plea, but he knew better than to try to find out.

He drove to the courthouse to attend the sentencing hearing. But when he caught sight of Dom and Amelia going into the building together, his courage failed him.

He left without looking back.

Chapter Nineteen

"I really wish you'd quit."

Hilary hurriedly closed the webpage about Dom's continued disappearance from public life and loaded the job application he was supposed to be working on. He drew deep on his cigarette and met Jasper's accusing look as he came into the room, buttoning his cuffs. Jasper frowned and opened the window.

"You could at least do it outside."

Hilary didn't answer and skimmed the application criteria, even though he couldn't even begin to figure out how to fill it in. Jasper pressed a hard kiss to the crown of his head.

"You'll find a new job, babe," he murmured as he shrugged on his jacket. "Don't worry."

Hilary stubbed out the cigarette and didn't meet Jasper's eye.

"I know you don't think I could handle knowing what got you fired, Hil. But isn't it time for us to be honest with each other?"

"I resigned," Hilary said for the hundredth time.

Jasper sighed and made for the door. "Well, I'm off. Don't wait up. You know how late these producer parties can run."

"Jasper," Hilary said. Jasper paused with his hand on the door handle, "I want a divorce."

Jasper's face paled. "What?"

"I haven't been able to admit it before. But, in my defense, neither have you."

Jasper sat on the edge of the sofa, looking stunned. "Admit what, Hilary?"

Hilary fought to unstick his suddenly dry tongue. "You don't want this. You don't want me."

"That's not true."

"It is." He hesitated then took Jasper's hand. "It's okay."

"I…I don't understand."

Hilary made himself meet his husband's eye. "You need to concentrate on you—on your career. That's all right. But until you care less about whether the whole world loves you, no one else stands a chance." Wetness glinted in Jasper's eyes and Hilary's stomach dipped. "I'm sorry."

"I can try harder…"

"You shouldn't have to," Hilary said, squeezing his hand.

"But we can't divorce. We just can't."

"Why not?"

"All the work we've done, all that positive PR for gay marriage. It'll all be undone."

"I think we do more damage to the reputation of gay marriage by staying in an unhappy one to save face."

"I'm not unhappy," Jasper said desperately. "I love you, Hil. I do. I just…." He scowled at the carpet. "I don't know how to make you happy. I've tried, but I've never been able to figure it out." He looked at Hilary, his blue eyes swimming with tears. "I'm a terrible person."

Hilary sighed. "You're not a terrible person, Jazz. You just won't admit what you want."

Jasper swallowed. "I've messed this up, haven't I?"

"It wasn't just you," Hilary said, leaning his head back and staring at the ceiling. He felt Jasper's penetrating look.

"You...?" Hilary heard him take a breath. "You and Dominic, right? That's what got you fired?"

Hilary closed his eyes.

"I knew it. I told myself I was wrong, but I knew something had changed. The minute you took that case..."

"I'm sorry, Jasper."

Jasper took a shaking breath. "Why him, Hil?"

"I... He understands me, all of me. Inside and out."

"He bullied you. Abused you."

Hilary rubbed his aching eyes. "He didn't know how to admit what he wanted, either. Apparently, it's really not that easy."

* * * *

Hilary drove without acknowledging what he was doing. His mind was a hard, aching blank. His chest hurt. His throat was dry, despite the drained bottles of water on the passenger seat. The land rolled away in green embankments. Mountains glowered in the distance. Finally, he was turning off the last twisting A-road onto an even more winding country lane. It was only as it started to get dark that the satnav's robotic voice declared that he'd reached his destination.

He stared at the large red-brick farmhouse through the windscreen with a strange feeling simmering under his ribs. A Land Rover was in the garage, a tractor next to that. A dog barked somewhere then went quiet. Chickens pecked at the cobbles outside a large barn behind the house.

Hilary sat there for almost ten minutes before he made himself get out of the car and ring the bell.

Dom opened the door. He was in a loose T-shirt and hard-wearing work trousers. His hair stuck up in all directions, and his face and bare arms were tanned. He stared at Hilary in silence.

"How did you find me?"

"Beck found you," Hilary said. "Or…she found out your dad left you this place. I just hoped…" He met his gaze then looked hurriedly away. "I'm sorry about your dad."

"Don't be," Dom said. "Dying was the best thing he ever did for his family."

Hilary looked around the quiet farmyard, bathed auburn in the late summer sunset. "I…I don't know why I'm here."

"You'd better come in, then."

Hilary followed Dom down a narrow hall clustered with battered bookcases with framed watercolors on the wall.

"There's only tea, I'm afraid."

"That sounds great."

Dom made the tea in a spacious kitchen, the windowsill crowded with plants, the walls hung with pots, pans and a dizzying array of cooking utensils. Hilary accepted the steaming cup and sipped. It tasted good, fresh and strong. He felt his trembling ease but still couldn't lift his head to meet Dom's piercing gaze.

"I thought you should know that Merriweather is having his sentence reduced in exchange for cooperating with the prosecution," Hilary said, running his fingers along the grain of the wooden table.

"I know."

Hilary looked up. The heat in Dom's eyes and the sight of his strong, large hands curled around the untouched mug of tea sent something flickering through Hilary's flesh. "She paid one of Lizzie's neighbors to tell her when Dean would next be over for dinner. He wasn't there by accident, Dom. She planned the whole thing, to get rid of them both and you in one sweep. She probably knew he'd have your DNA on him—or she made sure it was." Hilary paused to gather himself. "Merriweather…did not take the news well. He thought Dean was there by accident and that he did it all for you, not her. Now he knows what her real plan was—to remove Lizzie, Dean and you—it's all coming out."

Dom didn't reply. Hilary looked away again, unable to control his expression.

"Did you mean it?" Dom said as the silence threatened to swell out of control.

"Mean what?"

"When you said you loved me." Dom leaned forward on his elbows, his hand resting on the table close to Hilary's. "Did you mean it? Or were you just trying to stop me from blowing my brains out?"

Hilary hesitated. "I meant it."

Dom swallowed. "So what are we going to do about it?"

"I…I don't know…" Hilary stared into his tea, his stomach churning, his skin on fire.

"Hilary, did something happen?"

Hilary sipped the tea to loosen his tongue. "I've asked Jasper for a divorce."

Dom didn't speak.

"I don't know why I couldn't be happy," Hilary went on. "He was perfect."

"People are rarely perfect."

"But...I've worked so hard..." Hilary hated that his voice shook.

"You've always been everything you needed to be, Hilary. You never needed anyone else for that."

Hilary tightened his grip on the mug.

Dom stared at their hands, so close on the tabletop. "My own divorce will be final in a few weeks."

"I know..." Hilary said. He couldn't resist any longer and put his hand on Dom's. His skin was warm, soft, despite the hard knuckles and strong sinews. The touch sent fire dancing up Hilary's arm, and he felt steadier, like a whirlwind inside him was finally blowing out. Something changed in Dom's face, too.

"So...sheep farming, huh?" Hilary said, looking around the kitchen with a half-smile.

"My dad's idea of a joke, I think," Dom said levelly. "Another not-so-subtle jibe about my place in the world. But the joke's on him. Turns out I like it."

"That's good," Hilary said weakly. "Amelia went ahead with the Elizabeth Wood Foundation, I heard..."

"I gave her most of my companies in the divorce settlement," Dom said, voice level as a winter pond. "But only if she agreed to make sure that happened, if the Woods wanted it. But she was happy to do it. She feels responsible, too."

"It's a good thing...that charity."

Dom shrugged a shoulder. "I wonder now whether it would have helped someone as desperate as Lizzie Wood."

"She didn't have to do what she did."

"She obviously felt she did," Dom said quietly, "to protect her family."

"She believed what she read and decided the only way her brother would be involved with you is if you manipulated him...or worse." Hilary watched the purple evening gathering outside the window with an ache in his throat. "Perhaps she should have found out about you for herself before setting out to fight."

"I think she was just scared about losing her brother," Dom said after a pause, his voice so low Hilary could hardly catch the words. "Dean talked about getting away. Paris. I could tell he was distancing himself from something. Perhaps it was her. Perhaps she sensed it, too."

"So she should have talked to him...to you."

Dom looked at their hands. "It's usually easier to lash out at others than admit the problem is closer to home."

Hilary winced. He took a breath. "I missed you."

Dom raised his eyes. "I missed you, too."

"I was going to call..."

"Why didn't you?"

"I was scared."

Dom lifted Hilary's hand to his face. He brushed his lips over the knuckles, causing Hilary's breath to catch in his throat. "Scared of what?"

"Scared that I was right," Hilary forced out. "That it really is too late."

Dom came around the table, stood over him, tilting his face up to his. He kissed his lips, gently at first, then more insistently when Hilary shivered and opened his mouth.

"There's no such thing as a lost cause," Dom whispered against his lips. "Not if someone is left to believe in it."

"Jasper hasn't agreed yet," Hilary said, his voice shaking. "He wants to work it out."

"What do you want, Hilary?"

"I want to be certain again," Hilary said, his voice wobbling. "To know who I am."

"I've never known you to doubt yourself before."

Hilary screwed up his face to keep his tears from flowing. "Everything was worked out. It was all in place. But now I have no job. No marriage. No future. And I'm still not sure I understand why."

"Sometimes we're not meant to know why," Dom said, running his fingers over his cheek. "Sometimes we just have to accept that there is no certainty. You taught me that."

"They didn't disbar me..." Hilary murmured. "But I don't know what firm would accept me now. And...I don't even know if I'd want the job if they did."

"You were born to help people," Dom said. "You'll find a way to do that. Find a way to be certain of yourself again."

"How can you be so sure?"

"You helped me do it," he said, brushing Hilary's hair back from his face. "I can help you, if you'll let me."

"How?"

Dom hesitated. Nervousness flickered in his eyes and Hilary held his breath. "There's a small firm in the market town down the road, council-funded. They do a lot of pro bono work with young people. Their senior partner is about to retire, and they need a replacement.

I know it's a huge step down, but you said you preferred helping people who would make the most of that second chance."

Hilary narrowed his eyes even as his heart swelled in his chest. "How do you know about this?"

Dom hesitated. He looked away. "I asked."

"Why?"

"Because I hoped," Dom said, returning his gaze to Hilary's face. "No, I believed. Believed you might come after me."

Hilary wrapped his arms around Dom's shoulders. He kissed him again. Dom drew him to his feet and pulled him close. He slid his hand up his T-shirt, and Hilary whimpered, feeling his strength falling away in chunks. He clung onto Dom's muscled frame, strong enough for both of them.

"I want you, Dom," he whispered against his mouth. "I know that, now. Just you. I love you."

Dom snuggled his face into Hilary's hair. He went still, holding Hilary close like he might slip away if he didn't hold tight. "I love you, too, Hilary. I always have."

"Is it too late?" Hilary whispered.

"There's a lot to fix," Dom murmured. "I know that. But we can do it together—whatever it takes."

Hilary nodded. "I believe you."

Want to see more from this author? Here's a taster for you to enjoy!

Straight to the Heart
S. J. Coles

Excerpt

James Solomon knew it was unprofessional—unethical, even—to be grateful for the murder of a high-profile businessman two days before what would have been his parents' fortieth wedding anniversary. But his robust professional pride couldn't put a dent in the very real relief he felt when the call had come through.

He climbed out of the rented car outside Benson Industries HQ and breathed in the brisk sea breeze. The early morning was still gloomy, casting everything in shadow. Gibson slammed the passenger door with a sigh as a woman in a sheriff's uniform hurried over to meet them.

"Agents, thanks for coming so quickly."

"No problem, Sheriff," Gibson replied, her face schooled professionally blank. "The sooner we start, the better. Sheriff Coyle, right?"

"That's right," the middle-aged woman said, her smile doing nothing to warm the pale set of her face.

"Agent Lisa Gibson," Gibson responded, shaking the other woman's hand then indicating James. "Agent James Solomon. We've had the incident reports, but can you fill us in using your own words?"

"Sure. Follow me," Sheriff Coyle said, her voice a bit steadier. She preceded them to the wide, glass entrance and swiped a card through a reader. They paced past the empty reception desk and down a marble-tiled corridor. The place was deserted, the black eyes of cameras the only things watching them. "The vic is Derek Benson, fifty-five years old," the sheriff continued. "Born here in Winton, then got a job with the FDA in Maryland after college. Struck out on his own at age thirty. Now he's the owner, CEO, director — you name it — of Benson Industries."

"Specialist pharmaceuticals, right?" Gibson asked, scanning reports on her phone.

"That's right. Pulling in some pretty serious business these days. Some big names on the client list. That's why we called you guys in."

"So what happened?"

"Benson was found by the janitor in his office this morning, shot three times in the chest."

"Time of death?" Gibson asked.

"Our ME is putting it around nine p.m. last night, though he says he can be more accurate after the postmortem."

"And you said the security camera footage is missing?" Gibson asked, eyeing another camera as they strode past.

"Yeah," said the sheriff with a weary exasperation James could more than identify with. "The security system backs up everything onto disk. The disks from eight p.m. last night to three this morning have been taken."

"No online backup?" James ventured, not hopefully, as they stepped onto an elevator.

Coyle shook her head. "I don't think Benson trusted the cloud and all that. They're dusting the Security Room for prints where the disks were kept now."

"Did Benson often work that late?" Gibson asked as the elevator hummed up to the seventh floor.

"He put a lot of hours in, sure, but there was some kind of business presentation last night. All the heads of department and senior staff were here from seven-thirty onward. Plus, some of the lab rats were working late on a deadline."

"Lab rats?" James queried, as Coyle led them out onto a level that was all glass walls and spacious offices with big desks and bold, minimalist furniture.

"The technicians," she said, glancing this way and that, as if wary of what might be hiding in the maze of glass. "We have a list of everyone who was in the building at the time from the swipe system, though so far no one saw anyone leave the conference room or the labs."

"How many people are we talking?" Gibson, warily.

Coyle pulled a battered notepad from a back pocket and flipped through it. "Thirty-one."

"That's a lot of people with opportunity," Gibson muttered.

"One of them was his wife," Coyle added. "Melissa Benson."

"His wife was at the business meeting?"

Coyle nodded. "She's a senior partner in the firm. She delivered one of the presentations."

"At what time?"

"Pretty much the same time they reckon he was shot," Coyle said and grimaced. "Sorry."

"Well, we wouldn't want it to be too easy. She looks younger than him," Gibson said, examining a photo of

Melissa Benson on the arm of her husband at some event on a news website.

"She's his second wife. He and his first divorced about ten years ago."

"Amicably?"

"I'm afraid so," Coyle said with another sympathetic expression.

"What did you think of the victim?" James asked, watching the sheriff's face.

"Me?" Her forehead creased. "I didn't know him."

"But you knew *of* him," James pressed. "Big company. Small town. You had to have some impression of what he was like."

Coyle slid him a sideways glance. "He did stuff for some local charities. Donated to a few nature conservation causes and the homeless actions — that kind of thing."

"But?" James prompted, seeing her face had tightened.

Coyle looked uncomfortable. "He hired most of his staff from out-of-town. They don't live here. They don't contribute to the economy and they can get the locals' backs up. Snobbish, some say. Elitist."

"What would *you* say?"

"I've never had much contact," Coyle hedged. "They're law-abiding and keep to themselves."

"What do you make of the wife, Melissa?"

"Reserved."

"She's not upset?"

"Oh, she's upset," Coyle said. "But she's not the sort to go to pieces in front of the likes of me."

"The report said the murder weapon was his own gun," James said, carefully logging the sheriff's last reply away for further consideration.

"Sure looks that way. He kept it in his desk." Coyle stopped at one of the glass doors, where a uniformed officer, looking a little green, stood at attention. The body of Derek Benson was slumped in a large, designer office chair under the window. Blood splattered up the glass behind him, looking like red rain suspended in the gray sky. The crime-scene photographer was taking close-ups of the bullet wounds while his partner, who looked old enough to have been the scene technician at the St. Valentine's Day Massacre, was bent over the desk, sweeping for prints as delicately as if he were applying makeup.

"We don't get much murder here," Coyle murmured. "Winton's a peaceful town. We get some drugs, some drunk and disorderlies, a bit of fraud. But stuff like this?" She shook her head.

"A big company shoe-horned into a small community," James ventured, watching both the officers' faces, "can cause friction."

Coyle raised her eyebrows. "Big companies are fine. But BI's too big—and only likely to get bigger."

"Oh yes?" Gibson prompted, pulling on some gloves and pushing open the door.

"That's what they're saying that presentation was about," Coyle said, hanging back near the door as Gibson bent over the body. "They're striking a deal with an international distributer for their newest antiviral."

"Do you know which distributer?" James asked, examining the photographs hanging on the interior wall. Black-and-white shots of the local harbor, mostly, plus a few of the hills west of the town.

Coyle frowned at her notepad, ruffling the pages. "It's in here somewhere. I'm sure it went in the report."

"It did," Gibson replied, giving James a hard look. "Loadstone Inc."

Coyle smiled a relieved smile, and Gibson went back to scrutinizing the crumpled form of Derek Benson. His chin was on his chest. A rope of blood-speckled saliva hung from a corner of his lined mouth. His skin was yellow-gray and his limbs stiff with the rigor of someone dead nearly twelve hours. His hands, hairless and manicured, rested in his lap. His eyebrows were heavy and dark. His thinning hair was iron gray, though still almost black at the nape. He wore an expensive suit and a dark, conservative tie. Blood soaked his shirtfront and pooled under the chair. The gun was on the floor by the desk. A desk drawer stood wide open.

"All three shots went right into his heart," Gibson said, leaning close to the wounds. "The killer knew how to shoot."

"There's a lock on the drawer but not a complex one," James said, examining the keypad on the drawer front.

"And there's no signs of a struggle," Gibson replied, surveying the rest of the meticulously tidy office.

James nodded. "Someone he knew. Someone he trusted too—or at least someone he wasn't afraid of or he'd have been standing."

"But that could be any one of the thirty-one people in the building last night," Gibson said sourly. She stood with her hands on her hips, glaring at the corpse like it had done her personal harm. "The question is, did he get the gun out himself or did the killer?"

"Business expansion," James said, tilting the computer monitor toward him. The screen saver was another artistic shot of Winton Harbor. James began entering the most popular password choices. "Not always a popular move."

"And why was he *here*?" Gibson frowned. "With a big-deal presentation evening happening in the conference room and the future of his company in the balance?"

"And he's sitting in his office four floors up," James affirmed, smiling when 'qwerty123' allowed him into the computer. "Writing an email to personnel, by the look of it." He gestured at the screen. Gibson came to his elbow and bent to examine the open, unsent email with 'Contract Termination' typed into the subject line and a blinking cursor in the blank form.

Gibson was quiet a moment. James moved to a set of bookshelves against the far wall and scanned the titles. Tomes on business management, chemistry, biology, academic journals on pharmaceuticals and FDA manuals took up most of the upper shelves. The lower ones held several battered volumes on the history of Winton and the surrounding area, plus some on blues, jazz and soul music, with a Frank Sinatra biography thrown in for good measure.

"I think we have all we need," Gibson said to Coyle, who was watching them with an expectant air. "The ME can take him away now." Coyle nodded and stepped back out into the corridor, dialing a number on her cell. "And how about you stop making digs at the local law enforcement, Agent?" Gibson scolded softly.

"If they slip up this early on, it'll end in roadblocks," he returned, watching Coyle through the glass. "And we need to establish local feeling about the situation."

"Consider it established. Are you getting anything on this guy?"

"He loved his town...and music," James mused, glancing around the office again. "But I think he loved his company more."

"His company grossed several million last year. I can see why he had a soft spot for it." Coyle was just hanging up the phone as they rejoined her. "Okay, Sheriff. We need you to round up the employees from last night. We'll question them here."

"Yes, ma'am," she said. "Most of them will be turning up to work at eight anyway."

"Good," said Gibson, looking at her watch and repressing a sigh. "Tell them they can only have the building back when we're done. That'll get them through the door."

Coyle nodded and hurried off.

"We're doing the interviews here?" James questioned.

"One," Gibson said, holding up a finger and moving back toward the elevator, "interviewing near the crime scene could get the killer twitchy and we might get a hit early, meaning I can be back in time for my husband's promotion dinner tomorrow. And two," she said, stabbing the elevator button with more force than was necessary, "getting everyone across town to the Winton Police Station with its single interview room and stone-age Wi-Fi will add hours to the whole damn circus. I'm not paid enough to be here any longer than necessary on what should have been my vacation week."

James set up his interview station in the room he was directed to, put the digital recorder on the desk, pulled out a new, leather-bound notepad and re-read the initial reports on his phone as the clock ticked toward eight a.m.

He frowned when his personal phone buzzed in his pocket. He pulled it out, saw the number and cut the call. Shortly after, a police officer ushered in a tall woman in a business suit. She was already flustered and annoyed. James could already see a queue of similarly well-dressed and irritated people lining up outside. He flipped open his notebook, indicated the chair opposite and began.

Three hours and seven interviews later James was hoarse, tired and frustrated. He flipped through his interview notes, reaffirming that they contained next to nothing. Benson was generally liked. Everyone was quietly hopeful that the deal with Loadstone Inc. would be good for the company and, James figured, for their own wallets. No one knew why Benson had chosen not to attend the presentation evening.

James waited for the next employee wearily, tapping his pen on the desk. When the door remained shut, he checked the corridor. It was empty but for a few local police officers attempting to calm two members of the senior management who were still waiting to be seen and extremely unhappy about it. He sighed, drew breath to call them in then spotted a vending machine farther down the hall. His blood sang out for caffeine.

He slipped down the corridor, punched in his selection and received an ominously greasy coffee in a plastic cup. He glanced back, saw the impatient employees being shown into Gibson's interview room and took the opportunity to step out of a side entrance that had been propped open by the crime-scene team. He found himself on a concrete path at the back of the building. There was a bench against the wall and cigarette butts littered the ground. He took a seat with a sigh and sipped the coffee. It was revolting but hot, and the caffeine began poking holes in his fatigue.

The land rolled steeply away from the path down to the sea. A couple of gulls, looking brighter than jewels against the low sky, wheeled in the salty breeze. He took a moment to just breathe the smell and feel the chill on his skin.

It was so quiet, so unlike the city with its perpetual roar of traffic, blare of sirens and thunder of planes. And the people... Hundreds of thousands of people cramming the sidewalks and the roads, jostling, honking, swearing, always seeming to be desperate to be somewhere else.

He found himself closing his eyes for a moment, letting himself enjoy the cold, quiet sea air, when his phone buzzed again. He stared at the screen for a long moment, then, when the guilt became too sharp, he answered.

"There you are," came the irritated, high-pitched voice. "You avoiding me, James?"

"I'm working, Angelina."

"*This* weekend of all weekends?"

"Yes," James said, controlling his tone with an effort. "I'm afraid the murderer didn't consider their timing."

His sister huffed. "You worked Christmas too."

"I know that—"

"Dad's starting to think you're doing it on purpose."

James kneaded the bridge of his nose. "It's the job."

"Bull," she snapped, and James winced. It took a lot to make his sister even half-swear. "Even FBI agents get vacation time occasionally."

"Get it, yes. But we sometimes have to cancel it, too."

"Dad's not getting any younger, you know."

"Dad's fine."

"He's grieving, James."

James took a moment to let the stab of remorse fade. "We're *all* grieving, Angelina."

She sighed again, sounding defeated. "He misses you."

James didn't reply.

"Yes, he does," she retorted in response to what he didn't say. "I know he said some dumb stuff about Glen, but you know what he's like. Mum wouldn't want you to —"

"Angelina," he put in, firmly, "I've got to go. I'm interviewing."

"Of course you are." Her disappointment was harder to hear than her anger. "I'll film Ryan and Jackson giving Dad his flowers, shall I?"

"Yes," he said. "Please."

A pause. "Stay safe," she said, but in a way that made it clear she might love him but didn't like him much right now and hung up. He rested his head against the wall and stared at the sky, waiting for the flush of shame to ebb.

"Bad day, huh?"

James looked up. A young man in a lab coat stood by the door, giving him a sympathetic look through thin-framed glasses.

"Working day," he replied noncommittally.

The younger man smiled, pulling a pack of cigarettes from his faded jeans and offering them. When James waved them away, he gestured at the bench. "Mind if I...?"

James did mind, but he couldn't think of a professional way to refuse. He glanced at the door, knowing he should get back. But it was so quiet out here.

He shifted over to allow the young man to sit. James picked up the scent of good coffee and herbal shampoo. He blinked and shifted farther away. The man lit a cigarette with a silver Zippo. The tobacco smoke filled the air, thankfully masking the other, more appealing scents, and the wisps wove together above his head before whipping away in the breeze.

"You're one of the FBI agents, huh?"

"Agent Solomon," he confirmed.

"Poor old man Benson," the other murmured after a pause, smoke wreathing from his lips. "I can't believe it. Shot, huh?"

"Unfortunately, yes."

"Man..." The young man shook his head. James examined him out of the corner of his eye. He had long, caramel-colored hair pulled into a loose tail. Home-cut bangs framed a fine-boned face. James noticed with a start that the eyes behind the glasses were the most startling pale green he had ever seen, the color of bottle glass or young leaves. "It's unbelievable," he continued. "Shit like this just doesn't happen around here."

"So I believe."

"It'll be sex or money, right?"

"I'm sorry?"

"Murder." The young man had an impish grin on his face. "It's always about sex or money, right? Or both?"

"We're pursuing several lines of inquiry." He laughed, a bright sound at odds with the chilly, silent morning. "I'm sorry, and you are?" James asked with a spark of irritation.

"Leo." The man held out his hand, unaffected by or not noticing his tone. "Leo Hannah."

"And what's your connection to the victim, Mr. Hannah?" James said, not taking the offered hand.

"Just Leo. I work here. Lab rat," he added, still unfazed, tugging on the lapel of his white coat.

"And what exactly do you do?"

"Uh, well"—he scratched his forehead with a thumbnail—"I'd have to look at my email signature to give you the proper title, but basically, I look into microscopes and play with the analysis machines."

James watched the younger man take another deep draw of his cigarette. Under the lab coat he wore a loose T-shirt printed with some band logo and low-slung jeans. There were battered sneakers on his feet. His hands were long-fingered and fine, with a number of tiny scars and work-hardened pads. His face was boy-like, the green eyes large and fringed with thick lashes, making him look younger than James reasoned he must be. His manner was easy and unguarded, in stark contrast to everyone James had interviewed that morning. He entertained a half-notion for a long moment then heard himself asking, "Did you know Mr. Benson well?"

Hannah snorted smoke out through his nose. "Nah. He's the one with the shiny office on the seventh floor, and I work in the basement. You get me?" He threw James another disarming smile. "But I do know you've got your work cut out for you."

"How so?"

"Well," Hannah said, raising one eyebrow, "I've only been here a couple of years, but even I know you either loved the boss or you hated him."

"Your colleagues have not ventured the same opinion."

Hannah snorted again. "Top brass? No, they wouldn't."

"Why not?"

Hannah rubbed his thumb against his fingers just under James' nose. James caught again the subtle scent of mint and coffee and closed his throat. "Dollar-dollar, yeah?"

"I'm sorry. You'll have to explain."

The man's mouth turned up at the corner. He examined James like he was a slightly diverting article in a usually boring newspaper. James resisted the urge to break eye contact. "Top brass want to be in the pocket of whoever takes over, right?"

"I suppose."

"Well"—he shrugged like it was obvious—"until they know who that's gonna be, everyone's gonna play it cool, right? Especially with the cops. Then you can tell the new boss what a good team player you are."

"And you're not a team player?"

"Not while my team has a killer on the roster, no."

"Uh-huh," James replied and pulled out his notebook. "So you would say the senior management had a wide range of feelings about Mr. Benson?"

"That's a very college-educated way of putting it, but yeah," Hannah replied. "You only had to see them in a room together to see the DHs either worshiped the ground his size tens trod on or wanted to slip a land mine under them."

"DHs?"

"Department heads. Benson is...*was*...too old-school for some of them. Had principles."

"Good principles?"

"Strong ones," Hannah replied. "He demanded loyalty, you know...and respect."

"These department heads... They would be Horatio Torez, June Michaels and Harold Boon?"

"Yeah, those guys. Super top brass."

"Could you be more specific about their relationships with Benson?"

Hannah hesitated then continued, focusing on the burning end of his cigarette. "Michaels and Boon always looked like it was only the size of their paychecks stopping them from beating Benson's head against the table. But Torez? Well..."

"Yes?" James prompted.

"Let's just say I've never seen a guy so into another guy that wasn't into him back."

James took a moment to untangle that. "Torez is gay?"

The green gaze slid his way again. James tried to figure out what was going on in the appraising look. "Both ways, I think. But he keeps it on the hush-hush. He was in the military, you know."

James hadn't known. He made a note. "And how do you know about his orientation?"

Hannah shrugged again, and James wondered if it was a little too easily. "I know someone he dated for a while."

"And Benson?"

"Happily married...twice, I believe. To women, I mean. Been with number two, Melissa, for a while now. You must have that in your files."

"But they were close? Torez and Benson?"

"Hell yeah. Torez is into that whole respect thing. Big on chains-of-command. Benson was like his commanding officer and a father figure all rolled into one, I guess? Torez had a pretty rough upbringing. That's not a secret. I put all this in my statement, by the way—for the lady cop."

James cocked an eyebrow. "'Lady cop'?"

"The pretty one. Older, but still got it."

"You mean Agent Gibson?"

"Sure, that sounds right," he said, grinning again. "She took it all down. Although..."

"What is it?"

"I didn't mention it before because...well, there's no proof. That's what you guys want, right? Evidence? Proof?"

"What do you have?"

"Just a feeling, really."

"About what?"

"A feeling there's been, something, I dunno... something funny between Torez and the old man recently."

"'*Something funny*'?" James repeated.

"Yeah. Sassy said she's heard they've had a beef, though no one knows what about."

"Sassy?"

"Sallyann Andrews, one of the mail runners," Hannah explained. "She hears everything that goes on. Likes to pass it on, too."

"So she heard a rumor. What makes you think it's true?"

Hannah contemplated the sea for a long moment, his forehead creased. "Torez came down to the lab last week for a meeting. He sure looked like a man with a weight on his mind."

"When did Sassy first mention hearing about this disagreement?"

"Uh, a few weeks ago? A month? I'd have to check my work schedule to be sure."

"If you could do that and give me a call," James replied, pulling a business card from his pocket.

"Sure, happy to...James?"

"Agent Solomon is fine."

"Sure thing," Hannah smiled again, wider. James wondered if there was a glint in his eye or if it was just his dry spell playing with his radar. "And hit me up if you need anything, yeah? I grew up here and know the place pretty well. You got my number on file, right?"

James examined his face for a long time but couldn't make anything of the boyish guilelessness. "We do."

"Seriously," Hannah added, his smile dropping. "Anything I can do to help. I liked Benson. I didn't know him well, but he gave me a shot, you know, when no one else would. Kinda feel like I owe the old man."

James stood, pocketing his notebook and checking his watch. "Thank you for your cooperation."

"Sure thing. Oh...and, Agent?"

"Yes?"

Hannah nodded to the plastic cup in his hand, still half-filled with lukewarm dregs. "If you want a decent coffee, there's a place on the seafront. Arbuckles. That shit'll knock your socks off. Tell 'em Leo sent you." His smile made his eyes shine like stained glass. James hurriedly suppressed the thought just as Gibson appeared at the side door, looking harried.

"There you are," she said, her glance sliding to Hannah, who raised a hand in greeting as he lit his second cigarette. She nodded politely then gestured James to follow her in.

"What is it?"

"I want you in on this one," she said, pacing back toward the interview rooms.

"Who?"

"Renford Muntz...the janitor."

"The one who found the body?"

"That's right."

"You think he's good for it?"

"I don't know. I can't tell if he's guilty or just hates cops. Keep your eyes open. Mr. Muntz," Gibson's tone stiffened with politeness as she opened the interview room door. The janitor was hunched at the table, chewing on a splitting thumbnail. His deep-set eyes flicked up as they entered then dropped again to the tabletop. "This is my colleague, Agent Solomon. If you don't mind, I would like to go through your statement again with him present."

"Why?" the man grunted without looking up.

"He's a good judge of character. If you truly have nothing to be afraid of, he's a good guy to have on your side."

The man huffed, spitting out a gnawed piece of nail. James studied him as he took a seat next to Gibson. Muntz's dark, wiry hair stuck up in all directions like he'd been running his hands through it. His skin was sallow, and his stained coverall strained at the seams as he bent his large frame over the table. There were bags under his eyes and dirt under his fingernails. His jaw moved constantly, and he blinked more than James thought was normal.

"So tell me again how you found Mr. Benson."

"Again?"

"For Agent Solomon's benefit. Please."

He heaved a large sigh and recommenced tugging at the remains of his thumbnail. "Like I said, I came in at four like always. I do the top floors first 'cause those stuck-up assholes don't want me around once they start pretending to work."

"You do what, exactly? Cleaning?"

"No, there's a cleaning crew for that, ain't there? But it's my job to make sure that they done their job right."

"Okay, so you were inspecting the senior management's offices," Gibson continued without inflection. "Then what?"

"I saw him through the glass. I called the police."

"Your swipe card confirms you arriving at three-fifty-five am, Mr. Muntz. The call to the sheriff didn't come through until four-twenty-five. Did it really take you half an hour to get up to the seventh floor, see Mr. Benson had been attacked and call the police?"

"I did some other offices first, didn't I?" he snapped, shifting in his chair. "And when I got to his, I didn't see the blood at first. Thought he was sleeping."

"Do you know where the disks from the security system are kept?" James asked.

Muntz shrugged, staring hard at his fingers. "Sure. Security room. First floor."

"The disks with all the footage from last night are missing."

"Guess the killer musta taken them."

"Mr. Benson was in the process of writing an email when he died," Gibson said. "To the Personnel department. Do you know anything about that?"

"No. Why should I?"

Gibson paused. James watched Muntz. Sweat shone on his lined forehead. "A number of your colleagues mentioned you and Mr. Benson have had a few disagreements recently," Gibson stated, "about your behavior toward your colleagues, among other things."

"Lying bastards." Muntz's hands twitched then were still again.

"It's not true, then?"

"Course it's not."

"Why do you think they would say so?"

"'Cause they've all got it in for me. That's why."

"Who specifically, Mr. Muntz?" James asked.

"All of them," he spat out. "Everyone. They all want to see me out on the street."

"Why do they want you *out on the street*, Renford?" Gibson asked, her voice carefully level.

Muntz shifted his bulk in the creaking chair. "I don't know, do I? I'm different, I guess."

"How are you different?"

"I ain't rich, for one. And they think I'm dumber than shit. But they don't know half the stuff I know about this place. I been here *years*. Known Mr. Benson longer than any of them. Jealous…that's what they are."

"Who do you think would want to hurt Mr. Benson?" James said, watching the ruddy face carefully.

Muntz's bloodshot eyes weighed him up. A corner of the mouth twitched within the bristled depths of his beard. "How should I know?"

"You just said you know the company better than anyone," James remarked. "Don't you have any idea?"

The big man leaned forward on the table. "You want my guess?"

"I do."

"One of the DHs. Yeah, one of those guys."

"The department heads?"

"Yeah. That idiot Boon or that stuck-up bitch Michaels."

"And why would either of them want Mr. Benson dead?" James said, leaning his elbows on the plastic tabletop to mimic him, watching the twitching, sweat-sheened face closely.

"They hated him. That's why."

"Lots of people hate other people, Renford. It doesn't mean they kill them."

"This big deal," he said, "means big changes, right?"

"I imagine so."

"Well, they'd get more of all this new money if they were in charge instead of him, right?"

"Yes, I imagine that's right," James said. "So one of them will take over the company now? Get all the benefits from the expansion for themselves?"

"'Course. It's always about money, ain't it?"

"Most of the time," James agreed.

"Well then."

"Just Boon and Michaels?" James asked lightly. "You don't think Horatio Torez would have wanted the same thing?"

The man scratched at a mark on the table. "No."

"Why not?" Gibson prompted when the man offered no more.

"I dunno," he said, slamming a fist on the table. "Just *no*, all right?"

About the Author

S. J. Coles is a Romance writer originally from Shropshire, UK. She has been writing stories for as long as she has been able to read them. Her biggest passion is exploring narratives through character relationships.

She finds writing LGBT/paranormal romance provides many unique and fulfilling opportunities to explore many (often neglected or under-represented) aspects of human experience, expectation, emotion and sexuality.

Among her biggest influences are LGBT Romance authors K J Charles and Josh Lanyon and Vampire Chronicles author Anne Rice.

S. J. Coles loves to hear from readers. You can find her contact information, website details and author profile page at https://www.pride-publishing.com

PUBLISHING

Sign up for our newsletter and find out about all our romance book releases, eBook sales and promotions, sneak peeks and FREE romance books!